THE AMERICAN CAPTAIN

A SEA NOVEL

THE AMERICAN CAPTAIN

BY

JAMES KEFFER

www.penmorepress.com

The American Captain by James Keffer

ISBN-13: 978-1-957851-50-1Paperback)
ISBN 13: 978-1-957851-49-5 (e-book)

BISAC Subject Headings:
FIC014000FICTION / Historical
FIC032000FICTION / War & Military
FIC047000FICTION / Sea Stories

Editing: Lauren McElroy . Chris Wozney
 Cover Illustration by
Emillia Rakić PR Emily's World of Design

Address all correspondence to:
Penmore Press LLC
920 N Javelina Pl
Tucson, AZ 85748

Dedication

To John Adams, second President of the United States and Father of the US Navy. Thank you, sir, for your foresight and dedication to our nation's security.

Acknowledgements

I have always wanted to write a book. I still have several pages of an attempt at a mystery novel I wrote on our family typewriter at fourteen that was inspired by my love of Sherlock Holmes. Later on in life, it was my introduction to C.S. Forester by the movie *Captain Horatio Hornblower* combined with a book on the Battle of Waterloo that led to my first effort, *Hornblower and the Island*. Shortly after I posted the first draft of this on Smashwords.com, I was put in contact with Alaric Bond, whose *Fighting Sail* series was a sensation.

I owe Mr. Bond a great debt on two fronts: One, it was he who put me in touch with Michael James, then at Fireship Press, who agreed to publish *Hornblower*. Second was an email he sent me. It was after the second or third Brewer book had come out and was doing rather well. I emailed him a question, and he mentioned in his reply that I should consider stepping out on my own, get out from under Hornblower's shadow, so to speak. Not to abandon Brewer, mind you, just to establish a character who was completely my own. It started the wheels turning and led directly to the birth of Hezekiah Albritton.

Thank you, Mr. Bond.

CHAPTER ONE

Sitting in a country tavern—a pint of ale in his fist and good friends all around—was all he needed these days. Everyone who went in or out bade him hail or farewell, and he raised his tankard to each and every one. They expected him to be there now and took comfort from his presence during this troubled year of 1814. It was like he was a rock on which they could ride out the storm.

His name was Hezekiah Albritton, and he was a captain in the Navy of the United States. His family had been in America since just after the Mayflower landed, and locally they were regarded as the closest thing New England had to English country squires. His family's wealth came from a combination of privateering during the wars and shrewd land speculation in the west. His grandfather had built the family an estate outside of Boston in a town now known as Quincy. Albritton had inherited the estate years before when his father had died while Albritton was at sea. He'd renamed the place "Shiloh" after someone showed him the word in the Bible and told him it meant "peace."

Many boys who grew up in that part of the country heard the siren's voice in the waves of the cold Atlantic, and Hezekiah Albritton had been no exception. He'd joined the fledgling Colonial Navy in 1776 as a midshipman, right after his sixteenth birthday. He was a lieutenant by the time the war ended. Unfortunately, the Navy ended with the war, and

Albritton then had to make his living as second mate on a cargo ship that carried lumber and foodstuffs to Britain and returned with the hold filled with manufactured goods. It was a boring existence after the excitement of the war, but it had allowed Albritton to hone his seamanship and navigation skills to a fine edge.

His life changed in the mid-1790s when what became known as the Quasi-war began with France over their seizures of American merchant ships bound for England. The French Revolution had France at war with nearly all of Europe, and England was America's largest trading partner. The U.S. government authorized the construction of several large frigates as well as some smaller ships, and Albritton immediately applied for service in the new Navy, but he was rejected.

He'd refused to accept defeat and made his way to Philadelphia. Fortunately for him, the president of the United States was none other than his old Quincy neighbor, John Adams. Albritton secured an audience with the president and made his request for reinstatement in person. Adams immediately agreed and wrote out a lieutenant's commission for Albritton on the spot. Albritton fought well against the French, and had gone on to earn promotion and acclaim in the Barbary pirate wars in the Mediterranean.

He was promoted to captain in 1808 by President Jefferson. When the current war had begun, in 1812, he'd accepted command of the small frigate USS *Virginia* that had just been completed at Norfolk. She was armed with twenty 12-pounder guns and eight 32-pounder carronades. On his first cruise in Caribbean waters he took three English merchant ships and one of their sloops into Charleston as prizes. In November, 1813, he relieved Isaac Hull as captain of the USS *Constitution*. He took the ship on an eight-month cruise in the Atlantic that saw him take eleven British merchant ships as prizes, recapture three American ships, and twice defeat British frigates in single combat. In the second of these battles, which took place just outside of Boston harbor, Albritton had been wounded by splinters in his thigh, just before the enemy hauled down their flag. The *Constitution* and her prize sailed into Boston, and Albritton was sent home to Shiloh to recuperate. Albritton's recovery was slow. He'd celebrated his fifty-fourth birthday alone at home, his first on dry land in several years.

Hezekiah was the last of the Albrittons. He'd married his childhood sweetheart, Mary Young, in 1788. His captain had given him 30 days' leave as a wedding gift, and Albritton and his bride moved into a cottage built on a high bluff just outside Boston where she could watch for him to come back to her. He was at sea when he received the two most important letters of his life, the first from Mary announcing she was pregnant, and the second from his father telling him that Mary had died in childbirth without ever holding their child. To make matters worse, the letter went on to say that the child, a girl whom his father had named Mary after her mother, had only lived three days before expiring herself.

Those were dark days for Albritton. It was four months before his ship docked at Boston, and his first trip was to the gravesides of his wife and child. He dropped to his knees and wept. He stayed there for nearly two days, never leaving their graves, and then he rose and left the cemetery. He would not return for ten years.

He returned to the cottage and arranged for all his belongings to be moved back to his father's house, and he sold the cottage before going back to sea, this time as first lieutenant on a brigantine. He took his grief out on the British until the war was over. There was little prize money to be had from the Continental Congress, or from the Confederation Congress which followed it. Fortunately for

Albritton, the last merchantman they captured was carrying gold back to England. His captain, knowing they would get no prize money for the ship, had proposed that they divide the gold amongst themselves, and that the percentage each man received be determined according to the rules of prize money distribution. Albritton's share amounted to several thousand pounds.

The tavern was warm on this cold winter evening, and Albritton was glad for his tankard and his seat close to the inn's great fireplace. The combination of the comfort in his hand and the warmth for his body seemed to set the world to rights for him, and he needed that as his nation closed its third year of war with Great Britain.

The tavern was his favorite place to pass an evening. It was called the Washington Arms because of the owner's contention that George Washington had once slept there when he'd arrived to take command of the Continental Army outside of Boston in 1775. Albritton enjoyed swapping stories and the latest news with the locals there, even if all the news lately was about the war.

He nodded and raised his tankard in acknowledgement of the greetings of a passer-by. He knew what the locals thought about him, but he never let it go to his head. Yet it was a natural assumption; he certainly looked the part at six feet, three inches in height. He had a stocky build with broad, well-muscled shoulders and a barrel chest. His life at sea kept him fit despite his years. His chestnut hair was beginning to recede, but that didn't bother him as he always kept it short anyway. He never appeared in uniform when he was home from the sea, although tonight he was dressed in his heavy naval greatcoat as a concession to the cold and wind.

"Good evening, Captain," a familiar voice said. "Would

you care for some company?"

Albritton looked up and smiled. "Good evening, Mr. President. Please, sit down and join me."

John Adams, second President of the United States and lifelong Braintree and Quincy resident, sat down opposite the captain and signaled the barmaid for a tankard of his own and a refill for his friend. Albritton watched the ex-president settle into his chair and open his heavy overcoat to reveal a plaid mackinaw underneath. The barmaid arrived with the drinks and set them down on the table. Adams dropped several coins on the tray.

"Thank you, sir," Albritton said. The two men raised their glasses, saluted each other and drank.

"Well, my dear Captain," Adams said, "how goes the war?"

Albritton shook his head. "Truly, I do not know, Mr. President. I've heard nothing from Washington City in the months I've been home."

Adams shook his head. "Your solitude should not last much longer. We need to hit the British, and hit them hard. You are still our best hope for that. You've not failed us yet."

"That's kind of you to say, sir."

"Nonsense. I saw years ago that you were the one to lead us," Adams said. "And you have more than surpassed my expectations, young man."

Albritton raised his tankard in a gesture of thanks, and both men drank.

Adams set his tankard on the table, leaned in, and lowered his voice. "You say you've had no word?"

Albritton shook his head. "Nary a one. I tell you, John, at times I wonder if they've forgotten me."

Adams grunted dismissively. He chuckled to himself, thinking anyone who met Hezekiah Albritton was not likely to forget him.

"I'm sure you will be hearing from Mr. Jones soon," he said, referring to the current Secretary of the Navy. "I understand our British cousins left us a present in the Navy yard when they burned the capitol."

Albritton nodded. "So I've heard. A frigate and a sloop, both now nearing completion. For some reason, they weren't put to the torch when Tingey ordered the yard burned. The British left them completely alone." Commodore Tingey was the commander of the Washington Naval Yard. He'd ordered the yard burned to prevent it from falling into the hands of the British.

The ex-president grunted. "Probably didn't think they were worth the effort. I hope the frigate will be yours?"

The captain shrugged. "Possibly, but I wonder what is left to arm them with? Surely, between Tingey and the British, the foundry and warehouses were destroyed?"

"That I do not know," Adams said. "But for the life of me I cannot image the secretary—or even the president, for that matter—leaving you out of this fight."

Albritton grunted, a dismissive gesture to be sure, but Adams could read the frustration in his friend's eyes and knew he agreed with him. Adams stared into his drink.

"Something on your mind, John?" the captain asked.

Adams glanced from side to side as surreptitiously as possible and lowered his voice. "Have you heard anything about a meeting that is supposed to take place in Connecticut?"

Albritton shook his head.

"I'm not surprised," Adams said. "I had a visit from certain... *gentlemen*, I shall say, although I confess that I use the term rather loosely. They wanted me to be part of the Massachusetts delegation to a meeting that is scheduled to take place very soon in Hartford." Adams sat back and looked around again before taking a drink.

"And the purpose of this meeting?" Albritton prodded.

The former president frowned. "My visitors said the intent is to call for a second Constitutional Convention. They want to rewrite the document to include various additional articles that would protect Yankee interests. If their call for a new convention is rejected, then they will propose seceding from the Union of States and make a separate peace with Great Britain."

Albritton stared wide-eyed at his companion. To him, this sounded dangerously close to treason. Even the threat of making a separate peace with the enemy during time of war could not be thought of by any reasonable person in any other light. "Dear God!" he said in a voice barely above a whisper. "What does Sam think of this? Does he even know?"

Adams grunted. "My dear cousin thinks it is a wonderful idea. As long as friends of Mr. Jefferson are in power, he will countenance almost any form of rebellion."

The captain grinned. "I can well imagine. What else did they say to you? What do they want to add?"

Adams drained his glass and set it off to the side. "They want to do away with the three-fifths compromise."

Albritton's eyes went wide for just a second, but more than long enough to tell the ex-president what he thought of that idea. "If I may ask, Mr. President, whose idea was this convention?"

Adam's brow rose in derision. "Harrison Gray Otis." The captain scowled as his friend continued. "It was his suggestion that the New England states send delegates to a convention at Hartford."

Albritton shook his head in disbelief. "I've known Otis for years. I've never considered him a foolish radical."

"That's the thing," Adams rejoined, "he's not, at least not in my opinion. In fact, I think he's not the radical we need to fear. Have you heard the rumor that our dear governor has sent a mission to England regarding a separate peace?"

"Bah!" Albritton scoffed. "Caleb Strong is a fool."

"True," Adams agreed, "but he had enough political muscle to be reelected governor."

"*Bought* enough muscle, you mean." The captain nodded a greeting to a newly arrived patron. "Why did they come to you?"

Adams shrugged and took a drink of his ale. "Presumably because I had nothing to do with the writing of the Constitution in the first place. I was in England at the time, if you recall."

"I do, but surely Otis doesn't believe that a man of your reputation would join this... travesty?"

Adams smiled at the word. "It's true that I've always said this nation should be one of laws and not men. However, let me point one thing out to you, Hezekiah: you and I may not like the things Otis and his kind are proposing, but for now, at least, they are attempting to do their business *according to the law*. I understand some of them are making mutterings about seceding from the common union, but for now they are attempting to call a convention, which is precisely what the law requires."

Albritton frowned at his drink. "Tell me honestly, John— how good are their chances?"

Adams sat back in his chair, observing the crowd as he considered his friend's question. "Honestly, I'm not sure. The attendees at Hartford will all be from the New England states. It is my understanding that they will debate and come up with a report that will list their grievances with the conduct of the war and propose constitutional changes or amendments as a remedy. I expect their call for a convention to go unanswered, simply because no other states will be in sympathy." He leaned forward on one elbow. "Truthfully,

Hezekiah, this all seems to me to be an attempt to embarrass the government. Nothing more." He looked over at the couple who had just come in. "Party politics," he added in disgust.

"So you don't think they will actually secede?"

"Good Lord, no. Otis and his ilk may be out of their minds, in my humble opinion, but they're not stupid." He shook his head vigorously. "You need not fear Massachusetts or anyone else leaving the Union. No, I'm afraid all they will do is destroy the Federalist Party in the eyes of the nation." He grunted. "I'm glad Washington isn't still alive to see it."

The captain could only shrug in agreement and order another round. The two men talked of proposed improvements to the area for after the war and their hope that peace would come soon.

The clock in the corner struck nine, and the captain drained his tankard and stood. Adams smiled; Albritton was certainly a creature of habit. He always left the inn at nine o'clock to make his way home. Adams drained his drink as well and stood.

"It was good to see you, Hezekiah," he said as the two men shook hands. "Why don't you come to dinner tomorrow night at Peacefield? Abigail will be delighted. Eight o'clock?"

The captain bowed, more of an exaggerated nod. "I shall be delighted, sir."

"Good!" Adams fished two cigars from his pocket and offered one to his companion; the captain politely declined. Adams lit his and puffed deeply as the two made their way to the door. "I have a carriage tonight; may I offer you a ride home?"

"No, thank you, sir," Albritton said. "I enjoy the walk."

"As you wish." Adams climbed into his rig and tossed his friend a salute. "Until tomorrow, then."

The captain waved as his friend whipped up the horse

and was gone. He watched the carriage disappear into the darkness before turning for home himself. He pulled his collar up against the chill, lowered his chin to his breast to deflect the wind and, ignoring the pain in his thigh, forced one foot in front of the other toward home.

The conversation with Adams bothered him more than he was willing to admit. His recuperation had reached the point where he could take command of a ship again; surely his superiors in Washington knew this. He had heard that Isaac Hull had taken *Constitution* back to sea, but surely there were other ships? A misstep caused a pain in his leg and made him wince. He frowned. *Here is another reason to get back to sea!* he thought. *There are no rocks or roots on the nice, smooth deck of a ship!*

He resumed his trek homeward and thought about his friend. Whatever you thought about his politics, one had to admit that John Adams was the best friend the Navy had ever had in the short history of the United States. It was he who'd created the Navy department and gotten Congress to authorize the original six frigates that were now devastating the Royal Navy. *If we only had a hundred more,* he thought, *we might be able to make the British take notice of us.* It couldn't last, however, and he knew it; sooner or later the British would respond with ships as powerful as the six, and the Americans would be overwhelmed by sheer numbers. Albritton looked up at the stars and sighed. It was a blessing that most of the Royal Navy's frigates were tied up in the war against Napoleon.

He turned up the lane toward home. His father had planted birch trees three paces off and five paces apart on either side of the lane when Albritton was barely out of diapers. Now they gave the approach to the house an air of regal dignity that he always found both calming and welcoming. The lane emptied into a *cul-de-sac* in which the drive circled around a huge, ancient oak to allow carriages to drop visitors at the front door. He paused to lean against the oak's trunk and admire the house in the moonlight. The central block had been built in the Georgian style by his grandfather nearly a hundred years before. He'd added the solarium onto the east side of the house two years before he died. Albritton remembered stories from his youth of the old man basking in the sun there. Albritton's father had built the two-story New Wing off the back of the house just before Albritton was born. The bottom floor held a library with a large oaken desk at the far end; the upper story consisted entirely of the new master bedroom.

Shiloh's master ascended the steps. The front door opened for him.

"Welcome home, sir."

Albritton nodded as he handed his hat and coat to the man behind the door. Hawthorne had entered the family's service five years before Albritton was born as a fifteen-year-old groom and worked his way up to being valet for the master. He'd served Albritton's father faithfully for nearly twenty years, and now he was devoted to the son and managed the estate during Albritton's absences.

"Good evening, Hawthorne," the master replied.

"Did you have a pleasant evening, sir?"

Albritton shrugged as he removed his gloves. "Pleasant enough. I had a chance to speak with the president."

"Indeed?" Hawthorne accepted the gloves. "I hope Mrs. Adams is well."

"Apparently. I've been invited to dinner tomorrow night at Peacefield."

"Ah," Hawthorne said with a rueful look. "Perhaps this would be an appropriate time to inform you of a letter that came for you today."

"From Washington?"

Hawthorne nodded. "From the Navy Department, sir."

Albritton dropped his head and sighed. *There goes dinner.* "Very well. Bring it to me in the library."

Hawthorne bowed. "As you say, sir."

Albritton made his way through the entrance hall and past the staircase to the library. A fire was blazing as he went to the table in the corner and poured himself a whiskey. He carried the drink back to the fireplace and downed a large swallow as he gazed at the picture over the hearth. A gift from an artist friend, it was a life-size portrait of her in her wedding gown painted from memory and presented on the tenth anniversary of her death. He'd hung it in the library where he didn't have to share it with anyone. He thought it an excellent likeness; to him, she looked exactly as she had when she'd walked down the aisle on their wedding day.

He felt the familiar tug at his heart and grunted as he downed the rest of his whiskey. A gentle clearing of a throat drew his attention to the door, where he saw Hawthorne holding an envelope on a tray. Albritton broke the seal and withdrew the single sheet inside.

Captain,

> *I would like to see you in Washington City at your earliest possible convenience. Please come at once.*

Yours Truly,

William Jones
Secretary of the Navy

Albritton shook his head ruefully as he wandered back to the roaring fire, bouncing the folded letter off his fingers. *Too bad*, he thought, *I was really looking forward to dinner at Peacefield. I haven't seen Abigail for a long time.* He studied the portrait again and debated starting for Washington the day after tomorrow. Finally, he sighed and handed the letter back to Hawthorne.

"Make the arrangements for the earliest possible moment," Albritton said. "Alert Xavier."

"Yes, sir," the servant said with a bow. "Your bags shall be packed by noon."

Xavier was the captain's coxswain. He'd first come into Albritton's service in 1801 when the then-Lieutenant Albritton had saved his life during a boarding action on a Tunisian xebec.

"Thank you, sir," Xavier said after they'd returned to their brig. "I am in your debt."

"Forget it," Albritton replied. "You would do the same for me."

The younger man shook his head. "In my family, a debt owed must be repaid. I consider myself in your service, sir, until such time as the debt has been satisfied."

Albritton surrendered gracefully, thinking that allowing this man to be a servant of sorts during his remaining time aboard would satisfy this debt. Six months later, he received orders to report to USS *Constellation*. He returned to his room to pack his kit, only to find Xavier there packing it for him.

"What are you doing?" Albritton asked him.

"Packing," Xavier said simply. "When do we leave?"

"We?"

"The debt is not yet paid in full."

The two men departed, bound together by the debt felt by Xavier.

There came a day in 1807, when Albritton was first lieutenant on the sloop USS *Knox,* when things changed. Their ship was in a battle against two pirate luggers in the Caribbean, and Albritton led a boarding action against one of them. He'd just finished fighting two pirates directly in front of him when he heard a strangled cry behind him. He ducked and spun in time to see Xavier pull his saber from a third pirate's chest. A quick look of thanks was all they had time for.

That night, Albritton called Xavier to the quarterdeck.

"Well? Has the debt been settled now?"

Xavier shrugged. "Some may say so, but I would like to remain as I am."

"But why?" Albritton asked. "You are free now. You can return home with honor, if you wish."

"Perhaps, but I have found purpose during these past six years in your service. Also, I believe we have done well together, both in our country's service and to the benefit of our crewmates. Besides," he added with a half-smile, "I'm not sure you could get along without me."

"Really?" Albritton replied in jest. "Just because it took you six years to save my life one time –"

"Five," Xavier interrupted.

Albritton was stunned. "I beg your pardon?"

"I have saved your life five times in the past six years," Xavier said. "This is just the first time you noticed."

Albritton opened his mouth to protest but closed it again when he saw the look on the other's face and knew he was telling the truth. Neither man spoke of it again.

When Albritton was promoted to commander and received his first ship, Xavier became his coxswain and remained so in every ship Albritton commanded.

Albritton and Xavier left on the evening tide aboard a coastal schooner bound for New York, where they landed just in time to book passage on a luggar headed for Baltimore. Once there, Albritton borrowed two fast horses and the pair raced for Washington City. They stopped and took rooms at a rooming house in Woodbridge but stayed only long enough for the captain to put on his uniform before remounting and heading for the capitol.

They reined in their horses as they reached the city. Albritton looked around at the destruction and was amazed at what he saw. He had heard that the British had spared many of the privately owned structures, and he saw now that it was true. Public buildings, however, bore the full measure of British fury. The Capitol building and the Presidential Mansion were charred ruins. The Navy Yard was much the same, its warehouses and foundries burnt almost beyond recognition. Yet in the water he saw what was becoming known as "the Miracle": USS *Columbia* and USS *Argus* floating there unharmed. It seemed inconceivable that the British would allow a 44-gun frigate and a 22-gun sloop-of-war to remain for their enemies to use; Albritton could only conclude that the British army had been in such a hurry that they'd concentrated on buildings rather than ships. He caught a view of the ships across the yard and was pleased to see workmen and sailors on board.

An ensign met him upon his arrival and led him to the hut where Secretary Jones had set up his temporary office after the British abandoned the city. Two marines were on guard duty at the door.

"This is Captain Albritton," his escort said. "Secretary Jones is expecting him."

The guard eyed the newcomers before nodding. "Aye, sir. Wait here, please." He disappeared inside the hut before returning and holding the door open. "The secretary will see you now."

Albritton thanked his guide and motioned for Xavier to wait for him before following the man in. The room was spartan, with only three lamps for light and, for warmth, a Franklin stove in the corner. The single window gave a good view of the harbor. Several tables were covered with boxes. The secretary rose from the table closest to the stove; Albritton judged this to be his makeshift desk, as it was covered with stacks of papers.

"Captain Albritton," Jones said as he came around his desk, and the two men shook hands. "A pleasure to see you again. Thank you for coming so quickly. Coffee?"

"Thank you."

The secretary rang a bell on his desk, and a door in the corner that Albritton had not noticed opened to admit a steward. "Coffee for two, please."

"Aye, sir."

Jones indicated a chair before his desk. "Sit, Captain, please." The secretary sat behind the desk. The door opened and the steward entered carrying a tray containing a coffee pot and two cups. He set it down on the edge of the desk, came to attention, and retreated from the room. The secretary stood and poured for them both, handing Albritton his cup before resuming his seat. Albritton sipped his coffee and smiled, pleased at the taste; Jones had a reputation for enjoying the finer things. He took another drink and set the mug on the desk, then sat back to wait.

The secretary set his cup on the desk and went through the motions of clearing the surface before him. "Captain," he said, "as you probably saw on the way in, the British left us an incredible gift."

"Yes, I saw them. Any idea what happened? I can't imagine the British not destroying two warships so close to completion."

The secretary spread his hands and shrugged. "No idea at all. Reverend Samuels insists it is a miracle from God. Our usual sources of rumors within the British command have been completely silent in this area, although we do know the British army commander who burned the public buildings in the city has been recalled to England." He picked up his cup and studied the clouds for a moment before speaking. "Whatever the reason, the president feels that we shouldn't look a gift horse in the mouth. We need to get both ships to a safer harbor immediately." He paused for another drink. "Captain, I want you to get both ships ready for sea, take them to Boston to complete fitting out, then take both to sea to raid the British sea lanes."

Albritton nodded. "Area of operation?"

"That will be decided before you sail from Boston. We had thought that you could leave the *Argus* in the South Atlantic while you took *Columbia* into the Pacific to threaten British whalers." He shrugged again. "As I said, it's still under consideration. Any thoughts?"

Albritton crossed his arms over his chest and rubbed his chin between his thumb and forefinger. "I like the idea of the Pacific, though it is a long way for crews to bring their prizes home." He shook his head. "They'll expect prize money."

The secretary shrugged. "Of course."

Albritton stepped to the window. "I saw the crews working on the ships as I passed by. Does that mean Goodson is already aboard and working?"

Jones scratched the back of his head. "Yes, about that... I'm afraid you don't have Mr. Goodson with you for this voyage. He has been promoted to commander and placed in command of the sloop USS *Arbuckle*. At this moment, he is on his way to the Caribbean."

"Then who is to be my new first lieutenant?"

"Michael Chandler is the man's name. He's done good work on *Constellation* and *President*. He's just returned from a voyage to the Caribbean in *Enterprise*. He was put in command of a brig taken as a prize with orders to sail for Charleston. On the way there, he captured two more British merchantmen."

"That doesn't explain how he ended up on my quarterdeck."

"The commodore at Charleston gave him the honor of delivering his captain's reports to me personally, along with those concerning his adventures while in command of the brig. We needed a first lieutenant for *Columbia*. He had the rank and experience."

"Hmph." Albritton looked out the window again. He didn't like the idea of going to sea without Goodson. The two had sailed together for the better part of fifteen years, and Goodson had been the only first lieutenant he'd ever had. He shook his head. Chandler was a mystery, and trust took time to build. Time they didn't have.

He resumed his seat. "And who commands *Argus*?"

"Commander James Calloway," Jones said. "Heard of him?"

Albritton thought for a moment. "Yes, it seems I have. Wasn't he the captain of the *Chesapeake* when she struck to HMS *Leopard* in 1807?"

The secretary nodded. "The very same. Court martial found him guilty of failure to prepare his ship for combat, as well as surrendering without firing a shot." He paused to recall the facts to his mind. "He was relieved of his command and discharged from the Navy. He's been shipping out on merchantmen for the past five years. He was reinstated as a lieutenant when the war began. He was assigned to USS *Constitution* where he performed stellar service under Isaac Hull against HMS *Guerriere* and later under Charles Stewart against HMS *Cyane* and HMS *Levant*. In fact, both men mentioned him by name for conspicuous gallantry under fire." Jones sat and scratched his chin. "Since then, he has made a steady advancement. His last assignment ended four months ago after a successful cruise off Newfoundland in the brig *Constant*. He's been aboard *Argus* for the past two days."

Albritton rose. "Well, I should see my ship. Thank you, Mr. Secretary."

Jones came around the desk to shake hands. "Your orders will be ready tomorrow. Come back at 3:00pm to report your readiness for sea."

The captain came to attention. "Aye, sir."

Albritton found a boat to row him and Xavier out to his ship. Before tying up, he ordered the coxswain to circle the ship. He wanted to get a better look at *Columbia* and also judge her trim. The boat pulled slowly around the frigate, and Albritton was generally pleased with what he saw. The boat made her way gently toward the entry port. The captain timed his jump perfectly and climbed to his new command. He set foot on the deck just as the bosun's pipe blew.

An officer stepped forward and raised his hat. "Michael Chandler, sir," he said formally. Albritton caught a strong Southern accent. "I am your new first lieutenant."

"Pleased to meet you, Mr. Chandler," the captain said formally.

Chandler ushered him to the side where his officers were waiting to be presented. "Captain," he said, "may I present your second, Mr. Mitchell; your third, Mr. Hill; and your fourth, Mr. Williams."

"Gentlemen,"—Albritton nodded in greeting—"I look forward to making your acquaintance. Mr. Chandler, call the hands aft, if you please."

The men came aft. The captain stepped forward and pulled the paper from his coat pocket that gave him command of *Columbia*. He read it before them all in a loud, clear voice. When he finished, he refolded the paper and put it back in his pocket, then turned to Chandler.

"Dismiss the hands, if you please, Mr. Chandler. I want all officers and senior warrant officers in my cabin in fifteen minutes."

He turned his back on the first lieutenant without waiting for a reply and made his way toward the companionway stairs. He saw Xavier step down ahead of him, and he followed without delay. At the bottom of the stairway, he turned aft and saw the marine sentry snap to attention. The man opened the door, and the captain and his coxswain entered.

Commander James Calloway watched as Captain Albritton arrived and took command of *Columbia*. He frowned as he saw the man go below. He handed his spyglass to a midshipman and began to pace across the fantail.

When he'd received the summons from Secretary Jones, he'd expected to be given an independent command. Finally, he'd thought, he would be permitted to *do* something great, something that would forever erase the great blot on his record, the one great mistake of his career. He would put 1807 behind him once and for all. Only it hadn't turned out that way. Jones had told him he was to have *Argus* and would sail in company with Albritton in *Columbia*, and that he would be subject to Albritton's orders. He grimaced at the memory. So. There it was. *Still* they did not trust him in independent command. He would continue to wear the stigma of 1807 like a heavy cloak.

His teeth ground together in frustration. Looking back, he did not see how such a thing could have happened. He'd never expected HMS *Leopard* to open fire on him, forcing him to surrender USS *Chesapeake* to save the lives of his passengers and crew. Calloway shook his head as he reached the rail and turned around. And that court-martial he'd gone through—talk about a kangaroo court! He'd expected no mercy from Rodgers, who'd presided over the court, but he'd thought Decatur was his friend. Some friend! Well, that score would be settled one day.

The captain ceased his pacing and stared at the frigate. He turned and looked down the deck. *Argus* was ready for sea. Not ready for combat, but his orders—thankfully, this time—had been specific in that regard. He was to have his ship ready for sea. Albritton would take the two ships to another harbor, where they would be made ready to put to sea and harass the British.

"Mr. Pinkney!" he called to the quartermaster's mate at the wheel. "I shall be in my cabin. Call me for anything that demands my attention."

"Aye, sir."

CHAPTER TWO

Admiral Sir Richard Goodwin Keats, governor of Newfoundland, set the reports down on his desk and turned to look out the window. It looked cold and breezy outside, but then it was always cold and breezy on Newfoundland. He had arrived at St. John's two years before, prepared to endure a dreary diplomatic posting, but the advent of the Second American War had rescued him from that. The harbor here was nearly as busy as that of Plymouth these days and seemed likely to remain so for the foreseeable future.

He raised his cup of tea to his lips and recoiled at the discovery that the liquid had gone tepid. He set it down and made to reach for the bell on the corner of his desk, but he decided against it. He rested his elbow on the arm of his chair and rubbed his chin with his thumb and forefinger as he considered the report he'd just finished reading. He frowned; how could his good colleagues in the army have been so stupid? To leave two prime warships so near to completion intact was nothing less than a courts-martial offense in his opinion. He grunted as he remembered the sight of General Ross, the man who'd spared the warships when he'd burned the American capitol, boarding the merchantman for the voyage back to England. If those ships were allowed to disappear into the Atlantic, British shipping would soon begin to suffer.

Keats threw himself from his chair and began to pace back and forth. He hated cleaning up messes created by the army, but this one had fallen squarely into his lap. He paused before the map on the wall which detailed the entire shoreline from Newfoundland to the northern coasts of Brazil. Pins with different colored flags outside major American ports denoted the various blockade squadrons whose sole purpose was to keep the troublesome American frigates in port. The pin outside Washington had a yellow flag.

The governor stepped over to his desk and rang the bell. His aide appeared in the doorway.

"You rang, sir?"

"Yes, Simmons. Please get me the file for Yellow Squadron. Is my nine o'clock here yet?"

"I believe Captain Knighton has just entered the building, sir."

"Very good. In that case, bring us a pot of tea right after you show him in."

"As you wish, sir."

The man closed the door, and Keats returned to studying the map. The trouble was that America had a big coastline, and the Royal Navy didn't have enough ships to close all the ports properly. However, he still had to deal with the new threat. He sighed and returned to his seat.

The knock at the door heralded the entrance of Simmons.

"Governor, Captain Sir Thomas Knighton."

The captain marched into the office and halted before the desk. He came to attention, his hat under his arm. It was the first time the two had met, and Keats could see that the stories he'd heard were probably true. Physically, Knighton was thin as a rail to boot and not what anyone would call imposing. This was a man who could be easily overlooked—until one met his eyes. Those eyes held power and carefully controlled fury, and they announced Knighton as a man to be reckoned with.

Keats rose. "Thank you for coming, Captain." He paused as his aide set a silver tea service on the corner of the desk and handed him a file before retreating from the room and shutting the door behind him. "Please, be seated."

Knighton took his seat as the governor poured him a cup of tea and placed it on the desk, then refilled his own. Both men drank deeply.

"How was the voyage over?" Keats asked.

The captain shrugged. "No real problems. We have some repairs that need done due to a storm that came up suddenly, including a spar to replace, but that's all."

"Good." The governor picked up the document on his desk. "I have an assignment for you. This is a report from spies in the area of Washington City. You may have heard that when our army brethren burned the American capitol, they conveniently neglected to put to the torch two warships that were nearing completion. One is a 44-gun frigate and the other a 20-gun sloop."

"Yes, I'd heard something of the sort," Knighton said. "I take it the Americans are readying them for sea?"

Keats held up the report. "That's what this says. I'm sending you to Washington to reinforce Commodore Hollingsworth's blockade squadron, but your orders will read that your specific targets are these two ships. Should they slip past the blockade, your job is to find them and sink them. I take it the *London* is up to the task?"

"Oh, yes, sir," Knighton said. HMS *London* was one of the new class of razee-frigates cut down from 64s to maintain their thicker sides. Their main armament was twenty-six 24-pounders to try to match the American frigates, and twenty

32-pounder carronades on the spar deck. She also carried two additional 18-pounders on the fo'c'sle as bow chasers. "Tell me, Governor, do we know whom the Americans will put in command?"

Keats shook his head. "The report doesn't say definitively. The rumor is that they will turn to Albritton."

Knighton's eyes widened a bit, and he nodded.

"You've heard of him?"

"Yes, Governor. I chased him in the Caribbean last year, but the weather was on his side. He got away. I understand from others I've spoken to that he is considered the Americans' best."

Keats smiled ruefully. "With respect to all their other captains who've beaten us, yes." He was pleased when Knighton took the intended rebuke in silence. "Still, if he *is* on the American quarterdeck, it will make your mission that much harder." The governor rose, signaling the end of the meeting. The captain followed suit. "Report to me when ready for sea," Keats said. "Your orders will be ready for you then. Good day, Captain."

Knighton came to attention. "Good day, Governor."

Albritton stood in his day cabin with his back to the great stern windows, hands clasped behind his back, as his officers entered the cabin. He listened politely as the first lieutenant introduced them one by one. Then the captain cleared his throat.

"Gentlemen," he said, "I look forward to making your acquaintance. For now, we have an urgent mission to get our ships ready for sea as quickly as possible, before the British realize what we are up to and assemble a squadron powerful enough to completely seal the entrance to Chesapeake Bay. It won't be easy; I understand the enemy frequently have ships roaming the channel looking for merchantmen to take or warships on the move. Not easy, gentlemen, but it can be done, and it will be done."

"Where do we go, sir?" Chandler asked.

"That hasn't been decided yet. I hope to find out when I report to the secretary tomorrow. All I've been told is that we must make ready for sea immediately, and that we will be sent somewhere to finish fitting out for an expedition against British shipping." He paused to let the news sink in. "Mr. Chandler, how soon can we be ready for sea?"

"Sir," the premier said, "we're ready now, providing we don't have to go very far."

Albritton's eyes narrowed. "Can we make, say, Boston, or Charleston easily?"

"Yes, sir, providing we don't have to fight along the way. We only have eighteen 32-pounder carronades on the spar deck along with six 24-pounders on the gun deck."

Albritton was astonished at the news. He hadn't had the chance to tour the ship yet, but even so he'd thought her armament would be complete! Now he knew what Jones meant about going to another port to finish fitting out.

"And *Argus*?" he asked.

"She's at full strength," Chandler said. "Two long 12-pounder guns and twenty 32-pounder carronades."

"Is she ready for sea?"

"Commander Calloway reports that she is."

The captain grunted. "Thank God for small favors." He took a deep breath as he considered his options, only to come to the conclusion that he had none. "Very well," he said, "I shall report to the secretary tomorrow that we are ready. Now, gentlemen, if you'll excuse us, the first lieutenant and I have matters to discuss. I shall call you back individually shortly."

Chandler rose. "Dismissed!"

The assemblage filed out in short order, and Albritton sat on the settee. Chandler gave him a questioning look. The captain grinned.

"Time to meet the most important man aboard," he said. "Call my steward, if you please, Mr. Chandler."

"Aye, sir," came the cheerful reply. *"Sommers!"*

A lanky man entered the room. A receding hairline gave him a distinguished high forehead, which sat atop deep-set blue eyes. His leathery skin told of years at sea, and his easy manner meeting a new captain spoke of experience as a captain's steward. He was not imposing physically, save for his height, but there was something about him that exuded not only confidence but competence.

Sommers looked to the first lieutenant. "Sir?"

Chandler nodded toward the captain. "Sommers, I'd like you to meet our captain. Captain Albritton, this is Sommers, your steward." The servant bowed. "If you'll excuse me a moment, Captain," Chandler said, "I'll allow you two to get acquainted."

"Thank you," Albritton said. Chandler came to attention and left.

"Please, Mr. Sommers, sit down," Albritton said.

The servant sat in a chair across from him. "Not 'Mister,' Captain," he said, "just Sommers."

"As you wish. Tell me about yourself, Sommers."

"My first voyage was as a ship's boy back in '79, Captain," the servant began. "I sailed out of Lorient on *Bonhomme Richard* with John Paul Jones. I was ten years old." He grinned and shook his head at the memory. "I was thrilled and scared to death, all at the same time. I made it through the fight with HMS *Serapis*, but I was too scared to move when word spread that the ship was going down and Jones ordered, 'Abandon ship!' Would you believe it—'twas the captain himself who carried me over to *Serapis* before our ship sank!"

"John Paul Jones carried you?"

"That he did! Scooped me up onto his back, piggyback style. *'Come on, Sommers,'* he said. *'It's time to go!'* And off we went."

"And how did you become a captain's steward?"

"Well, sir, I've always been interested in cooking. My second ship was a privateer out of the Outer Banks of North Carolina called *Intrepid*. The cook on her was an old man, and I learned the trade from him. He taught me to keep the crew happy with good food, and I've been doing it ever since."

"Well, Sommers, here's your first test," Albritton said. "Pass the word for the first lieutenant, if you please, and then how about some coffee?"

"Aye, Captain," Sommers said as he rose. "I put a pot on when I heard you'd come aboard."

He rose and went off on his task, completely missing the bemused look on his captain's face. He returned with a steaming cup on a tray. Albritton took it and held it up to his nose. The aroma was delightful, so he blew on the rim and tested the brew with a sip.

"Sommers," he said, "this is the best coffee I've ever had on a Navy ship!"

Sommers bowed. "Glad you like it, Captain. When you get a chance, I'd like some time to talk to you. That way I can get a taste for what you like in your meals, how you like to entertain, that sort of thing."

"I'll make the time," Albritton said as a knock on the door heralded the arrival of the premier. "Hello, Mr. Chandler; care for some coffee?"

"Thank you, sir."

Albritton nodded to Sommers, and two fresh cups quickly

appeared before the steward retreated to his pantry.

"I see you and Sommers are getting along, sir," Chandler commented.

"If his food is as good as his coffee, I may adopt him." Albritton took another drink and set his cup down. "Please, sit down, Mr. Chandler. Tell me about yourself. Where do your people hail from?"

"Charleston, sir," Chandler said. He took a drink of his coffee before continuing. "My family has a plantation six miles outside the city. Tobacco, mostly, but before I left, my father was talking about changing to a different crop."

"How big a plantation?"

"Three thousand acres."

"That's sizeable," Albritton said. "Must take a lot of manpower to run it."

Albritton watched the change come over the other's face. It was like a door slamming shut. "Yes, sir," came the cold reply. "My father owns three hundred Negroes."

"I see," Albritton said. "I hope I haven't offended you, Mr. Chandler."

"Not in the least, Captain; I am what I am. You're from New England, aren't you?"

Albritton nodded. "Massachusetts. Quincy, just outside Boston."

Chandler grunted. "I suppose you don't see many Negroes up there?"

"On the contrary, the blacksmith two streets over from my house is a Negro. Samuel Johnston. Best blacksmith in four counties."

"Runaway?"

Now it was Albritton's turn to go cold. "I don't know, Mr. Chandler; I never asked him."

The captain was pleased to see Chandler had the good

sense to at least appear chastised. "Sorry, sir."

"No need, Mr. Chandler." The captain rose, and the first lieutenant followed. "Please send in the lieutenants, one at a time."

Chandler came to attention and left the room. Albritton watched the door after he had gone, wondering what he would find beneath the aristocratic crust of his first lieutenant.

Interviews with his lieutenants went off about as well as he'd expected. Jonas Mitchell, the second lieutenant, had joined the service in 1805 as a midshipman and had experience fighting Barbary pirates in the Mediterranean. Peter Hill was the third lieutenant. He'd joined in 1807 and had seen action against pirates in the Caribbean. The fourth lieutenant was Samuel Williams. He, too, had joined the Navy in 1807 and had just won his commission in 1812. He had yet to see action. All in all, Albritton thought they were a fine team to take to war.

His interviews with his "young gentlemen" went well, for the most part. The senior midshipman was eighteen-year-old Charles Franklin, who turned out to be the grandson of Benjamin. The remaining five ranged in age from a seventeen-year-old with experience on three other ships to a thirteen-year-old making his first voyage. *Well,* thought Albritton, *could be a lot worse. We'll see how well they learn.*

The warrant officers came next. Albritton had them in as a group, although he dealt with them individually. The sailing master was a grizzled veteran, about Albritton's age, by the name of Frank Warren. He'd been fortunate to learn his craft on Indiamen of the British East India Company, working his way up to sailing master. He left that lucrative position in protest of the impressment of American seamen by the Royal Navy and returned home to fight for his country. Albritton questioned the purser, Joseph Petry, very closely about his account keeping and came away satisfied but determined to keep an eye on him. He warned the bosun, Patrick Jones, against using a starter too liberally. The carpenter, Anthony Wade, and the gunner, Frederick George, were both men of good reputation in the fleet. Finally, the captain was pleased to see that his surgeon, Henry Brown, did not have a bulbous red nose, a sign of fondness for alcohol.

"Gentlemen," the captain said as the interviews concluded, "you are the backbone of the ship. How well you do your jobs determines what I have to fight with. Do your jobs well, and I have no doubt we shall return from our voyage with prize money galore. Dismissed."

The warrant officers rose as a group and filed out of the cabin. Xavier entered, and Albritton introduced him to Sommers. He turned to his first lieutenant. "Mr. Chandler, let's go over the watch list."

The following afternoon found Albritton once again standing before Secretary Jones's desk.

"Well, Captain? What have you to report?"

"Ready for sea, Mr. Secretary," Albritton reported. "Have you decided where yet?"

"The general consensus is that Boston's our best choice. Do you agree?"

"I do."

"Good!" Jones tapped his desk with his fingertip. "When can you leave?"

Albritton thought for a moment. "Tomorrow night. I think it better to do it over two nights— the first would be moving the ships down around Norfolk, and the second will see us break out into the Atlantic."

"Why not do it all in one night?"

"Two nights means we can moved slowly down to Norfolk," Albritton said. "That means we can hide as much as possible. Also, I will not be entering Gosport."

"Oh?"

Albritton shook his head. "Two reasons, Mr. Secretary. One, the British will be watching it very closely. Two, there are a couple of inlets to the west where we can hide both ships during the day."

Jones smiled and nodded. "I shall leave the details in your capable hands, Captain. Once you make Boston, prepare your ships for sea and sail when convenient. Your orders will be delivered to you onboard your ship later today. Any questions?"

"Just one: with what am I to fight? *Columbia* is short on both carronades and 24-pounders."

The secretary smiled. "It just so happens, Captain, that USS *President* is at Boston for a lengthy refit. There will be a provision in your orders that her armament is to be transferred to you when you arrive. Anything else?"

Albritton shook his head.

The secretary came around his desk and shook his guest's hand. "Good luck to you, Captain, and good hunting."

"Thank you, sir."

Outside the hut, Albritton pulled his cloak tighter against the cold, stiff wind.

"Hezekiah?" came a voice cutting through the wind. "Hezekiah? Is that you?"

Albritton turned to see Commodore John Rodgers approaching with his hand already extended. Albritton shook it warmly.

"It is you!" Rodgers exclaimed. "How are you, old man?"

"Better, now that I've seen you!" Albritton declared. "How

are your wife and young son?"

"Fine. I have sent them to Minerva's parents in Philadelphia." Rodgers looked out over the bay and nodded toward *Columbia*. "Yours?"

Albritton nodded. "What are you doing here, John?"

"*President's* in for a refit at Baltimore," Rodgers explained. "So I was ordered down here for consultations."

"Good for you," Albritton said as he clasped his friend on the shoulder. "It'll be good for you to be home for a bit."

Rodgers turned grim. "You've not heard, then?"

"Heard what?"

"The British raided my village last year. They burned my house to the ground."

Albritton stared for a moment, mute with shock. He squeezed his friend's shoulder. "I am sorry, John."

"I intend to make them pay, Hezekiah," Rodgers said with a grim smile. "I understand we are about to commission *Guerriere* with 50 guns at Philadelphia. I am here to make sure she goes to me."

"Are you free for lunch?" Albritton asked.

"Exactly where I was heading! Come, join me!"

The two men set out on foot, their heads bent in conversation against the wind. They came to a tavern and entered, taking seats near to the fire. The barmaid came over, and Rodgers ordered for both of them.

"When do you sail?" Rodgers asked.

"Tomorrow night." Albritton paused to allow the barmaid to deliver their ales and take their order. "We head to Boston to finish fitting out, then we take *Columbia* and *Argus* to sea to bedevil our English cousins one more time."

"Who commands *Argus*?" Rodgers asked.

Albritton raised his eyes to hold his friend's. "They gave her to Calloway."

Rodgers set his tankard down and sat a little more erect than before. The stern look and pressed lips left no doubt as to his opinion.

"John?" Albritton prompted.

Rodgers shrugged. "You had to be there, Hezekiah—back in 1807, I mean. I presided over his court martial. Brand new frigate, and he takes her to sea totally unprepared to fight. The deck was still strewn with supplies not yet stored, and his gun crews were totally ignorant of their duties." Rodgers took a quick drink, obviously reliving unpleasant memories. "He *knew* the British were patrolling off the mouth of Chesapeake Bay, and he knew why. It was criminal not to be ready to fight." Another pause, another drink. "Do you know the worst part? Calloway never owned up to his responsibility for what happened. Three or four killed and over a dozen wounded, and he never stood up and accepted responsibility for what happened to his ship. He actually showed up at the court martial expecting a slap on the wrist, some sort of reprimand in his file that nobody would pay attention to! By God, I wasn't going to have it! The verdict was unanimous, and Calloway was dismissed from the Navy. Of course, with the start of the war, and the Navy being starved for experienced officers, they took him back." Another shrug. "To be fair, I understand he has done good work since coming back, but this is his first command, so far as I know."

Albritton thought about what his friend had said. "Am I going to have trouble with him?"

"I hope not," Rodgers replied.

Their food arrived on a large tray that was set on the next table. A plate appeared in front of each man, containing two or three mutton chops covered in gravy, and a baked potato. A bowl of peas was placed on their table along with several slices of fresh hot bread on a plate along with a gravy boat.

Both men dug in with gusto. When their plates were almost clear, Rodgers sat back and pointed at his companion with his fork. "You know, Albritton, you're fortunate to be here just now. Why, just after the British left, we were eating army rations for six weeks!"

Both men cleaned their plates, drained their ale, and settled the bill before stepping out into the street again. "So, where are you off to now?" Rodgers asked.

"I need to get back to my ship. My orders will be coming aboard shortly." Albritton shook hands with his old friend. "Thank you for lunch, John."

"My pleasure. Take care, Hezekiah."

CHAPTER THREE

Albritton was met by his first lieutenant as he stepped on to *Columbia's* deck.

Chandler came to attention and touched his hat before speaking. "Orders came aboard about an hour ago, sir. I put them in your cabin."

"Thank you, Mr. Chandler. I shall send for you presently."

"Aye, sir."

Albritton went below. He found Xavier cleaning his captain's brace of pistols. The coxswain gestured to the sealed packet at the captain's place at the head of the table.

"Orders arrived, Captain," he said simply.

"So I see," Albritton said as he removed his coat and hat. Sommers appeared to take them from him. "Tell me, Xavier, what to you think of *Columbia*?"

The coxswain shrugged. "She's a pretty ship, sir."

"And the crew?"

"I'm sure you'll work them up before long, sir."

Albritton sat and picked up the order packet. Satisfied that the seal was intact, he pulled out a penknife and cut the binding around the packet. He broke the seal and opened the envelope, taking out the three pages. He scanned them hurriedly the first time through, then re-read them closely. He was ordered to take his ships to Boston, where they would provision for an extended voyage of at least six months' duration. Their objective was to harass the enemy's commerce, taking such prizes as the captain considered worthy while burning or sinking the rest. The only mention of Calloway and USS *Argus* was a single sentence, which said that he would be accompanied by USS *Argus* under the command of Commander James Calloway and that Commander Calloway was to act in accordance with Albritton's orders.

Albritton read the orders through one more time before setting them down. He leaned back in his chair, crossing his arms over his chest and stretching his legs, which he crossed at the ankles. He stared at the orders and considered.

"Sommers!" he called.

The steward appeared. "Sir?"

"Can you do a dinner party for four? Tonight?"

"Aye, sir, but I'd have to run ashore and do some shopping. When were you looking to eat?"

"End of the second dog watch."

Sommers smiled. "Leave it to me, Captain."

"Good." He rose and went to the door. "Pass the word for the first lieutenant."

"Aye, sir," the sentry replied.

Albritton barely had time to sit on the on the settee in the day cabin when the first lieutenant was shown in.

"You sent for me, Captain?"

"Yes, Mr. Chandler. I'm throwing a dinner party tonight. Xavier will be taking a boat ashore so Sommers can do some shopping. I presume you will be available to attend?"

"Of course, sir."

"Good," Albritton said, rubbing his hands together and warming to his subject. "I want to write a note. Have the third lieutenant—what's his name again?"

"Hill, sir."

"Yes, Mr. Hill. Have him deliver the note to Commander Calloway aboard the *Argus*. We shall invite him and his first lieutenant. Do you know his name, by any chance?"

"I believe the first lieutenant is a Mr. Wilson, sir."

"Very good." Albritton moved to his desk and sat down. He took out a sheet of paper and a pen. He opened the inkwell, dipped the pen, and began to scratch out a note. He signed it at the end and folded it closed before sealing it with wax. He handed it to Chandler.

"Have Mr. Hill leave at once." He closed the inkwell and stood. "Let's see just how good Sommers is, shall we?"

Four bells rang out as Commander Calloway and Lieutenant Wilson stepped up on to *Columbia's* deck. Lieutenant Chandler, accompanied by Lieutenant Mitchell, stepped up and saluted. The visiting officers replied in kind.

"Commander Calloway," Chandler said formally, "I am Lieutenant Chandler, the first officer. This is Lieutenant Mitchell, our second."

"Pleased to meet you," Calloway replied. "Mr. Wilson, my first officer."

"Thank you both for coming," Chandler said as he stood to the side. "Captain Albritton is waiting below, sir. If you'll follow me?"

Chandler set off and led the men below to the captain's cabin. The sentry opened the door, and the three officers found Captain Albritton standing in the middle of his day cabin.

"Sir," Chandler said by way of introduction, "may I present Commander James Calloway of HMS *Argus* and his first, Lieutenant Wilson?" He turned to the visitors. "Gentlemen, allow me to present your host, Captain Hezekiah Albritton."

The three officers bowed together, then Albritton stepped forward and shook each man's hand heartily. "A pleasure, sirs, I assure you," he said, waiving them to seats on the settee. He walked over to the desk where a large decanter of amber liquid stood beside four glasses. "Commander, may I offer you some bourbon?"

"Bourbon?" Calloway was confused.

"Excuse me," Albritton said as he poured. "That's what I call it. It is a rather unusual whiskey I found. It comes from Bourbon County in Kentucky, so I just call it bourbon. It is quite unlike anything I have ever tasted."

He handed a glass containing two fingers of the amber liquid to each man before picking up his own. He raised it in a silent toast and drank. The other three men hesitated only a moment before following suit. He smiled at the look of astonishment that covered each man's face. Young Lieutenant Wilson coughed.

"Extraordinary, Captain!" Calloway exclaimed. "However did you come across it?"

"A friend," Albritton replied. "He was in Kentucky on business and brought me a barrel by way of payment of a debt." He looked at the liquid in his glass before draining it. "Best payment I ever received, if you ask me."

The others could only agree. Sommers appeared and refilled their glasses.

"About fifteen minutes to supper, sir," he said to Albritton.

"Thank you, Sommers." They rose and made their way to the table. Albritton took his seat. "Well, let's get some work done while we wait. Commander, is *Argus* ready for sea?"

"Aye, Captain," came the reply. "I understand we're heading to another port to make ready for a long voyage?"

Albritton picked up his glass, but set it down again. "That's true. We sail for Boston. Once there, we'll provision for an extended voyage commerce raiding."

Calloway's eyebrows rose at the prospects, and he shared a look of anticipation with his premier. "May I ask where, sir?"

"The final orders are to be delivered to *Columbia* sometime tomorrow," Albritton confided. "I expect our areas of operation to be the Caribbean and North Atlantic."

"Marvelous!" Wilson exclaimed, slapping the table with the palm of his hand. He noticed the look on his host's face and the elevated eyebrow. "Sorry, sir."

Albritton favored him with a slight nod and let the matter pass. He turned to Calloway. "My plan is to escape from the bay over two nights. The first will take us to an inlet on the York River where we can hide for a day or two. As soon as the winds are promising, we'll move past the British squadron during the night at full sail and disappear into the Atlantic. Nobody will see us again until we appear at Boston."

Calloway pursed his lips and looked at the table as he digested what he had heard. "And after we leave Boston?"

Albritton paused a moment as Sommers and his stewards entered carrying platters and bowls. "What do you mean?"

Argus' captain stirred uncomfortably. "Do you have any idea what the orders will say about my position?"

"We shall know that when they arrive," *Columbia's* captain replied. Seeing it did not satisfy, he continued, "If the orders are unchanged from the secretary's conversations with me, you will be placed under my command and will operate according to my instructions."

Calloway's eyes closed and his gaze dropped. He was obviously disappointed. Albritton noticed and almost allowed the moment to pass, but at the last moment reconsidered.

"Is something wrong, Commander?" he asked.

Calloway raised his head and opened his eyes, his gaze totally dispirited. "No, Captain. That's about what I expected."

Albritton's eyes narrowed at the words. He turned to Calloway and said, "Commander, let me make one thing perfectly clear. I do not care one whit about 1807. I *do* care about 1814. Everything I have heard from Secretary Jones and others has been very complimentary of the work you have done since your return to the Navy. It's the reason you have command of *Argus*. Well deserved, in my opinion." He sat back, his eyes boring straight into Calloway's. "Do we understand each other, sir?"

Calloway just stared at him for a moment or two before the slightest hint of a smile could be seen at the corner of his mouth. "Aye, Captain," he said, "and thank you."

Albritton nodded once, and the incident was closed. He rose and picked up his glass. "Gentlemen, I propose that we put our business aside for a while and enjoy this feast before us. But first, a toast: To President Madison! May he lead us to victory!"

The others echoed the toast, and they drank.

The captain set his glass down and looked out over the table. "Now, what delights have the good Sommers and his men set before us? Commander, I believe that is a roast leg of mutton before you; would you be so kind? Thank you. Mr. Chandler, help yourself to the roast chicken! I have stewed potatoes in a bowl here, and I believe you have the peas and carrots, Mr. Wilson! Gentlemen, help yourselves and pass it around!"

The conversation lagged as the food made its way around the table. Chandler whistled in appreciation as Sommers came in with a plate of fresh, hot bread and a crock of butter. The four men dug into the feast with abandon.

"Enjoy it while you can, gentlemen," Chandler said. "I

doubt we'll see anything like this in the great Atlantic!"

The four of them laughed heartily. In no time the bone was all that was left of the mutton and the chicken was plucked clean. Sommers cleared the table before returning with an aromatic apple pie.

"Really!" Chandler exclaimed. "Sommers! This is too much!"

Albritton scooped each man out a generous slice. Wilson looked up.

"Captain, request permission to join *Columbia*."

"Why so?"

"Your cook is better than ours." The *Columbia* men laughed, and Wilson continued. "Tell me, what's the penalty for kidnapping a captain's steward?"

"Death by hanging," Calloway said.

"Ha!" Albritton cried. "You'd not get off so easy, sir! I'd court-martial you and sentence you to eat with the crew the remainder of the voyage!"

"God save me!" Wilson cried. "Truly a fate worse than death!"

The officers adjourned to the day cabin for coffee and cigars.

"Tell me, Captain," Calloway inquired, "I've never been to Boston—will we be able to get prize crews there?"

Albritton considered for a moment. "Yes, I should think so. Our worst problem will be provisions. I have no idea what the state of the harbor warehouses might be. We may be forced to find a couple of fat British merchantmen quickly to fill our holds!" He shrugged. "We'll have to see when we get there."

"Forgive me if I overstep," Wilson said, "but just how will the prize money be distributed?"

"It is my understanding," Chandler interjected, "that the

orders will place Captain Albritton in command over both ships. If that is so, he'll be entitled to the squadron commander's share."

"As well as a captain's share for *Columbia*?" Wilson asked.

"Obviously," Chandler replied. "Is that a problem?"

"No, of course not." The first lieutenant shrugged. "Privilege of rank."

"Yes, well," Albritton stepped in, taking control of the conversation, "let's hope we have a great deal to argue over. Assuming both ships are ready for sea, we shall move tomorrow night." He rose, and the others followed. "Thank you, gentlemen. Mr. Chandler, will you show our guests to their boat? Commander Calloway, a moment, please."

"We shall wait for you outside, sir," Chandler said. He led Lieutenant Wilson from the room.

After the door closed, Calloway spoke up. "Sir, I apologize for my first. I shall speak to him regarding his place."

"Thank you. I wanted to let you know that I shall send for you tomorrow so we can go over our orders together before we depart."

Calloway came to attention. "I shall await your convenience, sir. Good day."

Albritton stared at the door long after it had closed behind his guest, wondering if the man would ever be able to leave 1807 behind him.

HMS *London* was sailing SSW on the starboard tack on its way to join the blockade squadron at the mouth of Chesapeake Bay. Captain Knighton paced the quarterdeck, wishing he could make his frigate fly. They were four days into an eight-day trip that had been delayed by two days due to slow dockyard repairs. He could only hope that Albritton and *Columbia* were still at Washington when he arrived.

He frowned again as he reached the rail and made his turn. The knot that was forming in the pit of his stomach told him otherwise. The one good thing that had come out of their delayed departure was that they'd received intelligence confirming that indeed Hezekiah Albritton had been given command of *Columbia*. Knighton drew a deep breath and held it a moment before exhaling slowly in an attempt to calm himself, but he could not help it. The very thought of capturing or sinking *Columbia* and entertaining the pride of the American Navy at his dinner table excited him. It would be the crowning achievement of his career.

He pursed his lips. All that would become much harder if Albritton managed to make his escape into the Atlantic. The first thing to do upon their arrival was ask the commodore to send a schooner to make an extensive search of the bay and especially the Naval Yard at Washington. Hopefully, that would not take more than a few days, depending on how many inlets were big enough to hide Albritton's two ships. The letter he carried from Admiral Keats gave him the authority to use any resources in pursuit of *Columbia* and *Argus*; the only stipulation, the only limitation on him, was that he could not requisition any ships and leave the blockading squadrons undermanned.

He made another turn and reviewed the intelligence he'd received from the governor. USS *Columbia* was supposed to be the first of the next-generation of American frigates. They were slightly bigger than *Constitution* and her sisters and incorporated improvements the Americans hoped would keep their edge over the newest British models. Knighton stopped at the rail and looked out over the glassy sea with his hands clasped behind his back. *Well,* he thought, *hopefully we'll have the answer to that question very soon.*

At the Washington Naval Yard, Hezekiah Albritton also chose to spend the forenoon watch on the quarterdeck of his ship, only he was awaiting the arrival of the orders that would turn him loose on British shipping in the Atlantic Ocean. He looked up at the spars hanging in a stately manner over the deck and was pleased to feel the sun on his face. The gentle sea breeze complemented the warmth perfectly; Albritton hoped it was a good omen for the coming operation.

Mr. Franklin, the senior midshipman, approached him and saluted. "Begging your pardon, sir, but there is a boat approaching. You said you wished to be notified."

"Quite right, Mr. Franklin," the captain replied. "Thank you. Kindly meet the emissary and bring him to me."

Franklin raised his hat. "Aye, sir."

Albritton turned and studied the shore for a moment before looking at the USS *Argus*. He thought it strange that he did not see Calloway on his quarterdeck, then he shrugged. *To each his own.* He turned back to the deck when he heard footsteps approaching. It was Mr. Franklin leading a lieutenant.

"Sir," Franklin said, "this is Lieutenant Croft, from Secretary Jones's office. Lieutenant, I present to you Captain Albritton of USS *Columbia*." The lieutenant saluted, and Albritton nodded in reply.

"What do you have for me, Lieutenant?" he asked.

"Sir, I have your orders from the secretary."

"Good. Follow me to my cabin."

Albritton stepped off for the companionway stairs and left young Mr. Croft to catch up. When they got to the cabin, Albritton went straight to his desk and sat down before holding out his hand for the package. Croft handed it over. Albritton checked to make sure the seals were intact before signing the receipt and giving it back to the lieutenant. Croft came to attention.

"If there is nothing else, sir?"

"No, nothing. My best to the secretary."

"Aye, sir. Good hunting, Captain."

"Thank you, Lieutenant."

When he was alone, Albritton pulled out a penknife and broke the seal. He withdrew the five pages inside and read them carefully. When he was done, he set them down and sighed.

"Sommers!" he called. The steward appeared.

"Yes, Captain?"

"Bourbon, if you please."

Commander Calloway sat in the stern sheets of his gig and steeled himself for the coming interview. He wondered what was in the orders Albritton had received. The best he could hope for was that the decision as to whether or not *Argus* could be released to raid independently had been left completely in Albritton's hands. The worst case would be that the two ships would be ordered to stay in company—meaning that Calloway would stay under Albritton's thumb for the entire cruise.

Calloway sighed and looked down at his sword's hilt, cradled in his hands in his lap. *One mistake,* he thought again, *one error in judgment, and I am branded for life.* He looked up at the approaching bulk of USS *Columbia. Who am I kidding?* he thought with a sigh. *I don't think I'll ever be free from the shadow of 1807. No matter what anyone says, no matter what they promise, someone higher up in the Navy Department will remember 1807, and I will be done.* He lowered his eyes again and tried to resign himself to his fate.

When he stepped up on *Columbia's* deck, Calloway was greeted by the first lieutenant, Mr. Chandler. Calloway wasn't sure what to make of *Columbia's* premier yet; he heard the undertones in his voice of Southern aristocracy. He was shown to the captain's cabin, where he found the man himself reading in the day cabin. Albritton closed his book and rose to greet his guest.

"Good to see you, Commander," the captain said. "Thank you for coming."

Calloway shook the man's hand warmly. "What are you reading?"

"*Robinson Crusoe*. I read it some time ago and loved it, but recently I heard that the book is based on actual events— a man was actually marooned on an island, as recounted in the book and lived to tell about it. So, I'm reading it again, only this time I'm looking at every single thing that he does and trying to decide if that is real or fiction."

"Yes, I heard that about the book, too," Calloway agreed. "I'd be interested to know what conclusions you draw."

"Gladly. Shall we sit and discuss our orders?" Albritton led his guest to the table where Sommers had a pot of coffee and two mugs waiting for them. The captain motioned Calloway into a seat while he filled a mug for each of them and slid one to his guest. He sat at the head of the table and pulled a sheaf of paper from his inside coat pocket, holding it up. "Our orders. They differ little from what we expected. We proceed to Boston and complete our provisioning. We sail at my discretion." He handed the papers over.

"Thank you." Calloway smoothed the papers on the table and sipped his coffee as he began to read. He skimmed hurriedly through the orders, searching for the relevant part until he found it. Albritton had complete discretion when it came to *Argus* operating independently. He sat back and released the breath he hadn't realized he'd been holding, then picked up his mug and took a long drink.

Albritton watched with narrowed eyes as his guest went through the orders. He raised his mug to get a drink, hoping the steam would shield his eyes. He thought he knew what the man was looking for and hoped he was wrong, but he wasn't; Calloway stopped suddenly at the appropriate paragraph. He read and re-read it several times before leaning back in his chair and ignoring the remaining paragraphs. He set his cup down.

"Any questions?" Albritton asked.

"None, sir. When do you wish to sail?"

"Dark of the moon is tomorrow night," the captain said, "so I want to move to our hiding spot off the York River tonight and use that extra darkness to aid our breakout into the Atlantic the following evening."

"*Argus* will be ready."

"Good. Your orders, Commander, are to always be within communication range of this ship. You are not to go outside that without my express orders. Do I need to put these in writing?"

"No, sir; I understand the orders."

Albritton stood. "Be ready to sail after dark tonight, Commander."

Calloway came to attention. "Aye, sir." He picked up his hat and left the cabin.

Albritton poured the remainder of the coffee into his mug and walked back to the settee in the day room. He set the mug down and leaned his head back on the bulkhead, closing his eyes for a moment to think. His fears appeared to be confirmed: Commander Calloway was still looking to prove something to someone. Who that someone was, Albritton had no idea; he doubted Calloway himself could name the individual. It was obvious from talking to the man, from observing his body language, that he was still haunted by

1807. Now he was Albritton's problem.

Wonderful.

Charles Franklin came off watch and retreated to the cockpit. He plopped into an empty chair and was handed a drink immediately. He looked up into the friendly face of James Lee, one of the youngest of the "young gentlemen" on board *Columbia.*

"Thank you, James," he said before taking a deep drink and sighing in pleasure.

"Welcome, sir," Lee replied. "Do you know when we sail?"

Franklin shook his head, expecting to be left to his drink. Lee hung around, and Franklin lowered his cup. "What?"

"Is it true?" Lee asked sheepishly.

Franklin sighed. *Not again!* "Is what true?"

"That your grandfather was Benjamin Franklin!"

Franklin picked up his glass. "Yes, I'm afraid it is."

"Wow!" Lee said. "My grandfather said he was a great man!"

"Is that so?"

"You bet! Knew him in Philadelphia when he was a printer. Said he told a lot of jokes."

"Sounds about right. I never knew him."

"Really?"

Franklin shrugged. "I wasn't born until five years after he died."

"Wow!" Lee said with eyes wide open. "Oh! I'm sorry! I hope I didn't hurt your feelings, talking about him like that."

The senior midshipman smiled. "No worries, James. I've heard lots of people talk about him just that way. I wish I could have known him, that's all."

"I, as well," Lee said with a smile.

CHAPTER FOUR

Darkness settled over the waters like a thick blanket on a cold night. Captain Albritton stood near the fantail alternately observing the sky and the deck. He felt more than saw Lieutenant Chandler approach and halt a respectful distance away.

"Yes, Mr. Chandler?" he asked without taking his eyes from some topmen ascending to their posts.

The premier raised his hat. "Ready to move any time you like, sir. The wind's freshening, so hopefully it will be a swift passage."

"And *Argus*?"

"Standing by, sir. Night signal ready to hoist for them to follow us."

"Very good." Albritton paused to listen to the ship's bell ring six times, then he gazed at the sky again. "We'll wait a bit. Do we have any eyes out yet?"

"Aye, sir, five gunboats are scouting down the Potomac. They left the yard about thirty minutes ago."

Albritton sighed and looked to his first. "You've done well, Mr. Chandler; everything that is within our control has been attended to. Now we get to see whose side God is on this night."

An hour later, one of the gunboats returned with the news that the channel was clear. The two ships raised sail and edged out into the Potomac. They crept downriver as silently as possible, every light out and extra lookouts posted. Albritton stood in the middle of his quarterdeck, hands clasped behind his back, pleased with their progress but irritated that he could do nothing about any British spies on the shore. Between the current and the wind, they were proceeding at a pretty good clip; if those spies had their backs turned, they might miss his force altogether.

An hour into their trip, the premier approached and touched his hat. "I've posted extra lookouts, sir. Mr. Warren says we'll make our turn at the York River in about two hours."

The captain stirred at that. He nodded and said, "Would you care to join me for a drink, Mr. Chandler?"

"Of course, Captain."

"Follow me." Albritton stepped off and led his first lieutenant to his cabin, a nod of thanks tossed to the sentry who held the door for them. Inside, he set his hat on the table.

"Sommers!"

The steward appeared in the pantry doorway. "Sir?"

"Coffee for two, if you please. We shall be in the day cabin."

"Aye, sir."

Albritton led his guest aft and sat down beneath his frigate's stern windows. He was pleased to see that Sommers had rigged curtains so they would not be betrayed by a gleam of light.

"Sit down, Lieutenant," he said. "Sorry we're not having bourbon, but I thought the coffee might help us stay awake this night."

"Perfectly all right, sir, I assure you. Sommers brews the best cup in the fleet."

As if on queue, Sommers appeared with two steaming cups on a tray. He set one beside each officer before turning to his captain. "Will there be anything else, sir?"

"No, Sommers," the captain said. "Thank you."

The steward bowed and left the room.

Chandler blew on the rim of his cup and gingerly took a sip. "Ah," he said, "as good as advertised. Tell me, Captain, how far will we have to go up the York after we make our turn?"

"Yes," Albritton said as he set his cup down, "about that... We're not going to the York River."

Chandler looked puzzled. "I understood we were to hide along the York, sir."

"I know. I told everyone that, including the secretary, but that was only for the benefit of any British spies who happened to be listening. No, Mr. Chandler, we will be hiding in a cove on the western shore of Mobjack Bay. Kindly ask the sentry to pass the word for Mr. Warren, if you please."

"Aye, sir." The first lieutenant rose and did as he was asked. Minutes later, the sailing master was admitted to the cabin.

"Mr. Warren," Albritton said without preamble, "we are not going to the York River. We are going to hide in a cove I know of on the western shore of Mobjack Bay."

Warren's eyebrows rose at the news. Then he looked toward the deck above them, and his eyes narrowed. Slowly, a smile began to creep over his face. "Aye, I can see it now."

Albritton smiled. "I thought you might."

Chandler grimaced. "I'm afraid I'm not at all familiar with that bay. Is it that much better than the York?"

Warren rubbed his hands together in anticipation. "Oh, yes! There's many a good hiding place on that shore that're hours away from any populated area."

"Mr. Warren, how long until we can make our turn?" Albritton asked.

The sailing master looked up again and then pulled his watch from his pocket. Albritton could see Warren's lips moving as he studied the hands. He decided to wait patiently for the answer. It was quick to come.

"An hour, sir, maybe and hour and a quarter, depending on the current."

"Very good. You may return to the deck, Mr. Warren. I shall be up presently."

"Aye, Captain."

"Now, Mr. Chandler," Albritton said, "we come to the tricky part of the whole operation. We must let Commander Calloway know our intentions."

"How do we do that, sir?"

"We cut our speed and allow *Argus* to catch up to us. We light their night signal at barely deck level in the hope that they will be the only ones to see it. As soon as we are close enough, we use a speaking trumpet to pass along a short message: *'Follow me.'* That's it, nothing more. Then we douse their night signal and light a single lantern on the fantail. Hopefully, that will be enough for them to see when we make our turn and follow us into the cove. What do you think?"

Chandler picked up his cup and drank the dregs, even though they were cold now; it gave him a chance to think. If Calloway failed to see *Columbia* as she dropped back, there could be a collision that could result in both ships being captured by the British at daybreak. But, if handled correctly by both ships, the captain's plan would allow a quick and efficient way to pass the information. He sighed and put his cup down. "I think it's the best option open to us, sir."

"Good," Albritton said. "Let's get to the quarterdeck."

When they got to the deck, Albritton was pleased to see not a shred of light—save the occasional use of a shielded lantern—on his entire deck. He turned toward the shore and saw few lights there either. They were joined almost immediately by Lieutenant Mitchell, officer of the watch.

"Captain, we are still on course. No traffic observed on the river."

"Any sign of *Argus*?"

"None, sir."

"Mr. Mitchell, we are going to take in a reef to slow the ship down. Who has the best eyes on your watch?"

"Middleton, sir. He's in the foretop."

"Pass the word for him, if you please."

"Aye, sir." Mitchell turned and gave the order.

"Where is the night signal for *Argus*?" the captain asked.

"At the mizzenmast, sir, ready to be lit and raised."

"I need you to rig it so we can raise it at the fantail and light it, but no higher than necessary for it to be seen aft. We shall also need a lantern."

"Aye, sir." The lieutenant was obviously confused, but he turned and gave the midshipman of the watch the orders. Almost immediately, a tar appeared and saluted.

"Captain," Mitchell said, "this is Middleton."

He was barely more than a youth, but something about the way he carried himself inspired confidence from his captain.

"Mr. Middleton, I have a very important assignment for you. We are slowing *Columbia* down to allow *Argus* to catch up. The reason for this is that I must pass a short but vital message to her captain. You are to position yourself so that you can see *Argus* as she approaches. When you see her, you give the word so we can light her night signal. Do you understand?"

"Aye, Captain," Middleton replied. "Do we know how far back she is?"

"No, but I expect not very. Take your station."

"Aye, Captain."

Mitchell reappeared. "*Argus* night signal in place at the fantail, sir. We are ready to light it and raise it just higher than the railing. There's a lantern ready to be lit and hung."

"Very good," Albritton said. "Stand by."

The captain stepped back and waited. Middleton took his place at the fantail to the left of the night signal, a spyglass in his hand, which he periodically raised to his eye. Suddenly, Albritton saw him kneel to steady the glass on the rail, then he raised his hand. Albritton rushed to join him.

"Report," he said in a loud whisper.

"Ship approaching." Middleton pointed. "I'm not sure it's *Argus*."

Albritton squinted into the darkness, unsure if he saw anything moving or not. He had to make a decision and hope Calloway made the same one.

"Light the night signal," he said. "Raise it."

Mitchell oversaw the lighting before giving the order to raise it. When it cleared the rail, he gave the order to hold it there.

"Now we see," Albritton said under his breath.

Two full minutes went by before they saw the proper reply from *Argus*. Albritton didn't fault Calloway the time; after all, he wasn't expecting the signal for another hour or more.

"Well done!" he whispered to Mitchell and Middleton. He went around them and grabbed a speaking trumpet on his way to the larboard rail.

Calloway realized what was happening and altered his course to come alongside.

Albritton thought he could barely make out the man's form through the darkness. He raised the trumpet to his lips. "Follow me!" he called out. "Follow me!"

"Aye, sir!" came the faint reply.

Albritton waved and returned to the wheel. "Alright, Mr. Chandler, let out the reef again. Mr. Mitchell, dowse the night signal and hang out the lantern. I don't like using a light tonight, but we have to have something for *Argus* to follow. Now, Mr. Warren, when and where do you recommend we make our turn?"

Warren went to the chart table where a hand was holding a shielded lantern. He picked up the chart, careful to make sure that it stayed under the light. "We're about here, Captain," he said, pointing with his finger. "I think we ought to move to about here," he slid his finger about an inch or so, "before making the turn. That will make sure we're in the middle of the channel. Where's the cove you want to use?" Albritton leaned forward and placed his finger on a small inlet about halfway up the western shore.

Warren grunted and placed his finger on a spot a little further north. "I thought you would head for this one, but yours will do. I recommend that before we enter the bay, we raise the night signal again."

The captain studied the chart for a moment before nodding. "I agree. My plan is to enter the cove just as the dawn breaks. We may need the light. As soon as we are both in, I want boats lowered to turn both ships around, so we are pointed at the entrance. We also need to establish a lookout position on the shore. After that, we can let the men rest. Opinions, gentlemen?" His eyes moved from Chandler to Mitchell to Warren, but none of them responded. He looked around until he saw Mr. Jackson, the midshipman of the watch. "Mr. Jackson, I want you to go to my cabin. My compliments to Sommers, and can he please send up a pot of coffee to the quarterdeck? Five cups.”

“Aye, Captain!”

An hour passed before Mr. Warren approached the captain again. “It’s time, Captain.”

“Very well, Mr. Warren.” Albritton pulled out his watch and held it close to his face. “We have 45 minutes before the change of watch—plenty of time to complete the maneuver. Mr. Mitchell, light *Argus*’s night signal and hoist as before. Mr. Warren, we will enter the bay as soon as *Argus* acknowledges.”

“Aye, sir.”

Argus raised her night signal, and *Columbia* swung to starboard and entered Mobjack Bay. Once safely out of sight of the river, both ships hove to until the first crack of light over the eastern horizon. As soon as he could see, Albritton led both ships up the western shore of the bay and into a cove more than big enough to hide them.

Mr. Chandler spoke up. “You may proceed, Mr. Jones.”

Once the orders were given, the premier picked up a speaking trumpet and relayed his captain’s instructions to *Argus*. Boats were lowered from both ships, and the crews assigned labored mightily to turn their respective ships about, so their bows faced the mouth of the cove. It was backbreaking, precise work. Care had to be taken to avoid running either ship aground in the limited space they had in which to work; a mistake like that might result in a delay that would allow the British to find them. Fortunately, Chandler had ordered a man with a lead posted to the nose of each boat to ensure sufficient depth was available. In the end, both ships were duly brought about and made ready for a quick exit the following night.

“Mr. Chandler, give all hands a ’Well Done’ from me. An extra ration of grog this evening for them as well. Please tell the bosun and his mates they may attend to any repairs that are necessary, but take care for the men to rest as much as possible today. They have had a long night, and the next may be even longer."

"Aye, Captain." Chandler stepped in close. "Sir, might I suggest that you get some rest as well? You were on deck longer than anyone last night and, as you say, tonight may well be worse. I will tend to the repairs with Mr. Jones and rework the watch bill for today to see that all hands get a few hours' extra sleep."

"Thank you, Mr. Chandler," Albritton said as he stretched his back. "I believe I shall take your advice. Please leave word that I am to be called at the first sign of a ship near the cove entrance. Be sure you get those extra hours of sleep yourself."

"Aye, aye, Captain!"

Albritton made his way below to his cabin. He sat at his desk, suddenly exhausted, and laid his head for a moment on his folded arms. The next thing he knew was Sommers' hand on his shoulder, and he realized he'd fallen asleep.

"How long have I been here?" he asked.

"Nearly two hours now, sir," Sommers replied. "I thought you might like something to eat. I have some cold ham and cheese at hand, perhaps with a glass of wine?"

The captain sat up and raised his arms high over his head to stretch his back before rising stiffly. "Yes, thank you, Sommers. That will be fine."

He picked up his copy of *Robinson Crusoe* off the desk and headed to the table. Sommers already had his place set with two slabs of ham and several selections of cheese on a plate along with a glass of wine. He sat and said grace before opening his book. He always said grace before a meal; it was a promise he'd made to his mother just before she passed away when he was eight, and he had honored it ever since.

Had anyone asked him, Albritton would have been hard

pressed to say which was more fulfilling to him, the book or the plate. He ate as he read, enjoying both, until his attention was caught by the plate being empty. He looked around, slightly embarrassed by his groping the empty plate and relieved not to see Sommers watching him. He finished off the wine and stood, taking his book with him to his sleeping cabin. He pulled off his boots and rolled into his cot. Suspended from the deck above, years of practice allowed him to settle in on the first try. He managed to read a few more pages before being suddenly awakened by the book dropping onto his face. He sighed and closed first the book and then his eyes.

It was still light when Albritton was awakened by a hand on his shoulder. His eyes opened to see Xavier standing over him.

"It's time, Captain," he said. "Just calling the first dog watch."

Albritton rolled out of bed and sat on his sea chest while he pulled on his boots. "The ship?"

"Mr. Chandler's in the day cabin waiting to report." Xavier shrugged. "She looks good, Captain."

The captain nodded and stood. Over the years, he'd realized that Xavier had as good an eye when it came to such things as almost any officer he'd ever known. Still, the proprieties had to be observed. He ran a comb through his hair and stepped out to receive his premier's report.

Chandler came to attention as his captain entered the room.

"Sir, Mr. Jones and his mates have gone over every inch of the rigging and pronounced themselves satisfied. The carpenter has examined the hull and reported no leaks or seepage, and every hand got an extra three hours' sleep." He gave a small sigh of satisfaction. "We are ready, sir."

"And *Argus*?"

"Lieutenant Wilson reports they are ready to move at your order."

Albritton stretched out his arms behind him to allow Sommers to slide his coat on. "Well done, Mr. Chandler. By the way, how much sleep did *you* get?"

The first lieutenant shrugged. "I tried, sir, but I could only sneak in *two* hours."

The two officers went up on deck and were greeted by a soft late-afternoon breeze. The sun had dropped below the treetops, giving them a shade which dropped the temperature another couple of degrees. Albritton noticed that his premier shivered.

"Cold, Mr. Chandler?"

The first lieutenant grinned as he crossed his arms over his chest. "To be honest, sir, there *are* times I miss Charleston." He grimaced as a fresh breeze hit the deck. "And this is one of them."

"Well," Albritton deadpanned, "if you need cheering up, I think I can safely say that it will be a good twenty-five or thirty degrees colder in Boston." The captain could not help but laugh at the look of disbelief mixed with horror on the other's face. "Cheer up, Mr. Chandler. Send a message to *Argus* and ask Commander Calloway to come have a drink with us."

"Aye, sir." The first lieutenant headed for the bow with a speaking trumpet to pass the message, and the captain could only chuckle when he saw a shiver. When the premier returned, however, Albritton did not like the look on his face.

"Mr. Chandler? Is something wrong? What did the commander say?"

"Sir, the commander was not aboard."

"Oh? Where is he?"

"Mr. Wilson said he was ashore, inspecting the lookout

station."

Albritton was surprised. "Really? Please ask the good lieutenant to have the commander report to me when he returns." He walked to the rail in the direction of the lookout he'd posted ashore, as though he could see though the dense forest that shielded his ships from view. A few moments later, he returned to the quarterdeck. "In the meantime, Mr. Chandler, I want a meeting with all officers in my cabin in fifteen minutes."

"Aye, Captain."

Chandler departed on his errand, and Albritton returned to his cabin. "Sommers!" he called. "My officers will be here in fifteen minutes. Wine for six, and water for the young gentlemen, if you please."

"Very good, sir."

Albritton went into the day cabin and sat in his usual place, in the center of the settee beneath the stern window, and looked around the room. *Definitely going to make some changes when we get to Boston,* he thought with a nod. *I need a chair. Yes, a chair. Leather, maybe, thick with a comfortable headrest.* He looked to his left. *Over there, beside the desk, where I can look across the room and see everyone.* He patted the settee to his right. *Maybe with a small table off to the right where I can put my drink.* He grunted. *A captain is allowed some small comforts, is he not?*

A knock on the door heralded the arrival of his officers. He stood and waived his lieutenants to their seats, and Mr. Franklin ushered his midshipmen to one side. Sommers appeared and distributed refreshments to all.

"Thank you for coming," he said formally. "First of all, I want to thank you all for your efforts last night. The first leg of our breakout was an unmitigated success. However, the battle is only half-fought. Tonight, our purpose is to evade the British squadron blockading Chesapeake Bay and break out into the Atlantic. I cannot stress enough that I have no intention of engaging the enemy tonight. That is *not* our mission. Our purpose this night is to slip as swiftly and silently as possible past our enemies and make our way to Boston. There we will finish preparations for our voyage to glory and prize money for all." He paused to look each man in the eye. "Does any man here have a problem with that?"

Nobody moved. The captain nodded. "Very well." He raised his glass. "Join me in a toast: To *Columbia*! May she wreak havoc among British shipping and make us all rich!"

"Here! Here!" echoed throughout the cabin, and every man drained his glass. The only exception was Lieutenant Chandler, who sat quietly and looked at his drink. Albritton made note of it as he set down his glass and rose.

"Gentlemen, please take your stations and make preparation to get underway after dark." The assemblage filed out, and he called to his first lieutenant. "Mr. Chandler, bring Commander Calloway down when he arrives."

"Aye, sir," the premier replied and followed the others out.

The captain drained his glass and stared at the door, wondering what was going through his first lieutenant's head.

An hour later, a knock on the door interrupted Albritton's study of a map of the bay entrance. The sentry admitted Commander Calloway. Albritton rose to greet his guest. "Commander, thank you for coming. Please, sit. Coffee?"

"Thank you, sir."

"Sommers! Coffee for two, if you please."

"Coming up, sir."

Albritton sat down and folded the map out of the way. Sommers arrived and placed two steaming cups on the table before retreating. The captain picked his up. "You inspected the outpost ashore? How was it?"

"I found it well hidden, sir," the commander said, "but still commanding an excellent view. The men were relieved every two hours to allow them to get some extra sleep. They will report back aboard after dark."

Albritton nodded. "Now, as far as tonight. I will signal when we leave. It'll be probably an hour or two after full dark. We will slide out into the bay, and then *Argus* will fall into line behind *Columbia*. We shall burn one light on our fantail. Our mission is to slip past the British and disappear into the Atlantic Ocean before dawn. We will not engage the enemy under any circumstances. Understood?"

Calloway stared, clearly surprised by what he heard. He opened his mouth, but closed it again without saying anything. He lowered his eyes to the clouds in his coffee. "Understood, sir."

"Good. Our job is to make it to Boston without delay. Don't worry, Commander—we'll have need of more prize crews than we can carry before we're done."

Calloway lifted his cup in a toast. "That's good news, Captain."

Darkness fell. Albritton paced back and forth across the center of his quarterdeck. He paused to look at the sky and nodded; between the waxing crescent of the moon and the overcast sky, the weather definitely appeared to be on the Americans' side. It was time to move.

"Mr. Chandler," he said, "get us under way, if you please."

"Aye, Captain," the first lieutenant said. He picked up a speaking trumpet and gave orders that sent topmen scrambling to their posts. "Mr. Franklin, kindly go forward and pass the word to *Argus*—we move out at once. Mr. Middleton, take your position at the fantail. Mr. Adams, light the lantern for *Argus*."

In front of them, *Argus* got under way, moving straight out into the bay. *Columbia* followed, turning for the mouth of the bay as soon as she cleared the cove. *Argus* fell in behind her, staying just close enough to keep sight of the lantern. Albritton kept to his place in the center of his quarterdeck, his eyes noting how the wind filled his sails. As soon as his ships cleared the bay, he turned to his sailing master.

"Mr. Warren," he said, "I want to be able to see the beaches of Princess Anne County as we pass. Mr. Chandler, call the hands to make all sail. Mr. Middleton, signal *Argus* to make sail."

"Aye, aye, Captain."

"Aye, sir." Chandler picked up his speaking trumpet again and called to the hands to make sail while Middleton moved the signal lamp from side to side. The sky above the American ships filled with canvas, and the ships shot forward toward the southern end of Chesapeake Bay. Three hours into the trip, the ships were breaking out into the Atlantic Ocean.

"Deck there!" came the call from the lookout. "Lights off the larboard beam!"

Nearly every man on the quarterdeck joined the captain at the rail. Albritton raised a glass to his eye and scanned the horizon, but he saw nothing.

"Lookout!" he called. "Verify your contact!"

"Definite contact, Captain!" came the reply. "I can see the lights of one ship. Possibly a frigate by the size of her!"

"Has she seen us?" Chandler called to the lookout.

"Don't think so, sir! She's not approaching!"

"Thank God for small favors," the sailing master muttered.

"Sir!" Middleton called from the fantail. "I'm not sure,

but I think *Argus* is veering toward the sighting!"

Albritton turned aft. The cloud cover had broken, and the moonlight was barely enough for him to make out Calloway's sails. He lowered the glass, then raised it again to confirm his suspicions. He lowered it again and glowered into the darkness.

"Mr. Warren!" he called. "Bring us around to larboard! We must get ahead of *Argus* and cut her off!"

"Aye, Captain!"

Columbia came around on a course to cut off her wayward consort. Mr. Chandler appeared at the fantail. "What is he doing?" he said to no one in particular.

"Once we reach Boston," Albritton said in a voice approaching a growl, "I intend to find out."

"How do you intend to communicate with him once we catch him?" Chandler asked.

Albritton considered the question for a moment, then said, "Have Mr. Warren bring us up beside him, quarterdeck to quarterdeck. I'll try the speaking trumpet. I'm going to step below. Please see that I'm called when we catch *Argus*."

Chandler raised his hat. "Aye, Captain."

Albritton made his way below to his cabin. Once inside, he collapsed on the settee, suddenly very tired. He leaned his head back and closed his eyes. Questions were racing through his mind, but he knew there were no answers yet. At the sound of a throat being cleared, he opened his eyes and raised his head to see Sommers standing in the doorway.

"Begging your pardon, Captain," he said, "but I was wondering if you would like something? I can make you some ham and eggs rather quickly, or I have some cheese if you just want something cold."

"Cheese would be fine, Sommers. Thank you."

"Very good, sir. Coffee?"

"Not just now, but perhaps you could bring a pot up to the quarterdeck in an hour or so for the officers?"

"Aye, Captain." Sommers stepped away and returned in a moment, carrying a plate with a selection of cheeses in one hand and a glass of wine in the other. "This is the last of the cheese we brought aboard last week, Captain. I'm afraid this is it until we make Boston."

"Thank you, Sommers." Albritton took a sip of his wine and selected a wedge of cheese. All too soon there was a knock at the door, and the sentry admitted young Mr. Franklin. The senior midshipman came to attention.

"Mr. Chandler's respects, sir. We are about to come alongside *Argus*."

"Thank you, Mr. Franklin."

The young gentleman came to attention and marched from the cabin.

When the captain came on deck, *Argus* was sailing just off to larboard. Lieutenant Chandler arranged for two hands to hold lanterns on either side of the captain as he spoke—there would be no doubt who was speaking. Albritton accepted the speaking trumpet from Franklin and stepped in between the lanterns. He raised the trumpet.

"Commander Calloway!" he called. "What are you doing? Why have you veered off course?"

"We are trying to identify the sighting, sir!" came the reply. In the darkness of the moon, Albritton was not sure who was speaking to him.

"You will desist immediately and retake your station!" he ordered.

No answer came. Albritton thought he saw an argument taking place on *Argus*'s quarterdeck, but here the lanterns that illuminated him worked against him. His eyes were accustomed to the aura of light which surrounded him; had no lanterns been there, had his eyes been accustomed to the darkness, he might have had a clearer picture of what was going on on the other ship. He was about to repeat himself when he thought he saw one figure push away another. He heard the reply come over the waves. "Aye, sir!"

The captain turned away and handed the trumpet to a midshipman. "Douse the lanterns," he said to his premier. "Make sure Middleton keeps his eyes open and his lantern lit."

"Mr. Middleton has gone below, sir," Chandler explained. "I sent him below with the watch so he could catch some sleep. Your coxswain volunteered to relieve him."

Albritton turned to see Xavier standing beside the shielded lantern, watching for *Argus* to retake her station astern. It wasn't the first time he'd seen Xavier go out of his way to help out one of the crew. The captain asked for a glass and scanned for the original sighting, but he couldn't see it.

"Lookout?" he called.

"I lost her, sir!" came the reply.

Albritton lowered the glass. His eyes scanned the invisible horizon in frustration, but part of him realized that this was exactly what he wanted. Still, discretion being the better part of valor, he turned to his sailing master. "Mr. Warren," he said, "come around to the southeast, if you please."

Warren nodded, a look of relief on his face. "Aye, sir," he said and turned to his mates at the wheel.

The captain turned aft. "Xavier, make sure we don't lose *Argus*."

"Aye, sir."

Mr. Chandler approached, and Albritton could tell he was nervous. "We got lucky," the first lieutenant said.

His captain shrugged. "Luck is part of the game." He stretched his back and head around to relieve the tension.

"We'll stay on this course for two hours, then come around to the northeast. At dawn, we shall turn due north until the noon sighting."

Chandler took a deep breath to calm himself. "Aye, sir. I'll see to it."

The captain pulled out his watch and stepped over to the fantail so he could see it by the light of *Argus*'s signal lantern. Xavier paid him no attention.

"Do you have him?" the captain asked.

"Aye, sir. He's out there."

Albritton closed the watch and put it back in his pocket. "You have the deck, Mr. Chandler. Call me if we have any sightings."

"Aye, sir." Chandler studied his captain's back as he disappeared below deck. He turned to see Warren standing beside him.

"What do you think?" Warren asked.

Chandler turned aft and stared out into the darkness. "I think we have a problem."

Captain Albritton stepped up on the deck with the morning watch in time to hear the last echoes of his ship's bell. He looked off the starboard bow to see the barest glimmer of dawn's light on the eastern horizon. He made his way aft to where Mr. Middleton had resumed his post sometime in the night.

"He still out there?" Albritton asked.

"Aye, sir," Middleton answered. "I saw him just a few minutes ago. He should be visible within the hour."

"Let me know when *Argus* is visible." Albritton stepped over to where the first lieutenant and sailing master awaited him. "Anything to report, Mr. Chandler?"

"Nothing, sir," Chandler replied in a weary voice. "No

further sightings."

"Thank you. Get some sleep, Mr. Chandler; you've earned it."

That line provoked a tired smile and a nod from the premier. "Thank you, Captain. Good night, sir." He made his way to the companionway and slowly descended.

Lieutenant Hill stepped up. "Good morning, sir." Hill was the officer of the watch.

"Good morning, Mr. Hill. I want extra lookouts posted during all daylight hours."

"Aye, aye, sir." The lieutenant bounced slightly on his toes. "How long to Boston, sir?"

Albritton looked at his subordinate. "As long as it takes, Mr. Hill."

The young man lowered his head, suitably chastised. "Of course, sir," he mumbled. "Sorry, sir."

The lieutenant made his escape forward, and the captain stepped over to the sailing master. "Mr. Warren," he said quietly, "How long is it to Boston?"

Warren tried his best to keep a straight face. "A week or so, Captain. I'll know better after I take the sighting at noon."

Albritton nodded, the smallest hint of a smile at the corner of his mouth. He turned forward, hands clasped behind his back. "Thank you, Mr. Warren."

In the cockpit, the mood had lightened with the coming of the dawn. Jackson, on his first voyage, was bouncing off the walls with joy.

"I can't believe it!" he exclaimed to anyone who cared to listen. "I mean, he did it! He actually did it! The captain sailed us right under the British noses, and now we're free in the Atlantic!"

"The captain's good at what he does," Franklin said.

"That's why he's still alive—why he brings his crews home alive, too."

"You mean nobody died on his last voyage?" Smith asked. Franklin noticed he seemed pretty nervous.

The senior midshipman shrugged. "There are always casualties in battle. I'm saying nobody died because the captain made a mistake."

Smith sat down beside him. "Is it true your grandfather was Benjamin Franklin?"

Franklin sighed. "Yes, I'm afraid it is."

"Wow! That must have been incredible!"

"Not really," Franklin said. "He died five years before I was born."

"Oh," Smith said, suddenly embarrassed. "I'm sorry. I didn't know."

Franklin patted him on the arm. "It's okay, Grant. It was a long time ago. If you'll excuse me, I'm due on deck." He rose before the younger man could say another word and headed up to the deck. He found a quiet spot near the port side bow chaser and leaned against the railing. He felt bad about cutting young Smith off like that, but he found it increasingly annoying that everyone thought having a Founding Father in the family was such a great thing. Franklin wished he thought so, too, but he couldn't. His only memories of his famous grandfather came from his father, William, whose relationship with his father soured early on when William sided with the British during the American Revolution. Franklin was born very late in William's life to his second wife, Mary Johnson d'Evelin. By this time, thirteen years into his London exile following the American victory in the war and ten years since the last time he had seen his father, William had been growing increasingly bitter with guilt. He had had nothing good to say about Benjamin Franklin.

"Is everything okay, Mr. Franklin?"

Franklin spun around to see Mr. Hill, the third lieutenant. He came to attention and touched his hat. "My apologies, sir; I did not hear you approach."

"Indeed." Hill stepped forward to stand beside the senior midshipman along the rail. "You seem to have something occupying your mind. Anything I can help you with?"

Franklin stole a sideways look at the lieutenant. He was older than any of the other officers, despite being only third, and he seemed very reserved by comparison. Franklin heard the man sigh and saw him lean down against the rail.

"That's better," Hill said. "It's always nice to relax a bit in a cool breeze."

Franklin shrugged. "I suppose."

"What's bothering you, Mr. Franklin?" Hill asked. "You may rely on my discretion."

"Do you have anyone famous in your family, Lieutenant?" Franklin asked quietly.

"No," Hill replied just as softly. "Am I to assume this has to do with your grandfather?"

Franklin turned to his lieutenant. "You know about that?"

"Mr. Franklin, the whole ship knows about that."

Franklin hung his head for a moment before turning back to the sea.

Hill observed the gesture and continued. "Did you know him?"

Franklin shook his head. "He died five years before I was born."

"So, what is the problem?"

Franklin turned to him again. "The problem is that everybody thinks it is such a bloody wonderful thing to have Benjamin Franklin as my grandfather!"

Hill met his eye. "And you don't?"

The midshipman turned back to the sea and hung his head. "I don't know what to think. I never knew him."

"I see. Your father was William Franklin, I take it? Tory governor of New Jersey prior to the Revolution?"

Franklin nodded.

"And how old was he when you were born?"

Franklin thought for a moment, caught off guard by the question. "Sixty-five, I think. I was born in London. Made my way to America as a ship's boy when I was thirteen. Friends of my grandfather arranged for me to join the American Navy as a midshipman."

Hill nodded. "And your father did not speak fondly about your grandfather, is that so?"

"How did you know?"

"Their relationship was not exactly a secret. Your grandfather was hurt badly when your father chose to side with the king."

"So I've heard," Franklin said. "Father said my grandfather disowned him publicly and branded him as a traitor. After the American victory at Yorktown, he said he feared for his life and fled to England."

"Understandable," Hill agreed. "A great many Tories did so at that time, I believe."

Franklin raised his head and sighed. "Father never forgave him."

Hill pursed his lips in thought. "Did they ever see each other again?"

"Once, that I know of," Franklin said sadly. "They met in London in 1785 when my grandfather was returning from France. Father said he hoped to reconcile, but the old man would have none of it." The midshipman shrugged. "That's what my father said, anyway."

Hill raised an eyebrow. "You doubt him?"

"I don't know what to believe."

"Tell me," the lieutenant asked, "have you read his autobiography?"

"Autobiography?"

"Yes. Your grandfather wrote the story of his life—or most of it, anyway. You've never seen it?"

"No," Franklin said. "I've been at sea most of my life. This is the first I've heard about any book about him."

Hill straightened and stretched his back. "Well, perhaps while we are in Boston we shall have a chance to step ashore and look for a bookstore."

"I think I'd like that."

"Good," Hill said as he stepped away. "Enjoy your day, Mr. Franklin."

On board HMS *London*, the mood was decidedly different. When his ship had joined the blockade squadron three days earlier, Captain Knighton went aboard the flagship, the 74-gun HMS *Tiger*, only to learn that his quarry was gone. Two days prior to his arrival, the admiral had received a message from spies ashore saying that the American ships were no longer in the Washington Navy Yard, and an extensive search of the bay had failed to locate Albritton or his ships. Knighton had found the admiral in the midst of writing a report stating that the American ships were most likely loose in the Atlantic.

Knighton returned to his ship, furious at the delays that had caused him to arrive after his birds had flown. He stormed below to his cabin and slammed his hat down on the table. He turned at the sound of a throat being cleared to find Flagstone, his imperturbable servant, standing in the pantry doorway.

"May I get you anything, sir?" he asked.

As always, Flagstone's calm demeanor had a calming effect on his master. Knighton drew a deep breath and exhaled slowly and loudly, hoping to drain his frustration. "Tea, please, Flagstone," he said, "and thank you."

The servant bowed and withdrew. Knighton went to the cabin door and asked the sentry to pass the word for the first lieutenant. He returned to the table just as Flagstone returned with a steaming cup of tea. He blew on the lip and took a sip, savoring the hot liquid going down his throat. He set the cup down as a knock at the door heralded the arrival of Lieutenant Percival.

"I'm glad you're back, Captain," Percival said, "but I take it the admiral only had bad news for us."

Knighton shook his head in wonder. Percival's habit of practically reading his mind was annoying at times, but this was not one of them. "Is it that obvious?"

"To me, yes." The premier took his usual seat on his captain's right and nodded his thanks as Flagstone placed a cup of tea before him. "I take it the Americans have gone?"

"Yes, curse the luck. The question is, now what do we do? The admiral received word from informants ashore that Albritton was only provisioned for a short voyage. That means one of two things: either he is heading for another American port to complete his provisioning, or he is looking for a convoy to raid and live off the spoils." He picked up his cup. "Opinions, Roland?"

Percival leaned forward, resting his elbows on the table and clasping his hands before his face with his forefingers steepled. Knighton smiled; it was the premier's favorite pose whenever he did his thinking.

"Let's presume he's heading for a port to complete his provisioning," Percival said. "Where would they go? I think we can rule out Philadelphia, as it would be too easy for us to blockade him inside. Newport is an option, as are New York and Boston to the north and Charleston and Savannah to the south. I take it we have no idea as to what Albritton's orders were?"

Knighton shook his head and took another drink of his tea.

Percival's brow furrowed. "I see. Knowing that may have narrowed the field a bit, but no matter. What do we know about our foe? Albritton is regarded as the best the Americans have—privately, sir, I will admit I agree with the assessment—and he is a man of careful preparation. As we do not know his orders, sir, may I suggest that our fishing fleet off Newfoundland may be his target? Or the West Indies convoy? Isn't she at sea? Albritton could be looking to intercept her."

Knighton sighed. "You're not helping very much, Roland."

"Sorry, sir," Percival said. "Got carried away. My reading, as I said, is that Albritton is a careful commander. He will want to make ready before he goes to sea. I believe he'll head home to do it."

Knighton looked up from his cup. "Boston?"

Percival nodded. "Boston."

The captain drained his cup. "I shall write to the admiral immediately to say that we are heading to Boston, and I'll ask that he include that information with his next reports to Halifax. Thank you, Roland."

Knighton wrote a report and sent it to the admiral. He meant it as a courtesy, but almost immediately a note came back ordering him to delay his departure until he was released by the admiral.

So, for the last three days, Knighton had been sitting here off Cape Henry, waiting for his leave to go from the flagship. He did not understand why he was being held like this. He did not expect Albritton to be in Boston any longer than two or three days at most before he would be ready to attempt a breakout, and this delay could cost him any chance of catching Albritton there. If he got away again, someone was going to pay.

CHAPTER FIVE

Captain Albritton stood beside his sailing master on the quarterdeck of USS *Columbia*, his attention divided between the wind filling his sails and the fogbank before him. Their current position was three hours southeast of Boston harbor. His original plan had been to wait and try to run the blockade at night, but when he'd seen that weather conditions heralded a thick fog, he'd decided to make the attempt during daylight using the fog as cover.

His expectations were not disappointed. The fog they entered completely enveloped them, as they proceeded toward the harbor and home. Albritton estimated current visibility to be less than half-pistol shot, which should be enough to hide them from British patrols. The nervous division of his attention was caused by the knowledge that their shelter could quickly turn into a neat little mousetrap if a British frigate should emerge from the fog.

Silence was the order of the day. Orders were passed to the topmen by runners, and every lookout had an extra man to relay messages. The ship's bell was silenced by stuffing it with a blanket, and every precaution was taken to render the ship completely mute.

One of the ship's boys bounded barefoot across the deck. He skidded to a stop in front of the captain and saluted. "Begging yer pardon, Captain, but Wiley sent me to say he heard a ship's bell!"

"Where away?" Albritton asked.

The lad turned and pointed. "Starboard beam was the best he could say, sir. We ain't seen nothin', sir, just heard a bell."

The sailing master looked to the captain. "Channel marker, do you think?"

Albritton shook his head and listened. He heard nothing, neither did he see anything when he scanned the fog to the north. He turned to the sailing master. "Wear ship to larboard. I want a large, slow, silent loop that will bring us around to the nor'east." To Mr. Adams, the signals midshipman: "Notify *Argus* we are making the turn."

"Aye, aye, sir!"

"Aye, Captain." The sailing master went to the wheel and spoke to his mates in a quiet voice. The wheel turned over, and the ship came around. A long, wide loop, just what the captain ordered. The ship straightened up with her bowsprit pointed to the northeast.

"Take in a reef, Mr. Warren," Albritton said quietly. "Slow us down. Notify *Argus*."

"Aye, sir."

Runners went aloft to carry the commands to the topmen, and the captain soon saw the sail being taken in. He looked around the blanket of fog that engulfed them and wished he had the power to open a window for a brief instant. He turned to see a hand approach and salute.

"Beggin' yer pardon, Captain," he said, "but Mr. Chandler sends his respects. Would you please come forward, sir? The first lieutenant thinks he hears music, sir."

"Music?"

"Aye, sir. I heerd it too."

"What music?"

The man looked slightly embarrassed. "Well, sir, sounded

like a fiddle to me."

"Dear God! Show me!" Albritton followed the sailor to the starboard foremast shrouds, where he found Mr. Chandler trying to pierce the fog with a glass. "Report, Mr. Chandler."

The premier lowered his glass and lifted his hat. "Music, sir. Fine on the starboard bow is all I can tell you. We've heard snippets of it twice, when the winds veered this direction for a moment. Wait—there it is!"

Albritton stared at the fog and concentrated. Yes! There it was! The faintest sound of a fiddle being played. A lively tune it was! If they were any closer, they might just have heard the sound of dancing on the deck as well.

"Well done, Mr. Chandler. I am going aft. We will put hard over to larboard and try to sneak away. Remember, silence on the deck is the order of the day!"

"Aye, sir."

The captain hurried aft. "Mr. Warren, put the wheel over! Hard to larboard! Bring us around to due west!"

"Aye, sir. So it were true?"

Albritton nodded. He went to the starboard rail and began to pace. He needed to think, to sort out what was happening. A wrong move now could spell disaster. Suddenly, a sound caused him to stop mid-stride and spin. What was that? On the larboard quarter! Yes, a ship's bell! He moved as quickly and quietly as possible to the rail. There it was again!

"Mr. Warren!" he hissed. "Hard to starboard! Bring us two points west of north!"

"Aye, sir!"

"Sir!" came the cry from the fantail. "We've lost *Argus*!"

Albritton looked grimly aft. He was not surprised, what with the sudden and extreme maneuvers he had put the ship through in a very heavy fog. Well, he could not worry about

Argus now; he would have to trust that Calloway would bring her through and make it to Boston. Right now, he had his own problems. Primary of which was, *what was going on?* Suddenly, he stopped as an idea occurred to him, and he did not like it at all. He went to the wheel and called the sailing master. "Mr. Warren! Come here!" He pulled a sheet of paper and a pencil from his coat pocket. "Look. Boston is here." He marked an X on the paper. He moved the pencil down and to the right, then drew a line toward the X. "This was our course when we entered the fog. Agreed?"

"Aye, sir."

"Good." He stopped the line and drew a small circle just above or north of it. "This is approximately where we heard the first bell." Warren nodded as his captain drew a large circle from their position around to larboard, straightening up on a course to the northeast. "This is us after the first loop." Warren nodded again, and the captain drew another small circle to the right and a little above their position. "This is where Mr. Chandler heard the music, and we turned due west." He drew the line of their course to the left, and the sailing master nodded again. Albritton stopped the line and made a small X below and to the right of *Columbia's* position on the paper. "And this is where we just heard the ship's bell. We turned hard to starboard and settled on a course two points west of north." He drew the change on the paper. "Now, Mr. Warren, what does this look like to you?" The captain tapped the tip of his pencil on the small circles and the small X in turn. Warren's eyes grew huge at the realization of where they were.

"Sir!" he hissed. "We've blundered into the bloody British blockade squadron!"

Albritton nodded. "That's what I make of it. They're making all that noise so they don't run into each other." He turned to Mr. Adams. "My compliments to the first lieutenant. Please ask him to join us at once."

The midshipman touched his hat and disappeared into the fog. Moments later, Mr. Chandler emerged from it as though he'd passed through a curtain. Albritton took him through the chart and revealed the conclusions he and the sailing master had come to.

"So," Chandler said, trying to make sense of it all, "the noises we've been hearing, the British are making them on purpose, for their own protection?"

"I believe so, yes," Albritton confirmed.

Chandler shook his head. "Incredible. Well, at least we know where they are. All we have to do is avoid them as we make our way into Boston." He grunted. "Too bad we couldn't happen to emerge from the fog in position to rake one or two of them in the stern along the way."

"There's nothing I'd love more, but now is not the time," Albritton said as he looked from his drawing to the chart held by Mr. Warren. "Mr. Warren, in your mind, transfer my drawing onto your chart. Got it? Now, where would you say we are? Approximately."

Warren's eyes flew back and forth between the chart and the drawing before he reached out and drew a small circle with his forefinger east of Boston. "Just about here, sir."

Albritton nodded in agreement. "That is my assessment as well. Gentlemen, we are going to turn west and load on all sail. My intention is to blow past the British squadron and into Boston harbor."

"And if they appear from the fog in front of us?" Warren asked.

"In that case," Albritton smiled, "I trust you to save us, Mr. Warren. Pass the word, Mr. Chandler. Call all hands to make sail, if you please."

The captain stood back and listened to the patter of bare feet on the deck as the hands ran and leapt to the shrouds and climbed for all they were worth. He heard the great sails loosed over his head flapping as they filled with the wind and caused the ship to leap forward.

"Mr. Warren," he said calmly, "due west, if you please."

"Aye, sir," the sailing master said, resigned to whatever fate might hold for them. His mood brightened slightly when he realized that the wind was with them, and they could steer a straight course west for their destination.

"Shall I clear for action, sir?" Chandler asked. "In case the British should appear?"

Albritton shook his head. "I agree with Mr. Warren. If they do appear, we shall either be past them or collide with them before they know what happened."

Chandler did not seem pleased at the prospect.

"Mr. Chandler," the captain said, "have the lookouts keep alert. Also, pass the word, if you please, and remind the men to keep silent. No talking."

"Aye, sir." He saluted and was gone.

The run to Boston took three hours and fifteen minutes. British ships were spotted twice during that time, but each time *Columbia* was gone into the fog before they could react. Once they reached the harbor, a pilot was sent to guide them to their berth.

"'Tis good to see you back again, Captain," the pilot said as the anchor was dropped. "With a fine ship like this in your hands, the British will run for the hills!"

Albritton shook his hand warmly and saw him off the ship. "Mr. Chandler," he said after the pilot was gone, "I am going ashore to see the port admiral. Xavier is going with me."

"Xavier, sir?"

"He knows the area well, and I need a message delivered.

As soon as the fog lifts sufficiently, have the lookouts watch for *Argus*. Give the men today to rest. Hopefully, tomorrow we start taking on provisions for our voyage."

"Aye, sir."

Albritton went below and found Xavier in his cabin giving Sommers tips about the captain's favorite shops and what delicacies to lay in store. Both men came to attention when the captain entered.

"Good, you're here, Xavier. We are going ashore." Albritton moved to his desk and sat. He took out a sheet of paper and began to write. "I want you to deliver this note to our friend in Quincy. You are to wait for a reply. On the way back, I want you to stop at Shiloh and tell Hawthorne to get my sea kit ready. Also, we'll need to make some improvements to the day cabin while we're here."

Xavier smiled knowingly. "Leave it to me, Captain."

Albritton folded the letter over and sealed it by pressing his seal into the hot wax. He handed it to his coxswain. Xavier took the letter and made his way out.

Sommers stepped up. "Begging your pardon, Captain, but as I don't know you all that well yet, I wanted to ask you if there's anything special you wanted to get while we're here."

Albritton looked surprised. "You mean Xavier didn't give you the list?"

Sommers smiled. "Well, sir, he was just beginning when you came in."

"Five chickens will be arriving from my home at Shiloh," the captain said. "That will keep us in eggs for the voyage."

"And what should I feed them, sir?"

"They get the crumbs from the bottom of the bags of ship's bread. We'll detail a ship's boy to see to it. If you tap gently on the bags before opening them, some of the weevils will fall to the bottom as well. Chickens love weevils,"

Albritton explained. "Bourbon and whiskey will be sent aboard as well, plus a large supply of pantry items for the voyage. Xavier will bring back money for you to use ashore."

"Aye, sir."

Albritton made his way up on deck and, after a word to the first lieutenant made his way over the side. He settled in the stern sheets of his gig along with Xavier, who conned the boat, and Midshipman Smith, who would command the men as they waited for his return.

When they reached the pier, the captain and his coxswain got out and made their way to the port admiral's office. When they got to the door, Albritton reached into his pocket and gave Xavier several coins.

"Rent yourself a good horse," he said. "We don't want him going lame in the countryside. I will have a boat here for you at noon tomorrow for the first of my things, and then again at noon the next day."

"Aye, sir," the coxswain replied. "I'll take care of things."

"I know you will. Thank you."

The coxswain touched his hat and left. Albritton knocked on the door and was soon shown into the office of Admiral Redmon.

"Captain!" Redmon said as he rose and came around his desk to shake his guest's hand. "It's an honor to finally meet you. We have been expecting you. Where is *Argus*?"

Albritton shook the man's hand and took the seat he indicated before the desk. "We got separated in the fog while avoiding the British squadron offshore. I didn't hear any gunfire on the way in, so hopefully that's good news. I look for her either tonight or in the morning."

"Good." The admiral resumed his seat and pulled a file off a stack on the side of his desk. "Now, about your provisioning. Here's a list of what we have for you." He handed over a sheet of paper. Albritton took it and scanned the items written down, then he frowned.

"Sir," he said, "these items would only allow *Columbia* to stay at sea for three or four months at most."

Redmon made an apologetic gesture. "Unfortunately, that's all there is available. The only reason you're getting that much is the orders from Washington said to give you priority."

Albritton dropped the paper in his lap and sighed. "I was afraid you would say that." He shook his head. "I know things have been tough. We appreciate anything you can give us."

"Thank you, Captain," the admiral said. He picked up a large folder from the stack and handed it to Albritton. "This is the latest intelligence on the British forces at sea, their dispositions and suspected intentions. My aide will show you where you can study them. I regret that I cannot allow you to take them with you, but some of this is brand new and we haven't had time to get it copied yet."

Albritton rose and accepted the packet. "Thank you, sir."

He made his way out of the office and met the admiral's aide outside. The man guided him to a small, private study and left him to his reading. Intelligence reports were generally dry, but Albritton did learn that HMS *London* had been seen at Halifax. It took him nearly four hours to make it through the entire folder, taking notes as he thought necessary. When he finished, he had another short interview with the admiral which mainly consisted of the man apologizing for not being able to give him more provisions. Albritton made his escape and reached the pier just before dusk. Mr. Smith handed him a folded note.

"Xavier said to give this to you, sir," he said.

Albritton opened the note and read it. "Thank you, Mr. Smith. Shall we go?"

Once back on board *Columbia*, the captain called his first

lieutenant and Mr. Petry, the purser, to his cabin and gave them the list of supplies that were coming aboard. Neither man was particularly happy.

Chandler dropped the page on the table. "Now what do we do?" he asked.

"Well," Albritton said calmly, "first, we are going to take whatever they can give us with gratitude. Second, Mr. Petry will go ashore and see what he can procure from the shops in the area. After he returns, we shall meet again."

Chandler made to reply, but thought better of it and closed his mouth. He swallowed hard and nodded. "Aye, sir. Will there be anything else?"

"Not at the moment. Dismissed."

Captain Albritton came up on deck and looked around. Everywhere, men were either making minor repairs or bringing on provisions or stowing them below decks. He nodded approvingly. He saw the first lieutenant standing beside the wheel in conversation with the quartermaster and beckoned him.

"You wanted to see me, sir?" Chandler asked as he raised his hat.

"Yes, Mr. Chandler. I am dining ashore tonight. Kindly have my gig ready at the turn of the first dog watch. I shall be taking Mr. Franklin with me. Please pass the word so he will be ready."

"Mr. Franklin? Aye, sir." Chandler saluted. "We'll be ready, Captain."

"Thank you, Mr. Chandler." The captain stepped off to watch the provisioning before going below. When he returned, he found the first lieutenant and the senior midshipman awaiting him at the entry port.

"Everything is ready, sir," Chandler reported.

"Thank you," the captain replied. "Ready, Mr. Franklin?"

"Aye, sir." It was obvious that the midshipman had no idea why he was accompanying his captain, and Albritton did nothing to enlighten him. When they reached the pier, Franklin was surprised to find a carriage awaiting them. The captain climbed in without hesitation, and the senior midshipman followed suit. No sooner had his bottom touched the seat then the driver whipped up the horses and they set off. The carriage passed west through the town and out into the countryside.

"If I may ask, sir," Franklin said, "where are we going?"

"I had an interesting conversation with Mr. Hill the other day," Albritton began, "and he mentioned how you wished you knew more about your grandfather. Now, don't think badly of the lieutenant—everything he said was in very general terms and nothing of any private nature was divulged. In any case, I thought I might be able to help you. I know a man who knew your grandfather intimately, both during the Revolution and afterwards. We are going to see him. He can tell you firsthand what he knows, and you can ask him whatever you like."

"I see," Franklin said as he watched the passing countryside. Albritton almost asked if he was nervous but decided against it.

An hour's easy ride brought them to a great white two-story house set not very far back from the road.

The carriage stopped at the gate, and the captain rose. "We're here."

The two men stepped down, and Franklin followed his captain up the walk. Albritton knocked on the door and stepped back. It was opened by a short, balding man in a waistcoat with a pair of spectacles pushed up on his head.

"Welcome, Captain," the host said as he stepped back. "Please, come in."

"Thank you," Albritton said. The two men stepped inside, and the captain made the introductions. "Mr. Franklin, may I present our host for the evening, Mr. John Adams, second president of these United States. Mr. President, this is Mr. Charles Franklin, senior midshipman on USS *Columbia*."

Franklin's eyes grew wide for a moment, then he bowed. "An honor, Mr. President."

"The honor is mine, Mr. Franklin," Adams said. "Come in, both of you, come in."

The two officers stepped inside, and Adams closed the door behind them. Franklin stared in disbelief when his host asked for his coat and hat, and he only handed his over after he saw his captain do so. Adams nodded his thanks and stepped into the next room.

"Hezekiah!"

The two men turned to see a woman marching toward the captain, her arms outstretched. She then wrapped them around Albritton in a bear hug and he returned the gesture.

"I thought I'd missed you when you were called away to Washington City," she said as she let her captive go and looked to Franklin. "And whom have we here?"

"Ah," Albritton said. "Excuse me. May I present Mr. Charles Franklin, senior midshipman of USS *Columbia*. Mr. Franklin, this is Mrs. Abigail Adams, wife of the president."

"Madam." Franklin bowed deeply.

"Franklin?" Abigail looked to the captain. "Any relation to Benjamin?"

Albritton smiled. "His grandfather."

"I see." She turned to Franklin and took his arm in hers. "You are most welcome in our house, Mr. Franklin." She led them into the dining room to the right of the front door. The table was beautifully set for four. The president came in behind them and stepped around to his seat at the far end of the table. Abigail took Franklin with her as she sat at her husband's right, placing him in the seat next to her. Captain Albritton sat on the president's left. They took their seats and the president signaled the servants to begin. As they filled the glasses and brought the soup, Adams turned to the captain.

"Captain," he said, "pleased as I am to see you, I can't help but wonder why you have returned."

"I have been ordered here, Mr. President," came the reply. "I had to take my two ships out of Washington City, and Secretary Jones ordered me to Boston to complete my provisioning before taking my ships to sea again to prey on British shipping."

The president paused to thank his servants and bless the food. As they picked up their spoons to partake of the soup, he said, "I must tell you, Captain, that you may find it... difficult to complete your provisioning. I'm afraid the war— particularly the British blockade of Boston—has sent prices soaring. The price of flour here is double what it is in Baltimore, and three times that of Richmond. Rice is four times more expensive here than in Charleston or Savannah. And neither cotton nor wheat can be brought here from Charleston or Norfolk."

"As bad as that, sir?" Albritton asked.

Adams nodded gravely as he sampled the soup. "Merchants are being driven into bankruptcy, and the people are being driven into debt." He paused to pat his wife's hand in appreciation. "We are doing alright so far; the farm provides what we need, and we are able to help our neighbors a little." He shook his head. "This war must end, and soon, or the consequences will be unthinkable."

Albritton said nothing as he turned his attention to his soup. He could not disagree with anything his host said, although he wished it had not been said in front of a midshipman. Still, he knew a reply was warranted. "We shall do our best, sir. Soon, I shall break out into the Atlantic, where British merchantmen shall supply all we need."

Adams barked in laughter. "Well said, Captain, well said!"

When they had finished the soup, the bowls were removed and plates were brought, followed by platters of pork and roasted goose, and bowls of stewed potatoes and beans. Slices of fresh hot bread were set where all could reach them, along with butter and jam. The president sliced the pork while the captain took care of the goose, each man careful to serve Mrs. Adams first before taking some for himself and passing the platter around until everyone's plate was full.

"Mr. Franklin," the president said, "did I hear my friend here say that you are the grandson of Benjamin Franklin?"

"Yes, Mr. President," the youth replied.

"Then your father would be William Temple Franklin," Adams pressed, "the former governor of New Jersey before the Revolution?"

"Yes, sir."

"My, my," Adams said, "you must be very proud."

Franklin shrugged. "I suppose, but, truth be told, Mr. President, I don't really know anything about my grandfather, other than stories told by old friends or enemies. Even my father in his old age would only tell me horrifying tales of my grandfather's excesses."

Adams looked to his left and met the captain's eyes for a moment; now he understood why Albritton had brought the lad with him.

"Well, young man," he said, "I'm glad you came. Not only for the honor of making your acquaintance, but also for the opportunity of sharing with you memories of my time with your grandfather."

Franklin set his fork down and looked up. "Did you know him, sir? Personally, I mean?"

"I did." Adams sat back in his chair. "I first met your grandfather during the Continental Congress in... 1775, I believe it was. He was representing Pennsylvania, and I represented Massachusetts. He was a wonderful colleague to me in those days, and afterward."

The midshipman considered for a moment, trying to decide what questions would be appropriate. In the end, he dove in wholeheartedly.

"Mr. President," he said, "I have heard men say that my grandfather's best days were behind him by the time of the 1770s, and that he actually contributed little to the movement for independence—that Mr. Jefferson and yourself were actually the true driving force in 1776."

"Let me say this," the president replied, "if you were to consider Jefferson the 'pen' of the revolution for his writing of the Declaration, you may consider me the 'voice' of it for the way I led the debates on the floor of the congress." He sat forward and rested his elbow on the table. "But, in my humble opinion, you would have to consider your grandfather as the 'heart,' for the way he worked behind the scenes to make independence happen. He taught me the art of negotiation in those days, and I was privileged to sit at his feet, so to speak, and watch him talk to the other representatives and convince them that independence was not only the right thing to do, but also that it needed to be done at once. It was he who personally convinced the delegation from New York to abstain during the vote so the result could be unanimous. That did not happen without Benjamin Franklin."

Franklin was silent as he digested what Adams had said.

Abigail turned to the midshipman. "The Congress thought enough of your grandfather to send him to France to negotiate a treaty with them."

"Yes," the president agreed. "In fact, I was sent to France in 1778 to aid him in that task, but by the time I arrived, your grandfather had already concluded the treaty with King Louis."

Franklin looked up. "I did not know that."

"It has been rightly said," the president continued, "that, without the French alliance, America would have lost the Revolutionary War. Since that alliance would not have happened without your grandfather, it follows that America would have lost the war were it not for Benjamin Franklin." He paused, hesitating only a moment before continuing. "I will be honest with you, young man; I did not always agree with your grandfather, and there were times we quarreled like enemies. That being said, I repeat: America would have lost the Revolutionary War without Benjamin Franklin and his contributions."

An awkward silence settled over the room. "Mr. President," Franklin said, "I don't know what to say."

Adams sat back and grunted. "That's quite all right, Mr. Franklin. Take it from me—you have every right to be proud of your grandfather. He was by no means a saint, and I'm sure there will be many quick to point out lapses in his judgment or failures in his character, but that only proves that he was human. None of us are immune to such charges. Your grandfather was the man for his times. I feel privileged to have known him and worked with him."

The midshipman considered for a moment before looking to his host. "Thank you, sir. I have waited a long time to hear such words from someone who was there and knew him. I'm glad I know the truth."

Adams nodded. "You are most welcome, Mr. Franklin. My wife and I will pray that your life will be as great a benefit to this country as his was."

Albritton rose, and Franklin followed suit. He then turned to his host and said solemnly, "I can only promise you this, Mr. President: I will try."

CHAPTER SIX

Albritton returned to his ship and discovered that USS *Argus* had arrived two hours earlier.

"Any communication from Commander Calloway?" he asked his first officer after hearing the news.

"None, sir," Chandler replied.

The captain blinked at that. It was highly unusual. *Very well*, he thought. *If that's the way he wants to play it, so be it.* He looked at his premier. "Signal to *Argus*: *'Captain report on board.'*"

Chandler grinned ever so slightly. "Aye, Captain."

"I'll be in my cabin," the captain said as he turned toward the companionway stairs. "Bring him to me when he arrives."

He made his way below and found Xavier and Sommers supervising some hands who were putting in place some furniture that Xavier had brought on board from Shiloh. Curtains to cover the stern windows, some small pillows to go on the settee. Lamps to hang from the deck beams above and brighten the atmosphere. The crowning touch was his favorite chair, placed off to the side of the day cabin close to his desk. He'd had it built during his first commission on USS *Constitution* and made sure it came along with him ever since. It was the most comfortable chair ever made—at least for him.

"Well, Xavier," he said as he set his hat on the desk, "looks a bit more like home now, doesn't it?"

"Aye," the coxswain said with an approving nod.

"How many barrels?" Albritton asked.

"Two of bourbon, along with two kegs," Xavier said. "That was all we had. The new shipment hadn't arrived yet; Hawthorne said it was two weeks overdue. I also brought three barrels of Kentucky whiskey, three cases of wine, and the last of the Cognac we got from that French captain."

"How much of Cognac?"

Xavier had to think for a moment. "A case plus three bottles."

Albritton frowned. "I didn't realize we were so low. Let's hope we run into an English merchantman who has some in stock."

Xavier chuckled, and the captain turned to his steward. "And how are we stocked at the moment, Sommers?"

"Fairly well, Captain. Xavier brought a goodly amount of spices and other pantry supplies from your house. I gather that your man Hawthorne keeps a stock ready to be sent to your ship at a moment's notice—a smart idea, that. I would like to go ashore tomorrow and get some cheeses, a ham or two, and perhaps a couple geese and a leg of mutton for your usual party after we sail."

Albritton grinned. "You've heard about that, have you?"

Sommers shrugged. "Xavier thought it best I was informed."

Albritton gave an exaggerated nod. "I see. Well, he is usually right."

Xavier ordered the hands out and gave the room a once-over before following them out.

Sommers stepped up. "Is there anything I can get you, Captain?"

Albritton settled into his chair and sighed. *Good as it ever was,* he thought. "Tell me, Sommers, did Xavier bring any coffee?"

The servant smiled. "Vast quantities, sir."

"I'll have a cup, then."

"Already brewing, Captain; it should be ready momentarily." Albritton looked up in surprise, but Sommers shrugged. "He may have mentioned your fondness for it, sir."

Albritton laid his head back against the plush headrest and closed his eyes for a moment. He was nearly asleep when he heard Sommers set the cup down on the small table to his right.

"Xavier said you like it set here, sir," he explained. "Is there anything else?"

"Not for now. Commander Calloway is expected soon; he may want a cup when he arrives."

"Very good, sir." The servant withdrew.

The captain picked up his cup and inhaled the delicious aroma. He carefully blew on the hot rim before partaking, but the scalding brew was worth it.

It was not until over an hour later that the sentry knocked on the door and announced the arrival of Commander Calloway. Albritton rose and shook his guest's hand.

"I apologize for my tardiness, Captain," Calloway said. "I had to finish my report, and there was a disciplinary matter that could not wait."

"I see," Albritton said as he resumed his seat. "We can discuss that later. Please, Commander, sit here. Thank you. Coffee? No? Very well. Do you have your reports?"

"Aye, sir." Calloway handed them over, and Albritton placed them on his desk.

"Thank you," the captain said as he picked up his cup again. "I would like to hear it from you, if you please." He sat back in his chair to listen.

"Well, sir," Calloway began, "we lost sight of you on the second turn in the fog. I turned to the east, thinking that open water was a fairly safe bet." Albritton nodded, and Calloway continued. "After a half hour or so, we turned north for a time, then nor'west. My thinking was to try to slide south along the coast to the harbor, using the fog as cover."

"And when did you figure out that we had blundered right into the heart of the British blockade squadron?" Albritton asked with a smile.

Calloway folded his hands in his lap and grinned sheepishly. "After the third time we heard a ship's bell pass us by. That was right after we made our turn to the nor'west. Never did sight any of them. It took us longer to find the shore than I thought it would, so we were all the more cautious working our way south, but we finally made it."

"Good job in bringing her in, Commander," Albritton said. "From what I've been told, the British have placed a fairly tight lid on Boston harbor. Very few make it in, and even fewer make it out." He took another drink. "But we are going to try." He pulled a paper from his desk and handed it to his guest. "This is a list of the supplies that the port admiral says is available for *Argus*." He held up a hand before Calloway could protest. "I understand your frustration; indeed, I share it. You should have seen the list for *Columbia*. You will take on provisions and water tomorrow. If you can complete that tomorrow, we shall try to break out tomorrow night. Of course, it will be a last-minute decision."

"What about trying during the day, sir, if the fog is still about? Perhaps we might slip out to the north, the way I came in, and make it to Salem? It might be easier to get out of there at night, sir."

Albritton studied his guest through the steam from his

cup as he considered the plan. "You may have something, Commander. I shall consider it, if we are still here the morning after. As for our supply problems, we shall have to hope we quickly come across a couple of fat English merchantmen."

Calloway grinned and bobbed his head in agreement.

Albritton continued, "Once we are at sea, we should at all times stay within signal range of each other. Any night signal raised will bring the other ship to close the gap with all speed."

"Understood, sir."

"Neither ship shall investigate a contact until it has been reported and acknowledged," the captain said. His guest hesitated in his reply, and Albritton's eyebrow rose—never a good sign to those who knew him. "Is there a problem, Commander?"

"Well, sir," Calloway hesitated, trying to pick his words with care, "what if the contact appears to be moving away? Am I to wait for an acknowledgement and perhaps allow it to escape?"

"There will be others." Albritton met his guest's eyes. "No investigation without acknowledgement, Commander. Not by you, and not by me."

"Understood, Captain."

The next day passed quickly, with both ships completing the stowing of provisions and taking on fresh water. The ship was moved into position to allow the remainder of her armament to be brought aboard. Sommers and Boothby, the gunroom steward, spent most of the day ashore, trying to gather together such delicacies as could be had in the town. Mr. Franklin was sent ashore with them so he might have a chance to visit a bookstore in search of his grandfather's autobiography.

Leaving the shipboard duties in Mr. Chandler's capable hands, the captain spent most of the day ashore, first visiting the port admiral and then making social calls. His time with the port admiral went about as he'd expected. He informed the admiral of his plans to attempt to leave under cover of darkness, and, failing that, to flee under cover of a morning fog to Salem and thence to the open sea. The admiral warned of a reported strengthening of the British blockade squadron, and he also gave Albritton some news: intelligence from Halifax had reported that the British had sent one of their razed two-deckers, HMS *London*, to hunt down *Columbia* and either capture or sink her.

"Indeed?" Albritton quipped. A razed two-decker was a line-of-battle ship cut down to one gun deck like a frigate, but still with the battleship's thick walls. Its speed was also supposed to be comparable to that of a frigate. "I had no idea we would be so popular. Who commands *London*?"

"Knighton." The admiral saw the captain's look of recognition. "You know this man?"

Albritton shook his head. "We've never met, but I heard that he commanded a frigate that chased me in the Caribbean last year. We escaped, and I later heard this Knighton took it personally."

"I see," the admiral said. "Still, better to be informed."

"Aye, sir." Albritton rose. "If there is nothing else, sir, I have calls to make."

Admiral Redmon rose and shook the captain's hand. "Of course. Let us know how it fares for you as you can. Good luck to you, and Godspeed."

The sun was waning by the time Captain Albritton returned to his ship. He was greeted by the first lieutenant as he arrived, and the two men made their way to the captain's cabin. Xavier met them inside the door and took his captain's hat, coat and sword.

"How was your visit to the port admiral, sir?" Chandler inquired.

Albritton sat in his chair and leaned his head back. "About what you might expect. He had nothing additional to offer us, save one piece of intelligence newly arrived from Halifax. It seems the British have assigned a frigate—one of their cut-down two-deckers—to hunt us down. HMS *London*. Captain's name is Knighton."

Chandler's eyes darted as he searched his memory, finally shaking his head. "I don't know him, sir."

"Nor do I, but I understand he chased me in the Caribbean last year, and it seems he has taken my escape personally." Albritton shrugged. "Something to bear in mind. Now, what does Mr. Warren think of our chances of slipping out of the harbor tonight?"

"Not much, I'm afraid. The last time I spoke to him, which was about an hour ago, he was expecting clear skies and decent moonlight."

Albritton frowned, then pursed his lips as he considered the options. "Well," he said finally, "have us ready to move in any case, just in case there is a sudden change."

"Aye, sir."

"Dismissed."

After the first lieutenant departed, Albritton declined the offer of refreshments from the faithful Sommers and closed his eyes. He was visualizing the waterways available for his quick exit from the harbor—he knew these waters so well that he had no need of a map. The northern route to Salem, suggested by Calloway, was certainly an option, although any fog would cause them to reduce their speed to barely more than a crawl. That meant Salem would be a five- or even six-hour trip, depending upon conditions, a long time to have to crawl along the shore.

He opened his eyes and rose, stretching to force the kinks out of his back. He began to pace back and forth, more for the exercise than for anything else. He hated this part of it—the forced waiting while conditions asserted themselves and he had enough information to make a decision. Fortunately, *Columbia's* day cabin was broad enough that he could take seven steps across before he had to make the turn. He could get a longer course on the quarterdeck, but he didn't want to be a distraction to the crew. He tried to ease his mind by planning ahead, so to speak; he had no plans yet for the days and weeks after they were free from Boston and the east coast. He considered making a long, lazy arc from New England to Bermuda, where they stood a very good chance of finding some English merchantmen to ease his supply issues. Of course, in that area he stood an equal chance of encountering British warships. Still, he thought it worth the risk, particularly if they might stumble upon a lightly defended convoy ripe for the picking.

And after that? Albritton thought they might repeat the maneuver, going east and then south so as to disappear into the vast Atlantic Ocean. From there they would have their pick of the sea-lanes to raid as they made their way south toward the southern approaches to the Caribbean. It dawned on him that he might use *Argus* independently in this region. At the very least, it might force the British to divide their forces.

The trouble with that idea was, of course, Calloway. He had to admit, the man had done well in bringing his ship into harbor safely after getting separated in the fog. Still, there was something about the commander that nagged at him, a voice in the back of his mind warning him not to trust him just yet. Calloway's reaction to the order not to investigate without notification and acknowledgement only added to his caution.

Albritton stopped pacing and sat down again in his chair. He rubbed his chin as he stared out the stern window at the town beyond. One trouble he'd discovered was that he had nobody to confide in on this ship. He knew no one save Xavier. He wished he still had Goodson as his first lieutenant; the two had sailed together for years and saved each other's lives more than once. A bond had been forged there, and Albritton could talk to him and bounce ideas off the man. Chandler was still an unknown quantity, forcing Albritton to keep his own counsel more than he otherwise would.

Dusk had fallen when Captain Albritton stepped up on his quarterdeck. He frowned as he looked heavenward and saw a sky full of stars and a bright moon. He made his way to the wheel, where the first lieutenant and sailing master greeted him.

"Gentlemen," Albritton responded. "I see you were right, Mr. Warren."

"Would that I weren't, sir."

Albritton looked around. "Mr. Chandler, have the officer of the watch report any changes in the weather."

"Aye, sir."

"I'm going below," Albritton said. "Perhaps I can pray up a thick fog around dawn."

The officers chuckled.

"I hope so, Captain," Warren said.

The captain went back to his cabin and did indeed offer a prayer, begging God for either a stormy, overcast night or a dense morning fog. He sat in his chair and thanked Sommers for a cold glass of wine. He drained the glass quickly and leaned his head back and closed his eyes. The next thing he knew, Mr. Chandler was shaking him by the arm.

"What?" he struggled to awaken. "Mr. Chandler?"

"Good morning, Captain. Mr. Warren reports he thinks a fog is rolling in."

That one word struck the captain like a thunderbolt. *"Fog?"*

He sprang out of the chair before he realized what he was doing, but luckily Chandler was there to steady him. "Easy, sir," the premier said as he latched onto his captain's arm and kept him from falling. Albritton shook his head clear and wiped the sleep from his eyes.

"Thank you, Mr. Chandler. Ask Sommers to brew coffee. I'll be up on deck presently."

"Aye, sir. I believe the coffee is already on."

Albritton decided against waiting for the coffee and followed his first lieutenant out of the cabin and up to the deck. As soon as his foot hit the quarterdeck, he could smell the change in the weather. The fog was already thick enough to hide the rising sun to the east.

"Mr. Warren," he called, "how thick to do you think it will get?"

The sailing master looked around before he answered. "Thick enough, Captain, thick enough. I think we can try Commander Calloway's suggestion of sneaking north along the coast to Salem and then breaking out to the open ocean at night."

Albritton studied the sky for a moment before pacing to the far rail and back again. He stopped, pursed his lips, and nodded. "Let's do it," he said. "Mr. Chandler, notify *Argus* to standby."

On board USS *Argus*, Commander Calloway was also chafing under the present circumstances. He stood in the middle of his quarterdeck, bouncing silently on his toes and looking straight ahead. Occasionally his eyes drifted aloft, wishing he could unfurl the sails, but his gaze returned to the deck quickly enough. *What is he waiting for?* he fumed silently. *We're wasting precious time! Surely we can sneak past the British in this soup!*

He cleared his throat in an attempt to swallow his frustration, and his first lieutenant took the opportunity to approach him.

"Anything from *Columbia*?" Calloway asked.

"No, sir," Wilson answered. "I can't imagine he would wait much longer."

Calloway grunted. "We shall see, won't we? I just hope he doesn't bollix up the entire voyage for us!"

Wilson looked around to see if anyone had overheard the captain's words, but nobody appeared to be within earshot. "I wouldn't worry, sir," he reassured his captain. "I'm sure we'll come back richer than Gouverneur Morris!"

Calloway sighed and clapped his premier on the arm. "I hope you're right, Aaron. I know I could make good use of the prize money."

A midshipman stepped up and saluted. "Begging your pardon, sir—there's a signal from *Columbia*."

Albritton turned to Mr. Warren and the quartermaster and nodded once. Warren knuckled his forehead and went for the speaking trumpet while the quartermaster conferred with his mates. The hands at the capstan began to strain, and the anchor began to rise and then broke the surface. The ship began to glide toward the harbor entrance, with USS *Argus* following close behind. The two ships slid silently from the harbor, turned north along the coast, and disappeared into the fog.

The captain stood in the midst of his quarterdeck, hands behind his back as his ship sailed silently toward the open sea. A single light was lit on the fantail to give *Argus* a point of reference in the fog. Lookouts were posted along the rails and in the shrouds, their ears open for any indication that another ship was close by. Two hands stood ready with the lead on the larboard side.

"Mr. Warren," the captain said, "kindly alter our course two points to starboard." To Mr. Chandler: "Notify *Argus*."

"Aye, sir."

Nothing was heard by any of the lookouts, so Albritton soon altered their course north again, and they made their run for Salem. The fog burned off an hour later, and the two Americans found themselves alone on the glassy sea. Albritton walked to the larboard rail and was pleased to see that the Massachusetts coastline was below the horizon.

"Mr. Warren," he called, "when do you estimate we shall arrive at Salem?"

The sailing master pulled out his pocket watch and stared at the face for several moments while he did calculations in his head. "Maybe three or four hours, Captain, assuming the wind holds. I recommend we alter course two or three points to larboard in about an hour or so."

"Very well. Let me know when you want to change course." Albritton turned and walked to the fantail. He was pleased to see *Argus* sailing in her place, even if she was slightly to starboard.

"I shall be in my cabin, Mr. Chandler. Inform me at once of any sightings."

"Aye, sir!" Chandler called to his captain's retreating back. He watched as Albritton disappeared below deck before turning to the sailing master. "What do you think of that, Mr. Warren? Am I very much mistaken, or is something occupying our captain's mind?"

Warren shrugged and eyed the companionway. "Who knows, Lieutenant? Offhand, I'd say none of us knows what might be troubling the captain. We left Boston with less than a full hold, which means we'll be scavenging at some point during the voyage." He turned to the premier. "Not the best way to start a commission, now, is it?"

In his cabin on board HMS *London*, Captain Sir Thomas Knighton set his drink down with a sigh of disgust. His ship was proceeding under all sail toward Bermuda. He hoped a search of the waters north of the island would give him the best chance of intercepting Albritton before he could do any major damage to British shipping in the Atlantic.

He jumped up and began to pace across the breadth of his day cabin. *Five days!* he fumed. *How could that idiot hold me for no good reason for five whole days!* Knighton grunted, wondering who the man's sponsors were at the Admiralty, knowing he had to have help to achieve a squadron command in the Royal Navy. Now Albritton was gone; he'd slipped past the blockade squadron and disappeared into the Atlantic Ocean. Knighton's last packet of information, sent over to him along with the orders releasing him from the squadron, indicated that the American ships were heading to another port to finish provisioning before setting out on their mission. Personally, Knighton believed Albritton had gone north to Boston or possibly somewhere else in New England; it was a coast that his adversary knew all too well. Of course, Albritton might have gone south for that very reason, in which case he would be trying to slip past the blockade at any moment. Knighton shook his head in disgust. No, he had to go to Bermuda. It was the most logical place to pick up the American's trail. He only hoped it didn't take too long. He stopped his pacing and sighed.

It was the sound of a throat being cleared that caused him to turn and see Flagstone standing in the doorway.

"Begging your pardon, sir," the servant said formally, "but is there anything else I can get for you?" His eyebrow rose slightly. "A refill, perhaps?"

An ever-so-small smile appeared at the corner of the captain's lip. He was being chastised, and he knew it and accepted it. Flagstone was the one man aboard who had earned the right to speak to him thus; years of service and even friendship had secured it for him. The servant had been his constant companion for more then twenty years and followed him on numerous ships and adventures in literally every ocean in the world. As soon as Knighton's rank had become sufficient to allow him a manservant, his father had sent him Flagstone. The two men had fought side by side and sometimes back to back and saved each other's lives a dozen times over.

"No, thank you, old friend," Knighton replied, "although a cup of tea would do nicely. Can you please pass the word for Mr. Percival?"

Flagstone's face was an immovable mask, but his eyes shone with approval of the choice. "As you wish, sir." He bowed and withdrew.

Knighton shook his head and chuckled to himself, grateful yet again for his father's foresight. How many times had Flagstone performed the same service, rescuing him from his demons like this? He just had time to sit before a knock on the door preceded the sentry admitting the first lieutenant.

"Report, Mr. Percival?"

"On course for Bermuda as ordered, sir," the premier replied. "The sailing master estimates another two or three days, assuming the winds hold."

"Excellent, Roland. Sit, please."

Flagstone entered the room bearing a tray with two steaming cups upon it. Knighton smiled as Percival accepted his cup without a second thought. "When we arrive at Bermuda, I will go ashore and see the port admiral. I will show him our orders from Admiral Keats; that should be sufficient to get us whatever provisions can be loaded overnight. I want to be out to sea again with the morning tide."

"Understood, Captain. Have you decided on our patrol arc yet?"

Knighton sipped his tea and considered. "That will depend on whether or not we have missed the Caribbean convoy bound for London. If the convoy has sailed, we'll patrol a line roughly east to west, north and west of the island in the hopes of catching them as they move south. If we are in time to catch the convoy, we shall join the escort. I'm sure Albritton will have it in his sights and will try his best to intercept it if he can. We will sail with them for a few days to make sure they are out of danger before turning back to our task."

Percival sat back and enjoyed his drink. Sir Thomas's plan seemed sound. The convoy would certainly be a prime target for the Americans; they would be drawn to it like a moth to a candle's flame. Provided the stars aligned properly.

Captain Hezekiah Albritton sat at his desk in his cabin and studied the report prepared for him by Mr. Petry, the purser, on the current state of the ship's stores. USS *Columbia* and USS *Argus* sat peacefully in the harbor of Salem, Massachusetts, having arrived just after noon at the end of their uneventful transit north from Boston, waiting for nightfall to attempt to break out into the Atlantic. The captain had asked the purser for the report on the ship's stores and was not pleased with what he saw. He sent for the naval port commander, and sent a message to Calloway inquiring about the state of *Argus*'s stores.

He was still staring at the report and frowning at its implications when a knock at the cabin door heralded the sentry's admission of the port commander and the first lieutenant to the room. Albritton stood as a lieutenant in full dress uniform presented himself and stood at attention. Lieutenant Chandler stepped forward to make the introductions.

"Captain," he said, "may I introduce Lieutenant Rickons, the US Navy's port commander at Salem."

"Lieutenant,"—Albritton nodded in greeting—"welcome. Please, be seated, both of you. Sommers! Drinks for three, if you please!"

"Aye, sir!"

The two officers sat while Sommers set three glasses of wine before them and retreated. They toasted the health of President Madison and drank deeply before getting down to business.

"Lieutenant," Albritton said to the newcomer, "I have two questions for you. The first is, what can you tell me about Royal Navy activity in the area?"

"I would call it inconsistent, sir," Rickons replied. "From time to time, a brig will appear off the harbor, or occasionally a frigate, but they never stay more than a day or so before returning to Boston. Of course, that will most likely change as soon as they discover you are no longer there."

Chandler's eyes grew wide at the younger officer's effrontery, but a quick glance in his captain's direction told him that the remark went unnoticed. Albritton stared out over the table, his eyes moving just enough to tell the premier his captain was thinking furiously.

"Possibly," Albritton said absently. He blinked and addressed Rickons. "The second question is, what can you do for us in the way of provisions?"

The lieutenant lowered his eyes and shook his head sadly. "Not much, I'm afraid. You see, Captain, the blockade has bitten deep hereabouts. Many of the farmers in the area are keeping what little they can grow to feed themselves and their fellow townsfolk. Inflation caused by the war has hurt us as well. Merchants are not willing to accept government bonds as payment; they're insisting on cash payments, and money is in short supply."

"Surely, you must have something on hand we can use," Chandler said.

Rickons pulled a notebook from his pocket and opened it, flipping through several pages until he found what he was looking for. "As I said, I don't have much available, but I can let you have twenty bags of flour and ten of biscuit, along with two barrels each of beef and pork. Your purser will need to inspect those, as we took them from a British prize that was brought in two weeks ago." He turned a couple pages. "Ah! I have recently received 100 gallons of vinegar and fifty bushels of melons and other fruit. When do you plan to sail?"

"Tonight, if at all possible," Albritton confirmed. "I would not be surprised if a British ship arrived in the morning to inspect the harbor." The captain rose. "Thank you, Mr. Rickons. I will send my purser ashore with you to inspect the meat and anything else you have to offer." To Chandler: "Signal *Argus* to send their purser ashore as well. Stewards may go ashore if they need to."

"Aye, sir."

"Dismissed."

The two lieutenants came to attention and left the room. After the door was closed, Sommers came to clear the table.

"Will you be going ashore, Sommers?" Albritton asked.

"I believe so, Captain. We are fairly well stocked at the moment, but one never knows what bargains can be had in a new port. Is there anything you wish me to look for?"

The captain pursed his lips as he thought. "Coffee. We can never have enough coffee." He sat and leaned back, rubbing his chin as he warmed to the subject. "A ham. A big one, if you can find it; two small ones, otherwise. I want to entertain my officers soon after we sail. Let me see, is there anything else?"

Sommers thought for a moment before shaking his head. "Nothing comes to mind, sir. I had thought to use the mutton I purchased at Boston for your entertainment; I shall, however, endeavor to purchase a replacement. Will goose do, if a ham cannot be found?"

Albritton shrugged. "I suppose so." He rose and made his way toward the door. "We all have to make sacrifices to the war, don't you agree?" he called over his shoulder. He opened the door and spoke to the sentry. "Pass the word for the first lieutenant."

"Aye, Captain!"

Albritton closed the door and came back to the table. He asked Sommers, "Will you be back in time for me to have three other officers for supper tonight? Nothing fancy, you understand."

"Aye, Captain, that should be no problem."

"Thank you." Just then a knock at the cabin door preceded the admission of the first lieutenant. "Ah, Mr. Chandler, there you are. Will you join me for supper tonight? I intend to invite Commander Calloway and Lieutenant Wilson as well; I think a war council would be a good thing before we leave."

"Right willingly, Captain," the premier replied. "Thank you. Shall I send an invitation to *Argus*? What time should I put on it?"

The captain looked to Sommers. "Will the turn of the first dog watch be alright?" The servant nodded, and Albritton nodded to his first lieutenant.

"Right. I shall send it over with Lieutenant Williams. Is there anything else, sir?"

"Yes. Follow me." Albritton led the way into the day cabin

and sat in his favorite chair. Mr. Chandler took a seat on the settee. Albritton took a deep breath. "I intend to leave tonight. If we wait, we may become trapped here by the British blockade squadron." Chandler made to speak, but Albritton stopped him with a gesture. "I understand about our supply situation, but remaining here will not improve that. We shall have to make due with whatever the purser can procure here and make up the rest from some fat Indiaman we come across in the Atlantic."

Chandler sat back, looking resigned. "As you say, sir. I sent Lieutenant Mitchell and a party ashore with the purser in case there is any question about the disposition of provisions."

"The second lieutenant?" Albritton questioned. "A little beneath him, wouldn't you say?"

Chandler shrugged. "Possibly, but he will carry weight over anyone *Argus* could send other than Mr. Wilson or the commander himself."

Albritton grinned. "I see. Very well, Mr. Chandler; get that invitation off at once, if you please."

The premier arose. "Aye, sir." He came to attention and left the cabin. Once he was gone, Sommers appeared in the doorway.

"Do you care for anything, sir?"

Albritton considered for a moment before shaking his head. "No, thank you. I'll sit here and think until time for lunch."

"Very good, sir." The servant withdrew and left his master in peace.

The ringing of the ship's bell, announcing the turn of the first dog watch, had not yet died when the door opened to the captain's cabin, admitting the first lieutenant leading two guests into the dining cabin. Albritton stepped forward and shook hands with both men, greeting them warmly.

"Thank you for coming, Commander, Lieutenant," he said as he led them into the day cabin. Sommers followed with a tray full of refreshments, and the officers sat down to await their call to dine. "I thought it would be good for us to meet one more time before breaking out into the Atlantic."

"You intend to move tonight, then?" Calloway asked.

Albritton nodded. "I think the British will be looking for us once they get word we're no longer in Boston harbor, and if they find us here, it will be all too easy for them to put a proverbial cork in the harbor entrance and trap us here for the duration. We've got to move tonight. How are your stores, Commander? Were you able to get any help ashore today?"

"Some," Calloway replied. "I understand your Lieutenant Mitchell was very helpful in making sure *Argus* received a fair share of what fresh fruits there were to be had. I wanted to bring that to your attention and commend him for his actions."

"Thank you. I shall be pleased to note that in my report."

Calloway nodded. "Other than that, we're low, as I imagine you are as well, but we have enough for the short term."

"Rest assured," Albritton said, "we shall be making a call on the first Indiaman we come across."

Sommers appeared in the doorway to announce that dinner was served. The four officers rose as made their way to the table. Albritton took his place at its head, with Mr. Chandler on his left and Mr. Calloway on his right and Mr. Wilson next to his captain. Sommers and the stewards brought in a tureen of hearty vegetable soup. Albritton took the ladle and filled each man's bowl. Once that was finished, there followed a platter with a roast goose upon it, bowls of carrots and potatoes, and fresh hot bread and butter. The captain rose and raised his glass, and they all drank to the president's health.

"No need to stand on ceremony this evening, gentlemen," Albritton said. "Commander, will you do the honors and carve that goose? I confess, my mouth waters at the sight! Come now, Mr. Chandler, Mr. Wilson, help yourselves to what's before you. Ah, thank you, Mr. Calloway!" he exclaimed as the commander placed the first slices of the goose on his plate. Leaning forward he sniffed and declared, "There's not a better aroma in the best inns in Boston!"

"Here! Here!" Chandler echoed.

"Sir?" Wilson interjected as he placed a couple of chops on his plate. "May I ask what your plan is? When do we leave?"

"Tonight," the captain replied, "as I said. I want to wait until full dark, but no later than midnight. We shall go to full sail as soon as we clear the harbor and head due east throughout the night. I want to put as much distance between us and Salem as possible." He paused as he sampled the goose and nodded his approval. "Every bit as good as it smells... At some point, we shall turn southeast and head for Bermuda. I hope to intercept the Jamaica convoy on its way to London. I imagine taking some of those beauties will fill our holds nicely, don't you think?"

Wilson was all smiles. "Oh, I do indeed, sir!"

When the supper was ended, the officers adjourned to the day cabin for wine and cigars. Albritton sat in his chair, with the others scattered around the room, all puffing merrily and sending clouds of smoke toward the deck above.

"Commander," Albritton said, "I called this meeting to make sure there are no misunderstandings regarding procedures once we sail. Do you have any questions?"

Calloway shook his head. "I don't think so, sir. Everything is pretty clear."

The captain held the other's eyes. "No problems?"

The commander did not flinch. "No, sir."

Albritton took a deep drag on his cigar and blew the smoke heavenward to give him time to think. He thought about questioning his guest further to make sure he would comply, but in the end said nothing. He drained his glass and stood. "Very well," he said, closing the meeting. "We shall leave after nightfall. Commander, watch for our signal. Both ships will be dark, save the single lamp on *Columbia's* fantail. Remain within signal range at all times. Questions?"

Calloway shook his head. "None, sir."

Albritton held out his hand, and the commander took it. "Good luck," Albritton said, "to all of us."

"Amen to that, sir," Calloway replied.

CHAPTER SEVEN

Captain Hezekiah Albritton stepped up on the deck of his frigate to find that darkness had settled over the harbor. Lieutenant Chandler met him with his hat raised.

"Good evening, Captain," he said.

"Good evening," Albritton replied. "How's the weather looking?"

The premier shrugged. "Not as dark as I would have liked; we will still have to deal with the moon peeking through clouds." He looked at the sky again and sighed. "I think we need to leave now, sir."

"I agree," Albritton said. "Signal *Argus*. Take her out, Mr. Chandler."

The premier touched his hat. "Aye, sir." He picked up a speaking trumpet and began issuing orders. Albritton stood in the middle of the quarterdeck and watched his men as they went about their duties. Topmen climbed the shrouds to loosen sails while the bosun directed hands at the capstan. He turned to see Mr. Adams signaling *Argus*.

A favorable wind began to fill the tops'ls, and the ships began to glide slowly toward the open sea. They cleared the harbor and immediately came under a heavy cloud that completely blocked the moonlight.

"Make all sail," Albritton ordered. "Inform *Argus*."

"Aye, sir," Mr. Chandler replied. He turned to Adams.

"Hoist the signal for *Argus* to make all sail."

"Aye, sir."

"Make all sail!" Chandler called aloft. "All hands! Make all sail!"

Albritton heard the unfurling of sails and felt the deck leap forward beneath his feet. He nodded to himself in satisfaction. His crew were well trained; now it just remained to be seen how they would react in the face of enemy fire. He stood back and watched as they left civilization behind and sped into the wide spaces of the North Atlantic Ocean. Satisfied they had not been seen, he turned and made his way to the fantail.

"Did *Argus* acknowledge the signal to make all sail?" he asked.

"I believe so, sir, but I can't say for certain," the midshipman replied. "It got very dark suddenly, and I could not make out their reply."

"Keep an eye out for them."

"Aye, sir."

Albritton stepped to the wheel where Mr. Warren was standing beside the quartermaster. "Make your course due east."

"Aye, sir," Warren replied. "Due east it is, sir."

"Mr. Franklin," the captain said, "cast the log, if you please."

"Aye, Captain!" Franklin replied. "Come along, Mr. Lee, Mr. Miller!"

Albritton turned to watch the procedure. He was pleased that Franklin was using the occasion to train the two youngest and newest midshipmen. Mr. Miller manned the glass and Franklin instructed Mr. Lee on how to cast the log and how to seize it on Miller's signal. It took two tries for the two young men to get in sync—Miller forgot to turn the glass the first time—but the second cast went off perfectly. Miller watched carefully as the last grain of sand fell.

"Now!" he called, and Lee grabbed the line. He hauled the log back in, carefully counting the knots. "Thirteen knots, sir!"

Warren smiled. "And that's not her best, sir, not by a long shot!"

"We shall see, I'm sure," the captain commented. "Mr. Chandler, I'm going below. Who has the deck?"

"Lieutenant Mitchell is officer of the watch, Captain."

"Fine. Have him notify me of any sightings."

"Aye, sir. Goodnight."

Albritton made his goodnights and went below deck. Once in his cabin, he sank thankfully into the comfort of his chair and closed his eyes for a moment in relief. Sommers brought him a glass of wine, and Albritton sipped and allowed his mind to wander. Mary appeared in his mind, smiling as she had the last time he'd seen her, more than thirty years earlier. She'd been beautiful, and he'd loved her from the first moment he'd seen her. They'd met when he was sixteen and she fourteen, riding her horse past his family farm. She'd stopped and commented on the heat, so he fetched her a drink of water. Their hands touched for a moment when she handed the ladle back to him, and their eyes met. *That's when I knew,* he thought. *That's when I decided to marry her.*

Then she was gone, the vision replaced by The Letters. Albritton felt the familiar pain grip his heart, and his jaw tensed. Sadness still came over him in waves at the memory, even after all these years.

A knock on the cabin door roused him from his thoughts. "Enter!"

The door opened and Mr. Midshipman Smith marched in

and came to attention. "Mr. Mitchell's respects, sir; there's a light sighted to the south. Mr. Mitchell requests you come up on deck, sir!"

"My compliments to Mr. Mitchell. Tell him I shall come up."

"Aye, sir!" The midshipman came to attention again and left.

Albritton rose and picked up his hat. He paused for a moment to take a deep breath and steady himself, then he made for the door. When he appeared on deck, he was met by Lieutenant Mitchell.

"Light to the south, sir," he reported as he handed his captain a glass. "Intermittent contact, but frequent enough that I judged it to be real." He pointed in the direction just aft of the starboard beam. "It was headed east when first sighted, but it seemed to come about and parallel us; that was when I sent for you, sir."

Albritton searched the black horizon for several seconds before he saw it, a spot of white that appeared on the horizon for a few moments and then was gone. It appeared again, maintaining the same relative position, indicating a parallel course.

"Who is manning the signal lamp for *Argus?*" he asked.

"Mr. Presley, sir," Mitchell said. Albritton looked at him; the name was unfamiliar to him. "Petty officer on my watch, sir. Good eyes," Mitchell explained.

"Ask him if *Argus* is still on station," the captain said.

Mitchell touched his hat and went aft. Albritton studied the horizon and caught sight of the light twice more before the lieutenant returned.

"Sir, Presley said his last sighting of *Argus* was more then three hours ago, during the last period of good moonlight. He also said the ship seemed farther aft than she had been."

The captain lowered the telescope for a moment and considered what the lieutenant had said. *Argus* had been there three hours ago, albeit further aft than before. Was Calloway just being cautious in the darkness, or was he trying to sneak away so he could pounce on an unsuspecting prize that might present itself in the moonlight? Albritton frowned; he did not like the thoughts that were forcing themselves into his consciousness—doubts about a fellow officer were dangerous in wartime.

"Steady as you go," he ordered. "Keep an eye on our friend out there; inform me at once if her position changes in any way." He handed the glass to the lieutenant. "I will be in my cabin."

"Aye, sir."

He returned to his cabin to find Xavier there, ready to help him prepare for bed.

"Think she's British?" the coxswain asked.

"Who?"

"That ship out there."

"You heard about that, did you?" Albritton handed over his hat, coat, and hanger. "Who else could it be?"

Xavier shrugged and turned to put his master's things away.

Albritton rose with the dawn. He dressed and went up on deck to find a cloudless morning. He took a glass and quickly scanned the horizon, but the only ship that was visible was *Argus*, sailing a half-mile off the larboard quarter.

"Good morning, sir."

Albritton turned to see his first lieutenant touching his hat. The captain returned the gesture.

"So, Mr. Chandler," he said, "it seems we have done it."

"I never doubted it, Captain," the premier replied.

"Signal *Argus* to take station to the north," Albritton said.

"Aye, sir." Chandler turned to Mr. Adams, the signals midshipman. "Signal *Argus* to take her station to the north."

"Aye, sir!" The reply came a moment later. "*Argus* acknowledges, sir!"

The captain and his premier watched as the sloop turned off to larboard to take her station. They plainly saw Commander Calloway standing next to the rail, waving to them as his ship sped off. Chandler grunted and shook his head.

Captain Hezekiah Albritton's head turned upward slightly as he heard the ship's bell ring, announcing the turn of the second dogwatch. He rose from his chair and stepped to the end of the dining table just as the sentry's knock came on the cabin door.

"Enter," he called. The door opened, and his officers stepped in, one-by-one, to shake their captain's hand in welcome and then move off into the day cabin aft. After shaking the hand of the last man—who happened to be Mr. Monroe, the lieutenant in charge of the marines aboard—Albritton joined his men. He stood by his chair while Sommers went around the room and allowed each man to take a glass of wine from his tray. The captain, by previous arrangement, accepted the last glass and raised it in a toast.

"Gentlemen, I give you the health of our president, and a successful voyage!"

Cries of "Here! Here!" echoed around the room, and the officers took their seats. The captain took another drink before setting his glass on the side table and sitting back comfortably in his chair.

"Gentlemen," he said, "I welcome you to my cabin. I know we have not sailed together before, so I will tell you it has been my custom for some years to gather my officers on the first night of a voyage so that we may share a meal and also for me to inform them of our orders." He paused to adjust his position before picking up his glass and raising it to them. "First off, let me congratulate each and every one of you for the work you did in getting *Columbia* ready to sail, both at Washington and then at Boston. I have not seen better work under more difficult circumstances by an American crew in this war. I salute you!" He raised his glass in salute; his men returned the gesture in silent acknowledgement, and they all drank. Albritton set his glass down and continued. "Please, extend my thanks and congratulations to your men. Every division and watch is to be commended."

The captain paused to clear his throat and look around the room. The officers assembled here were by and large strangers to him. True, they had performed well thus far; no crew he'd ever led could have performed better in taking *Columbia* from the Chesapeake Bay to Boston, and then escaping the British blockade to sail north to Salem—let alone having to leave Salem so quickly to escape to the wide Atlantic before the British could arrive and bottle them up in the harbor! The missing ingredient, the missing piece of the puzzle, was how they would react in the face of the enemy. *Well,* he thought, *that will be known soon enough.*

He looked them over, quickly but casually. Mr. Chandler had the makings of a fine first lieutenant, but Albritton had questions about his upbringing on a Southern plantation. The only other two he really knew at all were the senior midshipman, Mr. Franklin, and the sailing master, Mr. Warren. Both men seemed competent in their jobs. The junior officers were unknown quantities, as were Lt. Moore of the marines and the surgeon, Doctor Brown. The captain sighed. The best-case scenario would be two weeks of peaceful sailing during which he could drill the hands aloft and work up his guns' crews to perfection; whether he would get the chance or not was another question.

"I can now tell you," he continued slowly, "that our mission is to create havoc among the British sea lanes. The first part of the job takes place in the North Atlantic and Caribbean. We want to make the enemy pull as many ships as possible away from blockade duty as we can. I intend to raid every British convoy and merchant ship we come across, even to the point of keeping one or two of them with us as supply ships. When they are empty, we will send home every one that we can as prize ships. Who knows? We may even come across one filled with specie we can dole out amongst ourselves when we get home."

"I beg your pardon, sir," Mr. Franklin said, "but what do you mean when you say 'specie'?"

"Money," Chandler replied. "He means a ship carrying gold or silver coins."

Franklin's eyes went wide as saucers. "You mean that happens?"

"Of course," Albritton said in amusement. "I remember my last cruise during the Revolution. We came across just such a ship on our way back to Boston. My captain at the time, Captain Drake—we were on a privateer, by the way, not a naval vessel—knew that we would not get any prize money out of the Confederacy government, so just before we arrived back at Boston, he divided all the coinage in the prize ship amongst the crew, all according to the rules regarding distribution of prize money. He had a copy of the rules, which had been included along with his Letter of Marque."

"Letter of Marque?" Lieutenant Williams asked.

"It's the formal letter from the government," Albritton explained. "It identified us as a privateer in the service of the United States government and authorized us to attack all ships belonging to our nation's enemies." He shrugged. "It was supposed to save us from being tried and hung as pirates if we were ever caught by the British."

"We have lots of privateers serving with us in this war," Chandler said. "My cousin is on one in the Caribbean, or he was, last I'd heard." He turned to the captain with a smile on his face. "Tell me, Captain, do you happen to have a copy of the rules regarding the distribution of prize money?"

Albritton grinned and nodded once. "Why, yes, Mr. Chandler, I believe I do." A gentle laughter rolled around the room, and the younger officers looked at each other in eager expectation. The captain raised his voice. "Don't count your prize money just yet! We have to catch them first! Besides, there's a way you have to go about taking a prize; it's different than engaging an enemy in battle."

"How so, Captain?" Mr. Williams asked. Williams was the fourth lieutenant, but Albritton was coming to realize he was on the young side for the job.

The captain looked to his premier. "Mr. Chandler? Would you care to enlighten our young lieutenant?"

"Aye, sir. You see, Mr. Williams, a prize is worth more undamaged. If we put a broadside into her to get her to surrender, we may cost ourselves thousands of dollars in prize money, not to mention the supplies the ship carries that might be ruined."

"That's right," Albritton added. "Remember, we were not able to get as full a load of stores as we would like before we sailed. We want to make them surrender without having to fire into them. We put a shot off their bows and hope they heave to so we can board them. Once that happens, we will rely on the skill of your marine snipers, Mr. Monroe. I don't know of anything that controls the crew of the deck of a prize like marine snipers in our tops."

Monroe raised his glass as a promise. "We'll be ready, Captain!"

At this point, Sommers appeared in the doorway to announce that dinner was served. Once the assembly were seated, Sommers led the way from the pantry carrying a large tray with a huge ham on it, which he placed in front of the captain and Mr. Chandler, who was at his right hand. His stewards followed behind, the first carrying a platter with a fat roast goose on it. He was followed by others bearing bowls of green beans and stewed potatoes along with day-old bread from the best bakery in Salem. Two pies lay on a side table for dessert. The stewards kept the glasses full, and the smalltalk was almost nonexistent as the men gave the fare its just due.

When the plates and bowls were empty, Albritton led his men back into the day cabin for cigars and more refreshments. A steward made the rounds with a humidor as the officers chose their cigars. Only Lieutenant Williams, fourth lieutenant and youngest of the officers, abstained; he watched in curiosity as the others lit their cigars and blew the smoke toward the deck above.

"You don't smoke, Mr. Williams?" Chandler asked.

"No, sir," Williams replied sheepishly. "I promised my mother."

Genteel laughter rose at the young man's remark, but it died swiftly when Sommers entered with a tray full of empty glasses and a decanter filled with a dark liquid.

"Is that what I think it is?" Chandler asked with a longing in his voice.

Albritton smiled. "It certainly is. Don't spoil the surprise."

"Oh, aye, sir," Chandler whispered.

Sommers took the decanter and stood by the captain while a steward took the tray around so each man could take a glass.

"Where did your mother stand on whiskey, Mr. Williams?" the captain asked.

"She asked me not to overindulge, sir."

"Well, try your best." Albritton held his glass up so Sommers could put about an inch of liquid in it. Albritton waited while the servant went to each man and put the same in each glass, although he put only half that in Williams's. Albritton smiled but did not comment. He raised his glass. "Gentlemen, I give you *bourbon*." He saluted them with his glass and took a drink, then he sat back to watch the reactions. Hill and Williams took small sips; Hill's eyes went wide, and Williams coughed. Monroe took a drink and shook his head.

"Wow!" he exclaimed.

Mr. Mitchell drank delicately and nodded his appreciation. "Marvelous, Captain! Where did you get it?"

Albritton told the story again, as he had told Calloway back in Washington. The officers looked at their glasses and nursed the drink as though it was a holy relic. Only Dr. Brown drained his glass, much to the astonishment of the others.

The doctor shrugged. "I grew up in Kentucky, Captain. Bourbon and I are old friends. I'm glad to see you have made its acquaintance."

"Yes, well," Albritton said, trying to cover his surprise, "if I may continue about our mission... Our immediate need is to secure supplies; therefore, I plan to head east for a day or two before heading southeast to search for the Jamaica Convoy. Taking one or two of those ships should set us up for months."

Albritton smiled at the variety of reactions he saw on the faces around the room. Chandler, Mitchell, and Warren were contemplating the rewards, while the rest of them had no idea what he was talking about.

The first lieutenant turned to explain. "Two or three times a year, the British send a large—and very rich—convoy from Jamaica up to Bermuda and on to London. It usually has a significant escort, but it shouldn't be too hard to pick off a straggler or two."

"Precisely," the captain added. "Questions? Thoughts?"

"Sir," Lieutenant Mitchell said, "what about the fishing fleets off the Grand Banks?"

"I had considered that," Albritton replied as Sommers came through to refill any glass that needed it, "but those boats typically would not have the kinds of provisions we're going to need for our voyage. Not to mention the fact that in that area we would be more likely to encounter British frigates." He paused for a drink. "No, I think we need to stay with oceangoing merchantmen."

"A couple of Indiamen would be nice!" Williams explained.

"Indiamen are generally armed, aren't they?" Hill asked. "Twelve-pounders, at least?"

"I believe so," Chandler said. "I've even heard tell of the Royal Navy purchasing some of them from the East India Company and converting them to two-deckers for use against Napoleon's navy."

"Indiamen are armed generally to defend themselves against pirates," Albritton said. "That's not to say they would not give us a hard time if we gave them the chance; if we encounter one, we shall need to take all care, just as though she were a warship."

"Aye, sir."

"Now," the captain said, taking control of the meeting again, "I want the coming days and weeks to be used for training. I don't want to waste any time." He caught each man's eye to ensure he understood. "Mr. Chandler will work out a schedule for drills on the sails and the guns. We have to be ready as soon as possible; you never know when we may run into the British. Another thing," he added as he shifted in his seat, "there may come times when I deem it best to avoid a confrontation in order to further our mission. Remember, we are to cause the British as much trouble as we can. If I decide that we can best do that by avoiding a fight, that is what I shall do." He looked around the room before continuing. "I say this, because if and when it happens, you may hear grumbling in your divisions or when you have the watch. I expect you to deal with that immediately. That's why I am explaining to you my reasoning for my actions. Remember, you must control your men at all times."

"Aye, Captain," Chandler answered for them all.

Albritton rose, and the others followed. "Thank you for coming, gentlemen. Tomorrow we begin. Now, I must wish you a good night."

They came to attention as a group and filed out one by one. Soon, only Lieutenant Chandler remained.

"What about *Argus*?" he asked.

Albritton resumed his seat and waved his premier toward the settee. "The gist of what I said tonight was included in the orders I gave to Commander Calloway before we left Boston. He knows what is expected of him."

Chandler drew a deep breath and shook his head, an if-you-say-so kind of gesture. "If I may say, sir, there's just something about the commander that makes me uneasy. I'm not sure I trust him."

Albritton looked at his first lieutenant over the top of his glass for a moment before studying the amber liquid within, trying to decide how much to take him into his confidence. "He'll be fine," he said, deciding that the time had not yet come for full disclosure. "Will you be ready to begin drilling the crew tomorrow?"

"Aye, sir. The schedule is basically complete; I was going to go over it once more to see if I could improve it anywhere. Would you like to see it?"

"Yes, if you please. Why don't you breakfast with me at four bells of the morning watch?"

"Thank you, sir—I'd be honored."

"If there's nothing else?" Albritton rose. His premier came to attention.

"Good night, Captain."

When he was alone, Albritton resumed his seat, suddenly tired. Sommers obligingly brought him another bourbon, which he sipped thankfully. Whether he knew it or not, Chandler had touched on the one variable Albritton had no idea as yet how to control or even deal with: Calloway. He couldn't shake the feeling that the man was still haunted by the events of 1807 and felt that he had to atone or prove himself—but to whom? Secretary Jones had given him *Argus*, so he obviously trusted him with the ship, and Albritton himself had worked hard all his career to earn a reputation for being fair with his subordinates.

What am I missing? Albritton wondered as he took another sip. *Outside of the incident regarding the sighting, the man has done nothing outwardly to merit any suspicion or mistrust. All I have to go on is that feeling I've gotten in the back of my mind the few times he has been in my company. Aye, but there's the rub! I've only had that feeling a handful of times in my career, and it has never been wrong yet. There's something about Calloway that warrants watching.*

Albritton raised his glass again, only to find it empty. He briefly debated calling Sommers for another refill, but decided against it—bourbon was the one thing he thought it would be unlikely to find on a British ship, so he had to make it last. He rose and walked to the dining room where he set the glass on the table. He turned to find Xavier standing beside the cabin door, ready to help him get prepare for bed. It was a custom the coxswain had adopted not long after he'd entered Albritton's service. Albritton had questioned it at the beginning, but by now he had come to accept it as a duty born of devotion. He merely nodded to the coxswain, who followed him to his bedside and helped him get changed.

"What are you hearing from the crew?" the captain asked.

"They're glad to be away," Xavier answered. "Some of them were afraid we would be bottled up in Boston, and then they thought the British would find us before we got away from Salem. I heard one hand wondering aloud if maybe you might deserve your reputation after all."

The captain grunted. "That's always the question, isn't it? Good night, old friend. Make sure I'm up at two bells of the morning watch; Mr. Chandler will be joining me for breakfast at four bells."

"Aye, sir." Xavier left without another word, adjusting the curtains that separated Albritton's sleeping space after he went out. Albritton turned and examined the space, taking note that his cot was suspended a little lower from the deck above than it had been even ten years before. Not that he was complaining; he was, after all, fifty-four years old now, and some accommodations could be made. He was pleased to see that Xavier had attached a small shelf on the bulkhead near the head of the cot; he used it to hold his candle at night as well as whatever book he was currently reading. The only other thing in the room was his sea chest nestled up against the bulkhead next to the door to his personal head. Not a lot of room, granted, but it did have its advantages. *At least I don't have to sleep with a 24-pounder next to me,* he thought gratefully. He blew out the candle and rolled into his cot, with an ease learned over years of practice, and allowed the rocking motion of the cot to put him to sleep.

In the morning, four bells of the morning watch found him sitting at his dining table as the sentry knocked before admitting the first lieutenant. Mr. Chandler presented his training plan to the captain as Sommers brought them eggs with ham, toast and marmalade, along with piping hot coffee. Albritton studied the plan closely.

"It looks good, Mr. Chandler," he said. "I wouldn't change a thing."

"Thank you, sir. I presumed you would want me to keep the live fire to a minimum, especially with the 24-pounder shot. If it's all right with you, I shall implement the plan this morning."

The two men ate their meal with a minimum of small talk. Albritton was secretly pleased that his first lieutenant had picked up on the fact that his captain was not much for that kind of interaction, although he did not require his guests to adhere to it. When they finished, Chandler wiped his mouth and pushed back his chair.

"If there's nothing else, sir, I'd like to get started."

"Of course," Albritton replied. "I shall join you on deck shortly."

The first lieutenant came to attention and left the cabin. Albritton sat back and allowed Sommers to refill his coffee. It was going to be an interesting day.

Captain Albritton stepped up onto the deck to find a beautiful, sunny day. He walked over to the wheel where two of his officers were talking with the sailing master.

"Good morning, sir," Mr. Chandler said as they all touched their hats.

"Good morning, gentlemen. Mr. Chandler, is *Argus* on station?"

"Aye, sir."

Albritton walked to the rail. "Mr. Adams!"

"Sir?"

"I want someone in the tops during all daylight hours with a glass trained on *Argus*!"

"Aye, aye, sir!"

Lieutenant Chandler picked up a speaking trumpet and gave the orders that sent the watch on duty to their drills. For the next hour, men were sent racing up the shrouds to their stations to make some maneuver or other. The sails were not touched—not yet, anyway; Chandler's intention was to increase their speed in getting to their posts. When he finally gave them a break, several of the hands dropped on the spot where their feet hit the deck. Albritton looked to his premier.

"I intend to give them a ten minute break."

The captain nodded. "Carry on, Mr. Chandler."

Albritton stood back and watched his first lieutenant drill the hands aloft, and he noticed some improvement by the end of watch. When the starboard watch came on deck, they too were thrown into the upperworks unmercifully. At one point, Albritton watched as the third lieutenant, Mr. Hill, obviously unhappy with his men's performance, took to the shrouds himself and beat his men to the tops, screaming all the while for them to keep up with him. His men responded with renewed effort and improved their time with every run.

"Well done, Mr. Chandler," the captain said when the watch was over. "I see improvement in each watch. If they do as well on the guns, give them an extra ration of grog tonight. But make them earn it!"

"Aye, sir! Thank you!"

Albritton dismissed his premier and turned to his sailing master. "How do you think she's sailing?"

"The ship seems okay, Captain, but I'd like to put her through her paces as soon as you're satisfied with the progress on sail drills."

"Agreed. Speak to Mr. Chandler about scheduling a time."

Warren knuckled his forehead. "Thank you, sir."

"Who has the deck?" the captain asked.

"Lieutenant Williams is the officer of the watch, sir."

"Pass the word."

Albritton turned to see that *Argus* was still on station, hull up on the horizon and within signal range. He heard footsteps approaching and turned back to see Lieutenant Williams standing before him with hat raised. The captain replied in kind.

"Mr. Williams," he said, "this is your first cruise with your commission, is it not?"

"Aye, sir."

"Tell me of your service."

"I came in as a ship's boy on *United States*, sir," the young lieutenant explained. "I was made midshipman and transferred to *Enterprise*. I did two cruises on the *Constellation*, then I passed my boards and was ordered to report to *Columbia*."

"And how do you like being an officer thus far?" Albritton noticed that the young man was puzzled by the question. "Come now, Lieutenant, I'm not trying to trick you. I am asking your opinion of being an officer."

"I like it fine, sir," Williams finally said. "I know I have a lot to learn; I just hope I don't make too many mistakes along the way."

Albritton smiled. "I'm glad to hear you say that, Mr. Williams. The biggest danger on a frigate is a new lieutenant who thinks he knows it all. Let me give you the advice my first captain gave me. He said, *'Albritton, if you make it your goal not to make the same mistake twice, you will be far ahead of your fellows.'* Sound advice, Mr. Williams. You may return to your duties."

"Aye, sir," Williams said as he touched his hat. "Thank

you, sir."

Gun drill went well that afternoon. Mr. Chandler drilled the crews on the 24-pounders on the gun deck while Mr. Mitchell drilled the carronade crews on the spar deck. Each officer assembled an experienced crew to demonstrate the procedures on the weapon while the newer hands watched. Each gun had an experienced captain who drilled his crew over and over in their tasks. Once he thought they were ready, they were allowed to fire a live round.

The first lieutenant raised his voice to get the attention of his men. "I want to remind you of the most important thing about being on the gun deck during drill or when we are in action," he called loudly as he looked around at those assembled before him, "and that is *silence*! There is absolutely no talking by any member of a gun crew! Any information that needs to be passed must be whispered from your lips to his ear." He looked around again to make sure they understood the gravity of the issue. "Every gun captain must be able to hear the orders that are given regarding targeting and load, and that can't happen if their crews are babbling incoherently. In battle, there's no time for reminders or for asking nicely, so this is your one warning! *Keep your mouths shut!* The consequences will be both immediate and dire, I assure you."

No matter how carefully the hands were trained, there was usually one who got careless, and on *Columbia* it was a sponger on the No. 3 24-pounder of the starboard battery. They were conducting their live-fire trial, and the gun crew was given the usual warning to stand clear before the gun captain pulled the lanyard to fire the gun. This man, however, decided to lean in so he could see down the barrel just as the gun was fired. Fortunately for him, Lieutenant Chandler was watching for just such an act of foolishness and was able to grab the man by the collar and snatch him out of the way before the recoiling gun carriage would have smashed into him.

Chandler turned on the unfortunate sponger lying sprawled on the deck. *"Did you not listen?"* he asked sharply. "Did you think I was talking for my health? Do you understand now why I say these things to you? That gun carriage is moving fast enough to kill you if you get in its way! You, gun captains! It is your responsibility to make sure your men are safe before you fire your weapon!" He turned and offered a hand to the sponger and pulled him to his feet. "Never fear, practice makes perfect! Just remember—a gun has neither eyes nor brains. You have to get out of its way, because it's not going to stop for you."

At the change of the watch, the two lieutenants met with the captain by the fantail to report.

"We'll have them ready, Captain," Chandler said. "We've got a good stock of veterans, many of them battle-tested, to go with the landsmen. I want to do a timed reload next week, and then every other week afterward; that way they will be able to see their improvement."

Albritton nodded. "Good idea. And you, Mr. Mitchell?"

"The same goes for my men, Captain," the second lieutenant reported. "Good mix of old and new, and even before the end of drills today I began to see some improvement."

"Excuse me, sir."

Albritton turned to see Mr. Adams, his hat doffed in salute. He returned the gesture. "Yes?"

"Signal from *Argus. 'Commencing sail drills.'"*

"Thank you, Mr. Adams. Acknowledge, and please inform Mr. Warren."

"Aye, Captain."

Albritton turned to his companions. "Well, gentlemen,

shall we observe? Come with me." They moved to the railing and were joined by Mr. Warren. A midshipman handed out telescopes to each officer. It took only moments for Albritton to lower his. "Mr. Warren," he said, "hard to larboard. Put us within two cable lengths so I can get a good view."

"Aye, Captain."

"Mr. Adams, signal *Argus* we are only approaching to observe their exercise."

"Aye, Captain!"

The sailing master soon had them on a parallel course with a fine view of *Argus*'s men going through their drills. It was quickly apparent that this was not the first time they had been put through this particular drill. The speed at which the topmen reached their posts displayed a sure-footedness born of much practice. Calloway put his men through all the paces, obviously intending to impress both *Columbia* and her captain, and in the end he succeeded.

'Congratulations to all hands on a drill well executed!' came the signal from *Columbia*.

Albritton ordered the ship back to her station. He closed his glass and handed it to Mr. Mitchell before going below deck without so much as a word. After he was gone, Chandler put his fists on his hips and stared at the companionway.

"What do you suppose has gotten into him?" Warren asked.

"I have no idea," Chandler admitted quietly, "but I imagine we shall know soon enough."

CHAPTER EIGHT

Captain Albritton stepped up onto the spar deck of USS *Columbia* just as the noon sighting was being taken. He waited patiently for Mr. Warren to calculate their position. It was only a few minutes before the sailing master approached him with the chart in his hand.

"Our position?" the captain asked.

Mr. Warren touched the chart with his finger. "Here, sir."

Albritton smiled. The day had finally come when they could turn southeast and begin their search for the Jamaica convoy. "New course, Mr. Warren. Bring us around to the southeast under all plain sail. Extra lookouts, Mr. Chandler—we are now looking for the Jamaica convoy."

"Aye, sir!"

"Aye, Captain!"

"Mr. Adams!" Albritton called. "Signal the new course to *Argus*."

"Aye, sir."

Albritton could almost feel the mood of the ship change as she came around on her new heading. It was as if the hands knew that they were now looking for the enemy. The captain stood in the middle of his quarterdeck, watching everything but saying nothing as his men went about their business. A tiny smile crept into the corner of his mouth.

Mr. Chandler stepped up and saluted. "Sir! We are on

course southeast under all plain sail. Extra lookouts have been posted. Mr. Adams reports that *Argus* has acknowledged our signal and is on station."

"Thank you, Mr. Chandler," the captain replied. "Please note in the order book that I am to be alerted to any sightings."

"Aye, Captain."

The ship's bell rang twice, and the captain pulled his watch from his pocket as though to verify the time. He wound the piece before returning it to its resting place.

"Mr. Chandler, who is the officer of the watch?" he asked.

"Lieutenant Williams, sir."

"He has the deck, then. I shall be in my cabin. Call me if I am needed."

Chandler touched his hat. "Aye, sir."

When he got to his cabin, Albritton sat at his desk and got out his quill and ink to catch up on his log. He dipped the quill tip in the ink and began to write. His handwriting was tight but neat, something that had always amazed Mary when she was alive; she'd said it looked like the script of an intellectual, not a seaman. The thought of her brought Albritton's pen to a standstill, and for a moment he was back at Shiloh, staring at her portrait. He sat back and sighed deeply; he wondered if he would ever be free from the loneliness that had plagued him since Mary's death. Strangely, it was a freedom he both longed for and dreaded. He shook his head and picked up his pen again. When he finished his log entry, he put the pen and ink away and made his way to his sleeping cabin. He opened his sea chest and sorted through his books. He had his Bible, given to him by his mother when he was young and rebound twice since then due to wear, Washington Irving's *A History of New York*, Defoe's *Robinson Crusoe* and *Moll Flanders*, the first two volumes of *The History of England* by David Hume,

Thoughts on Government by his friend John Adams, and Shakespeare's *Sonnets* and a collection of his plays. His newest acquisition was *The Life of George Washington* by Mason Weems. Albritton picked up the book and flipped through the pages. He remembered Adams telling him the book was more fiction than fact, but he thought he would read it anyway to find out for himself.

He stepped into the day cabin and made for his chair. He paused when he got there and smiled—on the table beside, Sommers had quietly placed a glass of wine. Albritton sat, silently thanking his servant for his thoughtfulness as he sipped the red liquid and opened the book. Two hours and twenty-five pages later, he was beginning to think that Adams had been right. He closed the book in disgust and took it back to his sea chest. He exchanged it for Shakespeare's plays and returned to his chair. An hour later, Sommers appeared in the doorway.

"Excuse me, sir," he said, "but I was wondering what you wanted for supper."

Albritton looked at him blankly and pulled out his watch. "Is it that time? Where has the afternoon gone?" He closed the book and laid his head back for a moment. He stood and stretched. "What do you have?"

"I have a leg of mutton, sir, or perhaps you would like a duck that was shot the day before we left Salem?"

Albritton considered for a moment and shrugged. "The mutton, I suppose. Could you pass the word for Mr. Chandler and Mr. Warren to join me in one hour?"

Sommers bowed. "As you wish, sir." He withdrew.

His guests arrived, and Sommers served the meal. Mr. Chandler at his right sat back and admired the mutton, along with the carrots and stewed apples. Sommers filled their glasses and bowed before withdrawing.

"Mr. Chandler," Albritton said, "will you please carve the

mutton? Mr. Warren, help yourself to the carrots and stewed apples. What do you think, Mr. Warren? How long should we hold this course?"

Warren helped himself to the carrots and passed them to his host. "I recommend that we resume an eastern course, sir; I think that gives us the best chance of intercepting the convoy. If we don't find them in two or three days, I would turn south." He held his plate up so Chandler could load it with slices of mutton. "We might risk a quick look inside the harbor at Bermuda as we pass by, but my thinking is that if we don't find them by the time we turn south, we missed them."

The captain nodded as he heaped spoonfuls of carrots and stewed apples—which were fast becoming a personal favorite—on to his plate. "I agree with you. Still, let's hope we're not too late."

"Amen to that, sir!" Warren raised his glass.

"Tell me, Mr. Chandler," Albritton said, "do you like to read?"

The first lieutenant looked up, his mouth full of food. He gulped hurriedly. "Read, sir?"

"Yes," the captain continued. "I want to know about your education. I found that, where I come from, most educated people read."

"Well, ah," the lieutenant stammered, "I confess that I do not have a single book in my kit, sir."

"Really?" Albritton remarked. He chewed a mouthful of food. "Well, to each his own. What kind of education have you completed?"

"I completed two years at the College of Charleston, sir, before I left to ship out on a merchant ship bound for the Caribbean and South America."

"What were you studying?" Warren asked.

"History, law, and philosophy of government. The school was the first college chartered in South Carolina, and many of our founders were active in the Continental Congress as well as the Confederation Congress and the Constitutional Convention." He shrugged. "I suppose they wanted us to know why they did what they did; you know, the history behind it all."

"Noble sentiment," Warren said. "Why did you leave?"

The first lieutenant's eyes dropped to his plate. "I suppose you could say the sea called to me. And I listened."

"I see." Warren's eyes flashed to his captain.

"Well," Albritton said, "to each his own. I can only advise you, Mr. Chandler, not to abandon your education. Read everything and anything that interests you. The world is constantly changing, and we have to keep up with it."

"As you say, sir," the premier replied meekly.

The captain rose as Sommers and his steward came to clear the table. "Gentlemen, I thank you for a pleasant meal. Now, if you'll forgive me, I will turn in. Mr. Chandler, kindly step up on deck and order the course change to the east. Thank you. Goodnight."

"Goodnight, sir," Chandler replied. Both men came to attention and left. Albritton stared at the door for a moment before heading for the day cabin and his chair. He stared into space and considered his first lieutenant. He did not fully trust anyone who was not a reader or at least hungry to learn something new, and now he wondered whether Chandler would fall into that category. A throat cleared itself softly, and Albritton became aware he was not alone.

"Is there anything I can get for you, sir?"

He glanced up at his servant and almost shook his head, but he was suddenly hit by a craving for coffee and asked for a cup. Sommers bowed and retreated, returning a few moments later with a cup of the steaming brew on a tray. He set it down on the table before bowing again and leaving his master to his thoughts, all without a word. Albritton stared at the retreating form, and it dawned on him how fortunate he was to have the man aboard.

He sipped the coffee and sighed. He set the cup down, leaned his head back, and closed his eyes. Two hours later, Xavier arrived and helped his master to bed.

The morning brought a stiff breeze that sent the ship skimming over the waves. Johnson and Petrie, two hands of the larboard watch, were stationed just aft of the portside bow chaser as extra lookouts. They had only one telescope between them; Petrie, having the better eyesight, allowed his fellow to use it.

"Think we'll find the convoy?" Johnson asked as he swept the horizon.

"Aye," Petrie replied as he leaned across a 32-pounder carronade. "The captain's the best we got. He didn't make it this far without having a nose for prize money." He nodded sagely. "He'll find it for us." He stood up straight and stretched his back. "Or, if he don't, he'll find us another. I ain't worried about returning home with empty pockets, not from this trip."

Johnson lowered his glass for a moment and considered what he'd heard. He nodded his agreement and said, "Me, neither."

Petrie was about to say something when a glint on the water caught his eye. It was fine off the larboard bow just ahead. He shaded his eyes and squinted, but he couldn't get a better look. "Here, Johnson, let me have that glass," he said. His friend handed it over, and Petrie brought it to his eye and made the adjustments until the patch of water became clear.

"Johnson!" he cried. "Get the lieutenant! Quick!"

Johnson ran aft and brought Mr. Mitchell. "What is it, Petrie?" he asked.

Petrie handed over the glass and pointed at a patch of ocean. "What do you see there, sir?"

Mitchell scanned the sea and quickly saw what Petrie was pointing at: a small field of debris, drifting from their right to left with the ocean current. The lieutenant recognized it instantly as such things as a careless wardroom steward would chuck overboard after cleaning up following a wardroom party.

"Johnson!" Mitchell called. "Run aft and tell the quartermaster to heave to immediately. Go below; give the captain my respects and ask that he come forward at once."

"Aye, sir!"

Mitchell raised the glass again and studied the field. "Good work, Petrie," he said. "This may just be the break we've been waiting for."

The two men turned at the sound of footsteps approaching and saluted when they recognized the captain.

"Report, Mr. Mitchell," he said.

The lieutenant handed over the glass and pointed to the debris. "Debris field, Captain, drifting north with the current."

"So it is," Albritton said. He studied it for several moments before handing the glass to Petrie. To Mitchell: "How long do you think it's been there?"

"Not more than a few hours, sir," the lieutenant replied. "The fish have barely had time to find it."

Albritton leaned on the rail and studied the water. "I agree. Another few hours and we'd have missed it entirely. Who made the sighting?"

"Mr. Petrie, sir, and Mr. Johnson."

The captain turned to the two men. "Well done! Mr.

Mitchell, these men get an extra ration of grog tonight."

The two hands smiled brightly. "Thank you, sir!" Johnson said.

"Mr. Mitchell, we shall head north. Follow the current. Have the quartermaster put on every stitch she'll carry. Signal our course change to *Argus*. You two," he looked to Petrie and Johnson after Mitchell went aft, "find me that convoy."

"Aye, Captain!"

Albritton went aft just as the orders were going out to make all sail. Men who were racing to their posts skidded to a stop and got out of his way, trying their best to salute without falling over each other. The captain returned their salutes and exhorted them. "Jump to it, lads! We are going after the convoy!" A cheer rang out, and the men leapt for the shrouds and climbed.

The captain reached the quarterdeck to find Mr. Chandler there, speaking to the sailing master and the quartermaster. The three raised their hats in salute.

"Gentlemen," the captain said in acknowledgement.

"What have we got, sir?" Chandler asked.

"Debris field drifting north. The sort of stuff a steward would toss overboard. Our estimate is that it is less than two hours old. We're following it north to see if we can catch the ship or ships it came from."

"Well!" Mr. Warren said, rubbing his hands together in anticipation. "This may be a red-letter day yet!"

Columbia came around to the north and the deck surged forward as the additional sail grabbed the wind. The ship's bell rang eight times, and the watch was relieved. Mr. Williams came aft to the quarterdeck and stood by; it was his watch coming on, but he had to wait to the side while the captain and first lieutenant were on deck. He caught the captain's eye and touched his hat, and Albritton nodded in return. A few minutes later, Chandler walked over.

"Good morning, Samuel," he said.

"Good morning," Williams replied. "What's going on?"

Chandler told him about the discovery of the debris and how they were now heading north in search of the British ships. "The captain and I are about to go below. Mr. Warren will come, too, so you will have the deck. I want to remind you of the captain's standing order that he be called at any sighting. Don't wait to identify it, Samuel; notify the captain immediately."

Williams swallowed hard. "Aye, sir."

"Don't worry, Samuel," Chandler said, "you'll be fine. Who's your midshipman of the watch?"

"I have two this morning, sir, Jackson and Miller."

"Good. Assign one of them to keep an eye on *Argus*. Notify the captain at once if they signal. Send for Mr. Adams if the captain comes on deck, and have him stand by to signal *Argus* if the captain desires."

"Aye, sir."

Chandler looked up and saw that the captain was ready to go below. He patted the younger lieutenant's arm and gave it a reassuring squeeze. "Don't worry. Just behave as you have every other time you've had the watch, and you'll be fine. The captain knows you're good, otherwise he would have told me to remain on deck. Good luck."

Commander Isaac Melville looked around the deck of his ship-sloop HMS *Belvidere*, and frowned. His ship was old and badly in need of a refit. That was supposed to take place over the next month at Bermuda; unfortunately, some delays arose with the last five merchantmen that were to be added to the Jamaica Convoy. The convoy commander refused to wait for them, so *Belvidere's* refit was delayed in order that she, along with two luggers, could serve as escort for the merchantmen. They'd left port three days after the convoy and had been trying to catch up ever since.

Melville's eyes ran over his ship's armament. He had two 8-pounder long guns, six 6-pounder long guns, and six 24-pounder carronades. Weak, even for a sloop, but he hoped he would not have to use them. Nothing he saw told him that the ship was not ready for sea; she just looked... *tired* was the only word that came to his mind. Melville sighed and walked over to the quartermaster, who was standing beside the wheel.

"What's our speed?"

"Four knots on the last cast, sir," came the reply. "We're due for another with the next bell."

"Very well. I shall be in my cabin. Call me if I am needed."

"Aye, sir."

Melville went below deck, remembering to duck at the bottom of the stairs. When he got to his cabin, he sat on the settee beneath the stern windows and ordered a cup of tea from his steward. When it arrived, he took a tentative drink, allowing the revivifying warmth of the liquid to slide down his throat. He set the cup down and leaned back to rest his head on the high back of the settee and closed his eyes. He doubted that they would catch up with the convoy; there was a chance, of course, if they could maintain their speed, but he didn't think they would. The convoy had too great a head start.

Melville allowed the merest hint of a smile to encroach upon the corner of his lips; at least they would get their refit in England rather than Bermuda. He hoped to get a week's leave so he could go see Ella.

His thoughts were interrupted by a knock at the door. He answered, and the sentry admitted the senior midshipman.

"Begging your pardon, sir," the lad said, "but there are

ships approaching from astern. I think they're American."

Lunch on USS *Columbia* turned out to be a solitary affair, the captain for once opting to be alone with his thoughts. At his request, Sommers had set out a plate of fruit and cheese along with a glass of wine. He munched on the selections indiscriminately, barely taking notice of what he was choosing. His mind was fully occupied with the convoy they were chasing. The escort was bound to consist of at least two or three frigates, along with a 74 thrown in for good measure. Off the top of his head, his best chance would be to have *Columbia* lead the frigates away in the hope that *Argus* could sweep in and take a couple of the stragglers before they returned. Albritton frowned; it was a good plan, with much to commend it, but there were still dangers. *Columbia* would have to get close enough to the convoy to make herself the real threat, while at the same time not becoming so fully engaged that her escape route could be cut off.

When his plate was empty, the captain took his glass and moved to his day cabin. He set the glass down beside his chair and began to pace. Another danger presented itself: in order for the plan to work, Calloway would have to hold *Argus* in reserve, so to speak, until the British frigates were chasing *Columbia*. He did not know if the commander could do it. If *Argus* came in too quickly, the frigates would leave *Columbia* and defend the convoy.

Albritton ceased his pacing and sat down in his chair. He drained his glass in one great draught and leaned his head back. His eyes had barely closed when a knock at the door demanded his attention. Mr. Jackson entered the room and came to attention.

"Mr. Hill's respects, sir," the lad said formally, "and would you please come on deck? He believes we've sighted the convoy."

The captain was met on deck by the premier and Lieutenant Hill. Salutes were exchanged, and Albritton accepted a telescope.

"Let's go," he said as he led the others forward. When they arrived at the bow chasers, he put the glass to his eye and made out a mass of white on the horizon. He thought he could make out two ships that were hull up, but the amount of sail pointed to more ships than that.

"Lookout estimates five to seven ships, sir," Chandler said, "but at this point that's just a guess. It looks like we haven't found the convoy itself, Captain, only the tail end of it. Perhaps a group that left late and is trying to catch up."

"Deck there!" The cry came from the lookout in the foremast tops. "Looks like three of the ships are peeling off and heading our way!"

Albritton put the glass to his eye again and saw one ship break away from the starboard side of the chase and two ships from the larboard. The captain thought them to be the escort. "Looks like a sloop and two luggers."

"Agreed," Chandler said.

"Deck there!" the lookout called. "The remaining ships are piling on all sail!"

"They're running!" Hill said.

"Signal *Argus*," Albritton said. "We must take those ships!"

"Aye, sir!"

"Mr. Chandler, you may beat to quarters!"

"Aye, sir!" the first lieutenant replied. "All hands! All hands! Beat to quarters!"

Albritton looked off to his left to see *Argus* surging forward toward the ships ahead. The two luggers were veering off to incept the American sloop. The captain looked ahead and saw the British sloop steering straight for

Columbia. His lips pressed together in grim determination. He admired bravery and devotion to duty, but he did not relish the thought of having to blow a small ship of good men out of the water. *Damn the war.*

"Mr. Chandler! Run out the guns! We'll put a broadside into the sloop as we pass! Load the long guns with ball and the carronades with grape!"

"Aye, sir!"

"Stand by! Mr. Warren! On my command, we shall turn hard to larboard! Mr. Chandler! Tell Mr. Mitchell to stand by the starboard battery! Mr. Hill! Stand by!"

"Aye, sir!"

"Sir!"

Albritton turned in time to see Mr. Adams pointing in the direction of *Argus.* Calloway had crowded on all sail and blown right past the luggers without so much as even firing a gun into either one of them. *What is he doing?* he asked himself. Albritton forced himself to deal with the matter at hand—the approaching British sloop.

"Now, Mr. Warren!"

"Aye, sir!"

The wheel spun under the hands of the quartermaster and his mates, and *Columbia* came around hard to larboard. As soon as she straightened up, the captain looked to his premier.

"Fire!"

The roar of the guns was deafening. The 24-pounders seemed to go off first, followed a split-second later by the carronades. The wind carried the smoke away quickly, so the fate of the British ship was visible to all. The sloop seemed to disappear in the hail of the big shot hurled at her. At least four or five guns scored direct hits of their target while the carronades had devastating effect on anyone unlucky enough to be on the deck, as well as decimating the upper works. The ship was a wreck.

Captain Albritton turned his attention to the luggers left behind by *Argus*. The ships had come around and were following the American ship. *Columbia's* course of roughly WNW would take her right across their path.

"Mr. Williams!"

"Sir?"

"We are about to cut off the British luggers that are following *Argus*. Your guns are loaded with grape?"

"Aye, sir!"

Albritton nodded. "Stand by to fire!"

The captain waited until they were directly ahead of the British. "Fire!"

The larboard carronades went off in two sections. Albritton had noticed his fourth lieutenant running from gun to gun, and now he knew why. Apparently, Williams had divided his guns into two divisions and assigned a lugger to each. At such close range, the concentration of fire proved decisive. Luggers were lightly built craft in any case, but *Columbia's* carronade fire left both ships broken and sinking in the water.

"Hard to starboard!" Albritton ordered. "Make for the convoy, Mr. Warren! I'm heading forward! Mr. Chandler, you're with me! Bring a runner!"

The captain made his way quickly to the bow and raised his telescope to his eye. "Lookout! Let's hear you!"

"Convoy's scattered, sir!" came the reply. "Two are headed north, one to the nor'east, and two to the east!"

"What of *Argus*?" Chandler called.

"She's after the two to the north, sir!"

Albritton scanned the ninety degrees of horizon between north and east before lowering his glass. "My compliments to

Mr. Warren. He is to alter course and overtake those ships to the east."

"Aye, sir!" the runner said. He snapped off a salute and disappeared aft. In seconds the big ship came around sharply and headed east. In another minute, they felt the deck surge forward under their feet as Warren crowded sail onto the yards above them. Chandler looked over his shoulder when he heard the runner returning; the lad saluted silently, and Chandler nodded in return.

"How long do you think?" his captain asked.

"Mmm, three hours?" Chandler mused. "Maybe four, if the wind doesn't hold."

Albritton lowered his glass and snapped it closed. "I'm going aft. Keep the runner with you. Inform me when you think we might get their attention with a bow chaser."

Chandler touched his hat. "Aye, Captain." Chandler watched his captain make his way aft to the quarterdeck. He noticed the runner staring after him as well. "Tell me your name," he said.

The lad looked up to him. "Me name's Mouse, sir."

Chandler brought the glass to his eye again. "Anyone at home named Cat?"

"Aye," Mouse replied. "That's me older sister."

That got the first lieutenant's attention. The glass came down and his eyes snapped to the lad beside him. "Your mother named her children Cat and Mouse?"

"Aye."

Chandler studied the boy's face but could see no sign of deception or even jesting from the lad. He shrugged and turned back to his study of the chase, determined not to ask about Dog.

Three hours later, Captain Albritton was still standing in

the center of the quarterdeck when Mouse came up and saluted.

"Mr. Chandler's respects, sir," came the report. "He says, *'I think I can reach them now, sir!'*"

"Thank you," he replied. "My compliments to Mr. Chandler. Tell him he is to put one off their bow."

"Aye, sir!" The lad knuckled his forehead and was gone.

"Mr. Jackson!" the captain called. "Take a glass and jump into the mainmast shrouds. I want to know what happens!"

"Aye, Captain!"

Albritton watched out of the corner of his eye as the young midshipman took a telescope and climbed halfway up the mainmast starboard shrouds. He hooked a leg and an arm into the rigging for stability before leaning outward for a better view. Two minutes later, the 18-pounder bow chasers went off.

"Captain!" Jackson called. "One short, the other off the starboard beam!"

"Deck there!" cried the lookout. "The British are splitting up!"

"Agreed, sir!" Jackson shouted.

Albritton went to the starboard rail to see for himself. Sure enough, one ship went nor'east while the other went south. "Mr. Warren! New course SSW! We'll stay with the southern one!"

"Aye, sir!"

It soon became clear to Albritton that *Columbia* had the angle and would cut off her quarry. Sure enough, before long the runner, Mouse, reappeared with a request from Chandler to open fire. Again, Albritton gave permission for a warning shot to make the enemy heave to. A single 18-pounder bow chaser went off this time, and Jackson reported a geyser twenty yards off the Britisher's starboard bow. This time, the enemy lowered her colors and hove to. Albritton lowered his glass, a look of satisfaction on his face. Cheers erupted across the deck.

"Silence on deck!" Albritton shouted, and the din was cut off. "Bosun! Ready two boats for boarding! Pass the word for Mr. Chandler! Mr. Warren! Heave to at pistol shot! Pass the word for Lieutenant Monroe!"

The captain's words electrified the crew. The bosun went forward bellowing orders and a runner went forward in search of the first lieutenant. Albritton moved to the larboard rail and swept the horizon, hoping to see *Argus* appear from the nor'west, but there was nothing but empty ocean. He did not doubt Calloway's ability to take two merchantmen; what he feared was that the merchantmen would lead him into a confrontation with British frigates coming south in search of the straggler group.

"You sent for us, Captain?"

Albritton turned to see his first lieutenant and the marine lieutenant touch their hats in salute. "Yes, Mr. Chandler. Well done with the bow chasers, by the way. You brought them to heel very smartly indeed. Mr. Monroe, we're going to board our friend out there. I want a dozen marines made available for the first lieutenant as well as your best sharpshooters in the tops. Mr. Chandler, take two boats and board her. Put the dozen marines in one, and in the other I want a prize crew along with the purser and some hands to help him. I want a full accounting of that ship's cargo to see what we can use of it."

"Aye, sir," Chandler said. Both men saluted and headed off.

Mr. Chandler rode in silence in the stern sheets of the gig with Mr. Franklin beside him. A dozen marines armed with musket and pistol, sword and bayonet crowded in along with the boat's crew before him. He looked over his shoulder to make sure that *Columbia* had her larboard battery out. He was also comforted by the obvious presence of marine sharpshooters in the tops and along the quarterdeck rail.

When the boat reached the merchantman's entry port, Chandler nodded to the marine sergeant. The man stood and led his force up the ladder and secured the main deck for Chandler. When he and Mr. Franklin stepped up on deck, Chandler spoke up.

"Who is your captain?"

One man stepped forward from a group congregated by the wheel. "I am Jonas Kirk, master of the *Olympus*."

"I am Lieutenant Michael Chandler of the United States Navy. Your ship is now a prize of war, and your cargo is confiscated." He turned to the marines. "Sergeant, take a party below and ensure that all crew members are brought up on deck." The sergeant saluted and led six men below deck, returning three minutes later with five additional men.

"Secure the British aft of the wheel," Chandler said. "Signal the prize crew, Mr. Petry and his mates to get to work." He turned to Kirk. "Do you have any impressed American citizens amongst your crew?"

The British master just glowered at him and refused to answer. Chandler shrugged and stepped past him to address the men directly. "What about it? Are any of you impressed American sailors?"

"Aye!"

Three men pushed through the rest to step forward. Chandler bit his tongue at the sight of them, for the third man was a Negro. "Mr. Franklin, take these men forward and interview them. If you're satisfied, we can take them back to see the captain."

"Aye, sir," Franklin said. "If you three will follow me?" He turned and led them forward.

"Mr. Petry," Chandler addressed the purser, "take your men below and get to work. Mr. Kirk, will you hand over your cargo manifest?" Again, Kirk remained silent. Chandler shrugged. "Sergeant, take two men and search the master's cabin. Take any manifests you find to Mr. Petry. Bring any other papers to me. Mr. Petry? As fast as you can, if you please."

"Aye, sir. Let's go, lads." The purser led his mates and one marine below.

"So, Mr. Kirk," Chandler said, "why were you traveling separate from the main convoy? What? Still nothing to say?"

"The only thing I have to say to you, *Leftenant,*" the master replied in a low, menacing voice, "is, *Get off my ship!*"

"Tsk, tsk, sir!" Chandler chided mockingly. "Mind your temper, else I may begin to think that you don't like me! I should warn you, however, that I can be very unkind to people who don't like me." To his credit, the British master did not flinch, holding the American officer's eyes with undiminished hatred. Chandler found his opinion of the man rising.

The first lieutenant turned to the marine corporal beside him. "Hold them here. I'm going below."

"Aye, sir."

He went below and made his way aft to the master's cabin, where he found a marine private sitting at the table going through a stack of papers and sorting them while the sergeant was completing a thorough search of the cabin. He addressed the private: "Name?"

"Private Morton, sir."

"What have you found, Private Morton?"

"Nothing much, sir," came the reply. Morton put his hand on one of the two piles to his right. "This stack has to do with stores; we will forward them to Mr. Petry as soon as I have gone through them all." He moved his hand to the other stack. "And these have to do with anything else. You will need to go through these and decide what needs to go to the captain."

Chandler nodded. "And you, Sergeant? Find anything interesting?"

The big marine motioned to the bench beneath the stern windows. "One musket, one pike, a brace of pistols, a sextant, one case of Bordeaux, one case of Cognac, and several charts of the Caribbean. That's it so far, sir."

Chandler's brows furrowed. "No log yet?"

The sergeant shook his head. "Not yet, sir."

"Strange. Well, keep looking."

"Aye, sir."

Chandler went and sat down opposite Morton and helped him go through the pile of unsorted papers. Once the two men had everything sorted, the private took the stack dealing with the ship's lading to the purser while Chandler began go through the other stack. The first several sheets held nothing of interest, but the next thing he picked up was a packet bound by a blue ribbon. He thought this strange, and he flipped through the tops of the pages without at first untying the ribbon. What he saw, however, quickly made him change his mind. He untied the ribbon and read the pages hurriedly. The pages were a series of confidential Royal Navy announcements to merchant captains about a decrease in the RN presence in the Caribbean and surrounding waters, and the establishment of a regular convoy system between Port Royal and Plymouth via Bermuda to be escorted by the remaining RN assets.

Chandler set the pages on the table and sat back to take a deep breath. These pages were worth gold to American privateers, not to mention ships like *Columbia* and *Argus*. He folded the pages in half and rebound them with the ribbon before putting them into his pocket. He worked his way through the remainder of the stack but found nothing that provided any useful information. Just as he finished, the sergeant appeared and set another stack on the table. Chandler looked up at him.

"Found these in his sea chest, sir," the big marine explained. "Buried underneath his peacoat."

"I see. Well, Sergeant, does that complete your search?"

"Aye, Lieutenant."

"Then you may return to the deck. Keep the prisoners together. I shall be up shortly."

The sergeant came to attention. "Aye, sir!" He left the room.

Chandler turned his attention to the new material. He waded through the stack and pulled out a leather-bound volume that turned out to be the ship's log. He flipped through the log to find the final entry, made only this morning. Chandler worked his way backward to discover they had left Bermuda five days ago, three days behind the main convoy. The first lieutenant sighed; this was important news. There was no way now that they would catch the main body of the convoy. It had left three days before this group, and Chandler bet their speed would be better to boot. They'd overtaken these ships from the rear; the main body had too much of a head start.

He closed the log and quickly scanned the remaining papers, finding nothing of any real value. He gathered everything up for transfer back to *Columbia*, rose and went to the deck. When he got there, he was met by Franklin.

"Sir?" The senior midshipman touched his hat. "I've finished questioning the Americans."

"And?" Chandler prodded.

"They all seem legitimate. All were able to provide convincing details of their homes and families."

"And the Negro?"

"Him, too. Says his name's Ezekiel. Aged 25, or so he thinks. Claims to be a freeman who sailed out of Baltimore. His papers were confiscated by the British when he was impressed off the *Charleston* in 1808. He was rated able seaman and was a topman before he was taken. He also learned to read and write while on board."

"What's that?"

"It's true. Says he was allowed to sit in on the class when the master's wife taught the ship's boys."

Just great! thought the first lieutenant. *First they learn to read, then they think they know it all, then they start getting uppity!* He frowned. *Need to nip that in the bud, right now!*

Mr. Petry came up on deck with his hands full of lists and hailed Chandler, who scowled as he saw Ezekiel being led to the boat for transport over to *Columbia* along with the other two. *Damnation! The darkie will have to wait.*

The sun was beginning to set when the premier and the purser finally made it back to *Columbia*. *Olympus* was hove to under the big frigate's lee, and both ships waited for USS *Argus.*

"Well done, Mr. Petry," Chandler said. "I shall report to the captain with these lists and, pending his approval, we shall begin transferring the cargo to *Columbia* at dawn."

"Thank you, sir," the purser replied. "We'll be ready."

The two men parted ways, and the first lieutenant made his way to the captain's cabin, where he found Captain Albritton at his desk, catching up his log.

"Mr. Chandler, what good news do you have for me?"

Chandler set the papers down on the table, and the two men sat. "The ship's the *Olympus*, sir. Five days out of Bermuda; she was part of the tail of the Jamaica Convoy.

They left port three days after the main body."

Albritton sat back heavily, disappointed at the news. "That means we'll never catch them."

"My thoughts as well, sir," Chandler agreed. "Nevertheless, the ship has some things we can use." He scanned the lists and recited, "Ship's supplies in the hold is five casks each of salt beef and salt pork, a hundred bags of bread, ten bushels of oatmeal, five of peas, fifty butts of beer and a half hogshead of rum. Her cargo is mainly wheat and cloth bound for England."

"Well done!" Albritton slapped the table. "If *Argus* has done as well, we shall be independent for months! Were there any Americans among the crew?"

"Aye, sir, we got two prime seamen from her."

Albritton's brows furrowed in confusion. "Two? I thought Mr. Franklin said there were three."

"Oh," Chandler said quickly, hoping to cover his slip. "You're right, sir—my mistake."

"Good. See that their names are entered in the ship's books, and add them to the watch bill first thing in the morning."

"Aye, sir." Chandler busied himself gathering the lists. "Shall we begin transfer in the morning, sir?"

The captain shook his head. "No, let's wait until *Argus* returns. We have no idea what she needs. Better to move things once."

"Aye, sir. If there's nothing else, I have business with Mr. Petry."

"Of course, Mr. Chandler. Dismissed."

"Thank you, sir." Chandler came to attention and left the room.

Albritton stared at the door, bothered by his first lieutenant's apparent slip on the men gained from the

Olympus. Albritton knew full well there were three men, not two, and he also knew the third man was black. The captain reviewed the scene in his mind and came to the conclusion that his first lieutenant had just lied.

He stepped into the day cabin and began to pace as he turned the issue over in his mind, thinking about it and attacking it from every possible angle. He was so intent that he did not notice Sommers come to the door to ask if he wanted anything, nor did he see that worthy realize his master's need of privacy and silently withdraw. The pacing ceased when he came to the conclusion that he needed to wait. If the need arose, he would speak to Chandler, but he did not want to precipitate a problem. Satisfied for the moment, he picked up his book on Shakespeare and sat in his chair to read.

Lieutenant Chandler made his way to the gunroom as quickly as his dignity would allow. He was still undecided as to how to address the problem of the Negro with the captain. After all, he was a Yankee, and people from his part of the country had no experience dealing with his kind. No, he would have to handle this problem and then inform the captain later.

He entered the gunroom. "Boothby!" he called. The servant appeared as Chandler took his usual seat at the head of the table. "A glass of wine, and pass the word for Ezekiel."

"Ezekiel, sir?"

"Yes, Ezekiel! He's one of the new men off the prize! You know, the darkie!"

Boothby raised an eyebrow, but he only said "Aye, sir" and disappeared. Chandler put his elbow on the table and his head in his hand as he stared at the tabletop and tried to decide what to do. He saw the glass appear in the corner of his eye, but he had no time for that now. He was disturbed by a new voice coming from the doorway.

"Youse sent for me, suh?"

Chandler looked up, and there he was. Muscular despite a lean build, Ezekiel was about as tall as Chandler himself. His hair was cut close. His face was dominated by widely spaced, intelligent eyes and an understated nose beneath a high forehead. Were he a white man met on the streets of Charleston, Chandler might have taken him for a schoolmaster or college professor. But he wasn't, and this wasn't Charleston.

"Yes, Ezekiel," the first lieutenant said. "I want to ask you some questions, and I want the truth. Are you a runaway?"

"No, suh," Ezekiel answered firmly.

"Then why aren't you on a plantation where you belong?"

Chandler saw the other man's jaw set. "I was set free when my master returned to England. Right after Mr. Jefferson's first election."

"If you're a free man, where are your papers?"

"British took them when I was pressed," Ezekiel said. "They said I wouldn't need them no more. I told all this to Mr. Franklin on the other ship."

Chandler was on his feet in a flash. "Don't get uppity with me, boy!" he roared. Just at that moment, Mr. Mitchell entered the gunroom.

"I'm sorry," he stammered, obviously surprised and alarmed by what he had interrupted. "Shall I come back later, sir?"

"No," Chandler said as he sank back into his seat. "We were just finishing up." He pointed at Ezekiel. "You just mind yourself, because I'll be watching."

"Aye, suh." Ezekiel came to attention and left the gunroom.

"Trouble?" Mitchell asked.

"I beg your pardon?" came the reply—a little too sharply, in Mitchell's opinion.

"Ezekiel." Mitchell nodded toward the doorway. "Is he in some sort of trouble? I ask only because he has been assigned to my division."

"I see." Chandler sat back in his chair. "No, no trouble. Tell me, Jonas, where do you come from?"

"Pottersville, Pennsylvania," Mitchell replied. "Outside Philadelphia. Why do you ask?"

"Your family own any slaves?"

Mitchell shook his head. "No. Why?"

The first lieutenant shrugged. "Just wondering. If you're not used to working with his kind, they can try to take advantage of you, shirking their work and the like."

Mitchell nodded slowly at the advice. "I'll bear that in mind."

Chandler nodded. "You do that. I'll be watching."

Ezekiel went forward, his head down and his mouth clamped shut to contain his anger. *This is exactly what I was afraid would happen!* he fumed. *Say what you want about the British, but by and large they don't give a rat's behind about the color of a man's skin, so long as he can do the job! Now I've got to deal with a first lieutenant who thinks we're still on his daddy's plantation!? How on God's green earth am I –*

Ezekiel blundered into someone and both of them went over a nearby gun carriage. Ezekiel hit his head on the gun's breach and went to the deck, dazed from the blow.

"Hey," a voice came to his ears, "you okay, man?"

Ezekiel tried to blink the clouds from his eyes as he lifted his head. A heavy, dull ache immediately made its presence known, and he groaned and lowered his head again. He looked off to the side and saw an enormous hand attached to a face full of concern by a heavily muscled arm. He took the hand and allowed himself to be pulled slowly to his feet.

"Easy, man," the voice said. "You're gonna have a nasty lump on your head tomorrow." He felt the area. "No blood—that's good. Bet it hurts though."

"You'd win that bet," Ezekiel said. "Who are you?"

"Sorry. They call me Two Toes." He stuck out his hand. Ezekiel looked at it for a moment before accepting. The man before him was huge, practically a mountain of bone and muscle. His skin was dark, like the Indians he'd met in western North Carolina. Dark eyes were set over a prominent nose; his head was topped with black hair cut short.

"You an Indian?"

The big man nodded. "Cherokee. Can you stand if I let you go?"

"I think so." Two Toes let go but stood ready.

Ezekiel wavered a bit but kept his balance. "I'm okay."

"Good. What's your name?"

"Ezekiel."

"You come over from the prize?"

"Yes." His head swam and he put a hand up to it. "Is there someplace I could sit?"

"Sure." Two Toes took him by the arm. "My mess is just below."

The big Indian guided his charge down the stairs to the berthing deck and a short distance forward to a table on the starboard side just forward of the mainmast. The three men and a boy seated around the table stopped talking when the two approached. Two Toes eased Ezekiel down onto the bench.

"What you got there, Two Toes?" one of them asked.

"We ran into each other on the gun deck, and he hit his

head on a breach. Peewee, go find Henry, will you?"

"You bet!" The lad jumped off the bench and ran forward.

"Is it serious?" another man asked.

"I don't think so," Two Toes answered. "I didn't feel any blood, but he's dizzy and needed to sit down, so I brought him here. I'm hoping Henry will know whether we need to take him to sickbay or not." He looked concerned when Ezekiel groaned and laid his head down on the table.

The second man's eyes narrowed. He pulled his churchwarden pipe from his lips and pointed at Ezekiel with the stem. "He's the one, ain't he?" he asked. "The one from the prize?"

Two Toes nodded. "His name's Ezekiel."

Peewee reappeared with Henry in tow. Henry was the mess leader, more by mutual understanding than appointment or election. He claimed his ancestry went all the way back to the House of Plantagenet, which had ruled England between the mid-twelfth and late fifteenth centuries. Unfortunately, his ancestor had been an illegitimate son of Richard III, born shortly before his death and the fall of the House. Henry did not boast of his lineage, but neither did he hide it. It was family history, after all, and nothing to be ashamed of. He was a medium-sized man, early forties at a guess (Henry wasn't telling), brown hair going grey at the temples and a receding hairline, and a full beard he kept trimmed close to his face.

Henry surveyed the situation. "Well?"

Two Toes told him what had happened, and Henry sat down on the bench beside Ezekiel.

"Ezekiel," he said, "my name's Henry. I need to feel that bump on your head. This may hurt." He began to feel tenderly. "Where was it, Two Toes?"

"Behind and above his left ear."

Henry gently felt the area until Ezekiel hissed. "That's got it. Aye, a small bump, but it'll be bigger by morning. Peewee, see if you can't find me a cold, damp cloth or something else cold to put on it."

"Aye, Henry!"

Henry pulled his fingers away and looked at them closely. "No blood. That's good, but the bump is soft, which may not be. No way to tell just yet. Ezekiel, I need you to look at me." The Negro complied. Henry held up two fingers. "How many fingers do you see?"

"Two."

"Are they moving, or fuzzy looking?"

"No."

"That's good. I don't think we need to bother the doctor just yet; we'll see what the morning brings. Now, where's that boy?"

Just then Peewee ran up and held out a damp cloth. "Soaked it in cold water and wrung it out," he explained. "Best I could do."

"Better than nothing," Henry said. He folded it and held it to the bump, which drew another hiss. "Hold this here, Ezekiel."

The injured man complied and groaned. "Thanks."

Henry sat back and looked him over. "By the way, this here's George and that's William." The man with the pipe nodded. "You already know Two Toes and Peewee."

"Where were you heading to in such a hurry?" Two Toes asked.

"Wasn't going *to* anywhere," Ezekiel said. "I was leaving a meeting with the first lieutenant."

"I see," Two Toes said. Henry's eyes met his messmates' in mutual understanding. They all knew Lieutenant Chandler's background.

"Have you got a mess yet?" Henry asked.

"No," came the reply. "I just came aboard."

Henry looked at each member of the mess present, including Peewee, and held their eyes. Each understood the unasked question, and each nodded in agreement. Henry turned to Ezekiel.

"You're welcome to mess with us."

Ezekiel looked up, and winced at the pain. He caught Henry's eyes and saw at once the offer was genuine. He nodded. "Thanks."

"You can sling your hammock over there," Henry gestured to the deck above them to their right, "next to Peewee. We'll make adjustments later if it's necessary." He saw the look in the newcomer's eyes and crossed his arms over his chest. "We're not all like the first lieutenant."

Ezekiel nodded his thanks before resting his head in his free hand. Maybe this would be all right after all.

CHAPTER NINE

USS *Argus* appeared the next morning with two prizes trailing behind. Captain Albritton stood on his quarterdeck and watched as the ships approached. His emotions were mixed, part admiration for the taking of two prizes and part irritation for the way the ship had blown past the two luggers without so much as an attempt to put them out of action. The ships hove to, and Albritton turned to his signals midshipman.

"Mr. Adams! Signal to *Argus*, 'Captain report aboard.'"

"Aye, sir!" Adams went aft and was back in a few minutes. "Acknowledged, sir!"

"Thank you, Mr. Adams."

Albritton watched as boats made their way from the prizes to *Argus*, and he realized that Calloway was gathering information on their cargoes before reporting aboard. The captain turned toward the companionway stairs.

"Mr. Chandler!" he called over his shoulder, "I am going to my cabin. Please bring the commander down when he arrives."

"Aye, sir."

Albritton entered his cabin and called for his servant.

Sommers appeared in the doorway. "Sir?"

"We will be having a conference here shortly. We shall need refreshments for four or five. Mr. Chandler will be bringing our guests in soon."

"Aye, sir." The servant retreated.

It was about an hour before a knock at the door made the captain close his Shakespeare and rise. The sentry admitted Mr. Chandler followed by Commander Calloway.

"Lieutenant Wilson will not be joining us?" Albritton asked.

"He is overseeing the stowing of supplies from the prizes, sir," Calloway replied.

The captain's eyes flashed to his premier's; the two men were in agreement. When Albritton spoke, his voice was low and firm. "Commander, while our ships travel together, distribution of supplies taken from prizes will be made according to need, regardless of who takes the prize. Have you brought the manifests from your prizes, along with the current lading on *Argus*?"

Calloway cleared his throat nervously. "For the prizes, yes, but not for *Argus*."

Albritton nearly asked him why not, but decided it would be fruitless. Instead, he turned to Chandler. "Send *Argus's* boat back for the purser. Tell him to bring his book."

"Aye, sir." Chandler went to the door and passed the word to the sentry.

"While we're waiting, Commander, would you mind explaining why you blew past those two luggers without so much as a broadside to try to put them out of action?"

Calloway appeared confused by the question. "I was trying to get to the prizes before they escaped, sir."

"And if they had followed you and gotten in a position to rake you after you boarded the prizes?"

"Well," the commander said, "I hope you would have been close enough to come to my aid before they could do that. Sir."

"I see," Albritton said. He stared at his hand as he tapped the tabletop with his index finger. The sound was ominous. "Did you bring your reports?"

"No, sir, they were not finished yet."

Albritton's eyes went briefly from his hand to Calloway and then back again. "Commander, I feel the need to remind you who is in command on this voyage."

"I assure you, sir, that is not necessary."

"I believe it is," the captain's voice rose. "You certainly are not acting like you're aware of it. You take it upon yourself to allocate distribution of supplies without consulting me. You have not completed your reports. Just how am I supposed to know that you are aware?"

Calloway's eyes flashed, but he managed to keep his mouth closed. He swallowed hard and said, "My apologies, Captain."

The three officers went over the manifests from their prizes while they waited for *Argus's* purser. The haul was not bad at all; they were fortunate that the ships were only five days out of Bermuda. The purser arrived, and the group spent the next two hours dividing the spoils according to the needs of their respective ships. Lists were drawn up for what supplies went to which ship. Albritton signed them and sat back in his chair.

"So," he said with a sigh, "this should make us independent for at least four months. All leftover supplies will be loaded into *Olympus*, which will sail in company with us. Prize crews will sail the other two prizes into New York or Newport. Once they're gone, we head south." He reached out and tapped a packet on the table bound by a familiar blue ribbon. "This tells us that we may find good hunting in the Caribbean, although we may also find what's left of the Royal Navy there as well." He rested his elbow on the table and rubbed his chin between his thumb and forefinger. "Your opinion, Commander?"

Calloway shifted in his seat. "I believe it depends on your intention for our commission, sir. If you want a short voyage with the possibility of many prizes, head for the Caribbean. The downside of that is that we will most certainly attract the attention of whatever is left of the Royal Navy in Caribbean waters. However, if you want to make a longer voyage and hurt the British farther afield, then you make a quick diversionary strike at the Caribbean—if even that—and head out into the Atlantic before heading south. The South Atlantic is a rich hunting ground by itself, but you also have the option of operations in the Indian or Pacific Oceans as well. What *are* your intentions, sir?"

The captain shook his head absently. "Our orders give me a wide breadth of discretion in that regard. Honestly, I have not made up my mind yet." He stared at his finger on the table, then blinked and looked up at his guest. "Sound advice, Commander—thank you. Return to your ship and make preparations to move south at my signal."

"Aye, sir."

Captain Sir Thomas Knighton sat in the office of the royal governor of Bermuda, nursing his cup of tea and wishing it were something stronger. HMS *London* had pulled into the island's harbor at first light, and Knighton had come ashore seeking any new intelligence on his American prey. He was disappointed to find that he had missed the departure of the main body of the Jamaica convoy for England by ten days for the main body and by a week for a group of stragglers. He was loath to follow the convoy at this late date; surely by this time Albritton had either taken his prizes or was heading out to sea after missing them. The question was, where was he going?

Knighton sighed as he set the empty cup on the desk

before him. Across the desk, the governor read his orders from Admiral Keats. The governor was a petit man with heavily hooded eyes that gave him the look of perpetual sleepiness. His mannerisms could easily be taken as either extreme indifference or superb confidence. At the moment, Knighton was leaning heavily in favor of the former. After what seemed an eternity, the governor set the orders on the desk and folded his hands on them.

"So, Captain, what is your plan for catching the Americans?"

Sir Thomas clasped his hands in his lap and studied them intently, trying his best to remain respectful to the governor. "I intend to sink them, Governor. However, in order to do that, I must find them first, which brings me to you. I need information. Have you heard anything regarding the American Captain Albritton and his ships?"

The governor rocked his hands back and forth upon Knighton's orders. "No, Captain, I have heard nothing about any American frigates at sea."

Knighton made to rise and make his escape. "In that case, Governor, I must –"

The door burst open, and the governor's aide rushed in. "Governor! The harbormaster reports that *Daisy* has returned! Sir, she is alone."

Knighton saw the governor's eyes go wide for a moment before he lowered them to study his hands. He frowned and looked up to his aide. "Have the master report to me at once."

"He's already on the way." The aide bowed and departed.

Knighton looked to the governor for an explanation.

The governor frowned. "The *Daisy* was part of a group of ships that left here three days after the Jamaica Convoy. Five merchant ships escorted by a sloop and two luggers. We hoped they might be able to overtake the convoy and sail home under their escort's protection." He shook his head and swallowed hard. "Apparently, they didn't make it."

The captain's lips were pressed together firmly as they waited for the merchant master. Soon, a knock at the door heralded his arrival. He, too, was a small, thin man who removed his hat as he entered the governor's presence, revealing a high forehead with wispy, graying hair on the temples. His face had a high-bridged nose and close-set eyes that grew wide when he saw who was sitting in the room.

"What is your name?" the governor asked.

"Jonas Fitzpatrick, yer lordship," the man answered, his hands wringing his hat nervously.

The governor motioned toward the captain. "This is Captain Sir Thomas Knighton of His Majesty's frigate *London*. Please, Mr. Fitzpatrick, sit."

The master's eyes moved nervously from one man to the other as he shuffled to the seat next to Knighton and sat.

"Tell us what happened," the governor ordered.

"Well, sir, we was five days out when lookouts sighted two ships to the south. They were soon identified as a frigate and a sloop, both American. The commander in charge of our escort ordered us to disperse while he turned his sloop and the two luggers around to attack the Americans. *Daisy* and one other ran east, another went northeast, and the last two ran north."

"Did you observe how your escort made out?" Knighton asked.

The master's head dropped. "They split up; the luggers went for the sloop, while our sloop went for the frigate. The American sloop ran right past the luggers and took off after two ships that went north."

Knighton's eyes came up smartly. "Excuse me, but I don't wish to misunderstand you. You say the American sloop went past the luggers *without firing a shot?*"

"Aye, Cap'n."

Knighton sat back and shook his head. "Continue."

Fitzpatrick drew a ragged breath. "The luggers went for the frigate." Knighton shot him a questioning look, but the master only nodded. "It looked like they tried to box the American in, what with them on one side and the sloop on the other. But all they did was sail right into the American's broadsides." He shivered at the memory. "All three ships. Gone. Devastating."

"Go on, Mr. Fitzpatrick," the governor said when the man seemed to go silent. "What happened next?"

The master raised his head, tears brimming in his eyes. "I heard about the guns on the American frigates, but I never dreamed..." He turned to Knighton. "They sailed right into it, Captain. The big American got off two broadsides from each battery in quick succession, and by the time the smoke cleared, all that was left of the luggers was two wrecks in a big field of debris. As for the sloop..." Fitzpatrick shook his head miserably. "Dismasted, her deck a mess; from where I was, I didn't see anyone moving on board. I think she was beginning to settle in the water."

His words left his audience in stunned silence. The governor was heard to mutter *"Incredible!"* while Captain Knighton stared out into space through hooded eyes.

"Go on," he ordered. "What happened next?"

"*Olympus* and my ship split up. He turned south while I continued east. The American went south. I continued on my course for three days before turning and making my way back to report what happened."

Fitzpatrick watched as Knighton and the governor shared a look. The captain gave a single nod, and the governor looked up.

"Thank you, Mr. Fitzpatrick," he said formally. "You did the right thing in safeguarding your ship and reporting the attack. Report to the harbormaster tomorrow for instructions.”

“Aye, sir.” *Daisy's* master bowed slightly and left the room.

Knighton waited until they were alone before sighing heavily and folding his hands in his lap. “I thought something like this might happen, but I thought he would run into the main convoy with its escort, not stragglers guarded by a sloop.” He put an elbow on the arm of the chair and rested his chin in his hand. “He's long gone now. The question is, where?”

The governor stirred. “The best hunting grounds would be south of Nova Scotia or in the Caribbean.”

“It depends,” Knighton said. “If he's on a short voyage, he'll head north to stay closer to the American ports. But if he intends to stay out, he'll head south. Either the Caribbean or our merchant shipping off the South American coast.” The captain rose and went to study a large-scale map of the North and South Atlantic on the wall. Suddenly he turned and marched back to the desk. “Governor, I believe he's gone south. I will sail as soon as my ship is provisioned and make for Port Royal. If he has not been seen in the Caribbean, I will make my way south toward Rio de Janeiro. I shall write a report for you to forward back to the Admiralty.”

“Very well,” the governor said. “I shall send a note to the harbor master stating that your ship is to be given priority in all requests.”

“Thank you, sir.” The captain picked up his hat, nodded to the governor, and went back to his ship.

The small American squadron sailed east, passing Bermuda to the north. Albritton's plan was to have *Columbia* and *Argus*, in company with *Olympus*, head to a point far to the east of the island before heading south. At the moment, the captain sat in his chair in his day cabin, debating the question of what to do with *Argus*. His orders gave him complete autonomy on her disposition, and what he had seen so far did nothing to encourage him to turn Calloway loose on his own.

Albritton leaned his head back and closed his eyes, hoping to dull the growing ache in his neck. He could not believe Calloway had simply blown past those two luggers without even firing a shot. True, they were only luggers and therefore not much of a threat to either *Argus* or *Columbia*, but he should have put a broadside into them in passing, for safety's sake. He had the feeling that if he turned *Argus* loose now, they would either come home with as many prizes as they could crew or else be blown out of the water by a Royal Navy frigate.

Sommers appeared in the doorway. "Is there anything I can get you, sir?"

"Yes," Albritton said as he opened his eyes. "Pass the word for Mr. Chandler, if you please."

Sommers nodded. "As you say, sir." It was not very long before a knock on the door heralded the premier's arrival.

"You sent for me, sir?" Chandler asked as he stood at attention in the doorway.

"Yes, Michael. Sit, please." Albritton indicated a place on the settee, and the first lieutenant warily complied. The captain had never before used his first name, and it put him on his guard. The captain shifted in his seat before continuing. "I am debating within myself about turning *Argus* loose."

"I see." Chandler looked at the deck for a moment before raising his eyes to his captain's. "And?"

Albritton shrugged. "As I said, I am only considering at the moment. My thought had been to send him into the Caribbean and use his activities to draw the British attention while we head south."

The first lieutenant bobbed his head slightly while he thought it over. "Sounds like a good plan. Are you sure Calloway is the man for the job?"

"He'll have to be. He's the man on the spot."

Chandler shrugged, then nodded.

"Please have Mr. Adams signal *Argus*," the captain said. "*'Heave to. Captain come on board.'* Have Mr. Warren heave to and notify *Olympus*."

"Aye, sir." Chandler rose and went to the cabin door to speak to the sentry. When he returned, he asked, "Are you sure, sir?"

Albritton ignored the question, instead nodding to himself. "Calloway will do it," he said in almost a whisper. "He has to."

When Commander Calloway arrived, Chandler greeted him at the entry port and escorted him down to the captain's cabin. He opened the door and stepped back. "After you, sir."

"Thank you, Lieutenant." Calloway stepped into the room to find Captain Albritton standing beside his dining table. On the table was a tray with three glasses filled with a dark liquid. The commander came to attention until his captain stepped forward to shake his hand. Calloway nodded toward the table. "I hope that's bourbon."

"It is. You gentlemen help yourselves and follow me." The three men moved to the day cabin and sat, Albritton in his chair and the others on the settee. "Mr. Chandler, will you please toast the President's health?"

The premier raised his glass and made the toast, and they drank.

Albritton set his glass on the small table beside his chair. "I called you here, Commander, because I plan to detach *Argus* for individual patrol."

"Thank you, sir," Calloway replied.

The captain raised his hand. "Save your thanks. I have a job for you. The information we acquired with the capture of *Olympus* indicates that the British have stripped the Caribbean in order to strengthen their blockade of our coast and also, I imagine, to look for us. Your orders will be to sail for the Caribbean and make a nuisance of yourself. I want you to draw the British attention so we can make our way south unnoticed."

Calloway nodded his head. "I can do that."

"I shall leave it to your judgement," Albritton went on, "as to when to head for an American port. I would suggest Washington City, so you can report directly to Secretary Jones, but I will leave that to your discretion. You will need to act quickly to draw their attention to you. Above all, be sure to bring your ship and crew home safely. The nation needs *Argus*, and she needs her captain as well. Do you have any questions?"

Calloway nodded his thanks for the compliment before slowly shaking his head. "No, I don't think so, sir."

Albritton rose and shook his hand. "Good. If you will be so kind as to join me for supper, my clerk will have the time to copy your orders and certain documents you may need."

Calloway made a short bow. "I'd be honored, Captain."

The supper was a low-key affair, neither man saying much. Afterward, the captain's clerk entered and placed on the table copies of the commander's orders and other relevant documents.

"There you are, Commander," Albritton said. "You sail at once. I will disappear into the Atlantic while you get the Royal Navy's attention." He stood, and Calloway followed. The two shook hands. "Take care of your ship and crew."

"I will, sir." Calloway stepped back, came to attention, picked up his orders, and left.

USS *Columbia* sailed southeast and disappeared into the wide Atlantic. The captain stood on his quarterdeck as night closed in around them, covering them like a blanket. He looked out over the empty sea and marveled that a man could be so alone on a crowded ocean. He stared at the stars and wondered again if he did the right thing in turning Calloway loose.

Three days later, Captain Albritton sat at his desk, updating his ship's log. They'd had the ocean to themselves since bidding farewell to *Argus*. If today's noon sighting placed them where he thought it would, NE of Bermuda, he would order their turn south. He set his pen down and sat back in his chair. Two or three weeks south, then possibly a week on a SSW course with maybe a quick dash west to put them squarely in the midst of the trade routes into the Caribbean from South America. He nodded in anticipation— rich hunting grounds indeed. A short time there, then putting in somewhere to take on water before disappearing into the Atlantic again only to reappear off the northern coast of Brazil. Here, he had to take care; the British did a great deal of trade with that country, and it was also the base of their South American squadron.

A knock at the door drew the captain's attention. "Enter!" he called.

The sentry admitted Mr. Smith, midshipman of the watch. "Yes, Mr. Smith?"

The midshipman came to attention, his hat properly tucked under his arm. "Mr. Hill's respects, sir, and would you please come up on deck? There's a strange sail off the port bow."

"My compliments to Mr. Hill," Albritton replied. "I shall come up directly."

"Aye, aye, sir!" Smith turned smartly and marched from the room.

Albritton came up on deck and was met by Lieutenant Hill. He handed Albritton a glass and pointed toward a spot on the horizon. "I don't believe they've seen us yet."

Albritton quickly went to the rail and surveyed the scene. He lowered his glass and said, "Mr. Hill, hoist the British colors."

The lieutenant was confused. "*British* colors, sir?"

Albritton met his subordinate's eyes and raised an eyebrow. "You heard me, Lieutenant."

"Aye, sir."

Albritton raised his glass and studied the approaching ship. He could see someone—presumably the master—on her quarterdeck, studying them through his own glass. *I've got to play this just right,* he thought. *If I do, we may be able to get a ship intact, which means an extra ten to fifteen percent when she is sold as a prize.* He shrugged. *Not to mention the supplies and men we might gain. At this distance, he may not be able to tell the difference between a British uniform and an American one. We'll know when he either heaves to or turns to run.*

"Mr. Adams! Use the British signal flags we got from *Olympus* and signal that ship to heave to! Mr. Warren! Heave to as soon as our friend does!"

"Aye, sir!" came from both men.

The captain waited as the signal was raised. He saw the confusion on the merchantman's quarterdeck, with three men, whom he thought to be the master, first mate, and quartermaster, arguing back and forth. Albritton was just about to order the long nines to be made ready when the master apparently ended the debate and ordered the ship to heave to.

Albritton turned to Mr. Warren and nodded. The sailing

master gave the orders to take in the sails.

"Mr. Chandler, break out the British lieutenant's coat and hat we have in storage. Take a boat with a standard boarding party. No marines. Introduce us as the frigate *Liverpool*. Bring the captain and first mate back. Be sure not to let them get a look at our fantail. Bring them straight to my cabin. We must play this right, Michael; all must look well from their quarterdeck."

Chandler smiled broadly. "Aye, sir." He saluted and left on his task. Albritton paced his quarterdeck and glanced from time to time at the British merchantman, trying his best to imitate a concerned British captain. When Mr. Chandler appeared on deck, Albritton could not help but stare at the transformation—the premier looked every inch an officer of the Royal Navy. The captain had to smile—Chandler had even found a white wig somewhere, complete with a proper queue hanging between his shoulders. The first lieutenant glanced over and nodded to his captain before disappearing through the entry portal.

Chandler sat in the stern sheets of the long boat as it rowed toward the merchantman. He tried to keep his back ramrod straight, as he had seen so many Royal Navy officers do in the past. Beside him was Xavier; the captain sent him along, armed to the teeth with a sword, a brace of pistols, and a dagger. He conned the boat and was to board the merchantman with the lieutenant; to that end he had on a clean shirt and clean duck trousers, borrowed from one of the ship's lieutenants. The premier grunted to himself and hoped the coxswain returned them without any blood stains.

The two men ascended the ladder and stepped up on the deck. Chandler stepped forward and saluted the quarterdeck.

"I am Lieutenant Chandler," he said, "first lieutenant of His Majesty's frigate *Liverpool*. Which of you is the master here?"

One of the group gathered by the wheel stepped forward. He was a head shorter than Chandler but older by at least twenty years. His brown hair was graying at the temples, and his face was fleshy with noticeable jowls and dark, close-set eyes.

"I am Nathaniel Edwards," he said, "master of the *Albatross*."

Chandler bowed and stepped forward to shake the man's hand. "And your mate?"

Edwards' eyes narrowed at the request, but he called over his shoulder, "Evans!"

A short, stocky man with long, black hair stepped from the group by the wheel.

"My first mate," Edwards said. "Elijah Evans."

Chandler nodded to the mate and addressed the master. "My captain invites the two of you to his cabin for a drink. He needs any information you may have on American movements in this part of the ocean."

Edwards shrugged. "It'll be a short conversation, then. We haven't seen another ship in days. We got blown well off our course in a gale and suffered damage. Took us days to make temporary repairs, and now we're heading for the Caribbean to do the job right."

Evans joined them. "Where did you say your ship was out of?"

"I didn't," Chandler replied. "But we left Bermuda five days ago."

The mate's eyes narrowed. "You sound like an American," he said accusingly.

Chandler shrugged. "That's not surprising, seeing as how I was born in South Carolina. After the Americans ratified their constitution and elected a president, my parents decided they didn't want to live there anymore, and we returned to England." He smiled condescendingly. "Guess I never picked up the accent."

The mate turned to his master. "I don't trust him. Remember the papers? The Americans are known to have ships out."

"Shut your mouth!" Edwards snapped. He turned to study the frigate standing less than pistol shot to windward. "Regardless, it don't look like we have much choice, does it? Mr. Chandler, we accept your captain's kind invitation."

"Excellent," Chandler replied. He stood to the side and indicated the entry port. "Shall we, gentlemen?"

Chandler and Xavier led their two guests into the captain's cabin. Albritton stepped out of the day cabin in shirtsleeves.

"Captain," Chandler said, "may I present Mr. Edwards, master of the *Albatross*, and his mate, Mr. Evans?"

Albritton shook hands with both men. "Please, gentlemen, sit down. Sommers! Wine for our guests, if you please! Now, Mr. Edwards, tell me about your voyage."

Edwards repeated the account he had given to Chandler aboard the *Albatross*. Albritton listened without interrupting, simply nodding from time to time. "Well," he said when the master had finished, "we can help with your repairs if nothing else. Mr. Chandler, return to the *Albatross* with the bosun's mate and some marines to help with their rigging and other repairs."

"Marines?" Evans questioned.

"Our marines are used to being in the tops," Albritton explained, "so I've started using them to help with the rigging when it needs repaired. They know what they're doing, let me assure you."

"Aye, sir," Chandler said and left the room. Xavier stood inside the door, still wearing his armaments. Sommers came in and distributed the refreshments.

"Tell me," Albritton continued, "have you heard tell of any American ships about?"

"Not a word," Edwards replied. "We haven't so much as seen another vessel since we ran into that gale until we sighted you, Captain."

"Pardon me, Captain," Evans said, "but I don't believe I got your name."

"No? How thoughtless of me. My name is Hezekiah Albritton."

Edwards sighed. "I thought so."

Albritton was surprised. "Do I know you, sir?"

"No, we've never been formally introduced, but I had a friend on board the *Guerriere*, and he described you pretty well."

"Do you mean...?" Evans stammered.

Edwards nodded. "Americans." Evans glared at his captor and downed his drink in a single draught before smashing the glass upside down on the table. Xavier took a step forward, his hand on his sword's hilt, but Albritton stopped him with a gesture.

"Mr. Evans," he said sternly, "I trust there will be no further demonstrations of that sort, otherwise my attitude toward your disposition may change considerably for the worse."

"Evans," his master said, quiet but ominous, "that'll do." He turned back to Albritton and gestured toward the deck beams above. "And your ship? Surely not the *Liverpool*?"

Albritton shook his head. "I must apologize for the deception. You are aboard USS *Columbia*." He took a drink of his wine. "I hope you understand, my intention was to avoid bloodshed, both of your men and mine."

"Aye," Edwards replied, resigned to his fate. "I suppose I ought to thank you for that, if nothing else. So, what happens to me and my men?"

"*Albatross* will be sent back to the United States under a prize crew," the captain explained. "You and your crew will be aboard and will be treated as prisoners of war. I should warn you, however," he said, looking at the fuming mate, "that any trouble from any of your crew will be met with immediate force of arms. If necessary, you two gentlemen will be the first men shot." He held the eyes of each man to make sure they understood what his orders to the prize master would be. "Tell me, Mr. Edwards, will my first lieutenant find any impressed Americans amongst your crew?"

"I don't think so, Captain. We are not the Royal Navy."

"I'm sure," Albritton replied drolly. "Nevertheless, I shall have Mr. Chandler ask."

The master of the *Albatross* shrugged. "As you wish."

"Do you wish to tell me what your cargo is, or shall I wait for the good lieutenant to return with your manifests?"

"Oh, let's wait, shall we?" Edwards answered, annoyed at his captor's tone. "I wouldn't wish to dampen your anticipation."

"As you wish, sir." Albritton rose. "Sentry! Have the sergeant-at-arms take these two men below and clap them in irons. Hold them in the cable tier for now."

The two men stared at him with undisguised loathing in their eyes. Neither man said a word as they were chained and led away. When they were gone, Albritton sat heavily and rested his elbows on the table.

Sommers appeared in the pantry doorway. "Bourbon, sir?"

The captain stared at the man and actually considered his suggestion. He sighed. "No, thank you. I'd rather save it."

"I understand, sir. Would you like something to eat while you are awaiting Mr. Chandler's return?"

"Just something quick, if you have it."

"I have just the thing, sir." He disappeared and soon set a plate of cold meat and cheese on the table. The captain nodded his appreciation and helped himself to the plate.

It was more than three hours before Lieutenant Chandler made his appearance, his arms full of papers that he set on the table.

"What's all this?" the captain asked.

"My apologies, sir," the lieutenant gasped. He sat in the seat proffered by his host. "These papers include the ship's manifest plus intelligence I think will help us." He paused to accept a glass of wine from Sommers. "We struck gold with this one, Captain." He shuffled through the stacks before him and pulled out the manifests. "Let me see... Here: for meats, we have tongues, corned beef in rounds, smoked salmon, dried beef and codfish, plus hams! As for drink, we found the best brandy, gin, and port, chests of imperial and gunpowder tea, and barrels of flour well stored. We also found clothing of every description and quality and a full hogshead of tobacco—most likely pirated from one of *our* ships, I daresay. Sir, it's like an admiral's personal supply ship!" Chandler handed the manifests to his captain while he searched through the stacks for another paper. "As for the ship herself, sir, I'm afraid she's not worth keeping. Her timbers below show advanced rot. Most likely the British would have scrapped her once she reached her destination. I suggest we transfer her cargo to *Olympus* and *Columbia* and then set her afire. No need to waste a prize crew."

Albritton looked up from the manifests and nodded. "I agree. See to it once we are done here."

"Aye, sir." Chandler resumed his search of the stacks and pulled out a report. "Captain, this copy of the ship's orders says *Albatross* was part of a convoy bound for the Windward Islands. The convoy was to meet a sloop of war east of Bermuda for escort to that island for fresh water before proceeding to their destination. I'll bet we robbed the admiral of the West Indies Squadron, or perhaps even the governor of Jamaica, of his dainties!"

Albritton laughed, and the two men drank a toast to their unexpected bounty. Albritton tapped the table. "Michael, I want to make sure the crew shares in this bounty in some way. Give them the beef, if it's fresh. Also, pick us out one good ham for the officers and give the rest to the crew if there's enough for everybody. Also, tomorrow's Thursday, isn't it?"

Chandler thought for a moment, caught off guard by the question. "Yes, I believe so, sir."

"Good. We'll cancel muster for Sunday, and let it be known among the crew that we'll be serving a special dinner that day. Ham and some fixings from the prize. If the ham runs out, we'll substitute something else from the prize. Every man of us will get something special! Sommers!"

The servant appeared. "Sir?"

"You heard?"

"Aye, sir."

"We'll invite the entire gunroom for supper, then. Turn of the first dog watch—will that give you enough time to prepare?"

"Of course, sir."

A thought hit Albritton. "Mr. Chandler, who's scheduled to have the watch at that time?"

Chandler had to think for a moment. "Mr. Mitchell, sir."

Albritton frowned. "I don't want to pull him from the

deck. Please inform Mr. Mitchell he is invited to a private supper with me at six bells of the afternoon watch. Hopefully, that will make up for his missing the party."

Chandler grinned. "I'm sure it will, sir."

The news spread like wildfire throughout the ship. The crew could talk of nothing else but the chance to fill their bellies with what was billed as an admiral's fare. The captain even went so far as to call the cook to his cabin along with Boothby and Sommers, just to make sure the meal would be prepared correctly. After interviewing the cook, Albritton decided to assign Boothby to help the cook, with Sommers looking in as often as he could. The cook strenuously resisted this until the captain pointed out that if the cook botched this meal, with all the excitement created by the captain's announcement, the crew might well be driven to seek revenge. The captain broadly hinted that if that were to be the case he would not stand in their way. That caused the cook to reconsider and eventually accept the help.

Anticipation grew as the time drew near, and the preparations more than met expectations. The ham lasted almost to the end, the last three or four messes having corned beef substituted. In fact, when it became apparent that the ham would not last and that corned beef would be the substitute, two messes voted to pass on the ham and wait for the corned beef! The sides of whole baked potatoes and fresh bread and butter, as well as the lime juice, also came from the prize. Only the extra ration of grog came from *Columbia*. Albritton later heard that some of the messes, more affected by the extra grog than their fellows, wanted to nominate the cook for Mayor of London.

Six bells of the afternoon watch rang out when a knock came at the cabin door and the sentry announced Lieutenant Mitchell. The second lieutenant marched in smartly, hat safely tucked under his left arm, and came to attention.

"At ease, Lieutenant," Albritton said. "I've invited you here alone, because you have the next watch and so will miss the officers' gathering for supper."

Mitchell gave a half bow. "Thank you, sir. I am honored."

"Please, sit," Albritton said. "Sommers! You may serve the wine." Sommers brought the glasses, and the captain picked his up. "Mr. Mitchell, will you please toast the President's health?"

Both men stood and raised their glasses. "I give you the President of the United States, James Madison, his good health, and victory over the British!" Mitchell declared.

"Here! Here!" Albritton replied. Both men drank and resumed their seats. Sommers and his mates brought out a half-ham on a platter, a bowl of potatoes, bread and butter, and a glass of lime juice for each man. Albritton did the honors of carving the meat and placed a thick slab on the lieutenant's plate. Each man helped himself to the fixings.

"Thank you, sir," Mitchell said again. "You didn't have to do this."

"It is a pleasure, Lieutenant, believe me. Tell me, how is the crew doing? I mean, what's your general impression? Are the new men settling in well?"

Mitchell stiffened at the question, and Albritton knew he had struck the nerve he was seeking. The lieutenant swallowed his mouthful and took a drink of his wine before answering. "I believe they are, sir."

"Including the Negro? What is his name?"

"Ezekiel," Mitchell said as he cut open his potato.

"Yes. Is the crew accepting him?"

Mitchell seemed reluctant to answer, so Albritton repeated the question.

"For the most part, I believe, sir," came the reply. "However, we do have crewmen from the South aboard."

"Officers as well, do we not?"

Mitchell flinched, and Albritton knew.

"I believe so, sir," Mitchell said.

"Rest easy, Lieutenant," Albritton said calmly. "Tell me, if we are blessed with prize money on this voyage, what will you do with your share?"

Mitchell, relieved at the change of topic, began to slice himself a general chunk of ham. "Do you know, I've been thinking about that very thing, sir, especially now that we've got a couple of prizes under our lee already, so to speak. I'm from Pennsylvania, outside Philadelphia, but I've always liked the idea of moving west of Harrisburg and buying a farm. Did you know that Harrisburg just became the capitol of our state?"

"No," the captain shook his head. "When did this happen?"

"1812, just before the war began, I believe. I've heard they're building a fine state capitol building, although I imagine the war has interrupted construction." He shrugged. "Anyway, I hope to get a good piece of land and settle down after the war."

Albritton sat back and let his guest direct the small talk for the remainder of the meal. He had the information he wanted; the question now was, what was he to do with it?

On his captain's orders, Lieutenant Mitchell went on deck for his watch and placed the ship on a new course that hopefully would put them across the course of the rest of *Albatross's* convoy. The quartermaster agreed that a run of five days or so would put them in a position to

begin a north-south patrol and hopefully intercept the convoy before it could enter the Caribbean. Unfortunately, three days' patrol brought no sightings of the convoy. Reluctantly, Captain Albritton ordered the ship to turn SSE and resume their course toward the southern Caribbean trade routes.

The feast was better than anything any of them had ever seen. Henry's mess was one of the first, so they got some of the prime chunks of ham and soft bread brought over from "the admiral's yacht"—that's what the men nicknamed the ship. Henry chuckled when he heard the nickname and thought it pretty accurate. Boothby and Sommers helped the cook ensured the fare was everything the men thought befitting for an admiral's table.

The mess lounged around the table, sipping their grog and allowing the meal to settle into their stomachs. The doctor had come through a while ago, just observing—or so he said. He did warn the men not to overindulge (Henry had to explain the word meant 'eat too much') to avoid a bellyache. Henry was pleased to see none of his men seemed to have that problem.

He was also pleased to see that, as far as he could tell, Ezekiel was settling in to the mess just fine. Henry didn't think any of his mess mates had anything against Negroes, and he was pleased to see that he was right. They kept their distance at first—of course, that was only natural—Ezekiel did the same. But once they saw him in the yards and saw what he could do, they welcomed him readily enough. As for the rest of the crew, Henry only knew of one incident of trouble brewing. Two hands from the other watch had stopped by their mess a few days before and started to make comments about how dark the mess was becoming, but Two Toes stood and stared them down, the look on his face bearing an unmistakable warning for the two to move along. The men wisely closed their mouths and went away. Two Toes had sat back down, all without a word, and resumed his meal. Ezekiel looked at him, but the big Indian ignored him. Ezekiel looked to William for an explanation.

The topman pulled his pipe from between his teeth. "You're in our mess now." He shrugged. "Nothing else need be said."

Ezekiel nodded, both in understanding and thanks. Nothing else was said.

As they relaxed now after their feast, O'Brien held his cup up to their newest member. "Got to hand it to you, mate. I haven't seen anyone climb a yard like you do. Where'd you learn that?"

Ezekiel looked to Henry, who shrugged and said, "O'Brien's still a landsman."

"Ah," Ezekiel said with a nod of understanding. "To answer your question, I learned it on British ships."

"Can you teach me?" O'Brien persisted.

Ezekiel shrugged. "Sure."

The landsman saluted with his cup and drained it in a single draught.

"Have you ever been in a battle?" Peewee asked.

Ezekiel shook his head. "I was pressed by an Indiaman, believe it or not. They had a run of smallpox on board—this was in 1808—and they stopped the merchantman I was on and boarded us. Those Indiamen are almost as well armed as a warship, so our captain decided he had no choice but to submit. The British officer came aboard and demanded to know which crewmen had been exposed to smallpox and survived. I was one of five men who said yes, and we were all taken. I worked the Indiaman for two years before being transferred to *Olympus*, and now I'm here."

"You never tried to escape?" George asked.

Ezekiel shook his head. "Didn't want to. The British treated me well, for the most part, especially after they found out I was rated as a topman. The money was good on the Indiaman, and even after I moved to *Olympus* the pay was regular and enough to keep me going. The British seemed to care a lot less what color I was than the Americans did. The only real trouble I ever had with them was that the captain of the Indiaman didn't give me back my papers when I left his ship."

"Papers?" Peters asked. He was a landsman, too.

Ezekiel nodded. "My papers that said I was a freeman. Not a slave any longer."

"Oh."

Ezekiel shivered. "I will admit, I did have a time getting adjusted to British food."

They laughed at that. O'Brien gestured to the empty plates on the mess table. "Too bad we can't have grub like this all the time!"

Ezekiel smiled into his cup and began to relax.

Albritton stood at the door of his cabin and welcomed his guests individually. He was ashamed that he didn't recall one or two of their names, and he made a mental note to ask Mr. Chandler for a reminder as soon as possible.

Commander Calloway sat at his desk in his cabin, savoring a glass of Cognac and working on his log and reports for Albritton and the Navy Department in Washington. The Cognac was part of a bribe taken from a French privateer they'd captured shortly after entering the Caribbean via the Anegada Passage between the Virgin Islands and Anguilla. A shot across her bow convinced the pinnace to heave to, and Lieutenant Wilson was sent to bring the captain back for talks. The French captain produced a letter of marque from the American government and demanded to be set free. It was plain to Wilson from the moment he went on board that the French crew had plundered more than just British shipping, and the threat of a search of his hold was enough to convince the privateer's captain to give in. Calloway allowed him to purchase his freedom for a price, knowing that he would spread word of the American sloop's presence in Caribbean waters.

In the weeks that followed, Calloway and *Argus* had done nothing to hide their presence. In accordance with Albritton's instructions, Calloway raised as much havoc as possible without exposing his ship to superior enemy forces. They took two prizes, one of which was too badly rotten to keep. Calloway removed all stores to *Argus* and sent all prisoners to Charleston with a prize crew in the second prize, a small brig.

It was dawning on Calloway that he might have worn out his welcome. Twice in the past three days he'd had to alter course to avoid interception by British warships. Sitting in his cabin, Calloway took that to mean that he had successfully completed his mission of drawing attention to himself in these waters, and he was now free to get out of there before he was hunted down. He decided to change course under cover of darkness and make for Charleston to check on their prize before going on to Washington and hopefully another commission.

He sat back and drained the last of the Cognac from the glass. He couldn't help but smile; perhaps things were finally looking up.

CHAPTER TEN

Captain Sir Thomas Knighton sat at his desk. Three days earlier, he'd met with a British ship south of Bermuda that brought him news of an American warship prowling the Caribbean and supposedly taking three British ships as prizes. The next day, his ship had raced south through the Anegada Passage and was now on course to pass down the western approaches to the Lesser Antilles. St. Kitts and Nevis were now off his port beam, just below the horizon, and he ordered extra lookouts to be posted as of dawn.

Knighton dropped his pen and sighed. Something was not right. He leaned back in his chair, crossed his arms over his chest, and frowned as he remembered his interview with the merchant's master. The withdrawal of so many Royal Navy warships had resulted in an increase in the number of American privateers, but the master had reported an American *naval* vessel. He could not believe that a man of Hezekiah Albritton's reputation would go to the Caribbean and allow his presence to be so widely known so quickly. He would take prizes quietly, containing the crews so word would leak out only very slowly, the alarm only being raised when the ships were missed at their destinations. But this American, if the merchant could be believed—and Knighton had run into a few who turned out to be exaggerating, or downright wrong—was making no attempt at all to do this. In fact, almost the exact opposite was the case.

The captain shifted in his chair and rested his chin between his thumb and forefinger. *What is going on? Surely, Albritton has left the area and is headed out into the Atlantic by now! Why stay? Could he be trying to lure an unsuspecting frigate captain into a battle, as he did with my old friend Captain Dacres of the Guerriere? What purpose-*

At that moment, a knock at the door heralded the entrance of the midshipman of the watch.

"Sir," he said as he came to attention, "there's a strange sail on the horizon. The lookout thinks it may be an American warship."

Knighton followed the young gentleman up to the deck, where he was met by Lieutenant Jervis, commander of the watch. Jervis handed his captain a glass and led him to the rail. "I ordered an intercept course, sir," he said as he indicated the sail ahead of them on the horizon, "as per your standing orders, and sent for you immediately."

"Well done, Lieutenant," the captain said. "Your grandfather would approve." The lieutenant's grandfather was none other than Admiral Sir John Jervis, victor at the Battle of Cape Saint Vincent. The lieutenant had tried to trade on that when he'd first come aboard, until he found out that it would get him nowhere. Since then, the lieutenant's skills had improved considerably, much to his captain's delight.

Knighton found the growing dot of white. "Frigate?" he muttered. "No, I think the sail is too small. Sloop? Maybe a sloop of war? Possibly." He closed his glass and walked to the wheel.

"I have the deck!" he announced. "Quartermaster, the stuns'ls, if you please. We must close the gap."

"Aye, sir!"

Orders were barked via the speaking trumpet, and the hands jumped to the shrouds and made their way aloft. The stuns'ls appeared, and Knighton felt the ship surge forward. Lieutenant Percival emerged from the companionway. The first lieutenant approached him and saluted.

"What have we got, sir?" he asked.

"American ahead. Possibly a frigate, more likely a sloop. Come with me, Lieutenant. We're going forward for a better look."

The two men went forward to the larboard long nine where the captain put the glass to his eye again. "I think we're gaining on them. Slowly, but gaining."

"I don't think they've seen us yet, sir," Percival said. "They look like they're still under normal sail."

"Hmm..." Knighton raised his glass again. "I think you're right, Roland. Let's hope we stay invisible for a while." He lowered the glass and thought for a moment. "I want you to stay here and ready the bow chasers. I'm going aft; let me know as soon as you think you can reach him. Get a runner and keep him with you. Send another to the lookout."

"Aye, sir."

Captain Knighton went to the quarterdeck and began to pace—five brisk steps across the stern before turning on his heel and doing the same in the opposite direction. He had no idea how long he'd been at it before Lieutenant Jervis stepped up to interrupt him.

"Begging your pardon, sir, but you have a message from Mr. Percival." Jervis stepped aside and indicated the ship's boy standing beside the quartermaster. Knighton nodded, and Jervis called him over. The boy saluted nervously.

"Well?" Knighton asked.

"Mr. Percival sends his respects, sir," the boy stammered. "He said the lookout says the American has seen us and crowded on all sail. Mr. Percival also says he may be able to reach the American soon."

The captain deliberately softened his look to put the boy at ease. "That's good news,

Mr. ...?"

"Timmy, sir."

"Mr. Timmy," Knighton repeated. "Well done. My compliments to Mr. Percival. Ask him to let me know when he is ready to fire. Dismissed."

The boy stood there, looking from the captain to Jervis in confusion.

Jervis leaned in. "That means you can go now."

Timmy's eyes went wide. "Oh!" he said. "Aye, sir!"

The captain almost smiled as he watched the boy scamper forward. He looked to Jervis. "How many hours would you say until nightfall, Lieutenant?"

The younger man's eyes went automatically to the western horizon and then rose until they met the sun. Knighton waited patiently while he calculated the time.

"I make it about four and a half hours, sir. Maybe five— I'm not sure of the latitude."

The captain cast an eye at the sun before looking at his lieutenant. "I agree." He turned his back without another word and resumed his pacing.

Forward, Lieutenant Percival stood beside the ship's bow chasers, arms crossed over his chest, staring at the American through hooded eyes and praying the daylight held out. He looked over his shoulder when he heard Timmy return.

"Well?" he asked.

"Sir?"

"What happened back there?"

Timmy thought for a moment. "I learned what 'dismissed' means."

Percival smiled. "Good for you, Timmy."

The boy stepped forward and leaned on the rail. "Are we

going to catch them?"

"I hope so," the lieutenant replied. "Depends on the sun. I think we'll have enough time."

"I hope we do, too."

Commander Calloway stood at the fantail, watching the British frigate as it slowly gained on his ship. He lowered the glass and frowned. It was absolutely unforgivable that the enemy ship had been allowed to get so close before it was spotted. She was hull-up on the horizon! He immediately ordered all sail and changed course to put *Argus* at her best point of sailing, but he knew now that it would not do any good.

Lieutenant Wilson appeared at his side. "What do you make of it, sir?"

"It's early yet," Calloway said, "but I think he's going to close the gap before the darkness can save us. You?"

Wilson looked to the British and then scanned the sky to judge the height of the sun. His jaw set as though he had come to an unpleasant conclusion. "Agreed."

Calloway raised his glass again. "From what I can tell, he has long nines on his deck as bow chasers. I don't see gun ports cut into the bow, do you? That would allow him to turn his forward 18-pounders and use them."

Wilson shook his head. "I don't see ports, sir."

Calloway frowned, his lips pressed into a firm, thin line. "Long nines, then. Accurate, but without so hard a punch. How long, do you think?"

"Before they're in range?" He took his captain's silence as a yes. "With long nines? Maybe another hour; definitely less than two."

Calloway lowered his glass again. "I agree. Come, let's go below and see if we can come up with a surprise or two for them."

The two officers entered the captain's cabin and took off their coats, laying them over the chair backs and setting their hats on the table.

"Johnny!" Calloway called for his steward. "Wine for two, if you please!"

"Aye, sir!"

"Sit, Aaron. Thank you, Johnny. Now, here's what I suggest: As the wind blows now, how do you think we would do better with a sharp turn?"

Wilson considered. "I should say starboard, sir."

"Then as soon as they fire their long nines, we shall turn hard to starboard and let loose a broadside. I hope the smoke from their guns will hide us just enough that they will take a minute or two to react. As soon as we loose the broadside, we shall put the wheel hard over to larboard and reverse course, loosing another broadside as we cross her bow. Guns to fire as they bear; our aim is to take out her jibs and hopefully the foremast. Then we swing a wide arc to try to come across her stern and rake her."

"You realize we shall be at the mercy of her larboard battery," Wilson said. "We can't possibly swing wide enough to be out of their range. Not without giving them all the time in the world to react."

Calloway stared at the clouds in his drink. "I know. But I don't know what else to do. I can't go down without a fight, not this time." He looked up and raised his glass. "Here's to luck." He tossed what was left of the wine down his throat.

"Luck." Wilson was not completely surprised to hear what his captain said. He tossed down his drink and rose. "If you'll excuse me, sir, I'm needed on deck."

"Of course, Aaron."

Wilson gathered his things and came to attention before

marching from the cabin, determined to think of a way to save as many of his shipmates as he could.

Captain Knighton stopped pacing when he turned and saw Lieutenant Jervis approach him. A quick glance showed Timmy trying his best to stand still behind him.

"Yes, Mr. Jervis?" he asked.

"Message for you, sir." The lieutenant turned to wave the boy forward. Timmy stepped up and gave a proper salute.

"You have a report for me, Mr. Timmy?" the captain asked.

"Aye, sir," the boy replied. "Mr. Percival sends his respects and says to tell you, 'I think I can reach him now.'"

"Very well, Mr. Timmy," the captain said formally. "I shall come forward directly." Knighton watched him with one eye. "You are dismissed."

The boy caught the command and smiled as he saluted and made his way quickly forward. The captain looked to Lieutenant Jervis with one eyebrow raised. The younger man blushed and looked at the deck for a moment. "Aye, sir. I'll address it."

"Thank you. I'm going forward." Jervis saluted as his captain walked past him. Only then did he allow the smile to creep into the very corner of his mouth. *Imagine!* he thought. *Timmy smiled as he saluted! If we don't address this now, pretty soon he'll wink at me!* Despite himself, the captain felt the smile encompass his face, and he shook his head at the absurdity of it all.

When Knighton arrived at the bows, he ordered Timmy to report to Mr. Jervis at the wheel. Once the lad was gone, the captain turned to his first lieutenant.

"Just about there, sir," Percival replied to the unasked question. "With any luck, her captain will have to find new accommodations."

Timmy returned. He came to attention and ripped off a perfect salute, his face plastered with a serious look. Knighton returned the salute, and the boy went to stand off to the side. The captain turned back to watch his first lieutenant sight the larboard 18-pounder. Once he was satisfied, he moved on to the starboard gun, and Knighton was surprised to see Timmy walk up to the larboard gun. He closed one eye and sighted down the long barrel of the cannon just as he would a musket! The captain turned away before he burst out in laughter.

Mr. Percival appeared at his side. The two men waited until Timmy was done approving the aim of the starboard long nine before proceeding. The first lieutenant looked to the American and said, "Fire!"

Both guns went off together, and the smoke blinded their view of the fall of the shot. This was normal; the lookout's call that followed was not.

"Deck there! The American's turning hard to starboard!"

"*What?*"

Knighton ran to the starboard rail and soon saw the American sloop clear the smoke with his gun ports open and his battery run out. He turned aft and called loudly, "Down! All hands down!"

He hit the deck just as the volley struck. His arms automatically covered his head as he listened helplessly as the enemy's ball shot ripped across his deck and sent showers of murderous splinters in every direction, the screams of those not quick enough to heed their captain's warning bearing witness.

As soon as he thought it safe, Knighton got to his feet and looked forward. The American was coming around, reversing his course to give his larboard battery a crack at *London*'s unprotected bow. He searched the deck frantically until he found Percival, who had dived behind the larboard bow chaser, somehow managing to scoop up Timmy and shield him on the deck with his body. He helped the first lieutenant to his feet.

"Are you alright?" the captain demanded. "And Timmy?"

"Yes," came the bewildered reply, "both of us, I think."

"Good. Now listen to me. The American will fire again in a minute. As soon as the bow chasers bear, fire both guns, then dive for cover. I'm going aft; I shall warn the men as I go. After he fires, jump to your feet and go below. Get the larboard battery ready. Stand by for my command!"

"Aye, sir!"

Knighton made his way back, telling everyone he met who was still standing to dive to the deck when the American fired again. Fortunately for him, he gave the warning to a hand just as the man looked past him to see the American crossing their bows. The man grabbed the captain by the lapels and pulled him to the deck before rolling on top of him to protect him. Knighton was just about to protest when the roar of the broadside reached his ears, and he covered his head with his arms. Several seconds passed before the man got off him and helped him to his feet.

"I'm sorry, Captain," he stammered, "but I didn't think there was time to point it out to you."

"Never apologize for saving a man's life, sir," Knighton said. He patted the man on the shoulder. "Thank you."

He made it to the quarterdeck and immediately made for the wheel.

"Mr. Morgan," he said to the sailing master, "I expect the American to try to circle around us in order to rake our stern. Once he is past our beam, I intend to put the wheel over hard to larboard and rake him first. Stand by for my command."

"Aye, sir!"

The captain grabbed a glass and went to the larboard rail. Sure enough, the American sloop—he was close enough to identify now—was continuing around in a wide arc, no doubt aiming for Knighton's stern. The corner of Knighton's mouth turned slightly upward. *Well, he's in for a surprise, isn't he?* A quick but detailed glance at their upper works revealed no serious damage, certainly nothing that would prevent him from dealing with this American upstart. He returned to the wheel.

"Standby, Mr. Morgan," he said. His eyes were on the enemy sloop, judging the best moment to spring his trap. "Now!" he called, and ran to the waist.

"Mr. Percival! Run out the larboard battery! Order the guns to fire as they bear! Tell them to take care. I want them to surrender. I do not want to blow them out of the water!"

"Aye, sir!" the first lieutenant answered from below.

HMS *London* healed over to larboard and headed for the American's unprotected stern. Knighton stood beside the wheel, a grim look on his face. *Now it's my turn.*

Commander Calloway stood on his quarterdeck, feeling pleased with himself. So far, the battle had gone his way, but he had to move quickly before the frigate could recover. One rake of his stern, and *Argus* would disappear over the horizon before the British could recover.

"Captain!"

The call turned his blood to ice. He looked up to see the mizzen top lookout pointing out to the larboard quarter. He spun to see the British frigate turning to cut across his stern. The other ship's larboard battery was being run out. Calloway's heart sank. His worst fears were coming true before his eyes.

"Hard about!" he shouted to the wheel. "New course NNW!"

The quartermaster reacted immediately. He understood that his captain was trying to shield as much of their vulnerable stern as possible from the enemy's superior weaponry. He also knew that it would do no good in the end.

"They've seen us, sir!" the lookout called out.

"Yes," Knighton muttered as he watched the sloop try to pull away from him at an angle. "Quartermaster, steer three points to starboard!" He went to the waist. "Mr. Percival! Fire as you bear!"

"Aye, sir!"

The cannon below went off in twos and threes; Knighton got to see the first shots strike home before the smoke obscured his vision.

Commander Calloway watched as his ship settled into its new course, then he looked back to see the enemy turning to starboard to get a broadside shot.

"Quartermaster! Helm hard over! New course SSW!"

"Aye, sir!"

That was when they heard the report of the British broadside, followed a split second later by the devastating impact of round shot repeatedly striking his ship. Calloway was thrown to the deck, hitting his head in the process. The ship's mizzenmast was taken out, along with her rudder. USS *Argus* now drifted helplessly to the SSW.

Calloway made it to his feet, helped by a midshipman, but the pain in his head made it difficult to process the devastation he saw. At the base of the wheel was the headless body of the quartermaster, killed by a direct hit. He turned slowly to see the mizzenmast reduced to a ten-foot-tall stump.

"Captain? Captain, can you hear me?"

Some officer or other stood before him, but Calloway could not understand him. The lieutenant looked to the midshipman. "Look, see if you can get him below to the doctor. I'm going below to alert the first lieutenant."

"Aye, sir." The midshipman watched the lieutenant go below and looked up at his captain. "Sir? Sir, can you hear me? We have to go below, sir. I've been ordered to get you to the doctor."

"What?" Calloway answered as he tried to pull away from the boy. "I can't leave... must fight... ship's in danger."

"Sir, the first lieutenant is coming to take command," the boy said. "Sir, I've been ordered to get you below."

As the boy was dealing with his recalcitrant captain, neither of them saw their British adversary come around and pour another broadside into their stern. They probably didn't even hear the sound before the 24-pound ball hit them squarely and turned them both into a bloody cloud of mist.

Lieutenant Wilson was just coming up on deck when the second broadside hit, and he was thrown against the companionway opening, breaking two ribs as a result. He squeezed his eyes shut against the searing pain and sucked in what air his broken ribs would allow. He made it on to the deck and staggered over to what was left of the mizzenmast, leaning on it for support. He looked around at the devastation. He grimaced from the pain and called to a nearby midshipman to get him a damage report. The lad disappeared forward, and the bosun stepped up to him.

"Are you alright, sir?"

Wilson nodded. "I think I broke a rib or two in that last broadside. Where's the captain?"

The bosun nodded toward a bloody mess on the deck halfway between them and the wheel. "Quartermaster's dead, too. Ball took his head clean off."

Wilson squeezed his eyes shut and locked his jaw shut

until he was sure he wouldn't vomit. "Mr. Morgan?"

"Wounded. He was taken below to the doctor."

Wilson raised his head and managed to nod his understanding when a quartermaster's mate came up. "Mr. Wilson!" he cried. "The rudder's shot away!"

"What?" said the bosun.

The mate nodded vigorously. "Direct hits!"

Wilson leaned his head against the mast and closed his eyes to keep them from filling with tears. He had never felt so helpless in all his life, nor so close to absolute panic. A single thought made its way through the pain—*Save your crew. There's nothing more that can be done here.*

He nodded to himself and turned so his back was against the mast. "Bosun, rig a white flag and start waving it on the fantail. Have someone strike the colors."

"Aye, sir." The bosun grabbed a nearby hand. "Go below and see if the doctor can spare Jedson to look at the lieutenant's ribs. You," he pointed at a second man, "pull down the colors."

Captain Sir Thomas Knighton stood on his quarterdeck, watching for activity on what was left of the American's quarterdeck. The two broadsides they had poured into the sloop had reduced the ship to a hulk. The mizzen was gone, and the main mast looked like it was ready to follow. The stern and much of the gun deck was a shambles.

"Captain!" the lookout called. "They're hauling down their colors! And someone's waving a white flag on the quarterdeck!"

"I see it, lookout!" He turned to Jervis. "Wave your hat to that man so he knows I've seen and accepted their surrender. Pass the word for Mr. Percival."

Jervis spoke to a hand before going to the rail and waving

his hat. The American waved back in acknowledgement. Percival came up on deck.

"You sent for me, sir?"

"Yes, Roland," Knighton said quietly. "Please give your crews a 'Well done!' from me. Their shooting was excellent. The Americans have surrendered. I want you to take a boat and board her. Take one or two of the doctor's mates with you, if he can spare them. Report back to me as soon as you can."

"Aye, sir." Percival saluted and made his way forward, calling for the bosun as he went.

Percival rode over to the wreck in the launch, with marines in the gig right behind him. It turned out that the entry port on the starboard side was destroyed in the battle, so the British went around the stern to the larboard port. The marines boarded first, followed by Percival, who was surprised to be met by a midshipman.

"I am Lieutenant Percival, first lieutenant of His Majesty's frigate *London*." Percival saluted.

The American returned the salute smartly. "I am Midshipman Montgomery, of USS *Argus*. Our captain was killed in the battle, and our first lieutenant was wounded. He's right over here. If you will follow me?"

Percival nodded, and the two weaved a drunkard's path through a maze of bodies either broken or ripped apart, hopping over two different pools of blood to get to the mizzen mast where Percival found an officer seated on the deck, getting a bandage put around his rib cage.

"This is our first lieutenant, Mr. Wilson."

Percival saluted, and Wilson nodded weakly in return.

"I am Lieutenant Percival of His Majesty's frigate *London*," he said. "I have brought two of our doctor's mates with me, plus a supply of bandages and medicines. Can we be of help?"

"That would be appreciated. Mr. Montgomery, take them down to the doctor."

"Aye, sir." He led the men below.

Wilson grinned wryly—the combination of the pain and the medicine loosening his tongue. "I'd invite you below for a drink, but I doubt there's much left of my quarters."

"No," Percival replied. "If your bosun will be so kind as to make sure everyone in your crew knows of the surrender, I can have my men help with your wounded."

"And search my ship?"

"But of course."

Wilson looked at the bosun and nodded, and the man departed on his distasteful errand. After he was gone, Percival squatted down and addressed the doctor's mate.

"How is he?"

"Not good," the man replied. "I think he broke two ribs and maybe cracked another. I'll know better in a couple days. He'll be in a lot of pain for a while, but I think he'll be okay."

The British lieutenant rose. "Good." He turned to his sergeant of marines. "Let's start the search. I need a damage report for the captain. Have two men examine the hold and two others look for papers in the captain's cabin, or his clerk's."

"Aye, Lieutenant!"

Captain Knighton waited in his cabin for his first lieutenant's return. He had been notified twenty minutes earlier that Percival was enroute. The captain hoped he would bring back intelligence that would help them track down Albritton.

Lieutenant Percival arrived with his arms full of papers and a tin box under his arm. He set his burden down as neatly as he could.

"And what have we here, Roland?"

"This is everything we could get from the American sloop, sir," Percival said. "USS *Argus*. Captain's name was Calloway. He was killed in our second broadside. First lieutenant was wounded, but survived. I interviewed him before I searched the ship. He claims not to know much; says Calloway usually dealt with Albritton alone. I'm afraid our broadsides were a little too good; nearly all the papers in the captain's cabin were destroyed. Most of these came from the clerk's office, including the tin case." The lieutenant pushed the papers to the side to make room for the case. He pulled out his knife and forced the lock, then he pulled out the top paper and scanned it quickly.

"We hit the jackpot, Captain!" he announced. "This is a copy of the orders for USS *Argus* to make her way to the Caribbean, where she will conduct herself in such a manner so as to get the attention of the Royal Navy and thereby focus their attention on the Caribbean. And look at the signature at the bottom."

He handed over the orders, and Knighton quickly turned to the bottom of the final page. The signature was that of Hezekiah Albritton, Captain, US Navy.

"I knew it!" Knighton exclaimed. "This must be the sloop that escaped with Albritton. You say his orders were to make a show of himself in the Caribbean? Why? So we will think Albritton is there? Now we know he is not, therefore *Argus's* mission was to draw us in so Albritton could make his way unimpeded. But where?"

Percival could only shrug.

Knighton scratched his chin for a moment. "How about their ship? Can she make it to Port Royal?"

"I believe so, sir, but it will be a slow ride. We may want to send our carpenter over for a quick survey. Theirs was killed in the battle."

"If you think it necessary," Knighton replied, lost in thought. "Their first lieutenant—you said he was wounded?"

"Aye, sir. Broken ribs, their doctor said. He should be alright in time."

Knighton stood. "Return to *Argus*, Roland. Take the carpenter or one of his mates with you if you feel the need. Get the ship ready to sail to Port Royal. I shall accompany you. Hopefully, by the time we get there, their first lieutenant, what was his name?"

"Wilson, sir."

"Mr. Wilson will be ready to talk."

Captain Hezekiah Albritton stood in the center of his quarterdeck, enjoying the Atlantic sunlight warming his face. His ship was on course for the water northeast of Columbia to lie in wait for British merchant shipping heading for the Caribbean. He didn't plan to stay long, and he was concerned that an appearance off the northern coast of South America could tip off the British to his ultimate destination. He frowned when he realized that the thought of giving away his plans to the British would not leave his mind.

"Mr. Williams," he said to the officer of the watch, "I am going below. Kindly pass the word for the first lieutenant, the second lieutenant, and the sailing master to join me in my cabin."

"Aye, sir."

Albritton went below. He found the faithful Sommers awaiting him.

"We'll need refreshments for four, if you please," the captain said.

"Aye, sir."

The sentry knocked on the door before admitting the two officers and the sailing master.

"Welcome, gentlemen," Albritton said. "Join me in the day cabin."

The party followed him to the next room and took their seats. Sommers appeared with wine and distributed the glasses all around before retiring. Albritton set his on the table and addressed the company.

"I am becoming concerned," he said carefully, "that we may be tipping our plans to the British by appearing off the coast of Gran Columbia. I find myself wondering if it would not be better to stay hidden in the Atlantic vastness and prey on individual ships for supplies as we make our way south. Once we appear off the Brazilian coast, the cat will be out of the bag, so to speak, especially if we end up taking a prize or two off the Argentine coast before moving into the Pacific. Opinions?"

His guests sipped their wine as they considered what they'd heard. Mr. Chandler was the first to speak up.

"The primary concern," he said, "with that course of action would be water. Nearly anywhere we put in would alert the British where we're going. Unless you know of a desert island with good springs."

The group chuckled at that. Albritton shook his head.

"We would also need to be careful about prisoners," Mitchell contributed. "It may be necessary to keep one prize to act as a prison ship, although that course will demand some of our marines being posted to it for security."

"We'd also need to replenish our prize crews," Mr. Warren added. "The richest prizes we could find would be the British whaling fleet around the Galapagos Islands. They're worth more than most Indiamen. We don't want to take the whalers and not have the crews to sail them home."

"We could sell the oil and ships at a port in Spanish Columbia, couldn't we?" Albritton asked. "Or perhaps in Valparaiso?"

"Doubtful," Warren replied. "The Spanish government-in-exile is in London. The British have driven the French out of Spain. I don't think the Spanish will let us into their ports. Valparaiso, that's different. The Chileans revolted against Spain a couple of years ago, and Carrera has been declared dictator now. But the British are sure to have agents in the port, maybe even a warship."

Albritton pursed his lips; it was a habit of his while he was thinking. "Let's leave that point for the moment and go back to Mr. Chandler's warning about water. Where could we stop that would attract the least attention?"

"One of the French ports in Guiana?" Mitchell suggested.

"Oh, the British are sure to have those watched, wouldn't they?" Warren asked.

"A chance we'll have to take?" Chandler wondered aloud.

"I'd rather not," Albritton said. His lips pursed again, and then his eyes lit up. "There is one place we might try."

Warren looked at him and nodded. "Oh, aye!" he whispered in awe.

The captain looked at him in surprise. "You know of it? Have you been there?"

"Aye," Warren confirmed. "My ship was blown off course back in 1797, and we landed there to make some necessary repairs."

"Two islands, but only one spring with good water?" Albritton asked suspiciously.

Warren grinned and shook his head. "Nay! Two islands, right enough, but *three* springs!"

The captain smiled and nodded. "Aye, you've been there all right! Fetch us a chart, Mr. Warren!" The sailing master left his drink and proceeded on his errand. The two lieutenants looked at each other, dumbfounded.

"Sir?" Chandler said, "May I ask what you and Mr.

Warren are talking about?"

Albritton took a drink. "Have either of you ever heard of the Island of Lost Souls?"

"I have," Mitchell said. "It's supposed to be an uncharted island used by pirates in the last century. Anyone who knew its location was put to death if they chose to leave the group. But I always thought it was a myth, like the *Flying Dutchman* or Davy Jones's Locker."

"Oh, it's real enough, all right,"—the captain paused as the door opened to admit Mr. Warren, chart in hand—"but uncharted, its location a carefully guarded secret by those few who know it. Now, Mr. Warren," he noted a mark on the chart with the tip of his finger, "this is our present position as of the last noon sighting. Do you remember the coordinates of the Island of Lost Souls?"

"Aye, sir."

"Then you will pilot the ship personally," the captain said in a low voice. "Arrange for us to arrive during darkness. Ideally, we can secure a new water supply and be gone before dawn."

The sailing master studied the map. He bent low over it, his eyes going from one end to the other as he considered the captain's instructions. Finally, he stood and nodded. "Aye, it can be done, but 'twill not be easy."

"See to it personally," Albritton said. "We begin at once. Once we have secured the water, we sail for Brazil."

"Aye, sir," Chandler said, and he led the others out.

"Ezekiel!"

The topman looked up from the mess table to find one of the ship's boys standing there.

"Yes? What's your name, boy?"

"Edward. The first lieutenant wants you. He's at the

stem."

"Thank you, Edward." The boy scampered off, leaving Ezekiel to ponder the summons. His face was a blank mask, his lips pressed into a thin, hard line. Reluctantly, he pulled himself from the mess table and went up on deck. He found the first lieutenant sitting against the breach of one of the 18-pounder bow chasers. Ezekiel came to attention and saluted.

"You sent for me, suh?" he asked.

"Yes, I did," Chandler said. "Where have you been?"

"I came as soon as I got the word, suh."

The first lieutenant pushed off the breech to stand almost nose to nose with the seaman. "You stand at attention when you speak to me, boy." Ezekiel came to attention, his eyes staring straight ahead of him into space. "You're not on any British scow anymore," Chandler continued in a low, menacing voice. "This is an American frigate, so we know what that makes you, don't we?"

The premier stepped back, watching for any reaction from this... *person* in front of him; Chandler could never bring himself to call anyone of Ezekiel's stripe a man. He walked around him, watching all the time for the slightest sneer, or glare in the eye, anything that would give him an excuse, but there was nothing. Chandler paused behind him, staring at the back of Ezekiel's head as he thought. Finally, he turned and waved another man forward, then he completed his circuit around his quarry.

"This area is a pigsty," he said. "I want you to clean it up, both sides, from bow to the foremast."

"My watch didn't have the duty today," Ezekiel said.

Chandler shrugged. "Didn't say it did. I'm telling you to clean it. Any questions?"

"No, suh."

"And just to make sure you do a good job," Chandler

indicated a man who'd stepped into view to the right, carrying a rope's end. "This is Mr. Pouncey. He's a bosun's mate, but today he works for me. See, I remember how you people need... supervision. Just think of him as your own personal overseer. Get to work."

Ezekiel saluted and held it until Chandler returned it. The first lieutenant strolled aft, and Ezekiel turned to Pouncey.

"Permission to go below and get some cleaning supplies?"

"Granted," Pouncey said with a grin. "Be back in two minutes."

The tar made his way below and gathered what he could. He was on his way back when he ran into Henry.

"What are you doing, Ezekiel?" the messmate asked.

"I got to clean most of the fo'c'sle deck," came the reply.

"Why? We didn't clean it today in the first place."

"I know, but orders is orders."

"Ezekiel," Henry said in a low voice, "who ordered you to do this?"

"The first lieutenant," Ezekiel replied, keeping his voice low as well. "Now, I've got to go."

Henry nodded and let him go. He went aft. He knew just the man to be alerted about this.

Ezekiel returned to the bow chasers to find Mr. Pouncey checking an imaginary watch in his hand. "Made it with time to spare! Now get to work."

Ezekiel turned and began wiping down the starboard long nine. Soon he felt the impact of the rope's end crashing brutally across his back.

"Faster, you dog!" cried the bosun's mate.

Ezekiel could do nothing but pick up the pace. It took him nearly three hours to complete the work, during which time he had to endure the rope's end three additional times. There was nothing he could do about it; to retaliate or even stand up to the bosun's mate would leave him open to being brought up as a defaulter, which could lead to a flogging. He remembered his grandfather's back, and his father's, with the scars left by the whips used by the overseers. It was a life he thought he'd left behind when he won his freedom and went to sea. Even the British had treated him like any other sailor! But now, when he had a chance to serve his own country, to *fight* for his own country, he was being thrown back into this kind of treatment.

"Finished, suh," he reported at last.

Pouncey looked around and nodded. "Well done," he mocked, then his face grew serious. "Now, get below. Not of word of this, mind, or Mr. Chandler shall hear of it. Understand?"

"I understand." Ezekiel gathered his things and went below, and Pouncey made his way aft, tossing the rope's end over his shoulder and feeling rather pleased with himself. Neither man noticed Xavier leaning quietly against the foremast.

The two Americans drifted into the harbor of the Island of Lost Souls, guided by the light of a full moon, and dropped anchor. Albritton sent Lieutenant Chandler ashore to oversee the refilling of the water casks for both *Columbia* and *Olympus*. Once the boats were on their way ashore with the empty casks, Albritton went to his cabin. He was not entirely surprised to find Xavier awaiting him, but there was something different about the man.

"Sommers!" he called. "Coffee, if you please! Now, Xavier, what's bothering you?"

The coxswain stepped up to the table. "Captain, there's something I think you should know."

Albritton looked up from his coffee. Whenever Xavier had spoken that way in the past, it always turned out to be something important. Albritton had learned to pay attention.

"Yes?"

"Do you remember Henry?" Xavier asked. "Starboard watch mess captain in Mr. Mitchell's division?"

Albritton thought for a moment. "Is he the one who claims to be descended from British royalty?"

"Aye, sir, that's him. Henry came to me with a problem in his mess. One of his men he thought was being treated unfairly."

The captain's brow rose slightly, and he rubbed his temple with his fingertips. "Is this the mess with the Negro in it?"

"Aye, sir."

Albritton sighed. "Go on."

"Well, sir, Henry met Ezekiel heading up to the deck with his arms full of cleaning supplies. When Henry questions him, Ezekiel says the first lieutenant ordered him to clean the fo'c'sle deck, guns and all, from the stem to the foremast."

"Was it his watch that had the duty this morning?"

Xavier shook his head. "Henry says not."

Albritton pursed his lips, and his brows furrowed. "Go on."

"I got there just as Mr. Chandler was going aft. Ezekiel was working at his task, and it looked like he had Pouncey, the bosun's mate, watching to see that he did it right."

The captain's face grew dark. "An overseer."

"That's how I saw it. Pouncey had a rope's end."

The captain raised his eyes. "Did he use it?"

Xavier shrugged. "Three or four times."

"Needed?"

The coxswain shook his head. "Not that I could see."

Albritton closed his eyes and tapped the tabletop with his

index finger. He drained his cup of the lukewarm dregs and set it down again.

"Thank you, Xavier. Keep your eye on the situation, if you please. Report to me as needed."

The coxswain came to attention and left the cabin. Albritton rested his elbow on the table and rubbed his chin between his thumb and forefinger.

Dawn found the Americans at sea, the Island of Lost Souls left in their wakes. Their course was south, using the vast empty regions of the Atlantic Ocean as a hiding ground while they made their way toward the southern hemisphere. The war seemed far away to those on a ship with the whole ocean to themselves, but a cry from the tops reminded them that man was not meant for paradise.

"Deck there!" the lookout shouted below, "sail on the larboard bow!"

"Where away?" Lieutenant Hill, who had the watch, grabbed a glass and went to the rail.

"Southwest!" came the reply. "Maybe a point or two south!"

Hill scanned the area indicated and soon made out the tiny speck of white on the horizon. "My God, Gabriel's got the best eyes on the ship!" he said. He quickly turned to Mr. Lee, one of his midshipmen. "Mr. Lee, my respects to the captain, and let him know we've sighted a strange sail on the horizon."

"Aye, sir!"

Three minutes saw the arrival of Captain Albritton on the deck, followed by Mr. Warren and Mr. Chandler. Hill reported the contact to his captain and handed him a glass.

"Thank you, Mr. Hill," Albritton said as he went to the rail to survey the contact for himself. "Anything more from the lookout?"

"No, sir."

Albritton lowered the glass and thought for a moment before turning to Mr. Chandler. "Intercept course, if you please. Mr. Adams, signal *Olympus* to stay behind us just inside signal range."

"Aye, sir." Chandler picked up a speaking trumpet and began bellowing orders. The men scampered to their positions, and USS *Columbia* turned her bows toward the contact.

"I have the deck!" Albritton called out. "Mr. Hill, I am heading forward to get a better look. Mr. Chandler, Mr. Lee, you're with me. Let's go."

Albritton led the others to the bow. As soon as they got there, he raised his head and his voice. "Lookout! Let's hear you!"

"Still hull down, sir!" came the reply. "Cut of her sails may be that of a large sloop, maybe, or a frigate, sir!"

Albritton lowered his glass. "Mr. Chandler?"

The first lieutenant lowered his glass as well and shook his head. "I can't say, sir. However, I think she's where a British frigate ought to be, on a rough line from St. Helena to the Caribbean."

The captain raised his glass for a moment of study before lowering it again. He found he could not disagree with them. "You may clear for action, Mr. Chandler."

"Aye, sir." Chandler raised his hat and was gone, calling for the crew to clear for action as he went.

"Mr. Lee," Albritton called. "I am going aft. I want you up with the lookout to act as runner. Let me know as soon as he identifies our friend out there."

"Aye, sir." Lee, too, raised his hat and leapt for the shrouds.

Albritton made his way back to the quarterdeck, where he was met by a committee of Lieutenants Chandler and Hill and Mr. Warren.

"Ship cleared for action, sir," Chandler reported.

"Very well," the captain replied. "I left Mr. Lee as runner for the lookout. If our friend out there is a frigate, we shall beat to quarters immediately. As soon as we are in range, my plan is to put the ship hard over twice, first to starboard, then to larboard, and put two broadsides into her bows. With luck, we'll take her foremast, and then we'll just have to wear her down. Mr. Chandler, have the batteries below ready. Run them out when we beat to quarters. Once we turn, fire as you bear. The same goes for when we reverse course. Don't wait for my orders. Instruct your captains that their target is the foremast. Mr. Hill, you are in command of the fo'c'sle carronades, correct?"

"Aye, sir."

"I want them loaded with ball for the first broadside, then afterwards with grape."

"Aye, sir."

"But first, I want you to ready the bow chasers," Albritton said. "Let me know when you think we're in range, and I shall come forward. Hopefully, we can put two balls into her before we turn."

"Aye, sir!"

The captain nodded. "Dismissed, gentlemen."

The two officers stepped back, touched their hats, and departed, leaving the captain alone with the sailing master.

"Mr. Chandler believes it to be a British frigate, travelling the line between St. Helena to the Caribbean."

Warren shrugged. "Could be."

"I am more concerned that we've hit upon a convoy, and there are two or three more warships below the horizon."

"A convoy from St. Helena to Port Royal?" Warren mused. "Reasonable. Even possible. But not probable."

Albritton turned to him. "Why not?"

"Wrong time of year for a big convoy to head into the Caribbean," Warren said. "Hurricanes could begin any week now. They may risk individual ships, but I doubt they'd risk an entire convoy at a shot. Unless they're in trouble somehow, and it has to get through."

Albritton went to the rail and raised his glass for another look at the strange sail. The white dot on the horizon was rapidly growing; he estimated that the lookout should be able to identify the class of ship very soon. Estimating a closing speed of sixteen to eighteen knots, the captain estimated that the 18-pounders at the bow would be within range in two hours at most. Albritton moved to the fantail and began to pace. He had a lot to think about.

Hands behind his back, chin wedded to his breast, seven long strides took him from rail to rail where a smart about-face allowed his return. He needed something to occupy his mind over the next two hours. This was one of the times that he regretted passing on the opportunity he'd had years ago to learn how to play chess. He sighed and knew he had a more pressing need: that of turning his orders into action. The further south he went, and the more he made his presence known by taking or sinking prizes, the more likely the British would be to respond and send a frigate after him, or more than one.

His ultimate prizes were the British whalers in the vicinity of the Galapagos Islands. A single whaler with its hold full of oil would easily be worth $75,000! If the British figured out that these ships were his target, they could easily recall them to a friendly port and deny them to him. Add to this that only one-half of his prizes were likely to make it back to New York or Philadelphia for sale—the rest being sunk by weather or recaptured by the British—and Albritton knew he had to conserve his prize crews for the more valuable prizes.

He knew there were strong British forces at St. Helena as well as the British South American squadron based at Rio de Janeiro. This would force him to stay in the middle of the ocean for the most part if he were to have any hope of arriving at the Galapagos undetected. Complicating matters was his need to "live off the land," meaning he depended to a large extent on the taking of prizes to keep his ship's company fed. *Olympus's* hold would soon be exhausted, at which point he would probably burn the ship and take its prize crew on board.

All this brought his thoughts to the strange sail ahead. Was it alone, or escorting two or three Indiamen, or was it the scout ship for an entire convoy escorted by a squadron of frigates and brigs? In any case, he must be engaged. Perhaps he could be disabled quickly enough to allow *Columbia* time to raid one or two of the Indiamen before the help arrived. If it did turn out to be alone, once it was disabled, Albritton planned to sail north until they were below the horizon before turning east and then south again. There were a few neutral or French ports he could put into on the way for water or provisions, but by doing that there would be no way to keep his voyage a secret.

He reached the weather rail and turned to find Mr. Warren and Mr. Lee waiting for him.

"Yes?" he said.

"Begging your pardon, sir," Lee said. "The lookout sent me to say he believes the sail ahead is a frigate. When I hit the deck, Mr. Hill stopped me. He sends his respects, sir, and begs me to tell you that he believes he can reach the enemy now."

Albritton looked forward for a moment before turning to

his sailing master. "Beat to quarters."

"Aye, sir!" Warren picked up a speaking trumpet and bellowed the three words that sent hands scurrying to their posts for battle. The marine drummer boy began to play, and the marine sharpshooters sent their rifles aloft, six rifles per sharpshooter. US Navy Marine sharpshooters were renowned for their speed of fire, something that had never been matched by their British counterparts. The reason was simple: each sharpshooter had six rifles in the tops with him, along with one loader per rifle. He just handed back an empty rifle and immediately had a loaded one slapped into his hand. It made for a very crowded top, but the resulting rate of fire was well worth it.

"I'm going forward!" Albritton called. "Mr. Lee, you're with me."

"Aye, sir!"

The two officers went forward. When they arrived at the bow, Albritton said, "Mr. Lee, return to the lookout and inform him we are about to fire on the enemy. Have him watch for the fall of the shot."

"Aye, sir."

The midshipman saluted and scampered up the shrouds. The captain turned to Lieutenant Hill. "Are we ready, Lieutenant?"

"Aye, sir. Both guns are loaded and primed."

"Proceed."

Hill saluted and moved behind the larboard bow chaser and sighted down the barrel. Satisfied at the aim, he jumped to the starboard gun and did the same. Afterward, he jumped back to stand beside his captain.

"Fire!" he shouted.

Smoke and flame belched from both guns as their captains yanked on the lanyards. The noise was nearly overwhelming. Both men were blinded by the smoke, so Hill called to the lookout, "Let's hear you!"

"Both balls swept his deck, sir!" the lookout called down. "Right down his throat!"

"Reload and fire, Mr. Hill!" Albritton ordered.

Sixty-five seconds later, *Columbia's* bow chasers erupted again. This time the lookout reported seeing splinters fly.

"Secure the guns, Mr. Hill," Albritton said. "See to your carronades. Larboard first, then starboard. Fire as you bear. I am returning to the quarterdeck."

"Aye, sir."

Albritton made his way aft, ignoring the glances of the hands manning the carronades as he passed by. He was met at the wheel by the sailing master.

"She's turning, Captain!" He pointed forward. Albritton spun to see the British ship reversing her course.

"Hard to starboard, Mr. Warren!" the captain shouted. He only hoped that Chandler was ready with the larboard battery.

The ship came around, and as soon as the broadside was able, the first 24-pounders went off. A few moments later, the carronades followed suit. The guns went off in twos and threes until the broadside was exhausted. The deck was shrouded by smoke.

"Lookout!" Albritton shouted.

"Looks like two hits in the hull, Captain!" came the reply from on high. "Her sticks are all still there, and she's still turning in good order!"

"Reverse your course!" the captain called over his shoulder. He frowned; he'd hoped to disable the enemy ship by now and be on his way north. He drew a deep breath to calm himself and let it out slowly. No matter. He made his way to the starboard rail and raised his glass to his eye. All he could make out from this distance was that the enemy ship was still in good working order. She looked like a 36-gun frigate, likely armed with 18-pounders, nothing that *Columbia* couldn't handle if they were forced to fight it out. Still, he did not like to risk major damage this early in the voyage.

The ship straightened up on her new course, but it was several minutes before the starboard battery could open fire. The enemy's reversal of their course carried them away from their foe, and *Columbia* had to travel to cross her course again. When they did, they were going to rake her at long range.

The starboard fo'c'sle carronades went off first this time—carronades have a wider traverse then the long guns—followed moments later by the main battery and the quarterdeck carronades. Again blinded by the smoke, the captain looked up.

"She's hit, sir!" the lookout shouted down. "Looks like her stern and larboard quarter have exploded! She's wobbling off course, Captain! We may have damaged her rudder!"

"Mr. Williams!" the captain called for the fourth lieutenant, who was in command of the quarterdeck carronades. "Load your larboard guns with chain! Be ready to take out her rigging on my orders! Mr. Smith! Carry the same orders forward to Mr. Hill! Mr. Jackson! My compliments to Mr. Chandler. He is to load the larboard battery with double shot. He is to fire into the enemy hull when he hears the carronades fire."

"Aye, sir!" The two midshipmen saluted and dashed off on their errands.

"Hard to starboard, Mr. Warren. I want to take her down the larboard side."

"Aye, Captain. Pistol shot?" he asked, inquiring as to the range.

Albritton thought for a moment and nodded. "Sounds about right. We shall fire in passing. I don't want to give them a chance for a lucky hit."

"Aye, sir."

The sailing master steadied the ship on a course just east of south in order to recross the British stern and place her on the American's larboard beam. Albritton crossed the deck to the larboard rail for a better look at the damage their broadsides caused, but what the glass revealed was more devastating then he originally thought. The larboard side of the British stern was gone, along with the larboard galleries. He thought it possible that two or even three of the enemy's 18-pounders were disabled in the carnage. He could only make out the most general movement on the British quarterdeck, and he could only imagine the casualties.

The American was approaching his enemy's stern when the British suddenly came around to larboard and opened fire with the forward half of their larboard battery. Carronades loaded with grape over ball bloodied the American deck and damaged her rigging. Two quartermaster's mates screamed and dropped to the deck, blood flowing from the torso of one and the other missing part of his head. Albritton had the wind knocked out of him when he was tackled to the deck from behind. Cries from the wounded could be heard all over the deck. He also felt the ship shudder as 18-pounder shot impacted her hull. Suddenly he was pulled to his feet and heard Xavier's voice as a hand brushed him, checking for injuries.

"Are you alright, Captain?" the coxswain asked. "Are you hit?"

"No, thank you. Why aren't we firing?" He looked around, and saw Lieutenant Williams lying on the deck with a wound in his shoulder, and he remembered that Chandler was waiting to fire until he heard the carronades fire.

"You men!" he yelled to the quarterdeck gun captains. "Fire!"

The captains grabbed their lanyards and pulled. A moment later the fo'c'sle guns and the main battery below fired. Albritton moved to the fantail to view the damage. Again, it was colossal. The British mizzenmast was reduced to a ten-foot-tall stump, the spanker having pulled the mizzen topmast aft on to the quarterdeck. The enemy's deck was littered with dead and wounded, and it looked like several cannon in her larboard battery were disabled.

The captain turned and surveyed his own deck. He went to Mr. Williams and knelt beside his barely-conscious lieutenant.

"Mr. Williams? How bad is it?"

Williams tried to swallow. "I'll be alright, sir, I'm sure," he croaked. Albritton squeezed his hand reassuringly. "You two!" he called to a couple of hands nearby. "Take Mr. Williams below to the surgeon. He stepped aside as they lifted their wounded comrade and took him below. Albritton turned to see Mr. Lee on the quarterdeck. "Mr. Lee! Pass the word for Mr. Chandler to come up on deck, then organize the men to get the wounded below."

"Aye, sir!"

"Mr. Jackson!" he called to the midshipman.

"Sir?"

"Go forward and get me a damage report," the captain ordered. "Find out Mr. Hill's condition."

"Aye, sir!"

Albritton turned to see Mr. Warren struggling to man the wheel alone. Men were just removing the bodies of his dead mates. The captain stepped over and gave him a hand until two more mates arrived to take over.

"Thank 'ee, Captain," Warren said. "I'm afraid the days

are long gone when I could handle that monster by meself!"

Albritton patted his sailing master on the shoulder and turned to see Mr. Chandler arrive and salute. "You sent for me, sir?"

The captain gestured with his head toward the wreck of the British frigate and handed the first lieutenant his glass. "Just thought you might want to see the results of your good work. Give all guns' crews a *'Well Done!'* from me."

"Thank you, sir!" Chandler took the glass and lifted it to his eye. A soft whistle escaped his lips as he surveyed the results of his handiwork. He handed the glass back with a nod of self-satisfaction.

Mr. Jackson returned. "Mr. Hill sends his respects, sir. He hit his head when he was thrown to the deck during the broadside, but he says he's fine now. One of the forward carronades was disabled, along with the larboard 18-pounder. Mr. Hill says they are working to repair them, carronade first."

"Very well. Report to Mr. Lee and assist him with getting the wounded below."

"Aye, sir."

The captain turned to see his first lieutenant looking back at the British frigate. "Will you finish him off?"

Albritton shook his head. "I want to head down his original course to make sure he wasn't escorting an Indiaman, then we turn north."

Chandler turned at that. "North, sir?"

The captain nodded. "Eventually, that ship will be rescued or make port. What direction do you want him to tell his superiors we went?"

"Ah!" Chandler responded with an exaggerated nod. "North it is, sir."

"Mr. Adams!" Albritton called the signals midshipman.

"Signal *Olympus* to make course northeast. We should rendezvous with her in a few hours."

"Aye, sir!"

"Mr. Warren," the captain said, "follow the British frigate's course in case he was escorting an Indiaman. Just before we drop below the horizon, I want to head north. Make sure the British can still see us make the course change."

Warren grinned. "Aye, sir."

Two hours' sail brought them to the horizon. Since there was no sign of any Indiaman, Albritton ordered the course change to the north. Three hours later, they sighted *Olympus*, and the captain ordered all officers plus the sailing master and the purser to gather in his cabin.

"Thank you all for coming," Albritton said when the assembly was seated around the table. Sommers and Xavier handed out wine for all attending before Sommers withdrew and Xavier took up his normal post at the cabin door. "I have called you here for two reasons. First, to express my congratulations for the resounding victory over the British frigate. Please pass on my thanks to all divisions of both watches. This victory belongs to us all and is a direct result of the hard work in training put in by all hands. The second reason is to inform you of our plans for the immediate future. I plan to hold this northern course until well after dark before turning east. Some time around dawn, we shall turn south again. I may adjust that course, depending on where the noon sighting puts us. My hope is that we can meet one or two individual British merchant ships we can plunder and sink to maintain our supplies through the South Atlantic. I want to save my prize crews for the British whaling fleet in the Pacific. The Spanish are still allied with England, so I doubt we can expect a warm welcome at any of their South American ports. I would say that Santiago in

Chile is probably the first neutral port we can expect. Even then, the British will surely be there. At any rate," he continued, "I feel our best chance is to have the element of surprise. The British may be able to determine we are heading south, but they will have no idea of our final destination until word gets back to them that their whaling fleet has been, shall we say, somewhat diminished."

Grins arose around the table. Word had already gone around the ship as to the value of even one of the British whalers full of oil; one or two prizes like that might see even the lowliest tar aboard set for life, and every man around the table would be due many times that amount under the current laws regarding distribution of prize money.

The captain held up his hand to regain control of the meeting. "Now, before we can spend the prize money, we have to take the whalers. I call this session open. If anyone has any ideas that may help us keep the element of surprise, I'm listening."

Sommers came in and refilled the glasses of those who wished it. Albritton noted that Lieutenant Mitchell was the lone abstainer. As Sommers retreated, looks were shared around the table to see who would be the first to speak.

"I agree with your desire for secrecy, sir," Mr. Warren said. "I believe it increases our chances of success the longer we can keep it. However, it all depends on our ability to find and take British merchant ships sailing individually or in small companies, which would allow us to keep out to sea and away from ports, and there is no way to predict that."

"Sir," Mr. Chandler spoke up, "I have the bosun and his mates working at repairing the rigging that was damaged in our battle with the British frigate, but if we were to be badly hit, we would have nowhere to put in for repairs. I seem to recall some intelligence that was delivered shortly before we sailed which said that due to the superiority of our frigates in ship-on-ship duels, the British now had their frigates travelling in pairs whenever possible. There are also reports that they are now building frigates that will carry 24-pounders as their standard armament with 32- or 42-pounder carronades on the quarterdeck and fo'c'sle. I hope I don't sound like a coward, but we must be careful not to allow ourselves to be damaged beyond what we can repair ourselves."

"A good point, Mr. Chandler," the captain commented, "and one that may require me to reverse course and avoid action in order to maintain our surprise. Let me take this opportunity to remind you that if or when that happens, I shall rely upon every man here to help control the crew. Some of them may not understand why we avoided battle or elected not to take a particular Indiaman, especially when he had two or three friends ready to help defend him." He looked around the table. "Anyone else? No? Very well, you are dismissed. I ask you not to discuss this with the crew, or anywhere you may be overheard."

"Aye, sir," Chandler answered for them all. The assembly rose and filed out of the cabin until only Xavier remained. The captain was not entirely surprised to see him stay behind.

"Xavier?" he questioned, motioning his coxswain to a seat. "Something?"

The coxswain nodded. "You said you wanted to be kept informed."

Albritton's eyes snapped upward. "Ezekiel?" Xavier nodded, and his captain sighed and set his glass on the table. "What happened? More of the same?"

"Aye."

"How many times?"

"Three, that I know of." A look from his captain told him to continue. "I haven't seen Mr. Chandler at any of them; it seems to be Pouncey who is the one driving it now. So far, Ezekiel's been able to maintain his control, but I don't know how long he can continue before he cracks."

"Have you spoken to Henry?" the captain asked.

Xavier shook his head. "Not since he first brought it to my attention. But he knows that I'm watching."

Albritton sat back in his chair and sighed heavily as he closed his eyes and massaged the bridge of his nose with his thumb and forefinger. He feared something of this sort would happen ever since Ezekiel had come aboard. *Apparently, Chandler has never been on a ship with Negro hands aboard,* he mused. *Either that, or his captain deliberately allowed him to turn the ship into his own private plantation.* The captain's eyes narrowed and his mouth set in a firm line; he would not allow that to happen on his ship. But what to do about it? He thought for several minutes before settling on a plan.

"When is the next scheduled transfer from *Olympus*?"

"First light tomorrow," Xavier replied.

"Have Pouncey transferred to *Olympus*," Albritton said quietly. "Exchange him with a Yankee, preferably one who is either anti-slavery or at least has no problem with Negroes."

"Aye, sir. And Chandler?"

"He may end up captaining the next prize we send home," Albritton said regretfully. "In the meantime, I'll have to talk to him. Ask the sentry to pass the word."

"Aye, sir. I'll do it on me way out." His captain nodded his agreement, and the coxswain left.

Albritton had barely begun to formulate what he would say before the first lieutenant arrived. "You wanted to see me, sir?"

"Yes, Mr. Chandler. Please sit down." He paused while Sommers brought two fresh glasses of wine and removed the captain's old one. "Forgive me for being blunt, but some matters require it. I want to speak to you about the hand named Ezekiel."

Chandler blinked in surprise but recovered quickly. "Sir?"

"I understand you have been giving him extra duty. In fact, you have been treating him in a manner very close to that of a slave on a plantation."

"Sir, I must protest! I hardly exchanged a word with the man!"

"So I've heard. I also heard at least one of those words was 'boy.'"

"Captain!" Chandler exclaimed. "I may have called him on deck one time for extra duty, but I turned him over to a bosun's mate and never –"

"Oh, yes," Albritton waved the argument away, "I know all about Mr. Pouncey and his shall we say liberal use of a rope's end. I also know that where Ezekiel is concerned, Pouncey works for you." Chandler stared at his captain through hooded eyes but said nothing. Albritton leaned forward. "Have you nothing to say for yourself?"

"What would be the point?" Chandler said. "You've quite made up your mind. You appear to prefer one of them to one of your own kind."

Albritton sat back and looked at his first lieutenant. He rubbed his chin for a moment before reaching for his glass and draining it in a single draught. "Mr. Chandler, that was just about the worst thing you could have said. An attitude like yours can spread as a cancer amongst a crew, especially when it concerns a good sailor like Ezekiel. I cannot allow such attitudes to fester, so I will put this to you bluntly, sir, so there will be no misunderstandings between you and me. Either you decide that you will treat Ezekiel fairly as a member of the crew of this ship, or I shall have to make other arrangements. And Mr. Chandler, if I ever hear that Ezekiel was wrongfully or unfairly singled out again, no matter who does it, I'm coming to you. Do we understand each other?"

"Aye, sir." The first lieutenant's face was a blank mask.

"As of now, nobody knows about this but us," Albritton said. "I highly suggest it stay that way. Dismissed."

"Aye, sir." Chandler rose, came to attention, and left the cabin. Albritton stared at the door and wondered if he had just lost an officer.

CHAPTER ELEVEN

Days passed without so much as a glimmer of another ship. It seemed as though USS *Columbia* and her crew had the entire ocean to themselves. Captain Albritton spent much of his time on deck. He thought it important that his crew see him standing watch just like the rest of them. He was careful to make periodic appearances during every watch and was pleased when word filtered back to him that the men were encouraged by his presence.

Xavier or Henry kept Ezekiel discreetly under observation, and the coxswain reported to his captain that the topman had seemingly been left alone since Albritton's meeting with the first lieutenant. Pouncey had been transferred to *Olympus*, and his place had been taken by Whitmore, a New Yorker who'd grown up on the shores of Lake Champlain. Xavier told his captain that although Whitmore had no particular love for the Negroes, neither did he have aught against them; all he cared about was that the man could do his job. That was fine with Albritton.

What wasn't fine was the apparent change that had come over Lieutenant Chandler. The captain couldn't quite put his finger on what was going on, but something was up. Chandler did his job—his captain could find no fault in that regard—but the man's whole demeanor, or perhaps his personality itself, had changed. Chandler was withdrawn, almost to the point of silence when not on duty. He no longer associated with any of his companions in the gun room and even took his meals in his cabin. He was not moping; indeed, the few interactions Albritton had had with him on deck made him think that the man was turning his fury inward somehow. Still, every behavior of Chandler's that Albritton observed was correct and proper in every detail, including the first lieutenant's gentle correction of Mr. Lee's gross mistake with his sextant. The boy had been next to tears from the cruel ridicule of his fellow midshipmen, but Mr. Chandler put a stop to that and repeated his instructions until Lee finally got it right. The first lieutenant congratulated the junior midshipman not only on arriving at the right answer, but also on his persistence in not giving up until he had achieved his goal. The pat on the shoulder he received gave the boy a smile that told of his renewed confidence.

The captain was sitting in his chair in his day cabin that evening, nursing a glass of bourbon and wondering how he could get past Chandler's defenses and get him to talk about it. He was afraid that the first lieutenant would eventually snap under the strain, and if that happened, the consequences would be dire indeed. Yet even as he took a drink of the amber liquid, the captain knew that he could never be the man to get inside. Chandler had already identified him as the enemy of his private little war. Xavier would also be in that camp. Albritton downed the remainder of his drink and rose to get ready for bed, hoping someone would come forward who could help.

Lieutenant Mitchell went below after being relieved. He had just completed the middle watch and wanted nothing more than a good breakfast and four hours of uninterrupted sleep. He stepped into the gun room to find Mr. Chandler seated at the far end of the table with a steaming cup of coffee and a book.

"Good morning, Michael," he said.

"Good morning, Jonas," came the reply.

Mitchell sat and called to Boothby for breakfast and coffee. He leaned back in the chair and rubbed his face with both hands, trying to will himself to stay awake long enough to eat. "Looks like it's going to be a fine day," he commented. "Maybe we'll find a merchantman today!" When his attempt at conversation got no reply, he shrugged and leaned to one side as Boothby brought his breakfast and coffee. "Thank you, good sir! Blessings on your stove and coffee pot!" He picked up his spoon and dug in.

Chandler closed his book with a bang and rose to go to his cabin.

Mitchell spoke, as he would later say, without thinking.

"What is the matter with you, sir?" he lashed out sternly. "For weeks now, you have been a different man, especially when you are off duty. What is ailing you? Please, Michael, let me help you."

"You can't," Chandler said softly. "You can't possibly understand, because you weren't brought up like I was. You're like the captain."

"How's that?"

"Where did you say you were raised?"

"Pennsylvania. Why?"

Chandler shrugged with a there-you-go gesture. "A Yankee. Just like the captain."

Mitchell suddenly remembered the conversation he'd had with Chandler in this room, when he'd come in and found him with Ezekiel. "Yankee? Michael, does this have to do with Ezekiel?"

Chandler's head snapped back. "Who said anything about Ezekiel?"

"You did," Mitchell said, trying hard to keep his voice level and calm. "You mentioned I was a Yankee, like the captain, meaning I wasn't born in the South and so don't know about Negroes like someone of your birth and breeding."

Chandler looked down at his book for a second to compose himself. "Jonas, I really don't believe this is any of your business," he said in a low voice. "Please stay out of it."

"I can't do that, Michael. You are too important to just let go. Too important to me, too important to this ship." He pushed out the chair next to him. "Please, sit."

"Me? Important to this ship?" Chandler's voice dripped with disbelief. "You need to take that up with the captain, my friend. He's already made it quite clear where I fall in the order of things."

"Michael!" Mitchell said firmly. The first lieutenant's eyes snapped to him. Mitchell indicated the chair. "Sit. Please."

Chandler's eyes dropped to his book again, and he shook his head in a *what's-the-use?* sort of gesture. But he sat.

The next night, when the first lieutenant had the watch, Captain Albritton was disturbed in his cabin by an unexpected knock at the door. Xavier went to answer it and then appeared in the day cabin doorway.

"Pardon me, Captain," he said formally, "but do you have time to see Lieutenant Mitchell?"

The captain looked up from his desk and the log he was updating. "Of course," he said as he set the quill down and rose. "Send him in. Ask Sommers to bring him a glass."

Lieutenant Mitchell stepped in and came to attention. "Thank you for seeing me, sir."

"My pleasure, Lieutenant." The captain turned to take the glass from Sommers' tray and handed it to his guest. "Please, sit down and tell me what brings you here."

"Thank you, sir." The lieutenant sat. Albritton thought he looked distinctly uncomfortable. Mitchell took a drink and set the glass down. He leaned forward with his elbows on his knees and staring at the hands clasped in front of him. "I pray you'll not think me out of line, sir, but I am very concerned about Mr. Chandler, and I didn't know who else to come to."

"I see," Albritton replied softly. He rested his chin in thumb and forefinger and studied his guest for a moment. He thought Mitchell concerned and sensed nothing ulterior in his motives—at least, not yet. "Go on."

Mitchell drew a deep breath. "Permission to speak freely, sir?"

Albritton's eyes narrowed slightly. "Granted."

Mitchell let out the deep breath and sat back so he could look his captain in the eye. "Sir, it's about Mr. Chandler and Ezekiel. It's common knowledge you spoke to the first lieutenant about him."

"And how is that?" Albritton demanded.

"It's not hard to figure out, sir. Everyone saw what Ezekiel was being made to do around the ship, first by Mr. Chandler and afterwards by Pouncey. Then you have a meeting with Mr. Chandler, Pouncey gets transferred to *Olympus*, and suddenly Ezekiel is left alone. Add to that the change in Mr. Chandler's behavior when he's off duty, and it all points to Ezekiel."

The captain looked at the tabletop and considered for a moment. "Very well. Go on."

"Well, sir, I had a talk with Mr. Chandler last night in the gun room. No one else was about, sir. He mentioned me being a Yankee like you, sir; that's when I figured out that Ezekiel was what was troubling him. I got him to sit and talk to me."

"One moment," Albritton said. "Were the two of you alone the whole time?"

"So far as I know, Captain."

"Nobody passed the doorway?"

"I couldn't say, sir. My back was to the door."

Albritton nodded. "And where was Boothby?"

"I don't know, sir. In his pantry, I suppose. To tell the truth, I never thought about him."

"Very well. Continue."

"I think Mr. Chandler's in a bad way, Captain. He is having a very hard time in seeing Ezekiel as anything other than a slave who should be on a plantation."

"But he was freed, wasn't he?"

"Says so, sir, but he claims the British took his papers when he was pressed."

Albritton tapped the table top with his finger. "So, no proof."

"None, sir." Mitchell leaned forward. "Captain, Ezekiel is an able seaman and a topman. I had thought of making him captain of the foretop, but I didn't want to propose that to Mr. Chandler." A pause to search for words. "I have watched him, Captain, and I've spoken to others, such as the bosun and the quartermaster, and those men unanimously attest to Ezekiel's skill in the yards. The only thing Mr. Chandler can have against him is the color of his skin." Mitchell spread his hands, and his voice went up a notch. "What's going to happen if we find more Negroes who've been impressed and want to come back to an American ship?" He stopped, embarrassed at his lack of control. "My apologies if I've overstepped, sir."

The captain smiled and shook his head. "Understandable, Lieutenant. No, you did right in bringing this to my attention. Tell me this: do you think Mr. Chandler can overcome his upbringing?"

"Regarding the Negro question, sir?" The question was met with a raised eyebrow. "I don't know, Captain. That would be asking a lot, perhaps too much. I can't say for sure, sir."

Albritton pursed his lips as he thought. He stood and said, "Thank you for bringing this to my attention, Mr. Mitchell. Keep trying to be a friend to him, as you have opportunity. Don't force anything, but hopefully he may open up to you eventually if he thinks you are a sympathetic ear. Keep me informed as you see the need."

Mitchell heard the unexpressed dismissal and came to attention. "Thank you, Captain."

USS *Columbia* made her way south, careful to stay away from anything that smacked of a warship or convoy. Her patience was rewarded when they took a small brig, HMS *Zephyr*, loaded with foodstuffs and fruit from the Caribbean, bound for St. Helena. The crew of ten men filled the prisoner accommodations on *Olympus* to the breaking point. *Zephyr* was unloaded and set on fire so as to preserve available prize crews.

Captain Albritton saw the ship get under way before returning to his cabin to update his ship's log. He had not been there an hour when a knock on the door heralded a visit by the first lieutenant.

"Pardon the interruption, sir," Chandler said, "but I thought this should be brought to your attention. I've been searching through the papers we took from the master's cabin on the *Zephyr*, and I came across this." He handed his captain a report.

Albritton sat down at the table to scan the paper. He motioned Chandler into a chair and called for Sommers to bring refreshments. The paper was a report from a Captain

Sir Thomas Knighton to the Commanding Admiral, British West Indies Squadron, and it detailed the capture by Knighton's frigate, HMS *London*, of the American sloop-of-war *Argus* in the Caribbean. Knighton stated that the sloop's captain had been killed in the action, but he had interviewed the ship's first lieutenant, Mr. Wilson, who had been wounded but survived. Wilson claimed not to know the whereabouts or plans of Captain Albritton or USS *Columbia*, stating that the ship's captain had always dealt with Albritton personally. The reported ended with the notation that the ship and crew would be left at Jamaica.

Albritton let the report fall to table as he closed his eyes and rubbed the bridge of his nose. "So," he said softly, "at least now we know. I pray Calloway found the peace in death that he never found in life."

Chandler held out another paper. "This appears to be a cover letter, sir."

He handed Albritton a letter from the commanding admiral to the royal governors of St. Helena and the Falkland Islands, warning them that an American frigate, USS *Columbia*, under the command of Captain Hezekiah Albritton, was thought to be entering the South Atlantic Ocean and might appear in their respective areas for the purpose of plundering British merchant shipping. The admiral said he was sending a frigate and some support ships south, and he urged the governors to alert all naval forces in their areas.

Albritton stared at the page through slitted eyes before letting it fall to the table. He closed his eyes and let his hand close into a tightly clenched fist for a moment, only to open his eyes again and expel a held breath. The hand lay limp on the table.

"Captain?" Chandler said.

The captain looked to him. "Sorry. Just thought about

Calloway—what a waste." He shook his head and took a deep breath. "Well. To the future." He tapped the cover letter on the table. "This changes things, I think."

Chadler frowned. "How's that, sir?"

Albritton sat forward. "Calloway did his job well. The British figured out what we were doing and correctly deduced where we are going. Make that 'were going.'"

"*Were* going?"

Albritton nodded. "The British think we are heading south and that they've cleared the Caribbean. They're wrong."

Chandler looked interested. "They are?"

"Aye." The captain smiled. "Mr. Chandler, please go on deck and set a new course. I want to be off the eastern coast of Martinique." He tapped the table again as he thought. "Better make it a roundabout course. Try to approach the island without passing any British possessions."

Chandler grinned from ear to ear as he rose. "Aye, Captain."

USS *Columbia* sailed just to the east of north on her roundabout journey to the island of Martinique. On the second evening, a knock came at the captain's cabin door. The sentry opened the door for the sailing master to enter.

"Yes, Mr. Warren?" Albritton asked, then he noticed the look on the man's face. "What's wrong?"

Warren shook his head slowly in a manner that evoked deep concern. "Captain, I think we're in for trouble."

"How so?"

"It's just a feeling, you understand," Warren stammered, "but, well, I think we're in for a hurricane."

"What? Why?"

The sailing master shrugged and shook his head again.

"I'm not sure, but I'm sure—if you know what I mean. I've been through two or three, and the feeling I got on deck just now, the way the air is behaving... I think we're in for it, possibly as soon as tomorrow."

"Clouds?"

Warren nodded. "I did notice a slight darkening on the horizon just south of west."

"And it is the right time of year." Albritton's eyes darted back and forth as he search his mind and memory. Finally he nodded. "Well, better safe than sorry. Very well, Mr. Warren, let's get ready; there's not a moment to lose."

CHAPTER TWELVE

A hurricane was hazardous during the best of times; at worst, the gales could dismast the best ship, and the waves had been known to toss a ship about like a cork. Albritton, determined to minimize the damage to his ship, erred on the side of caution in his preparations. He sent down the royal masts and had all rigging not absolutely necessary unreeved and taken below. He had every heavy article in the tops sent below as well as the lighter sails such as the royals, stay-sails, and stuns'ls. He also ordered all the shot to be put below, leaving only five rounds per gun available. All guns were moved from the ends of the ship to midships and secured. The main rigging was set up, and the storm-stay-sails were bent.

The storm hit at full force just before dawn the next morning. HMS *Columbia*, for all her bulk and solid walls, was tossed about like a child's toy and forced to run before the wind. The crew buttoned up the ship as best they could against water rushing in, but the captain was still forced to order the pumps into action before the first day was out. The hands were changed at the pumps every two hours, and then every hour, but they were barely holding their own to keep the ship afloat.

The men themselves bore the worst of the punishment, as they were thrown about like a little girl's rag doll. Some of the men tied themselves into their hammocks to avoid being tossed and flying across the deck. Two men died in their hammocks; they were on the end, with their heads closest to the bulkheads when a sudden violent wave tossed the ship and caused a timber to crash into their bunks, breaking their necks. The sick bay was soon overflowing with men who had broken arms or legs from being thrown about during the storm, so much so that the doctor was forced to order those who were less injured back to their hammocks to rest.

The crisis point arrived on the evening of the second day, when a wall of water crashed down and poured into the ship through hatchways that had been opened to allow fresh air into the hull, knocking a pump out of action and tossing men over cannon and mess tables. The flood of water started a panic among even the experienced crewmen. It was stemmed by a bosun's mate known only as "Bo," who after being washed from his mess table and slammed against a bulkhead by the water pouring into the ship, stood and screamed at the men to keep their heads.

"What are you doing?" he called to the panicked seamen. "Remember your training, damn your eyes! You men, check the pumps! Get them back into action! You three! Get up on deck and get those hatches closed! Jonesy! Take those men with you and search the decks for injured who need to be taken to the sick bay! Move, you sluggards! Act like Navy men, not some women on a pleasure cruise!" The mate's stern words did the trick, reminding the men of who they were and what they had trained for. Henry rallied the men around him into action.

Up on the deck, the wave took everyone by surprise. Lieutenant Chandler had the watch, but he had no time to react as the wall of water crashed over the fantail and larboard quarter rail, throwing everything in its path forward. Chandler was swept off his feet and washed forward. He struck something with his chest—possibly a carronade. The sharp pain told him he had probably broken a rib, but he was unable to grab hold of anything. The wave swept him forward, and Chandler began to panic when he tried to gasp for breath and inhaled seawater. Suddenly a hand grabbed his arm, and his eyes went white with pain. He tried to scream but only inhaled more water and began coughing violently. Another hand grabbed the back of his collar and pulled him between two carronades to keep him from being swept overboard. Chandler was beginning to black out when the water was suddenly gone. Someone flipped him over so he was now on his hands and knees, and began pounding him on the back to try to get the water out of his lungs. He coughed up great gobs of water before he was finally able to draw fresh air into his lungs. Stars filled his eyes as he fought to take breaths in the midst of coughing fits.

"Easy, sir," a voice came to him. "You're okay. Breathe easy. That's it, sir. Breathe. Can you hear me, sir? Breathe easy."

Gradually, the coughing subsided and Chandler's eyes began to clear. He rolled over so he was sitting on the deck with his back against the carronade's gun carriage. The change in position set off another coughing fit, and he felt a pair of strong hands hold his head till the fit subsided. His head pounded as he laid it back against the gun carriage. Finally, he opened his eyes to see Ezekiel squatting before him.

"You okay now, Lieutenant?" he asked.

On the second morning after the storm abated, land was sighted, and *Columbia* and her consort limped into the deserted island's bay for some much-needed repairs. Mr. Jones, the bosun, set to work immediately with his mates and a party of volunteers to set the top masts and rigging taken down before the storm to rights. The first lieutenant took parties ashore to see to the replenishment of the water supply for both ships, while Lieutenant Hill was sent ashore with a party to search for fruits or vegetables in the forests.

"Pass the word for Lieutenant Monroe," Albritton called. The marine lieutenant soon appeared and saluted.

"You sent for me, Captain?"

"Yes, Lieutenant." Albritton pointed to a hill at the entrance to the bay. "I want you to take one or two lookouts and set up a post to watch for approaching ships. That hill seems as likely a spot as any, but if you find a better spot, by all means use it."

"Aye, sir. Red rocket to signal a sighting?"

The captain thought for a moment before shaking his head. "No, that might alert anyone you sight that we're here. I will have a glass on your position at all times. Signal with a mirror or something as effective." Albritton noticed the lieutenant didn't leave. "Is there something else?"

"Actually, there is, sir," Monroe said. "My men spotted wild boar roaming not far from the beach. Request permission to send some of my sharpshooters ashore to get the men some fresh meat."

Albritton was surprised by the request, and involuntarily made a quick survey of the coastline but saw nothing. He turned back to Monroe. "Your men could do this without wasting ammunition?"

The lieutenant gave him a look of mixed shock and disappointment. "Sir," he said quietly, "I have some men from Kentucky who were give their first rifles while still in their cribs. I guarantee it will not take more than one ball to bring down one of the beasties."

The captain had the sense to appear suitably chastised. "Ah, I should have known. My apologies to your men, Lieutenant, and tell them I look forward to tasting the results of their skill. Just make sure you bring back enough for everyone."

Monroe smiled and saluted. "Aye, sir!"

The day passed in a spirit of pleasant expectation. It was good weather for the work that needed to be done; some men even sang as they went about their tasks. Word quickly spread through both ships of Lieutenant Monroe's proposal to the captain, and the nearly constant reports of the marine rifles going off ashore filled everyone with the expectation of savory meat to come! The expectation turned to excitement when the word spread that Monroe had sent a request and been granted permission to roast the meat on spits over a bonfire on the beach before sending it back to the ships! Fires soon dotted the shore and the wind was just right to blow the aroma of roasting pork back to the ships. Lieutenant Monroe was true to his promise: enough pork was sent back to the ships to satisfy one and all, including—with Captain Albritton's express permission—the British prisoners on *Olympus*.

It took three days for the work to be completed, but USS *Columbia* and *Olympus* were finally able to sail with the morning tide. The captain set a course of northwest, with *Olympus* stationed to their south. He called a meeting for all officers in his cabin.

As was his custom, the captain held the meeting in his day cabin to keep the atmosphere less formal. He sat in his chair and looked around the room. Mr. Chandler was the last to arrive, having seen to the deck before coming below.

"Thank you all for coming," Albritton said as he opened the meeting. "I called you together to let you know the next step in our voyage. But first, I want to congratulate you on the repairs done to both ships. Please pass my thanks to every division of both watches."

"Aye, sir," Mr. Chandler said, answering for them all.

"Good. Now on to business. As my dear old granny once said, '*Now the fun begins!*' By now you should all be aware of the reports received stating that *Argus* was taken by a British frigate in the Caribbean and that Commander Calloway was killed in the action. What you may not be aware of is a captured British report stating their belief that we are heading south for raiding purposes, possibly to the River Plate or even to the Pacific Ocean. From what the report said, the British are concentrating their efforts in those areas to bring us to battle." Albritton paused to allow the news to sink in, then he smiled. "As you may also know, this was indeed our intention. However, since the British expect us to do so, I think it only right that we do our best to disappoint them. We are heading north for the Caribbean, Martinique in particular. I intend to go ashore at night and try to gather any intelligence on British warships and merchant shipping in the area and then be away before dawn. With luck, we shall have a month, maybe two, before the British realize what we've done and turn their forces around."

He paused again to allow the information to sink in. Heads nodded softly, and the faces around the table showed a general approval of his plans, except for a frown on Lieutenant Mitchell's face.

"Mr. Mitchell?" the captain asked. "You have something to add? Fear not; I call these sessions open for opinions."

"Sorry, sir," Mitchell said, "but a thought occurred. Do we have any information on what happened to *Argus*? Her crew?"

"Let me see," Albritton looked to the deck beams above as he searched his memory. "I believe the report said that the captain had been killed in the action, but the first lieutenant had survived but was wounded. Am I correct, Mr. Chandler?"

The first lieutenant nodded. "I believe so, sir."

"Yes. It also said that the survivors and the ship were

taken to Jamaica." Albritton sighed. "At least we know that Mr. Wilson survived, and that there were others."

Mitchell nodded. "Thank you, sir."

Albritton allowed them time to digest the information. Many had friends aboard *Argus* and would be concerned for their welfare. His eyes fell on the first lieutenant. He'd noticed something different about Chandler since their experience of the hurricane, but he hadn't had a chance to ask him about it. There was a look about him; something... It frustrated the captain that he couldn't put his finger on it. He made a mental note to invite the first lieutenant to his cabin soon, and also to instruct Sommers to be free with the bourbon.

Chandler entered the gunroom to find Mitchell sitting at the table, writing a letter, a steaming mug at his elbow. The second lieutenant looked up at his entrance.

"Ah," he said as he set down the quill, "how are you doing, Michael?"

"What? Oh, fine, Jonas, fine." Chandler sat down and asked Boothby for a cup of coffee and something to eat. After the servant departed on his errand, Chandler stared at the tabletop. Intrigued, Mitchell pushed his letter aside.

"Are you okay, Michael?" he asked quietly.

The first lieutenant's eyes flashed to the second's, but his face remained an unreadable mix of emotions. Chandler grunted. "Don't suppose there's any use in lying to you, is there, Jonas? No, I'm not alright."

"What happened?" Mitchell moved to the seat next to him so they could speak privately.

"The storm," Chandler whispered. "The hurricane. I nearly died. Wave came over the stern and swept me down the deck. Someone grabbed me and pulled me over against a carronade, or I'd have surely gone over the side." His eyes darted back and forth. "I understand battle. I choose to get involved, and I can do much to keep myself safe. But at that moment, I was completely helpless, being swept overboard by forces I could not combat or control. It was absolutely terrifying."

"My God," Mitchell said. "Thank God someone was there to save you! Do you know who it was?" Chandler's eyes met his, a look of utter disbelief and misery, and Mitchell knew at once who the first lieutenant's savior was. "Ezekiel."

Chandler nodded and looked away as Boothby arrived with his dinner. He nodded his thanks, not trusting himself to speak at the moment. Mitchell sat back and watched as the first lieutenant picked up his spoon in silence and attacked the bowl of stew before him.

The two men had talked enough during the voyage for Mitchell to know that the worst place for a man like Chandler to find himself was to be in debt to a black man. Mitchell imagined that, had this happened at home on the plantation, the Negro would simply have been sold in order to remove the stigma, but such a thing was not possible here. Chandler would be reminded nearly every day when he saw his savior walking the deck, going about his business. Mitchell knew Ezekiel well enough to know the man would never try to take advantage of his deed to gain favor, as some on the lower decks would. Ezekiel was simply better than that. Mitchell shook his head. Too bad Chandler did not realize that.

Mitchell sat back and sighed. "So," he asked plainly, "what will you do?"

Chandler nearly dropped his spoon as he looked up at his friend, the look on his face was like Mitchell had asked the proverbial stupid question. The first lieutenant opened his mouth to say something, but he closed it again and shook his head before staring at his stew.

"I have no idea," he whispered. He raised his head and

took a drink of his coffee. He set the cup down and sat back with the air of someone needing to bare his soul. Mitchell saw this and sat back to listen.

"I am at war with myself, Jonas," he said. His eyes shifted from the table to Mitchell to the deck beams and back again. "It's my upbringing. We were taught that when a man saves your life, that's a debt that can never fully be paid, other than by saving his in return. On the other hand, were I at home, Ezekiel being who he is would completely release me from that oath."

"You're a long way from home, Michael," Mitchell pointed out.

Chandler tapped the tabletop. "Ah! You've come straight to the heart of the problem, Jonas, old son. I may as well be on the moon for all the good my upbringing is doing me. Everything I learned in life, my place in the world—and Ezekiel's!—has been tossed overboard by the actions of this one Negro." He shook his head and laughed. "Do you know—it occurred to me—that, one week ago, had you questioned me about what happened on deck during that storm, I am almost positive I would have told you that I should push his hand away, had I seen it coming! That I would rather die than be indebted to one of his kind." He flinched and frowned. "Somehow that sounds a lot more... *wrong* than it used to. You and the captain see absolutely no difference between me and him in terms of being a man, a human being. I was taught from the crib that Ezekiel and his kind were one step above cattle. I believed it, Jonas! I lived it! I treated them exactly that way! Now what do I do?"

Mitchell sat with his arms crossed over his chest and said nothing. He was careful to keep on his face a look of sympathetic neutrality as he waited to see which side would win the battle for control of the first lieutenant's soul. Chandler picked up his spoon and pushed his stew around the bowl, only occasionally helping himself to a spoonful. Mitchell took a drink of his coffee and waited for events to develop on their own.

Finally, Chandler pushed his bowl away and sat back. Mitchell raised an eyebrow but said nothing. The first lieutenant scratched his head and sighed loudly. "Nothing makes sense anymore," he said. "I don't even know who I am now."

"Oh, posh!" Mitchell exclaimed. "What rot, as our British cousins would say. Of course you know who you are. You just don't know if you *like* who you are."

Chandler frowned. "What do you mean?"

"Come on, Michael," Mitchell said. He waved his hand back and forth in the air, dismissing Chandler's claims of ignorance. "Part of you is arguing that Ezekiel deserves to be treated as a man, not as an animal while another part of you is resisting that idea. Actually, fighting a life-and-death struggle would be a better way to put it. More accurate, too. And what weapons does it have, Michael? Only one—the color of his skin. Your entire argument is that this is a black man, so that condemns him to inferiority. What else can there be? You can't have any argument or complaint about his work on this ship. I'm his divisional officer, so I know firsthand the quality of his work. You can't doubt his intellect. The man took it upon himself to learn to read and write. Most important, you can't assail his character. He saved the life of a man who treated him like he was one step higher than dirt, when all he had to do was *nothing* and rid himself of all the evil in his life. That leaves one thing—*the color of his skin*. Pardon me for saying so, but that's a damned narrow reason for trying to keep a man down." Without another word, Mitchell got up and went to his cabin, leaving the first lieutenant staring after him.

USS *Columbia* arrived off the island of Martinique an hour or so after sunset. Albritton ordered the lights out as they began their run to the island. The ship hove to about five hundred yards from the island's eastern shore.

"What's the plan, sir?" Chandler asked in a hushed voice.

"Xavier will go ashore in the skiff," the captain replied.

"Xavier?" Chandler was confused by the captain's choice.

Albritton nodded. "We've done this before, Mr. Chandler. Xavier was born on the island and speaks French like a Frenchman. He knows who can be trusted to approach for information. He also knows to be back in time for us to be well away before dawn."

"I see, sir."

The two men watched as Xavier came up on deck, disguised as a local fisherman. The coxswain came to attention and saluted, and the two officers returned the gesture. Xavier nodded to his captain, then disappeared over the side. The skiff was quickly swallowed up by the dark and moonless night. Albritton stood there for several minutes with his hands clasped behind his back.

"Who has the watch?"

"Mr. Mitchell has the first watch," Chandler said. "Mr. Hill has the middle."

"I'm going below. See that I'm called when Xavier returns."

"Aye, Captain."

Albritton went below, hoping what he had told the first lieutenant was still true. The British had occupied the island since 1809, so he and Xavier had no way of knowing which of their contacts on the island were still free and willing to help them. He entered his cabin without a word, dropped his hat and coat on the table and went to his chair. He leaned his head back and took a long, slow breath, hoping it would ease the tension he felt taking hold of the back of his neck. He became aware that he was not alone and opened his eyes to see Sommers standing beside him with a glass of dark liquid on a tray. Albritton thanked his servant as he took the glass and sipped its contents, pleased to taste the bourbon as it slid down his throat. *How well he has gotten to know me,* the captain thought. He looked up to see Sommers standing at the door.

"I have a pot of coffee brewing, Captain," he said. "Whenever you're ready."

Albritton smiled as his servant retreated. He felt the tension subside as he nursed the bourbon and tried hard not to borrow trouble by worrying about things beyond his control. Less than two hours before sunrise, a knock came at his door. The sentry admitted Lieutenant Hill.

"Begging your pardon, Captain," Hill said as he came to attention, "but the lookout reports the skiff is returning."

"Very well, Mr. Hill." The captain rose from his chair and stretched. "Please have Xavier report to me when he comes aboard. Instruct Mr. Warren to set sail due east at the earliest possible moment."

"Aye, sir."

Albritton stepped to the dining table to stretch his legs, and he saw Sommers step to the pantry door. It was obvious he, too, had not been to his hammock.

"You, too?" Albritton asked.

Sommers shrugged. "You may have needed something if you awoke, sir."

"Ah," the captain acknowledged with an exaggerated nod. "Well, Xavier is on his way down. Coffee, if you please."

"Aye, Captain."

Soon, a knock at the door signaled Xavier's arrival. When the coxswain entered the cabin, Albritton could see at once that the man was exhausted. He led him into the day cabin and put him in a seat before taking his own. Sommers arrived with coffee; Xavier seemed revived by the steaming brew.

"Are you alright?" the captain asked.

"Aye, sir," came the reply between drinks. "You're not going to like what I have to say."

Albritton sat back in his chair and sighed heavily. "All right, let's have it."

Xavier set his cup down and leaned forward with his elbows on his knees. He counted off points on his fingers. "First, Henri and Pasquale have disappeared. Henri's daughter said she came home from the fields one evening as the sun was setting and found him gone. She thinks the British have him in the prison, but the governor won't admit it. He says the disappearance is 'under investigation.' Same goes for Pasquale. Seems most of our friends have been rounded up since the war began." The second finger went up. "Nobody who would talk to me could tell me anything about British forces or intentions. Apparently, the British are discouraging folks from going to town or anywhere else they may get a good look at the harbor and what's in it." The third finger went up. "I decided to see for myself, so I climbed a hill west of Pasquale's house where I could get a good look at the harbor. There was fair moonlight, and none of the ships was dark. I counted three heavy ships, frigates, or maybe a 74 along with maybe five sloops or brigs." He looked up. "Do you think they may be after us? I mean, will they be sent south where the British think we're going? If not, that's a lot of their so-called diminished strength in one harbor."

Albritton pursed his lips as he considered Xavier's report. That *was* a lot of firepower for one harbor, especially when the West Indies Squadron was supposed to be under-strength. Would the British send a 74 after him? The heavier firepower made sense; the 74 would carry 32-pounders on her lower deck. Put together with a frigate to prevent him from simply running away, the two of them could do serious damage to *Columbia*.

He felt the ship get under way and come around to the east. He needed to hide in the vast, empty Atlantic for a while so he could think. He also wanted to allow events to unfold before making his move to enter the Caribbean. *Hopefully, the squadron built around that 74 will move to the South Atlantic, or even the Pacific, to look for us,* he thought. *If not, we'll just have to cross that bridge when we come to it.*

He rose, and Xavier followed suit. "Thank you, Xavier. Leave me now, I need to think. Get some rest. No, I mean it... To bed with you, sir! We'll talk again tonight."

Xavier surrendered, glad in truth to have the opportunity to sleep. "Aye, Captain. Good night, sir."

After his coxswain left, Albritton began to pace. Something was not right, but he had no idea what. The hair on the back of his neck was standing up, and something in the back of his mind was screaming at him in a still, small voice to beware of a British trap.

In his cabin on HMS *London*, Captain Sir Thomas Knighton ate his breakfast alone. Ever since arriving at Martinique three days ago, he and his ship had been held captive by Commodore Ezra Morgenthau on board the 74-gun HMS *Goliath*. The commodore had tried to hijack his ship to join his new South Atlantic squadron like he was a press-gang on a Devonshire street. He sent over a copy of the letter from Admiral Keats, and it seemed now the commodore was trying very hard to justify retaining Knighton and *London* for his proposed journey south to track down USS *Columbia*. Knighton was not convinced that Albritton would go south now, let alone try to enter the

Pacific. It just didn't *feel* right.

It was *Argus* that did it to him. He was sure Albritton had sent the sloop into the Caribbean to draw the Royal Navy's attention and so allow *Columbia* to make her way southward unmolested. But now, with the sloop destroyed and her crew prisoners, might not the American captain change his plans and stay north? Could the information found on the sloop have been planted for the British to find? If that was true, it might mean that Albritton was planning to help himself to British commerce in the Caribbean after they sent their best warships south looking for him!

Knighton pushed his plate away and leaned back in his chair. How was he to convince the good Commodore Morgenthau of this? The commodore believed the intelligence that said Albritton was heading south, possibly crossing to the Pacific with an eye on British whalers. Knighton had no time to appeal to Admiral Kellering, who was commanding the West Indies Squadron in Jamaica. No, if he could not get the commodore to honor his letter from Admiral Keats, then he might very well be forced to commit an overt act of insubordination.

He rose and began to pace. His frustration was growing when a knock came at his cabin door.

"Enter!" he roared.

The sentry opened the door, and a timid midshipman shuffled in. Thankfully, he remembered his training and came to attention.

"Well?" Knighton said.

"Mr. Wells' respects, Captain, and there's a signal from *Goliath*. Our number. It reads, *'Captain come on board.'*"

Knighton took a deep breath to regain his control. "My compliments to Mr. Wells. I shall come up directly. Have the gig ready."

"Aye, sir!" The lad came to attention again and scurried

out of the room as fast as propriety would allow.

Knighton donned his best uniform and came up on deck. The trip to *Goliath* was swift over the calm harbor waters, and he was met by the ship's captain, Jeremiah Steele. The two exchanged salutes, and Knighton accepted the other's hand.

"Welcome aboard, Sir Thomas," Steele said. "The commodore is in his cabin. If you'll follow me?"

Steele led the way aft and into the 74's great cabin. Although it was not his first visit, Knighton could not get over how the room resembled one of those mansions on the northern outskirts of Southampton more than a commodore's cabin on a ship of war.

The two officers found the commodore in his day cabin. He was staring out the stern windows, hands behind his back. Morgenthau was a small man. He still wore the powdered wigs of the previous century to hide his increasingly bald scalp. The wig left him with a high forehead, which did nothing to give an impression of either intelligence or competence. His close-set eyes with heavy lids gave him a looking of perpetual sleepiness. Steele cleared his throat and said, "Captain Knighton, sir." Then he nodded to his companion and left the room.

Knighton thought this an odd behavior as he watched the captain leave, but he turned to study the commodore's back and wait for the man to take notice of him. Out of nowhere, the commodore's high, squeaky voice filled the cabin.

"Do you still think Albritton is not heading south?"

"Yes, sir, I do."

The commodore's head dropped, and Knighton heard him sigh. Morgenthau turned slowly and looked up at his guest from across the room. His gaze seemed to communicate total indifference, but Knighton knew otherwise.

"I think you foolish, Captain," the commodore said. "You are after personal glory rather than what is best for the Royal Navy."

And you're not? Knighton thought. Wisely, he said nothing.

Morgenthau shuffled over to his desk. He picked up a letter and looked at it for a moment before handing it over to his guest. Knighton saw it was the copy of the Keats letter he had provided.

The commodore turned back to the window. "Unfortunately, I cannot argue with Admiral Keats. HMS *London* is released. You may sail at your convenience."

Knighton folded the letter and put it in his pocket. Even though the commodore had his back to him, the captain came to attention. "Thank you, sir," he said, and he left the cabin.

USS *Columbia* had traveled east for three days on unusually calm seas under blue skies, when Captain Albritton decided it was time for another council of war. He stood at the head of the dining table in his quarters waiting for Sommers and his mates to finish doling out the refreshments. Before him were Lieutenants Chandler, Mitchell, and Hill (Mr. Williams had the deck), Mr. Warren, and Lieutenant Monroe of the marines. Xavier stood over against the wall.

"Thank you all for coming," the captain said as he opened the meeting. "I want to take this opportunity to keep you up to date on what my plans are for the remainder of our voyage. You have all heard by now what Xavier saw in the harbor at Martinique. We have no way of knowing where those ships are bound. I hope they will be heading south, but we cannot be sure. We cannot risk another landing on Martinique. The British have the island locked down. I still intend to make a pass through the Caribbean. If our intelligence is correct, we should be able to take several prizes and then lead them north to an American port."

"Sir?" It was Lieutenant Hill who raised the question.

"Go ahead, Mr. Hill. This session is for open opinions."

"Well, sir," Hill hesitated, "it's just that, in light of what happened to *Argus*, can we still trust that intelligence?"

"A good question, Lieutenant," Albritton said, "and one that I alone must bear the responsibility of determining the answer. There is no way to know for sure. The intelligence could be false, or at least outdated, or *Argus* might have been unlucky enough to blunder into the lone remaining frigate left in the Caribbean. I will still try my luck."

"Aye, sir." Hill looked less than convinced.

Albritton moved on swiftly. "I propose to make a pass through the Caribbean. We will double back and enter the Caribbean north of Martinique and turn south. Those ships should be gone by the time we return. After our cruise in the Caribbean, we shall hide in the Bahamas until it's safe to make for an American port with our prizes. Comments? Questions?"

"What about *Olympia*?" Mitchell asked.

The captain sat back in his chair and steepled his fingers in front of him. "I've been giving that a good bit of thought, and I don't see any reason to take them in with us. I propose taking what supplies we can from her, leaving her enough to get back to an American port, and allowing her to proceed home independently with all the prisoners and any injured the doctor wishes to send home. Comments?"

Albritton watched as heads swiveled around the table, wondering if any of them would bring up the content of the prize crew to sail her home. Finally, Chandler spoke up.

"Agreed, sir," he said.

Mitchell raised his hand. "What about her prize crew, Captain? Who's going to take her home?"

"Are you volunteering, Lieutenant?" Albritton asked with a grin.

"Not me, sir," Mitchell quickly backtracked. "I've never been to the Caribbean, and I'm looking forward to it."

Quiet laughter rippled around the table.

"Recommendations?" Albritton asked.

"For the prize crew?" Warren asked. "Is Mr. Hill too young? What about Franklin?"

"We may need Mr. Hill before all is said and done," the captain reminded them. "I'm fine with Franklin, especially if we give him a seasoned petty officer as first lieutenant. Any suggestions?" He looked around the table.

"Jenkins for the petty officer," Warren said.

"Agreed," Mitchell added. "He's in my division. He knows what he's doing."

"Very well." The captain sat back in his chair. "Mr. Warren, appoint one of the quartermaster's mates to act as sailing master. Lieutenant Monroe, detail six marines to accompany them. Mr. Chandler, bring Mr. Franklin to my cabin after we're adjourned. Any other questions? Good. Mr. Chandler, I want to set sail in the morning."

"Understood, Captain."

"Dismissed." Albritton rose, and the rest followed suit and began to funnel out of the cabin.

In the gunroom, Chandler called for Mitchell. "Jonas, did you mean what you said about wanting to make Ezekiel captain of the foretop?"

"Yes," came the reply. "Why do you ask?"

"Well, I've been thinking it over," Chandler said, "with my eyes closed, if you know what I mean."

Mitchell nodded. "I do."

"Good. Then you have my approval to go ahead. I'll make the notation in the muster book and inform the captain."

"Thank you, Michael." Mitchell hesitated, but then pressed on. "I hope I'm not overstepping, but I have to ask. Is this because of what he did? I mean, are you trying to repay the debt?"

Chandler looked at him for a moment before lowering his eyes. "Jonas, I can't fault you for asking, and I'll admit privately to you that I have wrestled with it in my mind for the past few days. To answer your question, No. I'm approving it because he's earned it by his performance."

Mitchell smiled and squeezed his friend's shoulder. "Good for you, Michael."

Chandler shook his head. "I've got a lot to work out in my mind yet, Jonas, but I will admit that I've been forced to see things differently than I have in the past. I mean, Ezekiel and I will probably never be friends, but I can't stand in his way without good reason." Chandler caught the other's eye. "And skin color alone isn't a good reason."

Mitchell nodded his approval and went his way. Chandler watched him go and was surprised to find that he felt rather pleased with himself.

Mr. Franklin was brought in and briefed on his new command, and hands were set to work transferring supplies to *Columbia* so all would be ready by first light. When the watch came on duty for the middle watch, Ezekiel and his messmates staggered wearily below and made ready to get some sleep.

"Say, Ezekiel," Two-toes said, "I heard you were made captain of the foretop. Is that true?"

"It is! The lieutenant gave me the word when we came on duty!" he answered.

The big Indian slapped him on the back and said,

"Congratulations! You deserve it!"

"I'm not so sure," Ezekiel said as he shook his head. "I'm just not sure."

Henry looked up from his seat. "You know all promotions like that have to be approved by the first lieutenant, don't you?" Ezekiel nodded. "Well," Henry continued, "that's a good thing for you, right?"

Ezekiel shrugged. "Maybe. What you don't know is I saved the first lieutenant from going overboard during the hurricane."

The other two just stared at him, and Henry let out a low whistle.

"So you think this is just payback?" Two-toes asked quietly. Ezekiel shrugged again and shook his head. "Maybe he'll think differently now," the Indian added hopefully.

"You know, it doesn't matter," Henry said. "Whether he approved it because Ezekiel saved his life or because what Ezekiel did made him change his way of thinking, either way Ezekiel is now captain of the foretop. As the saying goes, *Don't look a gift horse in the mouth!* This is a good thing."

The others could only nod their agreement.

The sun was barely above the horizon when Captain Albritton, Lieutenant Chandler, and Sailing Master Warren stood on the quarterdeck and watched *Olympia* sail off to the northwest. The captain turned his back on the departing vessel and sighed.

"Very well, Mr. Warren," he said, "let's get under way. Course due west. I want to pass north of Martinique at night; calculate your speed accordingly."

"Aye, Captain." The sailing master went off to work on his chart. The captain turned to his first lieutenant.

"Mr. Chandler, shall we go below? Mr. Williams has the

deck."

The two officers went below and sat down at the dining table in the captain's cabin. Mr. Chandler handed over the muster book and explained the changes he'd made after detailing the prize crew for *Olympia*. Albritton interrupted him and pointed to an entry near the bottom of the page.

"What's this? We have a new captain of the foretop?"

"Aye, sir," Chandler said. "I was about to inform you. Lieutenant Mitchell recommended him for the position, and I approved."

Albritton tapped the page with his finger. "Forgive me for saying this, but I'm surprised you would approve putting Ezekiel in that position."

Chandler said nothing at first, but he saw that the captain was waiting for an explanation. "I admit to seeing things a little differently than before, sir. I'm still working through a lot of things in my mind, but I do believe that Ezekiel has earned the position. Mr. Mitchell recommended him very highly. I've also spoken to Mr. Hill and Mr. Williams, as well as Mr. Franklin before he left, and they also testified to the man's ability and skill."

"I see." Albritton slid the book back over to the first lieutenant and allowed him to finish his report. Chandler closed the book and said, "Will there be anything else, sir?"

"No, Mr. Chandler, I think that covers it for now."

The first lieutenant came to attention and left the room.

Albritton stared at the closed cabin door for several minutes before calling to Sommers for a bourbon. The captain took his glass and went to sit in his favorite chair before taking a long, slow drink and wondering if things were beginning to look up.

CHAPTER THIRTEEN

Captain Albritton rose just after dawn and went on deck while Sommers made his breakfast. He noticed Mr. Warren standing by the wheel, holding his chart in his hand and frowning. It was the sailing master's worried glance skyward that drew the captain's gaze upward, and he immediately saw the cause of Warren's concern. *Columbia's* sails were not drawing very well at all. The captain stepped over to the logbook and saw that the ship had averaged about three knots during her overnight passage.

"Good morning, Captain," the sailing master said.

"Good morning, Mr. Warren. I take it you're not happy with the winds?"

Warren frowned and handed the chart to the captain. "We're miles behind where I estimated we'd be by this time. The wind's vanished, sir. At this rate, we'll be lucky to pass north of Martinique tonight with enough of a margin to be safely out of sight of the island by daybreak. You may want to consider waiting another day to make the passage."

Albritton looked at the chart, tracing his ship's course with his finger. "We're about here, you think?" He pointed to a spot east of the island.

"Approximately, sir," Warren confirmed. "I'll know more when I can take the noon sighting."

The captain took a last look at the chart before handing it

back. He crossed his arms over his chest and looked again at their sails, which were lagging for lack of a strong wind; his lips pressed into a firm line. Finally, he shook his head and turned to his sailing master. "You and the first lieutenant come to my cabin for dinner," he said, "as soon as you've figured our position. We'll discuss our options then."

"Thank you, Captain," Warren said. He saluted and went off to speak to the bosun.

Albritton took a moment to look at the cloud of lazy canvas floating over his ship and wished for the hundredth time that he could control the winds. He lowered his head and pursed his lips in self-recrimination. Then, clasping his hands behind his back, he went for a walk on his deck.

On the deck of HMS *London*, still in the harbor at Martinique, Captain Sir Thomas Knighton was also taking a tour, casually inspecting the deck along with his first lieutenant. "I still cannot believe it," Knighton fumed. "We've been stuck here for nearly a week, first by problems with our provisioning and fresh water and then by the wind seeming to take a bloody holiday!" He clamped his jaw shut and shook his head while he tried to regain his control. "Well, at least the good commodore is still here as well," he ventured. He glanced at the 74 across the harbor and the brig beside it and shook his head. "Who knows how far away Albritton is by now..."

Percival tried to calm his captain. "That's behind us now, sir. We have all we need, and we've been cleared to sail at first light. God is in control, Captain—we'll get him."

Knighton glanced in his direction from the corner of his eye. "I had no idea you were religious, Roland."

The first lieutenant shrugged. "When things are outside my control, sir, I turn to someone who can handle it."

The captain nodded in reluctant agreement. Tomorrow

would see them at sea again, and Albritton had to be out there somewhere.

One bell of the afternoon watch had come and gone before Albritton's guests arrived. The captain was seated at his desk, writing a letter to his friend President Adams. He put down his quill, replaced the cap in the inkwell and rose to greet Warren and Chandler. He motioned them to sit in the day cabin with him.

"My apologies for being late, Captain," the sailing master said, "but I wanted to recheck my calculations before presenting them to you." He held out his chart for the captain to see and pointed to a spot slightly northeast of Martinique. "I place us about here, sir, nearly fifty miles northeast of Martinique. The first lieutenant has checked my work."

Albritton's eyes met Chandler's. The first lieutenant nodded.

Warren continued, "My calculations are built on the assumption that the wind will stay consistent with what we have seen for the past 36 hours. If we leave now under all plain sail, we *might* make it south of the harbor by dawn tomorrow, but I cannot say for sure. If we lose the wind even a little bit, we'll be making the southern turn in daylight."

Albritton sat back in his chair and rubbed his chin with his hand. Sommers appeared at the doorway and said that dinner was served, so the three men rose and made their way to the dining table. Sommers had already brought out the meal, modest by his usual standards but definitely a "square meal" nonetheless. A platter of Atlantic cod in a butter sauce held the place of honor before the captain, followed by bowls of potatoes, peas, and rice to act as a bed for the fish. The men sat and began helping themselves to the fare before them.

"You know," Albritton said as he addressed his fish, "our current situation reminds me of rumors I heard when I passed through New York on the way to Washington to accept this command. I wish now I had had the time to stop and investigate, but I was under orders to report without delay. What I heard was that the inventor Robert Fulton was at work on a ship for the Navy."

"Fulton?" Chandler asked.

"He's quite the inventor," Warren explained. "He built a steam-powered ship called the *North River Steamboat* in 1807, which ran passengers from New York to Albany and back in 62 hours."

Chandler's eyes went wide at the news. "Astounding! How far is that?"

"Round trip?" Albritton thought for a moment. "Over 300 miles."

"Incredible!" Chandler sat back as his mind whirled. "One way, that's 150 miles in 30 hours, more or less, even in a dead calm!" He shook his head. "It's hard to believe."

"Not only that," the captain added. "I read somewhere that he tried to interest Napoleon in a submarine boat, but Bonaparte turned him down."

Chandler stared, wide-eyed. "Pardon me, Captain, but did I hear you correctly? A *submarine* boat? As in under the water?"

Albritton nodded.

"And Bonaparte turned him down? For God's sake, why?"

The captain smiled. "I believe he considered it suicidal."

The first lieutenant sat dumbly in his chair, the look on his face announcing to all present his opinion of the stupidity of the Corsican's judgment.

"Anyway," the captain continued as he helped himself to another potato, "the rumor in New York was that Fulton was working on a steam warship for the Navy to protect New York harbor from the Royal Navy."

"A steam-powered warship?" Warren asked.

Albritton shrugged. "Apparently. That is his area of expertise."

"Did you see it?" Chandler asked.

The captain shook his head. "As I said, I wish I had had the time to look into it, but I had to leave immediately." He paused to point at the first lieutenant with his fork. "Put that on our list of things to do when we get back. And I wish to admonish you both not to talk about this."

"Oh, aye, sir," Chandler said.

The conversation strayed to other areas as they slowly emptied the platter and bowls before them. When the meal was over, the captain rose and led them back to the day cabin for cigars and Madeira.

"Regarding our present situation," Albritton said, "I feel we must press on and risk the wind. To stay in this area another day would be to invite detection, and to disappear into the Atlantic and return would be to expose ourselves to a worse timetable than we are up against now. Opinions?"

The first lieutenant and the sailing master shared a concerned look before Chandler spoke up. "Captain, we agree with your decision, but I wish there was another option. If Mr. Warren is correct and the winds stay as bad as they have been lately, we may well find ourselves sailing down the western shore of Martinique in broad daylight."

Albritton looked at the sailing master, who nodded his agreement.

"Thank you, Mr. Chandler," he said. "I don't like it either, but I believe to stay would be potentially worse. We are in agreement, then. Mr. Warren, please return to the deck and set course for the Martinique Passage. All plain sail. We'll just have to pray the good Lord lends his breath to the winds."

"Aye, Captain." Warren drained his glass and rose. He came to attention and marched from the cabin. Albritton turned to his premier.

"Post extra lookouts, Michael," he said, "even at night. I want the ship dark after the sun goes down. Silence on deck should be the order of the night."

"Aye, Captain."

"Dismissed."

When he was alone, Albritton puffed his cigar thoughtfully and asked Sommers for a refill. He was not sanguine about running the passage at night under an uncertain wind, but he felt they had no choice. Better to risk being sighted inside the Caribbean than outside the island ring and have to fight their way in. He took a deep drag on his cigar and blew a large cloud of smoke toward the deck above. He leaned his head back and closed his eyes, praying that the 74 Xavier had reported was gone from the harbor at Fort Royal. He smiled at the thought of the place, officially the capitol of Martinique, although the nearby town of Saint-Pierre was the one known as the "Paris of the Caribbean"—or at least it had been, before the British came.

"Sommers," he called, "I'm going to bed. See that I'm called for the middle watch."

"Aye, sir."

Albritton took off his boots and set them against the bulkhead of his sleeping cabin. He climbed into his cot and lay there, staring at the deck beams above his head. He tried to clear his mind and allow the gentle sway of the ship to rock him to sleep, but nothing seemed to work. Eventually, exhaustion won out and his eyes drifted shut, his last thought being how much he missed Shiloh.

He awoke with a start to find Sommers at his side, his hand on his captain's arm. "Middle watch, Captain," he said.

Albritton rolled out of his cot and stood there for a moment, trying to will himself awake. He watched dumbly as Sommers turned and picked up something from on his sea chest, and was very grateful when it turned out to be a cup of coffee. He held the steaming mug in his hands and used the pain in his palms to help revive himself. The scalding liquid gave him the energy to put his boots on along with a clean shirt. He walked to the dining table and drained the dregs from the cup. He leaned on the back of the chair and shook his head—he felt as though he'd only just closed his eyes! He stood up and stretched his back and shoulders. He sighed, picked up his hat, and went up on deck.

When he got there, he found the first lieutenant standing near the wheel, talking with the sailing master. The two men saluted as he approached.

"Report?" the captain said.

"The winds have not been kind," the premier said ruefully. "We are still at least ten miles from the passage. I ordered the studs'ls set an hour ago, but they have not had any appreciable impact on our speed."

Mr. Warren spoke up. "At this rate, we will pass down the west side of the island in broad daylight." He paused for a glance at Chandler. "Captain, do you want to reverse course and hope for better winds tomorrow night?"

Albritton looked from one man's eyes to the other's, then up to the sails above them, half-filled and lazy. He pursed his lips as he studied the deck for a moment.

"Give me a minute," he said, and he turned to step over to the rail. *What to do? Do I stay or go? Who knows if the winds will be any kinder tomorrow?* He shook his head in frustration. None of this was new; he had considered these points the night before. Had anything changed since then? He shook his head. *So, proceed as planned.*

He went back to the wheel. "Proceed as planned."

The sailing master smiled and nodded. He went to the quartermaster's mates manning the wheel and began giving them detailed instructions for approaching the Martinique Passage. The first lieutenant simply stood there, his hands behind his back, his look of resignation barely visible on the moonlit deck.

"Mr. Chandler?" Albritton said quietly. "Have you thought of something else?"

"Sir? Oh, no, sir. It's just that, this takes some getting used to." He saw the captain's questioning look and continued. "It's still a bit new to me, sir. I've never had to make a decision like this and then be forced to wait to see if I was right."

Albritton nodded knowingly. "I see. I remember when it was new to me as well. You'd be surprised—there are some who cannot do it. They second-guess themselves and change their minds, and so their end is worse than their beginning." He shook his head—a dismissive sort of gesture—and looked to his first lieutenant. "What would you do, Mr. Chandler? If the decision was yours, I mean. Would you turn around and hope for better winds?"

The premier's eyes rose and then he took his turn studying their sails while he considered. When he looked back to his captain he replied, "I don't know, sir."

But Albritton shook his head. "Not an option, Mr. Chandler. You are the captain, and you have to make the decision. What's it going to be?"

Chandler looked out over the silent waters passing by and bounced on his toes as he wrestled to come to a decision. A quick look at the deck preceded his return to look his captain in the eye.

"Go, sir," he said firmly. "Better to march than tiptoe. Always assuming you don't think it to be a trap."

There was a grim smile on the captain's face as he looked

down the deck. He nodded. "I agree with you, Mr. Chandler. Now we have to pay for the meal."

"Sir?"

"We wait." The captain went forward and disappeared into the darkness, leaving the first lieutenant to wonder how he would ever learn to emulate such calm. After a few minutes, Captain Albritton reappeared and stepped up to his premier. "I have found," he said, "there are two ways to best deal with the waiting. One is to stay busy. The other is to sleep." He looked around the quarterdeck. "Who is the officer of the watch?"

"Mr. Mitchell, sir. He asked me to watch the deck while he stepped below for a moment."

Albritton nodded. "I am going below. See that I am called if necessary. As for you," he turned and nodded toward Mr. Mitchell who was stepping up on to the deck, "you have a decision to make. I shall see you at the turn of the watch."

"Aye, Captain." Albritton bade him a good night and went below. Chandler watched him go below. Mr. Mitchell approached him.

"Sir? Is everything all right?"

The premier smiled. "Yes, everything is fine. I'm going below. The captain said to call him if he is needed. Call me as well. Goodnight."

"Goodnight, sir."

The ship's bell rang eight times, signaling the end of the middle watch and the start of morning watch, as Captain Albritton stepped from the companionway stairs. The dawn was yet to come, and he was hopeful that somehow they might still be able to slip into the Caribbean unobserved.

Mr. Warren was standing by the wheel, studying his chart by the light of the lamp held by a quartermaster's mate.

"Good morning, Captain." Warren touched his hat as his captain approached.

"Good morning," Albritton replied. "Any idea where we are?"

"I looked at the log book," the sailing master said. "Over the last six hours, the log registered speeds of three or four knots. Based on that, I think we are about here." He pointed to a spot just to the north of the island. "We are about to enter the passage."

Albritton frowned; he had hoped to be at least ten miles west of here by this time. Still, there was nothing to do but go on. "Hold your course, Mr. Warren. Take us through at our best speed."

The sailing master's face took on a resigned look. "Aye, sir."

The captain turned to see the first lieutenant emerging from the companionway stairs.

"Good morning, Captain," Chandler said as he touched his hat.

"Good morning, Mr. Chandler," Albritton replied. "I hope you passed a pleasant night?"

The premier smiled. "Slept like a baby, sir." He saw a grin creep into the corner of the captain's mouth. "What's the situation?"

The grin disappeared. "The winds have not been kind, I'm afraid. We are only now entering the passage."

Chandler frowned. He looked out over the dark waters while he considered their options. "I take it we're pressing on?" The captain nodded. "In that case, sir, may I suggest that, once we have navigated the passage and are in the Caribbean, that rather than turn south, we continue on our course and disappear into its interior?"

Albritton eyed the cloud of sails above them, only dimly

lit in the predawn moonlight. There was some wisdom in the premier's words; he had to admit it, even if he wasn't particularly happy with the idea. It went against the strategy he had worked out in his mind over the past couple of days. Still, Chandler had proven his competence several times over since they'd left Washington.

"An interesting plan, Mr. Chandler," the captain said. "I shall keep it in mind."

"Aye, Captain."

Silence descended on the quarterdeck as USS *Columbia* made her way westward through the Martinique Passage. The tension increased palpably as the sun arose behind them, removing the cloak that had protected them all through the night. They kept to the northern third of the passage, careful to have a hand manning the lead to make sure they didn't run aground. The idea was to keep as much water as possible between them and the Martinique coastline.

Albritton's decision to use the Martinique Passage to enter the Caribbean meant a journey of more than fifteen miles, made longer than it had to be by their northerly course. At their current speed, that meant a passage of four to five hours through increasing daylight within sight of land. The American was taking a big chance on disappearing to the west before the British could react to their presence.

Standing on his quarterdeck, Captain Albritton was lost in thought. It was a trick he'd taught himself early in his career. He allowed his mind to wander until it fixed on something—preferably something unrelated to the current crisis—and he focused on that until events forced his return to the present. Just now his mind had settled on rumors he had heard passing through New York regarding the steam-powered warship Fulton was building to protect the city from the British. How he wished that he had been able to take the time to see this marvel! From what he had heard, the ship would not be built on a traditional hull like a sloop or a frigate; instead, it would be more like a small mobile fort with guns on all four sides. The steam engine was connected to a paddle wheel to drive the ship. Both were located in the center of the ship for protection against enemy fire. The engine was supposed to produce sufficient power to propel the craft at a maximum of five knots' speed. The most amazing thing he heard was that the captain would be able to reverse the engine to move the ship in the opposite direction without the need to turn around! Rudders positioned under the ship fore and aft of the paddle wheel would allow for maneuverability no matter which way the ship was going. Albritton shook his head in wonder and raised his head to survey *Columbia's* sails. Fulton's craft would not have such a cloud above it, as it was designed solely for harbor defense. He understood it to have only one mast for the lookout and signals, with perhaps a single yardarm and sail for emergencies. He closed his eyes and sighed, wondering if all this were really possible or simply a rumor put out for the benefit of British spies. Then he looked around his own ship and considered all the improvements she contained, from hull design to improved armament to increased protection, and a smile crept into the corner of his lips. Perhaps it was possible after all.

He became aware that he was not alone, and he turned to see Lieutenant Mitchell standing three feet away. "Yes, Lieutenant?"

Mitchell took a step forward. "We are entering the Caribbean, sir. You said you wanted to be told."

Albritton pulled his watch from his pocket, surprised at how quickly the time had passed. He followed Mitchell back to the wheel, where the sailing master and quartermaster stood, heads bowed in conversation over Mr. Warren's chart.

The two men came to attention and touched their hats as he approached.

"Gentlemen," Albritton greeted them. "How's our speed?"

Warren grimaced. "Not so good, Captain. We've averaged only about three or four knots through the passage."

The captain frowned; he was hoping for something better, but no matter. "The question now is, do we follow our original plan and turn south, or should we adopt the first lieutenant's suggestion and continue ahead to disappear into the Caribbean? And where is Mr. Chandler?"

"I relieved him at the turn of the watch, Captain," Mitchell said. "I believe he went below to catch up on some sleep."

"Good for him. Mr. Warren, any words of wisdom?"

The sailing master shook his head. "I'm afraid not, Captain. As far as I can tell, the wind will be the same either way we go."

"Very well. Give me a moment." Albritton turned his back on them and retreated to the fantail. He paced along the railing there, his chin on his breast and hands clasped behind his back. Twice, he halted to stare at the ship's wake, crossing his arms across his chest while he pondered something, then it was back to pacing. Finally, they saw him halt and look out over the stern one last time. His shoulders rose and fell with a deep breath, and he returned to the wheel.

"We go south."

CHAPTER FOURTEEN

Captain Sir Thomas Knighton stood in the center of the quarterdeck of HMS *London* and tried to contain his frustration. Even leaving this cursed harbor was turning out to be a chore—the winds were still not cooperating. HMS *London* had to make its way slowly to the open sea by kedging. Knighton grunted, his only consolation being that the commodore had to endure the same slow exit for the huge 74 *Goliath*. He resisted the temptation to go to the fantail and watch the crew struggle to turn the big battleship around and inch her toward the harbor entrance.

Knighton walked forward to the bow chasers. He raised his glass to his eye and watched the exertions of his boat's crew as they strove to tow their ship into the wind. His chest swelled with pride as he saw man after man straining on the oars against the frigate's weight. He could almost hear the coxswain as he urged the men onward to the point where they could drop their anchor. After that, it would be up to their shipmates on the capstans to haul the ship to the anchor and then pull the anchor back to the surface for the boat to take forward again. He lowered his glass and made a mental note to make sure the crew were rewarded for their efforts—always assuming they made it out of the harbor in a decent time.

The captain turned and made his way slowly aft, pausing to speak to the men detailed to the capstan and encourage them in their efforts. When he arrived on the quarterdeck, he found the first lieutenant waiting for him.

"Captain," the first lieutenant saluted. "At this rate, I estimate two or three hours before we're free of the harbor."

Knighton nodded. "That is my estimate as well. It will be worth it to be free of this place." He looked at the sails above lying useless but at the ready. "I wonder how great a head start Albritton has on us now?"

Percival shrugged. "Who's to say? Reports from the American sloop say he was heading for the South Atlantic, possibly even the Pacific Ocean to hunt our whalers. However, let me remind you that Captain Albritton has a reputation for being... *independent*, shall we say? He may not go there at all."

"Then how do you propose to find him?" Knighton asked somewhat testily.

Percival looked to the deck for a moment. He understood his captain's frustration and hoped it would pass. He looked forward down the deck as he said, "Honestly, sir, I would go north and wait for him outside Washington or Boston. Let him come to us. It may take longer, but it has a more certain outcome than waiting for chance to bring us together."

The captain followed his premier's gaze forward as he stood with his hands clasped behind his back, grinding his teeth in frustration. He had to admit, Mr. Percival's plan did have a lot to recommend it, but Knighton was not willing to play a passive waiting game. His whole being cried out for action. He had to be at sea, trying everything in his power to track down his quarry and bring him to battle.

He looked out over the larboard railing and was pleased to see they were passing the fort at the harbor's entrance. He saw an unknown soldier wave to them from the battlement; for a moment, he considered waving back before reminding himself that such things were beneath a captain's dignity. He looked up at the sails overhead and was rewarded with a slight movement as they caught the first whisps of the sea breeze that had abandoned the harbor. The sound of running feet drew his eyes back to the deck in time to see a young midshipman come rushing up to him and skid to a halt not three feet from him. The man came to attention as best he could and saluted.

"What's the meaning of this?" Knighton demanded of the young gentleman. "What gives you the right to come running across my quarterdeck, sir?"

"Begging the captain's pardon," the youth stuttered in the face of the captain's hostility. "Mr. Ferris sends his respects and begs that you come forward at once. He thinks there's an American frigate on the horizon heading south."

Captain Albritton stood by the larboard rail with his glass, observing—or trying to observe—the sea to their east, toward Martinique. Due to the peculiarities of the rising sun in the Caribbean, he found his view to the east blinded by the early morning glare. Albritton lowered his telescope and frowned. His eyes were shaded from the glare by his hat, if only just barely so. He disliked the idea of trusting to luck that they had sailed far enough into the Caribbean that they could pass out of sight of the island before turning south, but for the moment he had no way of verifying that assumption. He looked aft and saw Mr. Warren standing a short distance away, a frown on his face, shading his eyes with his hand as he tried to see the island through the glare. *He doesn't like it either,* Albritton thought. A small comfort, in its way.

He stepped away from the rail and stood there, hands behind his back and looking at the cloud of sail above his head. Their speed had not picked up as he'd hoped it would. At this rate, they would be lucky to find any merchant shipping at all, let alone cause enough damage and confusion to force the British to divert some ships from their blockade of the American coast to search for his ship.

Mr. Warren joined him; he, too, was observing the sorry state of their tophamper. He sighed and looked to the west.

"How long?" Albritton asked.

"Until we can see? An hour, maybe a little more." Warren shrugged. "Reflection off the water is what blinds us."

Albritton nodded. His eyes went skyward again. The faster they got out of here, the better. "Studs'ls?"

Warren shook his head. "Won't help. We need more wind, not more sails."

Captain Knighton stood at HMS *London's* waist and struggled to contain his frustration at the speed—or lack thereof—with which the boats were being brought back aboard ship. Objectively, he knew his crew was proceeding as quickly and efficiently as possible, which was why he suffered in silence. He went to the fantail and raised his glass to check on *Goliath* and the rest; he smiled when he saw the trouble the crew was having in getting the great ship moving.

He felt the deck under his feet begin to move, and he turned to observe the sails take in the wind. His brows furrowed when he saw how little they actually bent, but even so their speed would be better than what the boats could provide. Knighton went to the starboard rail and raised his glass to study the speck of white moving right to left across his horizon. He was confident that two things would work in his favor: first, the same wind that was slowing *London* would work against that ship as well, and, two, he thought he had the angle to get in front of the speck and cut her off.

"Mr. Jeffers!" Knighton called. A midshipman appeared and saluted. "Make to *Goliath*, '*Strange sail in sight. Am investigating.*'"

"Aye, sir."

He stepped over to the wheel to speak to the sailing master. "Mr. Morgan, make our course southwest. I want to get in front of that ship out there."

"Aye, Captain!"

"*Goliath* acknowledges, Captain!" Jeffers called.

"Very well!" Knighton nodded to himself; his duty was done. Now he went again to the starboard rail to watch as the gap closed. He raised his glass to his eye and watched as the speck slowly grew larger. Periodically he raised his eyes to the tophamper to assess its condition before returning to his glass. Much to his dismay, it was soon clear to him that he was going to lose this race; HMS *London* did not have the speed or the angle to cut off her quarry. He lowered his glass with a scowl, snapped the telescope closed, and tossed it to a midshipman as he stormed back to the quarterdeck. He looked around for his premier but didn't find him.

"Pass the word for the first lieutenant!" he called to the quarterdeck at large.

Knighton ignored the scramble that ensued, and presently Lieutenant Percival appeared and saluted.

"You sent for me, Captain?"

"Where were you?" the captain barked.

"In the bow, sir," Percival replied, nonplussed by his captain's irritation. "Sir, I don't think we're going to catch them."

Knighton raised his eyes and looked past his premier to the passing waves. "That was my estimation as well," he said coldly. His eyes went to the deck for a moment before meeting the premier's. "Return to the bow chasers. Let me know if you think we have a chance to hit her."

"Aye, Captain."

"Deck there!" the lookout cried. "Ship off the larboard quarter, hull-up on the horizon!"

Captain Albritton went to the rail and raised his glass to see for himself. He was quickly joined by Lieutenant Chandler and Mr. Warren. Sure enough, what appeared to be a frigate was approaching them from the direction of Martinique.

"Damn!" Chandler muttered.

"They must have closed on us while we were blinded by the glare," Warren said. "Good timing. Or just lucky."

Albritton lowered his glass. "Either way, it's not good for us. Mr. Warren! Studs'ls and stays'ls, if you please." He looked back to his premier. "Can they catch us?"

Warren shook his head uncertainly and looked at Chandler. The first lieutenant was silent as he looked from the frigate to *Columbia's* sails and back again, gauging the wind versus the gap. Finally, he shook his head.

"They won't cut us off as long as the wind holds. I can't say whether or not he'll come within range of his bow chasers." He looked to the other two. "Can we go a few points to starboard, just in case?"

"Deck there!" the lookout called. "More ships behind frigate! Looks like a 74 and maybe a brig!"

The captain looked aft, but it was hard to confirm the lookout's report from the deck. If true (and he had no reason to doubt it; the man in the tops was one of the best aboard), it meant that engaging the frigate was now out of the question.

Albritton looked to his sailing master. "Mr. Warren? The turn?"

Warren shrugged. "Can't hurt. She'll sail just as well on a turn of, say, four or five points."

The captain considered again before nodding. "Make the change, Mr. Warren."

"Aye, sir."

Albritton turned aft to study the British ship. "Mr. Chandler," he beckoned the premier to join him. "Am I correct in thinking that our friend out there looks bigger than the usual frigate?"

Chandler raised his glass for a moment before nodding. "I'd say so, Captain. I've heard the British were razing some of their old 64s by cutting them down to one gun deck and arming them with 24-pounders to equal the firepower of our frigates, but I didn't think they were operational yet." He shook his head and wondered. "Do you think this might be one of them?"

The captain raised his glass to study their pursuer. There was definitely something different about the set of her sails from that of other frigates he'd fought, but it had been such a long time since he last saw a 64 that he wasn't sure if that explained the different bow on the British ship. Then again, he thought it entirely possible that the British might take advantage of the reconstruction to reshape the stem in an attempt to get a few more knots' speed out of her. He lowered his glass and frowned. If it was one of the razed 64s, *Columbia* would have her hands full if it came to a fight.

Albritton handed his glass to a midshipman and began to pace. Out of the corner of his eye, he saw the first lieutenant step over to the wheel to converse with Mr. Warren. At least once per pass across the fantail, the captain threw a glance at the British frigate. Finally, he stopped and studied the state of their sails again.

"Captain?" Chandler asked as he and the sailing master stepped over.

"I was just thinking," Albritton paused as he looked forward and then at the fantail, "that it looks as though we are in for a long stern chase. Mr. Chandler, I want two gaps cut in the fantail. Bring one of the 18-pounder bow chasers aft to fire at the British ship."

"Aye, sir," the first lieutenant replied. "You said *two* gaps?"

"Yes," the captain smiled. "I want one of the 24-pounders brought up on deck and set to fire aft through the second gap." Chandler's eyes went wide. Albritton nodded and continued, "I also want you to send a crew to my quarters. Remove the panes from two of the stern windows and turn two more of the 24-pounders to fire aft from there."

"Sir?" Chandler gaped in confusion. He saw the captain's brows rise slightly and quickly added, "Are you sure, sir?"

The look in his captain's eyes made it clear he would brook no questions. "Carry out your orders, Mr. Chandler."

The first lieutenant swallowed hard. "Aye, Captain." He went off, shouting for the bosun.

Mr. Warren stepped up. "Nasty surprise you've prepared for that ship back there."

The captain shrugged and looked aft. "Let's hope so. If we can take out her foremast, we should be able to get away before that 74 can join the action."

Captain Knighton stood near the lee rail on the quarterdeck of HMS *London*, eyes straight ahead, oblivious to all going on around him. He clasped his hands behind his back, maintaining a look of outward calm and assurance, all the while raging furiously in his mind at the gods of wind and sea. It was a pose he'd perfected early as a young post captain.

A few minutes earlier, the American frigate—a lookout had tentatively identified the ship as a *Constitution*-class vessel—had turned away from them, and *London* had settled into a stern chase. Knighton struggled to contain the urge to rush to the rail to see for himself or even to bounce on his toes in anticipation. He *knew* inside himself that the gods had delivered his enemy into his grasp. That was Albritton's ship out there. It *had* to be. It was destiny.

Knighton looked at *London's* tophamper and frowned. The sails were drawing less than fifty percent of their capacity, giving the ship a top speed of maybe four to five knots. He ordered studs'ls and stays'ls, but he wasn't hopeful of any improvement. He shook his head, taking no comfort in the fact that the same wind was preventing the American from getting away.

He turned aft to check on the progress of the squadron. *Goliath* was clear of the harbor and was taking her boats aboard and setting all sail. Knighton looked again to verify that the commodore had indeed ordered the stuns'ls set, and he grunted. *I hope that gets him here in time,* the captain thought. The brig was coming a little faster; her boats were already stowed aboard and her tophamper was filled with every stitch that might catch a gust of the elusive breeze.

The captain turned forward again and frowned as he realized the American was edging away from him. That was the one problem with these *London*-class frigates. Being razed from 64-gun ships of the line gave them better protection than the average frigate, but the general shape of the hull did not allow them to achieve a frigate's speed, even with her reconstructed bow. Just as he was about to return to the fantail, his eyes were drawn skyward by the one sound he dreaded more than any other—that of flapping sails bereft of their wind.

HMS *London* was becalmed.

On the quarterdeck of USS *Columbia*, Captain Albritton sprang from the companion stairs in response to an urgent summons. He was met almost immediately by Lieutenant Williams.

"The wind's gone, sir!" he cried, then hurriedly saluted.

"So I see, Mr. Williams," Albritton said. "Calm yourself and order the boats out again. We need to get moving before the British."

"Aye, sir." Williams saluted and went forward, shouting for the bosun.

The captain accepted a glass and went to the fantail. He saw at once that the British also were becalmed and were lowering their boats to try to get into gunnery range. He lowered the glass; this was a race he fully expected to win. The only question was whether or not they could outrun the British until they could get into a wind again. He became aware that he was not alone. A quick glance to the right revealed Mr. Warren, silent and watchful.

"We'll win," Albritton said, guessing the sailing master's thoughts.

"Oh, I have no doubt," Warren agreed. "I just hope we don't tire out before they do. How many men do you think they have on that ship?"

Albritton grunted. "Fewer than we do," he said. "I hope."

Columbia's boats did indeed beat those of their British rivals into the water, and the frigate was soon edging forward in the water. Albritton estimated that his ship gained a half-mile or more before the British were moving. Now it was a race, and one dependent on endurance and not speed.

"Pass the word for the first lieutenant," he called. Mr. Chandler soon appeared and raised his hat.

"You sent for me, sir?"

"Yes. I know the boats just went into the water, but I wanted to be sure you had a schedule for relieving the crews."

"Aye, sir," Chandler assured him.

Albritton nodded. "I'm going below. Let me know if they manage to come within range of our stern guns."

"Aye, sir."

On HMS *London*, Captain Knighton stood between his bow chasers and glared at his quarry. His ship was finally moving, and his men were keeping pace with the Americans. He looked down to the guns on either side of him, hulking 18-pounders totally impotent at this range.

"How much do we have to close the gap before we can try a ranging shot?" he asked.

Lieutenant Percival raised his glass to his eye for a moment. "I'd estimate two hundred yards or better, sir."

Knighton's lips pressed into a thin, frustrated line. "There *has* to be a way to close the gap. What is it?"

Percival shrugged. "We'd need more boats for that."

The captain's head jerked around at that. "What did you say?"

Percival was confused. "I said we'd need more boats for that."

"Capital idea!" Knighton said. "Come with me."

The captain headed aft at a pace that forced his premier to step lively in order to keep up. "Pass the word for Mr. Jeffers," Knighton said when they arrived. The signals midshipman appeared and saluted. "Mr. Jeffers, make to *Goliath, 'Request more boats be sent to me so I can close the gap and fire on the enemy.'* I know it will be a long signal, but get it out at once."

"Aye, sir."

The midshipman headed aft to his signal locker and the signal book inside. Percival stepped up and spoke in a low voice.

"Do you really expect the commodore to send you any of his boats?"

"If he wants to avoid being blamed for the Americans getting away, he will." Knighton turned to his first lieutenant. "Be sure my signal is entered into the log, Mr. Percival."

The premier smiled and shook his head. "Aye, Captain."

Commodore Ezra Morgenthau stood on HMS *Goliath*'s quarterdeck and fumed. Captain Steele stood off to the side, trying his best to shield the unfortunate midshipman who delivered the signal from his commodore's attention.

"He wants what?!?!" the commodore roared again. "Is he *mad*? If we send him our boats, then how are we supposed to close on the Americans? Hasn't he thought of *that*?"

Morgenthau walked to the rail and stood there dramatically, arms behind his back and staring out over the ocean. Steele lowered his eyes to the deck, careful to hide his feelings of disgust at his commodore's posturing. After a few minutes, he stepped up to him.

"Sir?" he said in a low voice.

"Who does Knighton think he is?" the commodore replied in the same voice. "Who is he to make such requests of me?"

"If I may, sir," Steele replied, "Knighton is an experienced captain who would not make such a request if he didn't think it not only necessary but also likely to bring success. It is my estimation that the only way that *Goliath* can be brought into this fight is for the American frigate to be disabled. HMS *London* is the only ship in a position to do that. Besides, you are still commodore of this squadron; if you send the boats and Knighton succeeds in disabling the American, you would still get the lion's share of the credit for the victory. And if he fails, and the American escapes, you can always blame Knighton's request as the reason *Goliath* never got into the fight."

Steele stood silently beside Morgenthau, staring out over the waves and counting to himself. He reached fifty-six before he saw in the corner of his eye the commodore blink and turn to him.

"True," Morgenthau said, "every word. Order four boats to join *London,* three of ours and one from *Comet.*" He nodded with his head toward the brig off their larboard quarter.

"Aye, sir." Steele touched his hat and went to issue the orders.

The knock at his cabin door made Captain Albritton put his book down. "Enter!" he called, and Midshipman Smith was admitted. The young gentleman came to attention.

"Mr. Williams' respects, Captain," he said. "He requests that you come up on deck. Something strange is happening with the British frigate."

"Very well. My compliments to Mr. Williams; I shall come at once." Smith's backbone somehow straightened a fraction more, and he left the room. Albritton set his book on the table and followed.

On deck, he was met by Lieutenant Williams, who handed him a glass and pointed aft to the British ship. "Looks like they've gotten more help, sir."

"Pass the word for Mr. Chandler and the sailing master," Albritton said as he stepped to the fantail and raised the glass to his eye. He soon noticed what the lieutenant was referring to—an additional four boats had appeared in front of the British ship. He lowered the telescope and narrowed his eyes as he considered the implications.

The first lieutenant and sailing master arrived. "You sent for us, sir?" Chandler said as they both touched their hats.

Albritton glanced over his shoulder to acknowledge them before nodding aft. "It seems our friends have come up with something new."

Chandler brought a glass to his eye and quickly surveyed the scene. He grunted. "Four more boats? If they can stay out of each other's way, they'll close the gap for sure."

"Agreed," the captain said. "Recommendations?"

Chandler lowered his glass. "Well, it won't be long before they're within range of your little surprise," he said, nodding to the 24-pounder beside them. "I for one would rather not shoot at men in boats, but they're not leaving us much choice, are they?"

Mr. Warren shook his head. "Nay. Their captain's leaving them exposed like lambs to the slaughter."

The captain considered again. "Pass the word for Mr. Adams."

The senior midshipman was called and saluted upon arrival.

"Mr. Adams," the captain said, "if you look aft, you will see that the British have extra boats towing their frigate. I am putting you in command of our two stern chasers. Let me know when they get close enough for us to try a shot."

Adams touched his hat. "Aye, Captain."

Albritton nodded and led the others away. He said to the premier, "Assign a midshipman to the 24s pointed aft in my cabin. He is to fire if he hears Mr. Adams fire a second salvo."

"Aye, captain."

"So," Warren said after the first lieutenant departed, "we may not be out of the woods just yet, eh?"

"We're all right for now. In three or four hours?" The captain shrugged. "There's no way to tell just yet." He cast one last look aft before saying, "If you will excuse me, Mr.

Warren, I shall be in my cabin. Have me called at once if I am needed."

"Aye, Captain." The sailing master touched his hat, and the captain went below.

When he got to his cabin, he found Midshipman Smith in his day cabin along with crews for the two 24-pounders. "Mr. Smith, you and your men may wait outside. You are authorized to enter at once if ordered or if you hear Mr. Adams fire a salvo."

"Aye, Captain," the midshipman replied. "Come along, you men." They all came to attention and left the cabin. After they were gone, Albritton called for Sommers and asked for a cup of coffee. What he really wanted was bourbon, but he thought it best to keep his mind clear.

Back on the deck, Lieutenant Williams joined the sailing master at the fantail. "How long, do you think?"

"Before they close the gap? Hard to tell." Warren sighed and crossed his arms over his chest. "It's like Mr. Chandler said, if they stay out of each other's way, they could come on fairly quickly."

Two hours later, Chandler rejoined them at the fantail. He did not like what he saw. "They're gaining," he said simply.

"Aye, sir," the sailing master replied. "I estimate they may have us before dark."

Chandler nodded his agreement. "I'll go tell the captain." He headed for the companion stairs.

Warren shook his head. "I wish there was a way to get more speed out of the old girl, at least until the winds return."

Williams was standing a step or so behind the sailing master and to his left, so it was understandable that Warren did not see the change come over the lieutenant's face as the idea hit him. "If you will excuse me, Mr. Warren?" Williams asked.

The sailing master nodded without turning, and Williams headed forward, calling for the lead. Two hands brought it and cast over the starboard side. They sounded a depth of twenty-six fathoms before hauling it up and casting it again to be sure. They reported the same sounding. Williams thanked them and went back to the quarterdeck, where he found that the first lieutenant had returned and was speaking with Mr. Warren.

"Begging your pardon, sir," Williams said as he interrupted the conversation, "but I think I've figured out how to outrun the British."

"Well, don't keep us in suspense, Mr. Williams!" Chandler replied.

"A thought occurred to me," the lieutenant explained, "so I had the lead cast. In fact, I did it twice just to be sure. Both soundings came back at twenty-six fathoms. What about kedging?"

Chandler's brows rose as he realized what Williams was saying. Warren broke out in a grin.

"Aye! That would move us faster than those boats could bring on that British tub!" he said.

Chandler passed the word for the captain and had Mr. Williams repeat himself after Albritton arrived.

"Well done, Mr. Williams!" he said. "You may have saved us this day. Pass the word for Xavier." The coxswain arrived and saluted. "Xavier, we are going to kedge our way to freedom. We will use two boats. You take one and pick a good man to take the second. You take one of the kedging anchors about a half-mile out and drop it. The other boat will take the second out while we are hauling up the first and drop it as the first clears the water and is loaded back into your boat. That way, we will always be moving."

"Aye, Captain," the coxswain said with a rare smile. "We'll leave the British in the dust!"

Albritton nodded toward Williams. "His idea."

Xavier turned to the lieutenant and saluted. The captain's brow inched up at the rare event. "Well done, Lieutenant," the coxswain said soberly. He turned and went forward to get the boats in the water.

Williams stood beside his captain and watched him go. "Pardon me, sir," he said, "but what just happened?"

Albritton smiled. "Mr. Williams, you have joined a very select club. In all the years I've known him, I can count on one hand the men Xavier saluted voluntarily." The captain clapped him on the shoulder as he walked by. "Something to be proud of, I assure you."

Leaving the bemused lieutenant behind, Albritton went to the rail to watch the lowering of the kedging anchor into the boat. Xavier was already in the boat, supervising the placement of the anchor so as to make it easy to put over the side when the time came. The coxswain paused just long enough to nod his respects when he saw his captain, before returning his attention to the task at hand. Albritton walked across the deck to observe the same operation in the second boat. He was pleased to see Xavier had picked old Calvin to conn the boat; Albritton had heard good things about the petty officer's conduct and work during the voyage. Satisfied, the captain returned to the quarterdeck and waited there as Xavier took his boat forward about a half-mile out and put the kedging anchor overboard. He knew that Mr. Chandler had already ordered all their spare rope to be bent on the cables and played out into the boats with the anchors, ready for the men at the capstans to pull the ship to them.

Captain Knighton sat at his desk in his cabin, working on his log when he put down his quill, picked up his glass of

Madeira, and sat back with a smile. He glanced back at the log before him and began composing his report to the Admiralty in his mind. He took a sip from the glass and was entirely pleased with himself; for once, everything was going right. Thanks to the boats sent to him by the commodore, his ship was gaining steadily on the Americans. He estimated another four hours or so would bring the enemy within range of his bow chasers, with another two hours after that needed to bring them to pistol shot when he would open up with broadsides.

Knighton's face grew serious for a moment as he contemplated the coming battle. He was confident that his ship and crew were fully capable of defeating a *Constitution*-class frigate and restoring the glory lost by the Navy in those early battles. Still, he was not blind to his ship's deficiencies vis-à-vis the American frigate, and he knew he had to consider his tactics very carefully. He could not maneuver with the Americans, so his plan of attack was to get in close as quickly as he could. He would try to rake the enemy as many times as possible, but failing that he would trade broadsides with them, trusting that the weight of his shot would be sufficient to penetrate the American frigate's hull.

Knighton drained his glass and rose to pace. To his knowledge, a *Constitution*-class vessel had never been subjected to sustained 24-pound shot backed up by 32-pound carronades at close range. Percival had their guns' crews trained to be among the fastest in the Royal Navy. The captain nodded to himself as point after point seemed to fall into line in his favor. He hardly noticed the knock on his door that admitted Mr. Jeffers.

"Yes, Mr. Jeffers?" Knighton said automatically as he paced.

"Begging your pardon, sir," the midshipman said, "but Mr. Jervis sends his respects and asks that you please come on deck at once."

Something in the lad's voice arrested his captain's attention. "What's wrong?"

The young gentleman hesitated for a moment. "Mr. Jervis says the Americans are pulling away from us."

Knighton rushed from the cabin without even bothering to gather his hat. Mr. Jeffers closed the door behind him as he hurried to catch up.

"Report!" the captain cried as he stepped up on deck.

Jervis stepped up with a glass for his captain in his hand. "Sir, fifteen minutes ago, the lookout in the foretop reported he thought the Americans were pulling away. I waited until his observation was confirmed, and then I sent for you at once."

Knighton accepted the telescope with a nod of thanks and made his way to the rail. A quick examination showed nothing amiss, although he did think the Americans were farther ahead than before. "Any trouble with our boats?" he asked.

"None, sir," Jervis replied.

"Crews changed on schedule?"

"Aye, sir."

"Did the American catch a gust of wind?"

"Not that the lookout reported, sir."

"Find out!"

"Aye, sir." Unperturbed, Jervis sent a runner to the foretop. Upon his return, the lieutenant said, "The lookout says 'no' to the question of wind, Captain."

Knighton stepped back from the rail as he searched his mind for anything that might account for the American's sudden burst of speed. A quick glance at their tophamper showed the sails to be as useless as they were before. There had been short, occasional gusts of a light breeze over the past couple of hours, but nothing that would explain what he had seen. He looked out over the beam and was surprised to see *Comet* had come up and was pacing him. A quick glance aft showed that *Goliath* had fallen far behind; *Comet* must have used those gusts of wind to catch up.

"Mr. Jeffers!" he called. The midshipman appeared and saluted. "Make to *Comet*: *'Close with me.'*"

"Aye, sir!"

Soon the brig was edging her way carefully to close with the big frigate. As she settled in on *London's* larboard quarter, Knighton took a speaking trumpet and went to the fantail.

"Can you hear me?" he shouted.

"Aye, sir!" came the reply.

"The Americans are pulling away! See if you can overtake them and determine why!"

"Aye, sir!"

Knighton waved and stepped away from the fantail, signaling the end of his message. The officer on *Comet* saluted and retreated. The brig pulled away from the frigate and set about on her task. Knighton noticed as they did so that they held their boats ready in case they were needed again. He did not know who was in command of the brig, but the sight gave him reassurance that the man knew what he was doing.

Over the next two hours, the brig worked her way forward and to larboard, trying to get a look ahead of the American frigate. Knighton never left the quarterdeck, sometimes standing alone, sometimes pacing to pass the time, no man approaching him unless bidden. Lieutenant Percival appeared and stood by the wheel with Mr. Morgan.

Finally, the strong voice of Lieutenant Jervis cut through the silence. "Signal from *Comet*, sir! Mr. Jeffers!"

The signals midshipman appeared with his signal book, and the two men hurriedly decoded the signal. "Sir!" Jervis said, "it reads *'Enemy is kedging.'*"

Knighton's brows rose and he looked forward in disbelief. He turned back, still silent, the rapid motion of his eyes back and forth being the only evidence of the speed of his thoughts. His head came up. "Mr. Jeffers! Make *'Explain.'*"

The signal was sent. Knighton saw the reply rise on the brig and forced himself to wait as Jervis and Jeffers decoded it. Jervis turned to him. "Sir, it says, *'Enemy is using two anchors.'*"

The captain's chin rose slowly as it dawned on him what the American was doing. He looked around the quarterdeck and spotted the premier standing by the wheel.

"I'm going forward," he said. "Mr. Percival, you're with me. Mr. Jervis has the deck."

The two men marched forward, leaving the chorus of "Aye, sir" and "Aye, Captain" behind them. They arrived at the bow chasers, and the hands in the area stepped away to give the captain some privacy.

"Pass the word for a runner," Knighton said as he brought his glass to his eye. He could see nothing different about the American ship. He noticed again the stern chasers that the Americans had deployed. "Roland," he said, and the premier stepped up. The captain motioned with his head toward the American. "What size guns would you say our friend out there has pointed at us?"

Percival examined the ship and lowered his glass. "At least 18-pounders, maybe 24s."

Knighton frowned. "That was my estimation as well. The price of raking her just went up."

"Aye, sir."

Percival watched as his captain stared at the enemy vessel. The first lieutenant knew that his captain was trying to decide what to do. Knighton blinked and looked back to him. "Order two boats brought in and loaded with kedging anchors. We shall imitate the American method. They must be running the second out ahead while recovering the first anchor."

"Aye, sir." Percival passed the order on to one of the runners standing by, and the man hurried aft. When the premier stepped back to his captain, he did not like the look on Knighton's face.

"Mr. Percival," the captain said formally, "we must try to delay or disrupt the Americans in order to give us a chance to catch up. Signal to *Comet*, 'Engage the enemy.'"

Percival's mouth dropped open, but he caught himself and closed it again. Such an order was next to suicide, but his captain knew that already. "Aye, sir." He saluted and went aft. Knighton watched him go; he knew Percival would not send a runner with that order. He would give it himself.

Captain Albritton stood beside the after carronade of *Columbia's* larboard battery, his glass fixed on the British ship off his larboard quarter. She was a two-masted brig-sloop, cut for seven gun ports down the side, all closed. He could only guess at her armament, which could be anything from 4-pounder long guns to 32-pounder carronades. *Columbia* was in no danger from her, but there was always the chance of a lucky shot taking out a topmast along with all the usual attending damage, so she could not be ignored. He had ordered Mr. Chandler to clear for action as she approached.

He had been called up on deck after she had pulled away from her frigate and begun to approach. Her captain was careful to pull out to larboard, keeping his ship safe from a direct assault from either the stern chasers or the quarterdeck carronades. The lightly built ship needed much less wind to push her through the water, making her the ideal scout in this situation. The brig had obviously been sent to determine why they were pulling away, and he had watched as she related the information back to her frigate. Even now, he could see the frigate recalling her boats and preparing to imitate the Americans' kedging. Albritton grunted; the best the British could do was not to fall any further behind, and he doubted they would be able to do that well.

"Captain!" It was Mr. Williams, the officer of the watch. "The brig's moving, sir!"

Albritton rushed to the larboard rail. The brig was putting on all sail and moving off to the south. Given *Columbia's* current course of SSW, Albritton's immediate thought was that she was trying to circle the frigate out of gun range and get to the kedging boats forward. It might take her a while, but it was a very real possibility.

"Mr. Warren!" he called. "I want to change the ship's course two points to larboard. No, make it three, the next time the starboard boat goes out."

"We're just pulling in the larboard anchor now, Captain!" came the response.

Albritton nodded. "Mr. Williams, get the word to Xavier: three points to starboard when he goes out."

"Aye, Captain!"

"Beat to quarters, Mr. Chandler," Albritton ordered.

"Aye, Captain." He picked up a speaking trumpet and issued the orders that sent the crew to the action stations. Eight minutes later, he reported the ship ready for action.

Mr. Chandler and Mr. Mitchell were at their stations with the gun batteries below, so the captain called, "Mr. Adams!"

The senior midshipman stepped up and saluted. "Sir?"

"My compliments to Mr. Chandler," Albritton said calmly. "I want one ranging shot on that brig."

"Aye, Captain." Adams saluted and went below. Two minutes later, the gun port for the number three gun opened, and the nozzle appeared. The gun erupted, spewing flame and smoke, the effect being all the greater for being alone. From the quarterdeck, the captain and sailing master watched anxiously for the fall of the shot. They easily saw the plume of water shoot skyward about thirty yards off the brig's bow. The ship prudently turned to larboard before resuming her efforts to get ahead of the frigate.

"Well," Warren commented, "at least we know her captain's no fool."

Albritton grunted. "That's just what I was afraid of." The captain's gaze went from the brig to the British frigate, back to the brig, then to the kedging boats and back yet again. "Mr. Warren, do we have a chance of cutting them off before they reach the boats?"

The sailing master studied the scene through hooded eyes before finally shaking his head. "I don't believe so, Captain, at least, not unless the wind should return. I believe the best we can hope for is a timely gust that will push us into gun range before they can open fire on our boats."

Albritton frowned.

Captain Knighton came up on deck and went forward to meet his premier at the bow chasers. "Do we know what she's doing yet?" he asked, referring to the brig.

"I think he's trying to get ahead of the American," Percival replied. "Take out the boats."

Knighton frowned. "What makes him think the Americans will let him do that? All it would take is a puff of wind to give them enough steerageway to bring their guns to bear."

Percival shrugged as he stared at the brig. "Well, sir, perhaps her captain thought that this way, maybe he had a chance to survive."

Knighton's eyes flashed to his premier, but he said nothing. Percival was perhaps the one man in the Navy who had the right to speak his mind to Knighton.

The two watched as the frigate took a ranging shot at the brig that fell short by a comfortable margin. Even so, the brig turned to larboard to widen the range before resuming his course to get ahead of the American.

"Are we gaining?" Knighton asked.

Percival shook his head. "No, sir. In fact, I believe the American is still widening the gap, though perhaps not by so much."

The captain's face became a mask that hid his growing frustration; the only evidence of his mood was a narrowing of his eyes. He turned and marched aft.

CHAPTER FIFTEEN

Winds on the open seas are strange things. A ship could have full sails and make a good clip, but another a hundred yards away she could be crawling, or even in irons. It didn't happen very often, but it always happened at the worst possible moments.

Captain Hezekiah Albritton was reminded of this when a desperate cry shattered the calm of the quarterdeck.

"Captain! The brig!"

Albritton spun to see Mr. Adams with a fearful look on his face pointing toward the larboard bow. He followed the midshipman's direction to see that the brig had suddenly shot ahead, obviously caught in a strong breeze. The result was that the brig was now significantly outpacing *Columbia* and would soon be able to cross her bow and go after the kedging boats.

"I'm going forward!" the captain called. When he arrived at the bows, he found Mr. Chandler still there, keeping his eye on the brig.

"Report, Mr. Chandler!" Albritton said even as he put his glass to his eye.

"If nothing changes, I estimate the brig will alter course and cross our bow in the next twenty to thirty minutes," the premier reported.

"Who do we have out there?" the captain asked as he scanned for their boat.

"Calvin, sir."

"Recall him."

"Already tried, sir. Either he doesn't see the signal or he's ignoring us. I'm sure he can see the brig." Chandler lowered his glass, let out a long, loud breath and shook his head.

Albritton lowered his glass and looked around in desperation. To his dismay, he now saw it was the larboard 18-pounder bow chaser that had been transferred aft. He turned to the gun captain of the forward larboard carronade. "Can you bear?"

To his credit, the man checked before turning sadly back to his captain. He shook his head. "Sorry, sir."

Albritton turned back to the stem. His eyes fell upon the lone remaining bow chaser, impotent on the starboard side of the bowsprit. He tried quickly to calculate in his head if the gun could be shifted over in time, but when he raised his head he saw the premier looking at him. Albritton raised his brows in question, but Chandler sadly shook his head; the move could not be done in time to save the boat. The captain lowered his head in resignation.

"Pass the word, quickly," he said without raising his head, "Xavier is not to go out."

"Aye, Captain."

"Deck there!" the lookout cried. "The brig's turning! She's coming across our bows!"

The two officers turned forward to see for themselves. The brig was indeed crossing their bow and closing fast on Calvin's boat. They saw her gun ports open, saw her guns run out, and stood there helplessly as the guns belched out smoke and fire. The boat was swiftly hidden by geysers—a testament to the accuracy of the brig's gunnery. When the geysers were gone, so was the boat.

The captain heard a strangled cry catch in his first lieutenant's throat, and he saw the look of anguish and helplessness on Chandler's face. He turned forward again, raised the glass to his eye and soon found the debris floating on the water. The sight shook him to the core, then it did two things: it caused a hard pit to form in his stomach at the thought of the fates of the good Calvin and his crew, and second, it filled him with a terrible rage and thirst for revenge.

It was at that moment that fate intervened in the form of a flapping sound that none of them expected to hear. Albritton looked to his tophamper and saw the sails flutter as they filled with wind and the ship began to move. *Columbia* had stumbled into the same breeze that had allowed the brig to wreak her havoc.

Albritton reacted at once. "Michael, run below and take command of the larboard battery. Fire as your guns bear. Don't wait for my command." He turned to the midshipman to his left. "Cut Xavier's boat loose! We'll come back for them."

"Aye, sir!" Chandler touched his hat and was gone.

"Aye, sir!" The midshipman echoed and ran to the rail.

The captain made his way aft and found Mr. Warren. "Hard to starboard. I want the larboard battery to bear on that brig."

The sailing master nodded and knuckled his forehead. Albritton took his place on the larboard rail as the ship came around. Mr. Warren straightened her up, and the main battery began going off, two guns or three at a time as they came to bear on the unfortunate brig. The lookout later reported that at least five of the big 24-pounder balls had found the target, the last of which had detonated the magazine and blown the ship to smithereens.

The sound of the explosion and especially the sight of the ship literally disintegrating in a cloud of wood, fire and smoke brought an instant silence to *Columbia's* deck. No one who witnessed it would ever forget it, and while they mourned the lives of their fellow tars who were lost, a single phrase was on the lips or in the minds of one and all, *"That's for Calvin!"*

Now the hand of fate intervened again, for she is known as a fickle mistress. The wind now disappeared as swiftly as it had appeared, leaving Albritton and his crew in irons.

Every eye on deck was drawn skyward by the ominous sound of a sail flapping with the loss of the wind. Albritton turned aft automatically to check on the British frigate. She was still coming on, kedging with two boats as his own men had been. Now, with *Columbia* dead in the water, they would close the gap very quickly, possibly coming within gun range inside an hour.

The captain looked quickly around the quarterdeck before stepping aft and signaling for Lieutenants Chandler and Mitchell and Mr. Warren to join him. He moved to the fantail and turned to them. "Options?" he asked.

"Get the boats in the water, rigged for towing," Chandler said immediately.

"We can't get away now that the British are kedging," the captain pointed out.

"We have two more kedging anchors in the hold," Mitchell said. "We could bring them up."

"Ach!" Warren spat. "We'd never get them rigged and in the water before that frigate out there came within range of us."

"Agreed," the captain said. "Mr. Chandler, get the bosun. Let's get the boats into the water anyway, rigged for towing. Mr. Mitchell, get those kedging anchors up here." A hiss off to his right drew his attention to the second lieutenant.

"Boats!" Mitchell gasped in almost a whisper. His eyes flew aft. "Sir! Xavier!"

Albritton felt an icy hand grip his heart as he took a step aft and quickly saw the launch bobbing on the waves. It looked like Xavier had them rowing south, probably trying to get out of the way of the frigate and hoping they were unimportant enough that its captain wouldn't decide to stop and take them prisoner. He looked at the deck and breathed a silent prayer, *Forgive me, old friend.* He drew a deep, calming breath, and let it out slowly before looking up again. "There's nothing we can do for them now. We've got to save the ship first, then we can come back and look for them. You have your orders! Dismissed!"

The two lieutenants raised their hats solemnly and made their way forward. Mr. Warren stood to the side, silent but not unnoticed. Albritton looked down at the older man. "Xavier will be fine," he said.

The other shook his head. "I hope you're right."

The captain turned his attention forward to the boats being deployed to take the frigate in tow again, and the sailing master was forced to follow suit. Every few minutes, he turned back to the fantail to check on the British frigate's progress.

The Americans got their boats over the side and soon the frigate was making some headway again. However, its speed was not such as to out distance the British frigate.

The captain looked to the premier. "And the kedging anchors?"

"Still another hour before they will be ready to go to the boats, sir," came the reply. "It seems the men had some unexpected trouble in bringing them to the deck."

Albritton frowned as he turned aft. "They'll be in range soon."

Chandler shrugged. "If they have 18-pounders in the bows, yes."

Albritton stepped up to the stern chasers and patted the breech of the 24-pounder. "How long before they're in our range?"

The premier smiled and raised his glass to his eye, only to drop it a moment later. "We might try a ranging shot now, sir, if you like," he said, "although it will most likely be a bit short."

The captain's chin rose a bit as he considered. "But it may induce them to slow their advance?"

"That *is* possible, Captain, although I think it unlikely."

Albritton considered for a moment before nodding to the 24-pounder's gun captain. "You may load and fire."

The gun captain sighted down the barrel. "Off the bow may be the best we can do at the moment, sir."

"Understood," Albritton said. "Proceed."

The gun captain supervised the loading and running out of his gun before standing back with the lanyard in his hand. He pulled, and the gun fired. The smoke made breathing difficult for a few moments, then the premier called to the lookout.

"Thirty yards short and to larboard, sir!" the lookout reported.

"Mr. Adams!" the captain called, and the senior midshipman appeared. "You may resume your post over the stern chasers. Notify me at once when you think you might reach the frigate."

"Aye, Captain."

Captain Knighton paced across HMS *London's* fantail. He could not believe what he was seeing. This American captain had the god of luck in his pocket—nothing else could explain the miraculous wind that had allowed them to destroy HMS *Comet* and then get under way via towing, all before he could arrive and bring them to battle. Now their frigate had fired one of their improvised stern chasers, and the geyser that had landed not so very short of his bow indicated a 24-pounder pointed in his direction.

He was marching toward the lee rail when his eyes happen to rise, and he caught sight of the remaining American boat fleeing. He was tempted to order the quarterdeck carronades to blow it out of the water, but after a moment he decided that would be a petty act of vengeance, and such things were beneath a gentleman. His fight was with the behemoth ahead of him. He stopped at the rail and watched the boat as she strained against the seas, and he thought those men not so different from his own. He shook his head at the idea—a brotherhood of sorts, but one divided by war. Knighton watched the boat and shook his head. *Not today, my friends,* he thought as he wished them luck, *today I am after bigger fish.*

"Deck there! The frigate's closing, sir!"

The lookout's call brought the quarterdeck officers to the fantail. Adams stood between his guns, glass to his eye, gauging the closing distance and judging the moment when the enemy would be in range. He turned to see the captain and his officers standing behind him; their eyes met, and the captain nodded once. The acting senior midshipman returned the gesture and turned back to his guns. "Stand by to fire!" he called.

The gun captains sighted down their barrels one last time before standing back with their lanyards at the ready. They watched for the signal to fire. Adams raised his glass for a final check. "Fire!" he called.

The 18- and 24-pounder went off together, and Albritton honestly could not tell the difference between them. He closed his eyes until the smoke had passed, then he looked to the tops. "Lookout?"

"One just short," replied the lookout. "One off to starboard."

"Not bad, Mr. Adams," the captain said. "You may fire at will, so long as you bear."

"Aye, Captain."

Albritton turned and led his officers forward to leave Adams to his work. After the next salvo from the stern chasers, he heard the 24-pounders in his quarters answer; Mr. Smith was faithful to his orders and followed Franklin's second salvo. He nodded to himself as he turned to his men. "That should keep our friends out there busy for the moment," he said. "Without the wind, it looks like we're in for a fight. Return to your divisions. Tell them I have absolute confidence in them."

Chandler led the officers in saluting their captain, only his eyes grew large as he looked past him. "Sir!" he cried and pointed. "Look! Off the starboard bow!"

Albritton spun to see what his premier was pointing at, and a smile broke out on his face at the sight of a squall heading straight for them.

"Mr. Chandler," he said quickly, "go forward. Get word to the boats to take us into the squall."

Chandler headed forward, and Mr. Warren stepped up. "Captain," he said quietly, "I agree that the winds in that squall will get us moving again, but it will make recovering our boats extremely difficult."

"Mr. Chandler will be there to oversee the recovery." He paused. "I don't like it, Mr. Warren, but I don't know any other way right now to save my ship." The captain looked down at the smaller man standing beside him and saw only sympathy and understanding in his eyes. Warren touched his hat.

"Aye, Captain," he said. "Straight for the squall." He went back to the wheel and began issuing orders.

USS *Columbia* swung around and crawled toward the safety of the squall. The change of course interrupted the growing duel between the Americans' stern guns and the bow chasers of the British frigate. The British continued to close the gap due to their kedging, but it soon became apparent to everyone on the American quarterdeck that they would win the race to the squall.

Captain Knighton stood behind his bow chasers and watched as his quarry neared the safety of the storm ahead. Not only would the rain hide them, but it was also quite possible—probable, in fact—that they would pick up more than enough wind there to gain sufficient maneuverability to make their escape. He fumed at the possibility of losing them, but he knew better than to follow them in. That would only give the Americans a perfect opportunity to gain the weather gauge and turn back upon their pursuers from a position of supreme advantage.

"Mr. Percival," he said over his shoulder, "pass the word. Hard to starboard. Keep us out of the squall, but go around it and stay within easy reach of the edge."

"Aye, sir." The premier repeated the order to a runner and dispatched him to the quarterdeck. "May I ask your plan, sir?"

Knighton lowered his glass but stared at the storm ahead. "I am hoping for two things, Roland. First, that we pick up wind from the storm without having to subject ourselves to it, and second, that the Americans will kindly come blundering out of it and right into our broadside."

Percival chuckled, knowing that such fortune was possible but unlikely. "If you'll excuse me, sir, it's time to change the crews on the boats. I'll also have extra men standing by so we can get the boats back aboard quickly when we pick up the wind."

"Thank you, Mr. Percival."

Captain Albritton sat at the table in his cabin, nursing a cup of steaming coffee and contemplating the next few hours. As expected, the ship picked up the wind almost immediately after entering the squall. The boats were recovered without incident, and the captain ordered a change of course to starboard in an attempt to lose the British frigate. Once that was done, he came down to his cabin to dry off and decide what to do next. Sommers produced the coffee that was now warming his insides, but, truthfully, he appreciated the dry uniform more.

He sipped the coffee and considered. Somehow he doubted the British captain would give up very easily, so it seemed prudent to assume his ship was nearby. Still, that wasn't the only consideration preying on the captain's mind; no, he was more worried about the British 74 having time to arrive and regain maneuverability with the squall's winds. *Columbia* would not survive in a battle against both ships. That fact left him only two options. Either take on the frigate before the 74 could arrive, or else escape and leave both British ships behind. He rose and went to the day cabin. The two 24-pounders had been pulled back into the ship and the glass panes replaced just before the ship entered the squall. He made his way around the breech of one and found his chair tucked into a corner of the room. A little maneuvering made it possible for him to sit comfortably. He leaned his head back for a moment and closed his eyes, hoping to ease the tension in his neck and prevent the headache he felt coming on. He opened his eyes again when he heard the sound of Sommers clearing his throat.

"Excuse me, sir," Sommers said, "but Mr. Chandler is at the door."

Albritton sighed. "Very well. Send him in."

Sommers nodded and retreated, replaced a moment later by the first lieutenant.

"What can I do for you, Lieutenant?" the captain asked.

"I apologize for the interruption, Captain, but I thought you should know that it doesn't look like the British followed us in."

Albritton nodded. "You think he's given up?"

Chandler shook his head. "No, sir. If he weren't serious, he'd never have sent the brig after us the way he did. I think he's out there, waiting for us to come out."

"I agree. And that means that the 74 is most likely out there as well."

The first lieutenant shook his head. "Personally, I'd like to avoid a fight with that one, sir, if at all possible, but I *especially* recommend avoiding a fight with both of them at the same time."

Albritton grinned. "Mr. Chandler, you read my mind." The captain rose. "Return to the deck and talk the situation over with Mr. Warren and the officer of the watch. I shall be up shortly; have any options or recommendations ready for me."

"Aye, Captain."

Maintenance on a frigate had to be conducted no matter the weather, and so it was that Ezekiel found himself in the weather fore-chains helping to set the rigging. He turned to proceed to the next task assigned to him by the bosun, but he got distracted by a sound in the sheets behind him. As a result, he wasn't careful reaching for a rope and slipped off when he put his weight on it. He reached for the yard but missed it, and he fell overboard into the swirling sea.

Lieutenant Chandler was on the quarterdeck when the alarm of "Man overboard!" was raised.

"Where?"

"Larboard forward!" came the reply.

"I have the deck!" the first lieutenant shouted. "Back the main and mizzen tops'ls! Brail up the course! Tell the bosun I want a boat in the water right now!"

The deck exploded with hands rushing to their assigned tasks despite the driving rain. They had practiced this drill regularly, right alongside sail drill and gunnery drill. The crew never took it lightly, because they knew that proficiency can make the difference between life and death—and each man knew that the life in question could one day be his own.

The wind dumped from the backed tops'ls brought the ship quickly to a halt, and Mr. Jones had a boat over the side and into the water in record time. Chandler and Warren watched over the rail as the boat's crew pulled aft as swiftly as possible. Two hands in the boat's bows called out and searched the water for their missing man, and soon Chandler saw one of the searchers turn to the coxswain and point. The boat altered course, and a minute later they saw the hands pulling a man from the sea.

"Mr. Adams," Chandler called, "meet the boat when it returns. I want that man taken straight to the doctor. If the doctor clears him, have him report to me in the gun room."

"Aye, sir."

"Why aren't you going to meet them?" the sailing master asked.

Chandler shook his head. "I don't want to get in the way. Getting him to the doctor is the important thing."

Warren persisted. "But aren't you curious who it is?"

Chandler shrugged knowingly. "Just wait."

The boat returned, and the hand was helped up on deck and taken directly below. Not long afterward, Mr. Adams appeared out of the rain. "It was Ezekiel, sir," he said.

"Thank you, Mr. Adams," Chandler said with a teasing glance at the sailing master. "You have the deck. See that the captain is informed. I shall be in the gun room."

In the gunroom, the first lieutenant sat at the table, reading a book and sipping a glass of wine while he waited for his meeting to begin. A knock on the doorframe made him look up to see Ezekiel standing there. Chandler closed the book and stood. "Come in," he said and indicated a chair near his own. "Please, sit. Boothby! Another glass of wine!"

"Aye, sir!"

Ezekiel stepped over to the chair and sat cautiously. This treatment was not at all what he'd expected when Mr. Adams had told him to report to the first lieutenant. He nodded his thanks to Boothby when his wine arrived.

"Relax, Ezekiel," Chandler said. "I wanted to talk to you about what happened. Please tell me in your own words how you went overboard."

The tale was quickly told. Ezekiel credited a technique he'd learned on British ships for allowing him to hit the water in such a way that he remained conscious and calm as he waited for rescue.

"Amazing," Chandler commented. "I know of no such training in our Navy. I want you to be ready to give instruction to the crew about it during our next drill. It may save someone else's life." He noticed that his guest had not touched his drink. He nodded toward the glass. "That's for you, Ezekiel. Help yourself." Ezekiel's eyes narrowed and went from the glass to his host and back again.

"It's all right," Chandler insisted. "Go ahead." He sighed. "Look, let me be honest with you. I know now that how I treated you when you arrived was wrong. I've watched you, Ezekiel. You've performed well since joining this ship. And please don't think I'm doing all this to make us even for your saving my life. I didn't even know it was you when I ordered the boat out." He shook his head, not liking how this was coming out. "All I can say is, watching you has given me a lot to think about. For now, whenever I deal with you, or have to consider your rating or promotions, I plan to do so with my eyes closed, so to speak."

The two men's eyes met, and Ezekiel saw that the first lieutenant was simply being as honest as he could be. The tar nodded and drained his glass. He rose, and his legs were a little shaky. Chandler jumped to his feet and grabbed him by the arm to steady him.

"Thank you, sir," Ezekiel said.

"Not at all. Get some sleep; you can rejoin your men at the next watch."

"Thank you again." Ezekiel came to attention and shuffled wearily from the room.

A midshipman came in. "Sir? The captain wants you in his cabin."

Chandler nodded. "I'll come at once."

Lieutenant Chandler entered the captain's cabin to find the sailing master and the second lieutenant already seated at the table.

"Come in, Mr. Chandler," the captain said. Chandler took the empty chair on the captain's right and thanked Sommers as he set a cup of coffee before him. "Now, we need to discuss options, but first, Mr. Chandler, how's our man?"

"It was Ezekiel, Captain," Chandler explained, ignoring Mitchell's raised eyebrows. "The doctor has cleared him, but

I sent him to bed until he begins his next watch. I've interviewed him, and he seems fine."

Albritton hesitated for a moment but did not ask anything further. "That's good to hear. Now, gentlemen, do we know where we are?"

"Not precisely," Warren admitted, "but I have a pretty good idea. Right now, our course is basically NNW. What I don't know is when this squall might dissipate and leave us sailing in clear weather."

"We also have no idea what happened to the British frigate," Mitchell added.

"We shall cross that bridge when we come to it," the captain said. "For now, I think it prudent to presume that he is still around and may even be waiting for us when we emerge."

"Aye, sir," Chandler said.

"Options?" the captain asked. No one had anything to add. "Very well," Albritton said, "we shall continue on this course for the present. We shall meet again after Mr. Warren is able to take a sighting and determine our position. Thank you all. Mr. Chandler, will you remain?"

The sailing master and second lieutenant filed out of the room. After they were gone, Albritton sat down again.

"Did everything go all right during your meeting with Ezekiel?" he asked Chandler.

"Yes, sir."

Albritton looked into his premier's eyes and saw no deceit. He nodded and left the topic. "I expect to run out of this squall in the next day or so. After that, I am considering turning south and east. Perhaps we can pick off a ship or two coming from St. Helena or Rio."

Chandler nodded, not sure if his captain was looking for an answer. Albritton rose, signaling the end of the meeting. Dismissed, Chandler left the cabin.

CHAPTER SIXTEEN

USS *Columbia* sailed out of the squall shortly after midnight during the middle watch. The wind stayed strong and true as dawn broke. Captain Albritton rose early and stepped up on the quarterdeck to enjoy the sunrise. He was met by the officer of the watch, Lieutenant Williams.

"Good morning, sir," the lieutenant said as he touched his hat.

"Good morning." Albritton looked around the quarterdeck and then forward to the bowsprit. "I want extra lookouts posted during daylight hours."

"Aye, sir."

"Quartermaster!" the captain called. "New course due south. Mr. Williams, pass the word for –"

"Deck there! Sail on the starboard quarter!"

The two officers went to the rail and saw a tophamper visible above the horizon. Albritton didn't need to wait for the hull to appear; he recognized the sail.

"Beat to quarters!" he cried.

The drumbeat sounds filled the air, sending the hands to their action stations. Footfalls beat their way across the deck and hands scurried up the shrouds to man the yards. Albritton gave the orders that brought the ship around to close on her opponent. All doubt was removed when the ship came hull-up and he could see her bows. This was definitely the same ship that had followed them out of Martinique.

"Mr. Warren, we'll take her down the starboard side!" Albritton called. "Run us by at pistol shot, if you please! Mr. Adams, pass the word to Mr. Chandler to stand by the starboard battery! Pass the word for Lieutenant Hill!"

"Aye, sir!" came from both men.

Adams came back on deck. "Mr. Chandler's respects, Captain. Starboard battery standing by!"

Hill appeared and saluted. "You sent for me, sir?"

"Yes, Lieutenant. I want your carronades loaded with grape over ball. You will not fire as we pass the British. I want you to hold your guns in reserve. Mr. Warren! A moment, if you please!" The sailing master joined them, and the captain continued. "Mr. Warren, I will order Mr. Chandler to fire his guns as they bear. I am holding Mr. Hill's carronades in reserve. At the first possible moment, I want you to put the wheel over hard to starboard and take us across their stern. Mr. Hill, you may fire as your guns bear. Make sure every shot counts."

The lieutenant couldn't help but smile in anticipation. "Aye, Captain!" He saluted and returned to his guns.

"Are you sure, sir?" Warren asked.

"I believe that ship is one of the razed 64s we've heard about," Albritton explained. "If that's so, his sides are thicker than a normal frigate's and they may come close to our own as far as degree of protection. The one thing he cannot do is turn with us. I want to use the advantage." He shrugged. "I just hope they won't expect it, not so early in the battle."

The captain scanned the deck one last time to make sure all was ready for the coming battle. Lieutenant Hill commanded the starboard carronades; Albritton could see him running from gun to gun, conferring with the captains and encouraging the crews. His eyes rose to see marine sharpshooters in the tops, each with three loaders to ensure a rapid rate of fire. More marines were at the ready lining the starboard rail. He saw Lieutenant Monroe on the rail in the midst of his men, directing their placement and giving them last-minute instructions.

"Mr. Adams," he said at last, "my compliments to Mr. Chandler. He may fire as his guns bear."

"Aye, Captain." The midshipman disappeared below, only to return a moment later. He turned forward and received a nod from Hill to show he understood. Adams turned back to Albritton. "Orders acknowledged, Captain."

Albritton nodded. He took his place beside the wheel, hands clasped behind his back, and he waited. The two ships approached one another on parallel, converging courses; the British captain apparently in agreement with the American plan of passing at pistol shot. Albritton estimated they had almost ten minutes before the action started, so he stepped over to the rail where Adams was studying the British ship with a telescope.

"What do you make of her, Mr. Adams?" he asked.

Adams lowered his glass and frowned. "His starboard battery appears to be 24-pounders, sir. Looks like the rumors may be true after all." He drew a deep breath and let it out slowly, as though steeling himself for the coming battle. "Has a *Constitution*-class ship ever been shot at by 24-pounders?"

"Not to my knowledge," the captain admitted. "I can tell you that I personally have never been under fire from 24-pounders while in command of *Constitution* or *President*. 18-pound shot was the biggest I have received, and they did not penetrate the hull."

"What ship was that, sir?"

"USS *President,*" Albritton replied. "We were in the Mediterranean, and the guns were Tripoli shore batteries."

Adams nodded, and a moment later Albritton saw him swallow hard. "Mr. Adams, take a message to Mr. Wade, if you please."

"The carpenter, sir?"

"That's right. Tell him I want a detailed report after the action on what the British shot does to our hull."

"Aye, sir." The senior midshipman touched his hat and went forward.

Mr. Warren stepped up and nodded after the lad. "Giving him something to do beside think about dying?"

Albritton nodded once. "I remember what it was like, and I appreciated later how an officer gave me something to keep me busy."

The two walked back to the wheel and watched as the British ship neared.

"Any minute now," Warren said under his breath.

As the bows approached the point of passing, Albritton could see that along the British deck tars and marines were at the ready, just as his own were. He raised a speaking trumpet to his lips and shouted out the code word to start the action. Two things happened on deck: his marines opened fire, and Lieutenant Hill and all the crews of the carronades lay down on the deck. The lieutenant had objected when the captain had first instructed him, fearing a charge of cowardice from the men, but Albritton explained that he needed the guns crews alive and ready for the turn and raking the British stern, and the lieutenant seemed satisfied.

Nobody on USS *Columbia* could say afterward whose battery got the first shot in. The American guns went off in twos and threes as they bore, but most of the British battery —aside from one or two by the bow—went off as the ships came side by side. *Columbia* was rocked by the impact, and the captain had a difficult time keeping his feet. Two of the quartermaster's mates at the wheel were felled by British marine fire, and Albritton and Warren jumped in to keep the ship on course. Warren watched the progress of the ships, and at his signal they all put the wheel hard over to starboard.

As the ship turned, Lieutenant Hill and his crews jumped to their feet and stood at the ready. *Columbia* came around and crossed the unprotected stern of the British ship. Albritton was able to see the name *London* painted under the stern windows before Hill's arm dropped and the carronades erupted. The American ship crossed at barely half-pistol shot, and the effect of the carronade fire was devastating. The stern windows disappeared in a cloud of glass shards and the destruction of the fantail and railing sent showers of splinters down the deck.

Replacements arrived at the wheel and took over, allowing the captain and sailing master to step away. Albritton ordered them to steer away to larboard while they assessed the damage done by the British broadside and got the wounded below. A look forward along the deck revealed that fortune had smiled on them—not one of the spar deck carronades had been knocked out of action. However, the captain was experienced enough to know what that meant. The British had concentrated their battery fire on *Columbia's* hull, probably hoping to penetrate it on their first attempt. He resisted the impulse to run below and see for himself how bad the damage was—he knew he had to stay where he was. Hill and Williams were organizing crews to take the wounded below to the doctor as the ship made a large, lazy loop to larboard away from their quarry.

Captain Knighton stood amidst the carnage on HMS *London's* quarterdeck with a curse on his lips as he watched his enemy circle away. He was able to read the name *COLUMBIA* across her stern, and he was sure now it was Albritton on the other quarterdeck. The American had gotten a blow in on him with that dash across his stern; he had not expected that, and his ship and crew had paid the price.

"Get the wounded below," he said angrily. "I'm going below to speak to Mr. Percival."

He made his way to the gun deck and saw the devastating effects of the raking by the Americans. Blood and body parts seemed to be everywhere, but the cries of the wounded showed him that some were still alive.

Mr. Percival appeared and saluted. "We have three guns out of action, sir. We're trying to get some of them back into action, but a good number of hands are dead or wounded. We may need to take some from the yards."

"I'll consider it," Knighton replied. "What about the hull?"

"No breaches that I know of," the first lieutenant reported. "The three guns that were damaged were hit by 24-pounder shot that found a gun port. Those crews are gone. There are a couple of spots where the backing is cracked." He pointed to places in the hull where the impact of the American shot had cracked the interior walls. Another shot or two in the same place would mean the hull would give way. The captain observed the damage through hooded eyes and wondered if perhaps his strategy of closing and not allowing the American to maneuver might need some adjustment. Knighton went back on deck.

Mr. Morgan, the sailing master, approached him. "Orders, sir?"

"Where is the American?" the captain asked.

Morgan turned and pointed off their starboard quarter. "There, sir. She looks like she's coming around to parallel us. She's currently out of gun range."

Knighton studied the American for a moment before looking to his own tophamper. Then he stared at the deck for a moment or two as he sorted out ideas and calculations in his head before staring at the American again. HMS *London* had still held her NW course when she'd first observed her enemy coming over the horizon. Finally, he turned to Morgan.

"New course, Mr. Morgan," he said. "Steer due north and steady up on an intercept course."

"Aye, sir!"

"Pass the word to Mr. Percival! He is to ready the larboard battery and wait for the word! Mr. Jervis! I want the larboard carronades loaded with grape over ball! Wait for the word!"

"Aye, Captain!"

"Mr. Morgan, reduce sail, if you please!"

"Aye, sir!" Morgan issued the orders, then stepped over to his captain. "Sir, you *want* them to pull ahead of us?"

"Yes," Knighton said without explanation. Morgan nodded, touched his hat, and retreated.

"Looks like we hurt her badly, Captain!" the lookout cried.

"Thank you, lookout!" Albritton called. He stood at the fantail and studied HMS *London* through his glass. Her stern was a mess, but her hull retained its integrity and her tophamper was essentially undamaged. *This fight's a long way from over,* he thought. He noticed Mr. Wade standing by and called him over. "Report, Mr. Wade?"

"Aye, sir," the carpenter said nervously as he knuckled his forehead. "I've been all over the starboard hull, sir, and I don't see anywhere that the British shot penetrated. Has Mr. Chandler reported to you yet?" Albritton shook his head. "Well," the carpenter continued, "I have noticed a couple cracks on the interior of the hull, sir; if we take another shot or two in that same location, I think it's possible the hull may give way, sir."

"Thank you, Mr. Wade. Report to me immediately if you notice anything else."

"Aye, sir."

The carpenter saluted and went below, and the first lieutenant stepped up and saluted. "Captain."

Albritton returned the gesture. "Report?"

"Three guns out of action in the starboard battery, sir. I think we can get one or maybe even two of them back into action eventually, if we have the time. I wish we'd had time to bring those 24s out of your cabin and put them back in their batteries."

The captain shrugged. "Lessons learned. Besides, I think we may just be able to use them to discourage any raking by our friends out there."

"I hope you're right. Where are they?"

Albritton nodded to the larboard quarter, and Chandler turned. He nodded. "Hill did a good job."

"Yes," the captain agreed. "So did you, Mr. Chandler. Return to your guns and let me know as soon as you can about the possibility of getting any of your guns back in action."

"Aye, sir."

"Mr. Warren! Straighten up on a parallel course!" the captain called.

"Aye, sir!"

Albritton looked around the deck, and he noticed Mr. Adams manning his post at the stern chasers. He stepped over to the midshipman. Adams saluted.

"Did you happen to hear Mr. Wade's report, Mr. Adams?" the captain asked.

"Aye, sir," came the calm reply. The captain was pleased to see Adams had regained control of himself. "We build them strong in America!"

"That we do!" the captain agreed. "Mr. Adams, it occurs to me that your position here might suddenly become pivotal to our survival. When that time comes, I may not be able to direct your actions, so therefore I am giving you the order here and now. You are authorized to fire on the enemy anytime your guns bear, unless specifically ordered not to do so. Pass the word to Mr. Smith below. He is to fire when you do, and only when you do, unless specifically ordered to do otherwise. Understood?"

Adams came to attention and raised his hat. "Aye, Captain."

Albritton nodded and returned to his quarterdeck. He made his way to the larboard rail and signaled for the sailing master to join him. Suddenly, the voice of the lookout prevented that.

"Deck there! Chase is shortening sail!"

Telescopes were quickly raised, and sure enough *London* was taking in sail. Albritton frowned as he lowered his glass and considered.

"Do you think we hurt them worse than we thought?" Warren asked. "Shall I reduce sail, sir?"

"No," the captain said. "As we pull ahead of her, we shall feint to starboard before putting the wheel hard over to larboard. We shall cross her bows and put a broadside into her as we pass. I want the 24-pounders double-shotted and the carronades with bar over ball."

Warren smiled and nodded. "Aye, Captain."

"Pass the word for Mr. Chandler and Mr. Williams." When the two officers arrived, the captain pulled them aside and explained his plans. "There will be no time for me to give the order to fire," he said afterwards. "Be alert, and when we come back to larboard, you may fire as your guns bear. Mr. Williams, your accuracy will be particularly important. If your guns can take out their jib, or even their foremast, our chances for victory increase immeasurably."

"We'll be ready, Captain," the young lieutenant reassured him.

Albritton put his hand out and squeezed Williams' shoulder. "I have every confidence in you. And your men."

He dismissed them back to their batteries and walked to the larboard rail. As they gained on the British frigate, he could get a better look at the damage their broadside had done to the razed ship's hull. He lifted his glass and noted two or possibly three gun ports that had taken direct hits from Chandler's guns. *I need to make it a point to congratulate them on their gunnery,* he thought. He also noted several places where the hull looked as though it had been battered severely, with pieces of the outer hull seemingly broken off.

Albritton was also able to get a good look at *London's* guns as her starboard battery was run out, and he agreed with the earlier assessment of her main battery being 24-pounders. He lowered his glass and smiled grimly, pleased that *Columbia's* hull stood up to their broadside and, from the carpenter's report, would probably survive another two or three. He grunted—not that he intended to get hit with another two or three.

He walked back toward the wheel, his head down as he thought about what to do next. He wanted to disable the frigate and make his escape before the 74 could intervene in the battle. His main advantages were maneuverability and speed over the water, and he was determined to make full use of them. That was one reason he decided to try the dash across the British bows. He knew he had to be careful; the enemy's guns could still splinter his masks easily if they managed a direct hit.

Captain Knighton stood on his quarterdeck and studied

the advancing American frigate. He lowered his telescope and smiled grimly. *Just a little farther, my friend,* he said to himself, *then I shall give you a little surprise.*

He stepped aft for a better view and was immediately rewarded. The American's larboard battery was on full display. Knighton found he had to admire the battery, and he took note of two gaps in the line.

"Pass the word for Mr. Percival and Mr. Jervis," he said. The officers quickly arrived and saluted. "Gentlemen, we are going to give the Americans a surprise. As soon as they have passed us, I shall order the wheel put over hard to starboard with all sail. You shall order your batteries to fire as they bear. I am hoping that we can not only rake her stern but also take out at least one of her masts. That should allow *Goliath* to enter the fight, dooming the Americans. Questions?"

There were none, and he dismissed the officers back to their guns. He turned back to his quarry and waited another quarter of an hour, his hands clasped behind his back. At long last, he turned to his sailing master and said, "Now, Mr. Morgan. Call the hands to make sail. Hard to starboard."

At that moment, Captain Albritton was stealing a quiet moment in the battle to get something to eat for the first time that day. He sat at the table near the fantail, delighting in the plate of fish and onions laid out for him by Sommers. By his calculations, he had about twenty or thirty minutes before his maneuver could commence. If his luck held, in an hour *Columbia* would be disappearing into the Caribbean, leaving behind a badly damaged British frigate and a 74 that was just too slow.

His dreams were shattered by the midshipman of the watch, Mr. Jackson. The young gentleman was beside himself.

"Captain!" he said, so excited that his voice cracked, "The British frigate is heading for us!"

The captain was stunned. He jumped from his seat and marched to the rail where he raised a glass to see a more detailed version of what was plain to his naked eye. The British ship had crowded on sail and come around to her starboard, and she was now heading for *Columbia's* stern.

His first instinct was to put the wheel over to larboard, absorb the enemy's broadside as he dashed past, and then cut across her stern and deliver his own volley. However, he hesitated when he caught sight of Adams standing ready at his stern guns. Turning to larboard may or may not be completed in time to bring any of that battery to bear, but it would certainly take the three 24-pounders and single 18-pounder under the midshipman's command out of the action. Would it not be better to hold his course and force the British to expose themselves to the power of Adams's guns? But to do so would expose his ship to being raked by the British 24-pounders. Too late, he decided to order the turn to larboard. He gave the order and turned to check on the enemy ship as his own came around. Only then did he realize how greatly he'd underestimated the acceleration of his enemy.

Columbia came around, but she was not halfway through her turn when *London* fired. The American ship took the full impact of the British onslaught on her larboard quarter. Albritton ordered his men down, and most of them were able to comply before the broadside of British iron and the accompanying splinters arrived to spread death and mayhem.

Fate now intervened for the Americans. The British salvo knocked the quartermaster's mates manning *Columbia's* wheel to the deck, allowing the ship to steady up on a new course only midway through her turn. This in turn gave Mr.

Adams a perfect opportunity. He and his men had taken refuge behind their big guns and so had been spared injury. Now they leapt to their feet and went to work. In moments they were ready to fire, and Adams, true to his earlier instructions from his captain, gave the order.

"Fire!"

The 18-pounder on the left went off first, followed quickly by its 24-pound neighbor. Adams was pleased to hear one of the guns below him go off as well. He quickly ordered a reload of grape over ball. "Mr. Jackson!" he called to the midshipman of the watch. "Run below and tell Mr. Smith to reload with grape over ball. He is to maintain fire as long as his guns bear. Understood?"

"Aye, sir!"

Adams turned back to see his gun captains standing by, lanyards in hand. He glanced up to be sure of their aim. "Fire!"

Both guns spewed out fire and smoke. Adams stepped to the side and raised a glass to his eye. He could see his guns had struck home and done some damage to the enemy quarterdeck. The stern windows below were gone. He called to his gun captains.

"Belay that! Reload with bar! Let's try to get her rigging! Your target is the British mizzen!"

"Aye, sir!" both men called and got to work. The guns were elevated and ready in less than 100 seconds, and Adams gave the order to fire. He was rewarded when he got to see the British mizzen gaff splinter and her spanker fall to the deck.

Albritton was on his feet again and watched the success.

"Mr. Warren!" he called. "Bring us around! Hard to larboard! I want to cross their stern and rake her! Mr. Jackson! My compliments to Mr. Chandler. Tell him we are about to cross the British stern. He is to fire as his guns bear!”

"Aye, sir!" The lad saluted and went below.

"Mr. Williams! Stand by to fire as you bear!"

"Aye, sir!"

Columbia came around smartly and crossed her adversary's stern. The range was a little more than he would have liked, but Albritton shrugged. *Beggers can't be choosers,* he thought as the spar deck carronades began to go off in twos and threes, followed quickly by the main larboard battery below.

Captain Knighton lay on his quarterdeck, knocked from his feet by the force and impact of the American broadside into his stern. He tried to stand, but he was dazed from the impact with the deck. A hand grabbed his arm and pulled him to his feet, then held on to steady him. He turned and blinked until the image of Mr. Morgan came into focus.

"Report!" Knighton gasped.

"Coming in now. I sent men below and forward to check. With the gaff gone, any maneuvers we try will be sluggish at best."

Knighton raised his glance to the mizzenmast and immediately regretted the gesture, as his vision spun and his head ached mightily, but he forced himself to gaze at the stump of the gaff for a moment. The heavy guns at the American's stern had done him a good bit of damage.

"Wounded?" he asked.

"We're taking them below now, sir," Morgan replied. "Orders?"The captain stood straight and stretched his back. "Where are the Americans?"

Morgan handed him a glass and pointed off to their starboard quarter. Knighton turned and studied his foe through his glass. He could see the damage on the larboard quarter, but only part of their stern window was missing. He hadn't expected the American frigate to turn so quickly. He wondered how bad the damage was below, and he made a mental note to step below at his first opportunity. He sighed and lowered the glass.

"Hard to starboard, Mr. Morgan," he said. "After them. Have Mr. Jeffers signal *Goliath*, 'Am pursuing the enemy.'"

"Aye, sir," the sailing master said, "but the spanker..."

The captain cut him off. "I know. Do your best. Pass the word for bosun to lower the gaff and get it replaced at once."

"Aye, Captain."

"You have the deck. I'm going below to speak to the first lieutenant."

"Aye, sir."

Knighton stepped below into such devastation as he had not seen since he was a young lieutenant on HMS *Tonnant* during her duel with the Spanish 74 *Monarca* during the battle of Trafalgar. Blood and body parts littered the deck, and the carnage was worse from the mainmast aft. He counted some five guns out of action. He looked aft and saw that his quarters would take some time to put back together. He looked forward again and saw the first lieutenant heading his direction.

"Captain," he said as he came to attention. "Five guns out of action, sir. Two went during this last action."

"Wounded?" Knighton asked as he surveyed the damage.

"Taking them below now, sir. Captain, I only have enough men to man one battery or the other. Can I have some men from the yards?"

The captain thought about it for a moment before shaking his head. "They are already quicker then we are, and with the spanker gone the problem gets worse. Perhaps after the bosun replaces the gaff, but not now. What about your guns?"

"I have men working on two of them now, but if we go into action I will need them to man guns. How close is *Goliath*?"

Knighton shook his head. "Not close enough. We'll have to disable the American for her to have a chance to catch up."

Percival nodded and looked forward, and Knighton heard a heavy sigh escape his lips. "If there's nothing else, Captain, I'll get to work on those guns. I'd appreciate any hands you could send to help."

"Understood," Knighton acknowledged. Percival came to attention and ran forward. The captain watched him jump in to help a crew manhandle a 24-pounder long gun while two others rigged a pulley to get the gun off the deck and back onto its carriage when the time came. He shook his head in admiration of the efforts his men put forth.

He returned to the deck and went immediately to the wheel to speak with Morgan. "How are we doing?" he asked.

"Falling behind," the sailing master replied. "They would be faster than us, even if we had the spanker."

Knighton frowned as he looked forward. He could see his enemy cruising ahead of him under all plain sail. He turned to the bosun, whose men were working on the new gaff. "How long until the spanker is available?"

"Three hours, minimum, Captain," came the reply.

The frown sank into a scowl as the captain turned forward. *He's going to get away again,* he thought bitterly, *and there's nothing I can do about it!* He looked around again in desperation, and his eyes settled on a carronade. An idea struck him—*At least I can let him know I'm not happy about it!*

"Mr. Jeffers!" he called to the midshipman of the watch. "My compliments to Mr. Percival. Tell him to ready the starboard battery and stand by for my order to fire!"

"Aye, Captain!" The midshipman disappeared below deck.

"Captain?" It was Morgan. "A hit at this distance would be the wildest stroke of luck!"

"True," Knight shrugged. "But that's all we have. Maybe the gods will be kind and we can skip a ball right into her mizzen." He stood tall and put his hands behind his back. "He's going to get away—I have to do *something*!"

Morgan nodded and touched his hat. "Agreed, Captain."

"Stand by to turn to larboard, Mr. Morgan."

"Aye, sir."

Knighton saw Jeffers come back on deck, and he sent him below again with orders for Percival to fire as his guns bore, regardless of the range. The midshipman saluted and went below again. Knighton waited a full five minutes before giving the order to alter course. He had to allow Mr. Percival time to stare at the midshipman in disbelief and vent to poor Lieutenant Jervis before giving the orders to get the battery loaded and run out. He turned to the sailing master and nodded.

"Steer four points to larboard!" Morgan roared.

"Aye, sir!" replied the quartermaster. He and his mates put the wheel over.

The ship came around, and as soon as she straightened up, the starboard battery erupted. Knighton raised his head to the lookout.

"All short, sir!" came the report.

"Captain!"

Captain Albritton spun at the midshipman's cry and saw the smoke of the British broadside.

"They must be crazy!" Warren exclaimed. "They can't hope to hit us at this range!"

Albritton was silent as he watched for the splashes of the 24-pounder balls skipping across the surface of the warm Caribbean waters. He counted ten or twelve in the volley; once, twice, a third and then no more, but the third was only forty or so yards short of his stern. He stepped to the fantail and raised his glass in time to see the British frigate resume a pursuit course. He noticed her turn was sluggish; something must have happened to her tophamper during their last raking. He turned back to the quarterdeck and caught his first lieutenant's eyes. It was one thing to be called out by the enemy, but quite another to have it done under the eyes of his officers.

The captain stood a foot from his premier, hands clasped behind his back and eyes forward. "You have something to say, Mr. Chandler?"

The first lieutenant copied his captain's pose, his eyes on the British frigate. He shook his head. "No, sir."

Albritton's eyes went skyward. "That's strange, because I thought you were about to point out to me that we were being called out."

Chandler shrugged. "No, sir, not for me to say. Besides," he added, "you already knew it."

The captain looked down at his premier, but the other's eyes were fixed aft. Albritton turned around and watched the enemy ship. She was back on a pursuit course and falling behind. All he had to do was sail away and change course after it got dark. So why did he feel like he was running from a fight?

"Mr. Chandler," he said softly, "do the names Lawrence and Broke mean anything to you?"

The premier shook his head. "Can't say they do, sir."

"Captain Broke commanded the British frigate *Shannon*," Albritton explained, "and Captain Lawrence, as you might now realize, commanded the American frigate *Chesapeake*.

Broke was patrolling off Boston last year, and he caught Lawrence in Boston harbor. Broke called him out, and for a while Lawrence resisted the temptation. The story goes, one day Lawrence gave in and took his ship out to the *Shannon*. *Chesapeake* was taken, and Lawrence was killed in the battle. Do you know what Lawrence's mistake was?"

Chandler shook his head. "No, sir."

The captain turned and looked at his premier. "He wasn't commanding *Columbia*." Chandler smiled as his captain turned to the wheel. "Hard to larboard. Bring us about, Mr. Warren. Mr. Chandler, kindly ready the starboard battery. Wait for the word."

"Aye, sir."

CHAPTER SEVENTEEN

Captain Sir Phillip Knighton sat at a table that had been set up in a corner of the quarterdeck for him so he would have a place to eat and work until the action was over and his cabin could be put to rights. At the moment, he was smoking a cigar and trying to compose a report that Commodore Morgenthau could not twist into an excuse to relieve Knighton of his command. Every time he looked the report over, every time he went over the course of events, he didn't see anything he could have done differently. He'd met every challenge, only he'd come out on the losing end. It was all in the report. He frowned and signed the bottom of the page.

Percival appeared beside him. "Captain," he said, "the American has come about."

Knighton nearly jumped from his chair at the news, only to realize he still had the cigar in one hand and the report in the other. He looked from one to the other, then lit the paper with the cigar and tossed it overboard. After one more good draw, the cigar followed. He accepted a glass and went forward. At the waist, he leaned over the starboard rail and got a good look. Sure enough, the enemy frigate had come around. If neither of them changed course, the enemy would pass down their starboard side at close range.

"Mr. Percival," he said, "ready the starboard battery, if you please. Take what men you need so that you have a full complement for one battery. It's the best I can do at the moment," he added to the unspoken request on the premier's face. Percival closed his mouth and nodded. He saluted and went below.

Knighton stepped forward and watched the approaching frigate. "Mr. Jervis, I want the carronades loaded with bar. Tell Mr. Percival to double-shot the main battery. Our only chance is to hurt her on the first pass."

"Aye, Captain!"

He turned to check the progress on the new spanker and saw at once the new gaff would not be ready in time. "Mr. Morgan," he said quickly, "as soon as we've fired, come around to larboard. The larboard battery will fire as soon as it bears. Once they fire, put the wheel hard over to larboard and cross the American's stern. Pass the word for Mr. Percival!" The first lieutenant rushed from the companionway. "Mr. Percival, I need you to perform the impossible." He explained the three broadsides that would need to go off in quick succession, the third being held back until they could rake the enemy frigate. To his credit, Percival's only reaction was a widening of the eyes that was quickly brought under control. He saluted and disappeared below decks again.

"Mr. Jervis!" Knighton called. "You heard my orders! All three salvos of the carronades will be loaded with bar. Your orders are to do as much damage to their rigging as possible!"

"Aye, Captain!"

Knighton returned to the wheel and stood beside the sailing master. He had done all he could; now he could only wait for the enemy to arrive.

Captain Albritton stood on his quarterdeck and waited. Sails had been trimmed, and the guns were loaded and run out; carronades were loaded with grape over ball to sweep the British decks, and the 24-pounders had round shot. The captain looked around to satisfy himself that everything was ready when he noticed the quarterdeck carronades.

"Mr. Adams!" The senior midshipman stepped over from his stern-chasers and saluted. The captain pointed to the three starboard carronades on the quarterdeck. "I want you to take command of these three guns," he said. "Your orders are to hold your fire for the enemy quarterdeck. Understood?"

Adams saluted. "Aye, Captain."

The ships approached each other and passed. The Americans got their broadside off a split second before the British, and the smoke from the combined broadsides blinded both ships. Albritton heard the screams of the wounded and saw two carronades forward thrown into the air when two of the British 24-pounders struck their ports. One of the guns was thrown across the deck and went through the larboard rail and into the sea—incredibly, without hitting an American gun on that side.

The captain looked around and saw little other damage had been done to his deck. Hands not manning a gun on the starboard battery had taken shelter on the deck, and most of them were able to rise unscathed. The bosun directed hands to take the wounded below. He turned to Mr. Adams's carronades and saw he and his men on their feet and awaiting the order to fire. A quick glance told the captain that now was the time.

"Fire!" he called.

The carronades went off with one voice.

Knighton was knocked to the deck again by that last American broadside, only this time he found he could not rise. He lifted his head and tried, only to have a screaming pain in his arm and shoulder force him to lie down again.

"Captain!" a midshipman's face came into his fast-dimming vision. He heard the lad call for help, and all went black.

"Mr. Morgan!" the midshipman called, "it's the captain!"

The sailing master ran over and knelt. He saw blood oozing from the side of the captain's head, probably caused when he struck the deck. Of far more concern was the bloody mess that used to be his left arm. The sleeve of his coat was saturated with blood, and the arm itself was bent outward away from his body about halfway up the upper arm. He immediately fashioned a tourniquet and placed it just below the shoulder.

"Bosun! Bosun!" he called, and the bosun appeared. "Get the captain below to the surgeon. Pass the word for Mr. Percival to come up on deck."

"Aye, sir!" He signaled two hands to carry the captain below, and he followed them down the stairs.

"Mr. Pinkney!" Morgan said. "I need a damage report! Quick as you can, sir!"

"Aye, Mr. Morgan!"

Lieutenant Percival came up on deck. Morgan met him by the wheel. "You saw the captain?" he asked.

Percival nodded. "Looks like he'll lose the arm."

Morgan closed his eyes and lowered his head in a moment of silent prayer.

"Damage report?" Percival asked.

"Coming," Morgan replied. "Mr. Pinkney should be back any minute. How are things below?"

The first lieutenant shook his head. "Not good. Their 24-pounders have completely worn down our hull. If we try to stand with them, we may suffer great damage." He reached for a glass. "Where are they?"

The midshipman pointed aft, and Percival turned to see the enemy sailing away at speed. A quick inspection showed no visible damage worth mentioning.

"Sir!" It was the lookout in the mizzen tops. "The Americans are coming about!"

The two men looked aft to see the enemy was assuming a pursuit course under all sail. Mr. Pinkney reappeared and made his report to the sailing master. Percival noticed Morgan's eyes go wide.

"Mr. Morgan?" he asked.

Morgan swallowed and motioned for Pinkney to remain where he was, then he stepped over to the first lieutenant. "Mr. Pinkney has made his report, sir. The carpenter is plugging two holes in the hull, one forward and the other midships. He, uh, strongly recommends against trading broadsides with the Americans, or at least taking the next couple on the larboard side. Two more guns were put out of action in the last broadside. It appears the Americans held some carronades back in order to attack the quarterdeck, and that's when the captain was injured." Percival nodded. "Also," Morgan said, "he reports that an American ball struck the mizzen about fifteen feet up. The mast is still together, but it's weak. The bosun's trying to brace it."

The premier's face was grim as he looked at the deck. "Very well," he said, without lifting his eyes. "Tell the bosun to expedite repairs on the mizzen. We may need her first."

"Aye, sir."

"Well done, Mr. Adams!" Albritton called. Adams saluted and returned to his stern chasers.

Mr. Chandler came on deck. "Sir, we lost two more guns during that pass. The British seem quite good at finding our gun ports. That makes a total of five on the starboard battery. I believe we can get two, or perhaps three, back into action if we have the time."

The captain considered for a moment. "Any guns out of action on the larboard battery?"

"No, sir," Chandler replied. "All the action has been to starboard thus far."

"As I thought. Would it be possible to move one or two guns to the starboard battery without endangering the ship's stability?"

Now Chandler considered, taking into account the locations of the disabled guns. Finally, he had to shake his head. "I don't believe so, Captain—at least, not without taking the time to drag the disabled guns out of the way. I suppose it could be done, sir, but it will take quite a while."

Albritton frowned. "That's what I thought you'd say. Mr. Chandler, return to your guns and try to get as many as possible back into action. I am about to come about and chase the British frigate. I intend to overtake them on our starboard side. When we pass her, we shall circle broadly to starboard so that we come back across and rake her stern with our larboard battery. I need you to reload that battery at speed, as I intend to put the wheel hard over to larboard to pass down her starboard side. We will put another broadside into her, then put the wheel hard over again and rake her bows. Can you do it?"

Chandler nodded. "We'll be ready, sir. Am I to wait for the order to fire?"

"I shall give you the order on the first pass, the one down our starboard side. After that, you will use the larboard battery to rake the British stern. You will need a quick reload before we turn up their starboard side. Our guns did considerable damage to that side on our previous passes, and one more good broadside might breech it. Then, if all goes well, we will put the wheel hard over and cross her bows, again with the larboard battery. In those cases, you are to fire as your guns bear. Understood?"

"Aye, Captain. Loads?"

The captain considered for a moment. "Grape over ball for the raking runs, and double-shot for the broadsides."

"Aye, sir."

Albritton nodded. "To your guns, then. Tell your crews I am proud of them."

Chandler saluted. "Thank you, sir." The premier went below, and the captain turned to the wheel. "Bring us about, Mr. Warren," he said. "Pursuit course. Make all sail. I want to overtake them."

"Aye, Captain."

The ship came around and settled in on her course to overtake her British foe. It was immediately obvious that *Columbia* was sailing much better than her rival, and the Americans closed the gap quickly.

"You heard what I said to the first lieutenant?" Albritton asked the sailing master.

"Aye, sir," came the reply. "Down the starboard side on the first run."

The captain nodded. "Then loop off to larboard and bring us around to rake her stern. Stand by to put the wheel over immediately afterwards. I want to go down her starboard side at half-pistol shot if we can."

"Aye, Captain."

Albritton stepped away and turned his attention to the enemy. Through his glass, he could see men working on their mizzen. *We must have hit it on that last pass,* he said to himself. *Let's see if we can finish the job!* He went forward to find Lieutenant Hill.

"Mr. Hill!" The lieutenant stepped over to him and saluted. "It appears we've done some damage to the enemy's mizzen. I want to finish the job. Load the first half of your carronades with grape. They are to sweep the enemy deck. The second half I want loaded with ball. Their target is the enemy mizzen. Make that clear to the gun captains, if you please. After the initial run, reload with grape over ball for the remainder of the engagement."

Hill saluted and returned to his guns. The captain crossed the deck to speak to Lieutenant Williams, commanding the larboard carronades, and repeated his plans. Albritton made his way forward to his sole remaining 18-pounder bow chaser. The midshipman in command turned and saluted. "Captain."

"Mr. Miller." The captain stepped up and raised his glass. He could see the men on the enemy deck still working on their mizzenmast. He smiled; too bad they wouldn't get a chance to finish the job. "Mr. Miller, how long do you think until you are within range?"

The young gentleman looked toward the chase and chewed his lip as he thought. He shook his head. "Maybe another quarter hour, sir, if this wind holds."

The captain nodded. "I agree. Let me know when you're ready to fire."

"Aye, Captain."

Albritton returned to the quarterdeck. Everything was ready. They had to hit them hard on the first pass. He began to pace across the fantail, mostly to pass the time but also to try to keep his mind occupied. Out of the corner of his eye, he saw a messenger arrive from the foc's'l. He stood still and raised his head. The boy saluted.

"Well?" Albritton asked.

"Mr. Miller's respects, sir. He's ready to fire."

"My compliments to Mr. Miller," the captain replied. "In one minute, I shall alter course one point to starboard. That should give you a better aim. He may fire when he bears."

"Aye, sir," the lad said. "Thank you, sir." He ran forward.

"Mr. Warren," he said, "one point to starboard, if you please."

"Aye, Captain." He nodded to the wheel, and the mates put the wheel down a point. They looked forward and were rewarded a moment later when the bow chaser fired. They looked to the lookout for a report.

"Short and to larboard, sir!" the lookout cried.

"Pass the word to Mr. Miller," Albritton said. "He is to continue to fire as long as he bears, until ordered to cease fire."

"Aye, sir!"

"Mr. Warren, alter course as needed."

"Aye, Captain!"

Albritton moved to the lee rail and stood with his hands behind his back, watching as the bow chaser fired again. He saw the geyser erupt off the British starboard quarter. He turned to see Mr. Warren join him.

"Another quarter hour, and we're on him."

The captain nodded. "Take us past at pistol shot or less."

"Aye, sir." The bow chaser fired again, and the captain looked forward.

"Pass the word for Mr. Miller to cease fire and secure his gun. Pass the word for the first lieutenant."

"Aye, Captain."

The two men walked over to the wheel. Albritton stepped away when the first lieutenant appeared on deck. "Are you ready?" he asked.

"Yes, Captain," Chandler replied.

"Good. Remember the quick reloads on the larboard battery after we rake her stern."

"Aye, sir."

Albritton nodded, and the first lieutenant saluted and returned to his battery. Everything was ready.

Lieutenant Percival looked aft at the growing shape of the American frigate and knew he was in trouble. They had absorbed one hit from the enemy's bow chasers, and soon the ship would pass them and exchange broadsides again. He turned to check on the status of the mizzenmast and spanker and knew at once they would not be ready in time. He ordered the men to pause their work and take cover on the deck until the American had passed.

"I'm going below to check on the captain," he said to the sailing master. "You have the deck until I return."

"Aye, sir."

He made his way below to the sickbay and found the doctor tending to a hand. The doctor acknowledged him with a nod.

"How's the captain, Doctor?" he asked.

The surgeon finished dressing the wound and stood. He motioned over to the far corner of the room. "He's resting as comfortably as he can for now," he said as he led the first lieutenant over. "I hope to move him soon."

"Move him? Why?"

The doctor paused and faced the premier. "First," he said in a low voice, "I can't do anything more for him now. His arm will probably have to come off, but that can wait while I attend to more urgent injuries. Second, it's not always good for the injured to see their captain incapacitated."

Percival nodded, and the doctor led him to the unconscious form lying on a blanket. The first lieutenant took in the bloody bandages on his captain's arm and head and shivered. "Pass the word for Flagstone and Wiggins to make up the spare cabin in the gun room for him. I'm afraid his own is uninhabitable at the moment," Percival added grimly. "If you are going to move him, I suggest you do it quickly. The American is gaining on us, and we shall be exchanging broadsides very soon."

"Very well." The doctor pulled out his pocket watch and held it close against the dim light. "We shall move him in fifteen minutes. Is that in time?"

Percival considered for a moment and nodded. He put a reassuring hand on the doctor's arm and returned to the deck.

British marines began firing at *Columbia's* deck as the ship approached, and Lieutenant Monroe ordered his men to return fire. The American sharpshooters in the tops, with their high rate of fire, drew their counterparts' attention while the US Marines on the deck added their weight to the battle.

Captain Albritton stood on his quarterdeck and watched as *Columbia* drew even with her quarry. Surprisingly, the British held their fire until more than half of their guns could bear. Both ships fired at almost the same instant. Albritton heard the screams of the wounded, mostly from the guns' crews who could not take cover. He looked aft to see Lieutenant Hill standing behind his carronades, waiting for them to bear on their target. Hill waved to his captain and turned his attention to his first gun. He crouched behind the barrel along with the gun's captain, and Albritton saw him nod and jump out of the way. The gun captain took the lanyard and pulled. The gun erupted as Hill squatted to check the aim of his second gun. He spoke quickly to the captain and moved to the next gun, and so on down the line.

It was the fourth gun that claimed the prize. Right after it went off there came a loud *crack!* that was plainly heard above the din of the fray. All eyes on the American quarterdeck turned in time to see the British mizzen tumble to starboard. The mast got hung up over the rail and dragged in the sea, causing the ship to slow dramatically and veer away from *Columbia*. Albritton turned to shout at Hill, but he saw the lieutenant was already talking to the captain of his last carronade and instructing the man to change his target to the British mainmast.

Albritton sprang to the wheel to find Mr. Warren. "Belay the turn!" he ordered. "Steady as you go until we see what they can do."

"Aye, Captain!"

The captain looked forward to ensure that parties were busy getting the wounded below. Satisfied, he turned his glass on his wounded enemy. The British were taking in sail so as to better control the ship until they could cut away their wreckage. It was an opportunity too good to waste.

"Mr. Warren! Wear ship to larboard! I want to cut across her stern and rake her at half-pistol shot!"

"Aye, aye, Captain!"

"Mr. Williams! Stand by to fire as your guns bear! Pass the word—same instructions to Mr. Chandler!"

"Aye, sir!"

USS *Columbia* came around and settled up on a course to deliver a knockout blow to the helpless enemy. Albritton could see men with axes and pikes trying to free their fallen mast and force it over the side. One or two guns still active on her larboard quarter fired at them as they approached, but their shots went wide.

"Mr. Warren," the captain said, "after we fire, I still want to put the wheel over hard to larboard and give our 24-pounders another shot at their starboard hull."

"Aye, Captain!"

Albritton raised his telescope to his eye, hoping to see the enemy captain haul down his colors but knowing that it wouldn't happen. *Columbia's* guns went off as they crossed the unprotected British stern. Albritton thought he heard another *crack!* similar to when the British mizzenmast came down. When they were clear of the British stern, Mr. Warren put the wheel hard over to larboard. Albritton noted that he allowed room in case the British succeeded in getting their mizzen over the rail.

As soon as they commenced the turn and were free of the smoke, the lookout shouted down. "Deck there! We hit the British main!"

Albritton went to the rail to see for himself, and sure enough, the main topmast was leaning to one side! "Mr. Williams! Your target is his mainmast!"

The lieutenant waved his acknowledgement and ran to the forward carronades to relay the order. Their load of grape over a 32-pound ball would be devastating at such close range.

They were almost abeam before the larboard battery went off. The upside of that was that three-quarters of *Columbia's* big guns went off as a unit and made mincemeat of the British hull, opening two large holes on their gun deck. Willliams' carronades laid down accurate fire as well. The number three gun dealt a glancing blow to the British main topmast, but the sixth and seventh guns hit the mast square just fifteen feet above the deck, first damaging the mast and then sweeping it from the deck. Williams intercepted the last three guns and redirected their fire to the British foremast, and, incredibly, the final gun did some damage with a glancing blow just above the foremast yard.

"Mr. Warren," Albritton said with relief in his voice, "belay the order to cross her bows. Steady as you go. Give us some room to make repairs, then heave to."

"Aye, Captain," Warren said. "Congratulations, sir."

"Thank you."

Lieutenant Percival stood among the shattered ruins of

HMS *London's* quarterdeck and looked around, grateful to have survived the onslaught from the American frigate. The sailing master was sitting on the deck near the shattered remnants of the ship's wheel, careful to avoid the debris that was what remained of the mates who'd been manning it when it took a direct hit from a 32-pound ball from one of the American's carronades. Morgan was holding his hand around a large splinter protruding from his shoulder and waiting for medical attention. Percival noted the wounded were no longer being taken below to the sick bay; with the cease fire the doctor had sent word that the sick bay was full and that he would send help to the deck as soon as he could.

The first lieutenant leaned on the stump of the ship's mizzenmast and tried to take inventory of all he saw. The ship was effectively dismasted and quite unable to maneuver. This meant they were helpless against the American frigate. He looked about in desperation, hoping to see *Goliath* hull-up on the horizon and bearing down on them quickly, but all he saw was the enemy hove to out of range while they made emergency repairs and tended to their own wounded.

The report he'd just received from below carried more bad news. The last American broadsides had been very effective. The raking of their stern had disabled several guns, and he was informed that they did not have enough men to man those that remained. The last broadside had ripped open *London's* starboard hull so that no protection was now offered to those manning the guns. The midshipman whom he'd dispatched to gather a damage report said that to his knowledge Percival was the only officer still fit for duty.

Exhausted, the first lieutenant fell back against the mast and sighed. He wiped the tears from his eyes and tried to think of what to do. The captain was still unconscious, so the decision was his alone, and with no other officers fit, and the sailing master also out of action, there was nobody to consult with. He dropped his head to his chest and took a deep breath, then let it out slowly to try to calm his nerves.

"Mr. Pickering," he said to the nearby midshipman, "lower the colors."

"Aye, sir," the lad sobbed and saluted. He went aft and brought down their flag. He held it gathered in his arms and wept bitterly.

"Sir?"

Percival turned to see one of the loblolly men from sick bay. "Yes?"

"The captain's awake, sir, and he wants to see you."

Percival sighed and nodded. "Does the doctor know?"

"Not yet, sir," came the reply. "I came straight here."

The first lieutenant pushed off the mast. "Inform the doctor and ask him to meet me at the captain's cabin. He is in the gun room?"

"Aye, sir." The tar saluted and went below.

Percival made his way below, pausing just long enough on the gun deck to see the damage for himself before continuing on to the captain's cabin on the deck below. The berthing deck was in good shape compared with those above. The captain was in the end cabin, normally reserved for a chaplain but empty and available on this cruise.

The door was open so he stepped inside. Captain Knighton lay on a cot suspended from the beams above. The doctor was there, seated on a sea chest against the opposite wall. Knighton saw his premier enter and said, "Report." His voice was weak and thready. Percival looked quickly at the doctor, but the man only shrugged.

"We are helpless, sir," he answered bluntly. "We are dismasted, and the American's last broadside blew large holes in our starboard side."

The captain closed his eyes and grunted. "So much for

64s being able to stand up to the American 24-pounders."

"Yes, well," Percival stammered. "Captain, I am sorry to have to inform you that I have lowered our colors."

Knighton looked confused for a moment. "Surrendered?"

"Aye, sir."

The captain frowned and closed his eyes. He lay back on his pillow. "I'll break you for that."

Percival was about to plead his case when he felt a pull on his shirt sleeve and turned to see the doctor shaking his head and motioning to the door. The first lieutenant nodded and silently left the cabin.

"Captain! Look! Their colors!"

Albritton spun and saw the British flag being taken down by a young man, probably a midshipman. He bowed his head in silent thanks as a cheer rose from those around him.

"Mr. Warren," he said, "take us to within half-pistol shot for the larboard battery. Pass the word for Mr. Chandler to load the guns and run them out, then he is to report to the quarterdeck."

"Aye, Captain!"

Columbia moved slowly toward their defeated foe and came to a halt at half-pistol shot from *London's* shattered starboard side. Albritton stood at the rail and marveled at the extent of the damage his guns had inflicted. Mr. Chandler arrived and looked over his handiwork.

"My God," he whispered.

"Yes," the captain agreed. "I'd say that about sums it up. Take the launch and see what kind of shape she's in. I'd like to take her back as a prize, although from what I can see from here, she may not be worth it. I shall let you make that decision. Let me know."

"Aye, sir."

Lieutenant Chandler sat in the stern sheets of *Columbia's* launch and studied their prize as they approached. Close up, it was easy to see the lines of its previous incarnation as a 64-gun third rate showing through in her hull. Stoutly built and capable of handling anything up to an 18-pounder at normal ranges, they'd proved inadequate against the Americans' 24-pounders at pistol-shot.

The dismasted hulk was drifting slowly with the current, and Chandler thought it might be down by the bows a bit. The coxswain guided the launch to the British entry port, and a half-dozen marines scampered up to the deck. Chandler followed once the deck was secure. "I am Lieutenant Michael Chandler of the frigate USS *Columbia*," he said loudly. "Who is the ranking officer?"

A man stepped out of the group on the quarterdeck.

"I am Lieutenant Roland Percival of His Majesty's ship *London*." He took his sword from its scabbard and handed it to his American counterpart hilt-first. "I formally surrender my ship to you."

"Thank you," Chandler replied. "You may keep your sword. You and your men fought valiantly. Your captain?"

"Wounded. He is currently below in the gun room."

"I see." Chandler glanced over his shoulder as *Columbia's* bosun and carpenter stepped up on deck, followed by additional marines. Chandler turned back to Percival. "These men are our carpenter and bosun. They will inspect your ship." He turned and nodded. The carpenter and half the marines went below while the bosun went forward with the rest.

Chandler looked around at the wounded. "Do you need medical assistance?"

"Thank you," Percival replied. "Our doctor is a bit overwhelmed at the moment."

Chandler dispatched the midshipman who'd accompanied him back to the ship with orders to bring the doctor if possible and a supply of bandages and medicines.

The two men waited in awkward silence until the launch returned with the doctor and some of his helpers, all carrying armfuls of medicines and bandages.

"Pick a spot, Doctor," Chandler said. "Their own doctor is treating men below." The doctor nodded and got to work.

Just then the bosun returned. He shook his head. "There's nothing to be done, sir. I doubt she'd take the towing."

"Very well," Chandler said. "See what you can do to help the doctor."

"Aye, sir." He knuckled his forehead and went forward."

Minutes later, the carpenter came back on deck, pulling a British tar with him. "This here's one of their carpenter's mates, sir, name of Willoughby. I found him plugging holes at the waterline forward."

"Yes? Go on."

"Well, sir, we did a quick inspection of the hull, and we both agree that the ship's not worth saving. If we try to tow it, she'll never make Charleston."

Chandler turned to his counterpart. "Do you agree, sir?"

Percival looked to Willoughby, who reluctantly nodded his agreement. He said to the American, "I do, sir."

Chandler pursed his lips as he thought. "Very well. My captain has instructed me to destroy your ship if it was too badly damaged to take as a prize. Order all your boats brought alongside so we can transfer your men and wounded to our ship. Do you have a speaking trumpet? I must report to my captain."

One was brought to him, and he stepped to the rail. "Captain!" He saw his captain step to the rail with his own trumpet.

"Report, Mr. Chandler!"

"As we thought, sir, she's too badly damaged to take! Recommend we take her survivors on board and burn her!"

"Agreed!" Albritton said. "Quick as you can! We don't want to linger!"

"Aye, sir!" Albritton waved and turned away. Chandler turned back to Percival.

"I need to report to my captain, if he's awake," the British officer said. "Will you accompany me, sir?"

Chandler nodded and followed the other below. He was shocked at the damage to the British gun deck but said nothing as they continued below to the gun room. They found the captain awake and lying in bed. He sat up a bit when they entered. Chandler saw he was severely wounded in one arm, but he held his sword in the other.

Percival made the introductions. "Captain Sir Thomas Knighton, may I present Lieutenant Chandler of USS *Columbia*." Chandler bowed.

"Your captain is named Albritton?" Knighton asked.

"Yes, sir."

Knighton lay back, exhausted from the effort. He nodded. "At least I had my chance."

Percival was confused. "Sir?"

"Nothing," his captain said. "What is it, Mr. Percival?"

"Sir, the Americans have determined the ship is too badly damaged to take. They intend to burn her, sir."

"I understand," Knighton replied.

"We are taking your survivors and wounded to our ship, Captain. I shall send a detachment to carry you to the deck," Chandler said.

"Thank you for caring for my men, Lieutenant. As for me, that will not be necessary."

Chandler's eyes went wide, and Percival went to his captain's bedside. "Sir! Don't do this!"

"My time is done, Roland," the captain said. "Let me go with the ship."

"I won't!" Percival cried.

Knighton brought his blade up to his premier's neck. "I know that you did all you could. What happened was not your fault. But I will kill you if you attempt to take me from this cabin."

Percival pulled the blade from his captain's grasp and laid it on his chest. There were tears in his eyes. "Aye, Captain," he whispered.

He stood, and both lieutenants saluted. Knighton nodded. "Go now. Save the crew."

The two officers left without a word and returned to the deck.

The evacuation proceeded without incident as both crews did all they could to make sure everyone was accounted for. Chandler dispatched a team of volunteers below to set fire to the match leading to the magazine. The premiers were the last men off the ship.

Columbia raised sail as soon as the last man was aboard. Chandler presented Lieutenant Percival to his captain, who, like his premier, refused the lieutenant's sword. When informed of Captain Knighton's decision, Albritton merely raised an eyebrow and nodded. The three officers moved to the fantail.

"Time on the fuse, Mr. Chandler?" Albritton asked.

Chandler checked his watch. "Any minute now, sir."

Albritton turned to face HMS *London* and came to attention. "Gentlemen?" he said, and saluted. The two lieutenants followed suit. Thirty seconds later, an explosion was heard followed quickly by the ship being blown apart when her magazines exploded.

"Mr. Warren," the captain said, "make your course north. We are leaving. Plot a course for the Mona Passage and then for Charleston. Hopefully, we'll find Mr. Franklin and *Olympus* there. See to the prisoners, Mr. Chandler, if you please. I shall be in my quarters."

"Aye, sir."

Albritton went to his cabin and sat in his chair. Sommers came in with a glass of bourbon. He accepted it with a nod of thanks. He sipped in silence, mourning the loss of the British captain. He understood the man's thinking—Mr. Chandler had reported what happened in the man's cabin—but he hated the thought of a life of service ending that way.

He came up on deck the next morning and was about to speak to Lieutenant Williams when a call was heard from above.

"Deck there! Boat on the starboard beam! It looks like Xavier and his men!"

Albritton led the charge to the rail and raised a glass to his eye. Sure enough, he easily recognized the form of his coxswain standing in the boat and waving for all he was worth.

"Hard to starboard, Quartermaster! Get us close and heave to!"

"Aye, Captain!"

The captain waited on his quarterdeck as the boat came alongside and Xavier and his men were brought on board. The coxswain stepped up and saluted.

"Thank ye for stopping, sir," he said with a grin.

Later, in the captain's cabin, Albritton, the first lieutenant and Xavier sat in the day cabin drinking bourbon and smoking cigars.

"We watched most of the fight, sir," Xavier said. "We actually cheered when you brought their mizzen down!"

"Did you see the explosion?" Chandler asked.

The coxswain shook his head. "You were below the horizon for a bit. We saw the light in the sky, but we didn't know what happened. I bet their captain was mad."

Albritton shook his head. "He decided to go down with his ship."

Xavier's eyes went wide. "What's that?"

Albritton motioned to Chandler, who told Xavier about Knighton deciding to remain on his ship. Xavier drained his glass and set it down. He thought for a moment, then nodded solemnly. "Not a bad way for a man to finish his career." He shook his head sadly and rose. "If you'll excuse me, sir, I'll go to bed." He came to attention and left.

The captain watched him go and turned to his premier. "I don't think I've ever seen him so... 'moved,' I guess would be the word."

The first lieutenant drained his glass and rose. "I think I'll check in on deck and then turn in myself. Goodnight, Captain."

"Goodnight."

When he was alone, Albritton drained his glass and set it down on the table. He leaned back his head and closed his eyes, hoping the war would be over soon.

THE END

About The Author
James Keffer

James Keffer was born September 9, 1963, in Youngstown, Ohio, the son of a city policeman and a nurse. He grew up loving basketball, baseball, tennis, and books. He graduated high school in 1981 and began attending Youngstown State University to study mechanical engineering.

He left college in 1984 to enter the U.S. Air Force. After basic training, he was posted to the 2143rd Communications Squadron at Zweibruecken Air Base, West Germany. While he was stationed there, he met and married his wife, Christine, whose father was also assigned to the base. When the base was closed in 1991, James and Christine were transferred up the road to Sembach Air Base, where he worked in communications for the 2134th Communications Squadron before becoming the LAN manager for HQ 17th Air Force.

James received an honorable discharge in 1995, and he and his wife moved to Jacksonville, Florida, to attend Trinity Baptist College. He graduated with honors in 1998, earning a Bachelor of Arts degree. James and Christine have three children.

Hornblower and the Island is the first novel James wrote, and it is the first to be published by Fireship Press. He has self-published three other novels. He currently lives and works in Jacksonville, Florida, with his wife and three children.

IF YOU ENJOYED THIS BOOK
VISIT

PENMORE PRESS

www.penmorepress.com

All Penmore Press books are available directly through our website

Other books by this Author

Brewer's Private War

By

James Keffer

A chance meeting in a tavern on Martinique brings a man from Brewer's past back into his life. Brewer discovers this man - a mentor of his when he was a raw midshipman - has turned to piracy, and Brewer is determined to track him down and end his reign of terror over British shipping in the Caribbean. Captain Brewer soon discovers that still waters run deep when he is kidnapped by his former mentor and warned to stop while he still can. With the help of the US Navy, Brewer finds his quarry in the Bahamas, only to chase him to Washington City and find himself staring down the wrong end of a pirate's pistol!

PENMORE PRESS
www.penmorepress.com

Brewer's Revenge

By

James Keffer

Admiral Horatio Hornblower has given Commander William Brewer captaincy of the captured pirate sloop *El Dorado*. Now under sail as the HMS *Revenge*, its new name suits Brewer's frame of mind perfectly. He lost many of his best men in the engagement that seized the ship, and his new orders are to hunt down the pirates who have been ravaging the trade routes of the Caribbean sea.

But Brewer will face more than one challenge before he can confront the pirate known as El Diabolito. His best friend and ship's surgeon, Dr. Spinelli, is taking dangerous solace in alcohol as he wrestles with demons of his own. The new purser, Mr. Allen, may need a lesson in honest accounting. Worst of all, Hornblower has requested that Brewer take on a young ne'er-do-well, Noah Simmons, to remove him from a recent scandal at home. At twenty-three, Simmons is old to be a junior midshipman, and as a wealthy man's son he is unaccustomed to working, taking orders, or suffering privations.

William Brewer will need to muster all his resources to ready his crew for their confrontation with the Caribbean's most notorious pirate. In the process, he'll discover the true price of command.

PENMORE PRESS
www.penmorepress.com

BREWER

AND THE

BARBARY

PIRATES

BY

JAMES KEFFER

It is said that a man is shaped by his past, and so it was with William Brewer. Before he took command of *HMS Defiant* in a hurricane, before he hunted pirates in *HMS Revenge*, Brewer endured a crucible of fire. Fresh from the tutelage of Napoleon Bonaparte on St. Helena, Brewer signs on for a cruise under Captain Bush in *HMS Lydia* to the Mediterranean to battle the Barbary Pirates. Here Brewer learns to fight, but he also learns what it means to command men in battle and what it takes to order men to their deaths. Their enemy is a Scottish renegade who is responsible for the deaths of dozens of his fellow sailors over the years and the selling of hundreds of Europeans into African slavery. Along the way, Brewer is introduced to new heroes and new devils. He also receives sage advice from no less than the Duke of Wellington himself. In the end, Brewer has to use all he's learned and going beyond to save *HMS Lydia* from destruction at the hands of pirates.

PENMORE PRESS
www.penmorepress.com

Penmore Press
Challenging, Intriguing, Adventurous, Historical and Imaginative

www.penmorepress.com